ABIDING HOPE

BOOK FOUR IN THE HEALING RUBY SERIES

Jennifer H. Westall

Jennifer H. Westall
www.jenniferhwestall.com

Publisher's Note: This is a work of fiction. Names, characters, places, and incidents are a product of the author's imagination. Locales and public names are sometimes used for atmospheric purposes. Any resemblance to actual people, living or dead, or to businesses, companies, events, institutions, or locales is completely coincidental.

Book Layout ©2013 BookDesignTemplates.com

Abiding Hope/ Jennifer H. Westall. -- 1st ed.
ISBN 978-0-9976627-1-9

In memory of Uncle Charles "Charlie" Gandy

To be in his presence, was to know true joy.

Are not two sparrows sold for a penny? Yet not one of them will fall to the ground outside your Father's care. And even the very hairs of your head are all numbered. So don't be afraid; you are worth more than many sparrows.

—Matthew 10: 29-31

PROLOGUE

Matthew

June 1942
Southern Luzon, Philippines

I didn't dare move as I lay with my back pressed into the mud, peering up through the swaying cogon grass at a gray sky that refused to darken enough for my escape. Agony coursed through my body in more forms than I could count—hunger, thirst, infection, fever. And, most pressing, like a demon haunting me through every inch of the jungle, exhaustion nearly overwhelmed me. But at least it had stopped raining for now.

The voices of Japanese soldiers, only a couple hundred yards away at best, moved closer and spread in multiple directions. I'd made one wrong move after another since barely escaping Mindanao, but this latest slip-up might be the one to do me in. I'd been so hungry, so thirsty. In the broken-down barrio a few kilometers away, I'd risked exposure for a small cup of rice and some dirty water offered by a boy who couldn't have been more than ten. I'd tried to tell him to keep quiet, but I still didn't know enough of the language. Absent of any decent shelter in the area, I'd taken refuge in the tall grass near the base of a mountain. I'd closed my eyes for only a moment.

And then I'd heard the voices that had tracked my every move for weeks, maybe months. I'd lost all concept of time since I'd fought my way off Mindanao. They'd hunted me from one barrio to the next, through jungle and swamp, across one island after another. Led by a brutal commander named Kojima, they interrogated the frightened Filipinos who dared to help me, especially those who'd guided me to safety. I'd learned quickly to stay out of the barrios as much as possible, if only to protect the Filipinos. This time, the Japs were close—so close, I could hear Kojima barking orders. I couldn't risk crawling through the grass to the path that led west and up the nearest mountain. Not that I had the energy for such a maneuver anyway.

"Captain Doyle!" called the high-pitched, heavily accented voice of Kojima. "You surrounded all side! We know you lying in grass!"

I held my breath, afraid the blades above me would move if I exhaled. How much longer until sunset?

"You come out!" Kojima continued, his voice moving slightly east as he yelled. "You lay down weapon and come out. We give food and bed. You eat and sleep. No more hunger. No more fight. We not hurt you if come out."

I knew better. I'd seen how the Japanese treated prisoners on Bataan after the U.S. surrendered, marching them in columns, beating them for no reason, and shooting anyone who stopped to help stragglers. Surrender would lead to unimaginable torture. I was sure of it. But how was I going to escape again?

I can't go one more step, Lord, I prayed. *I'm through. If they find me, give me enough strength to fight. I'd rather die fighting than surrender to these monsters.*

The voices spread out, moving further east, encircling me. God had seen me through the brink of capture several times already. Would He save me again?

I heard movement just north of my position. I was almost completely cut off from the mountain. If night would just fall, I could slip away into the darkness. *Lord, show me which way to go. Bring the cover of night, and give my body strength. Help me find my way.*

Something moved in the grass within several yards of my position. An animal? The breeze? A Japanese soldier? The hair on my arms and neck prickled. I held my breath and listened. All I could hear were a few tropical birds in the distance. Were they warning me? It still wasn't completely dark, but maybe I could make it to the other side of the field.

North. The thought came to me from out of nowhere, but it made no sense. I'd just heard them moving in that direction. Surely I wasn't supposed to run right into the enemy's hands.

North.

Something whizzed over me and cracked as it hit the ground. A bullet.

I jumped up and ran north, trying not to run in a straight line and to keep my head down as far as possible. As I lumbered through the grass and mud, more bullets whizzed past me. Glancing around, I glimpsed the edge of the field, where the jungle began to offer precious cover. But dark shapes were running through it, bound to cut me off. I pumped my legs as hard as they'd go, but they were so heavy.

Pain like hot iron ripped through my right hamstring, and I fell onto my face. Scrambling to my feet, I kept going. Shouts rang out from behind and to the right of me, and then another spray of bullets ricocheted from in front of me. I dropped to the ground. I was surrounded. What could I do?

Run north.

If I didn't keep moving they'd be on me in seconds. North would send me right at them, but there was no time to reason through my options. I crawled north through the needle-like grass as it tore at my face. Bullets whipped in every direction. But something familiar caught my attention. English! Someone was yelling in English!

I took a quick peek over the top of the grass. In the dark shadows of the jungle ahead of me, I could make out several bodies in position behind trees, their weapons aimed beyond me. One of them waved his arm, signaling for me to keep coming.

"This way!" he called. "Come on! We'll cover you!"

Indescribable joy leapt through me at those words, and I took off running with every bit of energy I had left in my feeble body. I fell into the line of trees, landing on my back, panting so hard I thought I might have a heart attack. The gunfire raged on for a few more minutes. Then all went quiet. My right leg was on fire. I rubbed it, feeling the blood slipping beneath my fingers. I'd been shot.

A dark face leaned over me, blocking out the dim light coming through the tops of the trees. "Well, I'll be damned. If it ain't Matthew Doyle."

I knew that voice.

The figure dropped to a knee beside me, and I could finally make out his features. He looked on me with the same astonishment that must have spread across my face. "Henry?"

He grinned before grabbing me by the shirt and hoisting me to my feet. "Let's get out of here, boys. Them Japs'll overrun this position within minutes."

Ruby

June 1942
Melbourne, Australia

It was raining when Mike Sawyer and I stepped out of the taxi, so I covered my head with my bag and ran to the front steps of the small chapel on base. We stopped at the front door and shook the water from our clothing and hair. Mike gripped the handle on the front door and met my gaze with the same pity that had been etched into his expression for nearly two months, ever since he'd forced me to leave Matthew behind on Mindanao.

"Now, let's not get our hopes up," he said.

Despite his support in my efforts to persuade someone with enough authority to mount a return to the island, I still hadn't forgiven him. I hardened my expression so he'd know I meant business. "All I have left is my hope."

His eyes softened. "Grace, I just mean that you shouldn't go in here expecting—"

"I know what you mean," I said. "I'll be all right. Let's get inside."

We made our way through the small lobby and into the darkened chapel. The only light filtered in through dirty stained-glass windows featuring scenes from the Bible. In the back corner, two small flickering flames cast shadows over a statue of Mary.

Colonel William Dorsey stood from a pew a few rows ahead of me and approached us with his usual stiff manner. He shook hands with Mike before turning to me. "Mrs. Doyle, it's good to see you again. You're looking well."

My hand instinctively went to my midsection, cradling my only remaining connection to Matthew. "Thank you, sir. Do you have any news about Matthew?"

He frowned and glanced at Mike. "I'm glad you're both here this time. I know the waiting has been tough on you, Mrs. Doyle. I can appreciate your determination to locate your husband, and I've done everything in my power to be of assistance."

I didn't like the sound of that. He'd never stalled when we'd met before. He'd always gotten right to the point, insisting time was of the essence. "I appreciate all you've done, Colonel Dorsey. I know you've put yourself in a difficult position by sharing information with me. Is there anything new you can tell me?"

He let out a hard sigh and turned back to the pew where he'd been sitting. "I have something I must give you. It was supposed to be delivered by mail, but I wanted to speak to you in person." He turned back to me with a small yellow card in his hand. "I'm afraid it isn't good news. The army has declared Captain Doyle deceased."

My stomach nearly hit the floor, and I had to grip the pew next to me to keep my balance. "I don't...understand. How is that possible? Has new information come in?"

"No, ma'am." He held the telegram out to me, but I couldn't take it. Mike took it instead.

"Then how do they know that he's..." I couldn't form the word. "You told me only a few weeks ago, in this very chapel, that the reports from the men who were last with Matthew stated he was alive when they ran for the plane on Mindanao."

"Yes, ma'am. I know."

"He was still fighting."

"Yes, ma'am."

"Then what changed?" My voice shook, despite my effort to control it.

Colonel Dorsey cleared his throat. "I understand your confusion, and I wish I could give you more information, but I can't."

"Wait a minute," Mike said. "This says he died on May 5. We escaped from Mindanao on April 30. What happened between those two dates?"

I took the card from Mike to see for myself what it said as Colonel Dorsey answered him. "Listen, I have already shared enough information with the both of you to get myself fired, possibly worse. I've told you everything I can."

I was having a hard time making sense of everything, so I read the telegram out loud.

WE DEEPLY REGRET TO INFORM YOU THAT YOUR HUSBAND, CAPTAIN MATTHEW DOYLE, DIED IN THE HONORABLE PERFORMANCE OF HIS DUTIES AND IN SERVICE TO HIS COUNTRY ON MAY 5, 1942 ON THE ISLAND OF MINDANAO, PHILIPPINES. TO AVOID AID TO OUR ENEMIES, THE EXACT CIRCUMSTANCES OF HIS DEATH HAVE BEEN CLASSIFIED.

I looked from Colonel Dorsey to Mike. "This doesn't make any sense. Why would his death be classified?"

Mike eyed Colonel Dorsey with suspicion. "If this is true, then he survived after we left. He must've kept fighting. He must have—"

"I've told you everything I can," Colonel Dorsey interrupted. "I am sorry to be the one to have to deliver such painful news."

"But you haven't told us anything!" I protested, trying to stay calm. "I'm not giving up. I don't believe this for a moment. Matthew isn't dead. Until someone can tell me exactly what's going on, then I refuse to accept this. And you can tell Douglas MacArthur himself that I will find my husband!"

Colonel Dorsey shook his head. "I'm afraid that's going to be even more difficult. MacArthur is moving headquarters to Brisbane."

"What? When?" As the church began to spin before me, I sank onto the pew.

"Couple of weeks. All military personnel will be moving out." He glanced at Mike, who'd put his hand on my shoulder. "That'll include you as well, Lieutenant. I don't have specifics yet, but your squadron is being relocated."

"But not me," I said. "Because I'm not military personnel."

"Again," Colonel Dorsey said, turning back to me, "I'm very sorry to have to tell you both this. I know it must be difficult, but you should start thinking about your future. I can arrange for you to be transported back to the States if you'd like. Just let Lieutenant Sawyer know what your plans are, and I'll have my staff make the arrangements."

I did my best to squeak out a "thank you" in reply. But I couldn't even look up at him. He'd just yanked the very ground I stood on out from under me. How could I possibly think about the future?

***

"Grace, you need to think about what's best for you," Mike said as he handed me a cup of water. He took a seat in the rickety chair beside the sofa where I'd crashed shortly after returning to my apartment.

My thoughts swam, along with my stomach. Between lingering issues from my dysentery and the poorly named morning sickness that had no regard for the time of day, I felt weak nearly all day long. But Colonel Dorsey's news had zapped the tiny amount of strength remaining in me.

"I shouldn't have left him," I said, setting the cup on the coffee table without taking a sip. "I never should've gotten on that plane."

"You think it would've been better if *both* of you had died?" Mike looked at me like I'd lost my mind.

"He isn't dead. He's still out there."

"You don't know that."

"But I have to believe it."

Mike leaned back and studied me for a bit. I had a hard time thinking of him, of both of us, soaring above Cavite in his Stearman biplane, or him and my brother, Henry, cutting up on the golf course in Manila. But I knew that I *had* to hold onto those images, or the war would erase everything that had come before, leaving nothing but heartache and loss.

I'd had my fill of both of those. And I was determined to hang on to every ounce of hope I could find.

"I can stay here," I said. "I'll wait tables and whatever else I have to do until..."

"Until what?" he said quietly.

I couldn't answer.

"Even if we can turn this war around and retake the Philippines, that's going to take months, maybe years. What are you going to do once the baby comes? How will you take care of yourself and a baby on a waitress's salary and no one to help you?"

"I can't go back to the States. I promised Matthew I would wait for him here."

Mike shook his head and leaned forward onto his knees. "Listen, Matthew would want you to take care of yourself and your child. You need family and friends who can help you."

My eyes burned, but I was determined not to cry. "Matthew and Henry *are* my family. There's no one else."

"What about your parents?"

I shook my head.

"Aunts? Uncles? Cousins?"

I shook my head some more. "No. I said there's no one."

He stood in a huff and began pacing my tiny living room. It only took him about three or four strides to cross it. "You've mentioned nursing school before. What about that?"

"That would take a couple of years."

"You have so much experience already. Do you even need nursing school?"

His pacing was giving me a headache. I leaned back against the sofa and stared at the paint peeling from the ceiling. "Laura mentioned something about a new nursing training program they've started up in the States. The government pays for the program and gives a stipend to live on. I reckon I could look into it."

Mike's face brightened, and he stopped pacing. "That's the ticket. Why, I bet you could fly right through any old nursing program." He wagged his finger at me. "In fact, I have just the plan."

"Oh, you do?" I managed to pull myself back to a sitting position as he dropped once again into the chair beside me. This time he almost seemed excited.

"Listen here, my parents live in a great little section of Houston, and my youngest sister just married and moved out this past spring. They mentioned renting her room out."

"Oh, I don't know about that. I'm not sure the stipend would be enough to cover rent."

"I'll talk to them and explain things. They'd just love you. I'm sure they'd work something out."

I'd never been one to ask for help from folks. I'd been scolded for my stubborn independence countless times. Maybe it was time to accept the generosity being offered, but how could I leave Australia without Matthew and Henry? Maybe it was foolish, but I'd spent the better part of our time together refusing to listen to Matthew, and insisting on doing things my way. In his absence, the only thing I could offer was my promise to wait for him.

Seeing the conflict within me, Mike took my hands and met my gaze with compassion. "I know this is hard. Just let me help. I'll talk to my parents. I'll keep up with everything going on in the Philippines and send you regular reports. And I promise you, Grace, if Matthew and Henry are alive, I'll do everything in my power to find them."

Mike's kind words warmed my aching heart, even though I knew he had no real means to keep his promise. "Thank you," I said, my mind flitting back once more to happier times. Had I really once thought of this sweet man as an ape? My eyes burned, and my throat ached. "I reckon there's nothing more that I can do anyhow."

"So you'll go then? You'll move in with my parents?"

"Well, let's not put the cart before the horse. You'll need to speak with them. And I insist on paying some kind of rent."

"Of course," he said, jumping to his feet. "I'll get word to them right away. And I'll make arrangements with Colonel Dorsey, too. You don't worry about anything. You just keep yourself and that baby as healthy as you can."

I cradled my belly once more, saying a quiet prayer in my mind. *Lord, please guard and protect all of us. Keep Matthew and Henry alive and bring them home. And if that isn't Your will, grant me the strength to go on.*

CHAPTER ONE

Ruby

January 7, 1945
Houston, Texas

My journey from Memorial Hospital to the Sawyers' house ended every day with a step off the bus, followed by approximately seven hundred thirty steps down Alabama Street. I found that ironic. Sometimes I actually talked to the street in my mind. Most folks might think I was crazy, but I liked to think it kept me from *going* crazy.

Sometimes I asked the street if I should just pack up and head home. Let the Lord settle everything in my past the way He saw fit. Those were my braver moments. I pictured myself walking right into the courthouse and turning myself in to Sheriff Peterson. Underneath those thick black brows his eyes would nearly pop right out of his head.

But those were the few days I amused myself on the walk home. Most days, I asked the street if I should write to Mother and Asa or the Doyle family. Maybe the army had sent them some information. I could write them a letter posing as someone else, another soldier who'd known them. But I'd chickened out every time I put pen to paper.

By the time I made it to the Sawyers' heavy oak front door, I was usually exhausted in both body and spirit. But today was different. Today, the sun had peeked out from behind the clouds, and reminded me of what a great blessing had come out of all my troubles. Today, I walked through the front door with a smile on my face.

As I entered the foyer, the signs of a full house greeted me. Jackets were strewn over the coatrack, and shoes of all sizes and colors lay at its feet. Female voices chatted in the kitchen just around the corner. I assumed they belonged to Mrs. Sawyer and her daughter, Jillian.

I headed that way, dropping my books, purse, and a small package on the dining room table as I passed by. I poked my head around the doorway to find mother and daughter standing near the stove. Mrs. Sawyer stirred creamed corn in a large skillet, while Jillian tore apart a head of lettuce beside her.

Jillian saw me first and broke into a big smile. "Hi there, Grace! 'Bout time you got home." I'd been going by the name Grace for about eight years now, and it still felt strange. Every time I heard it, a needle prick of shame came with it. She came over and hugged me, her protruding belly making it a bit difficult to reach her. "We were about to start without you."

"Oh, we wouldn't do any such thing," Mrs. Sawyer said, her eyes crinkling up behind her glasses. "Don't listen to Jillian. She's just gotten impatient waiting on that baby to pop out."

"Ain't that the truth," Jillian said. "Any day now!"

I eyed Jillian skeptically. "I don't know. Looks to me like you've got a few more weeks in you."

Jillian's blue eyes widened in horror. She shook her head, and her auburn curls bounced around her shoulders. "Don't you dare say that! I can't take one more day, much less another week or two!"

We all had a chuckle as Jillian went back to the salad. "What can I do to help?" I asked.

"We're about done in here," Mrs. Sawyer said. "Why don't you go round up the rest of the family and tell them it's time to eat."

"Yes, ma'am."

I headed through the living room to the back door, opening it to the large backyard of the Sawyers' home. I stepped onto the wooden deck and shielded my eyes from the sun. Off to my right, Mr. Sawyer stood next to the large fire pit, while glazing a hunk of meat over the fire.

To my left, I heard the joyful little voice that I looked forward to the most every day. I walked down the steps onto the grass and snuck around the side of the house where Mr. Sawyer had put up a swing in the large oak tree. Mike stood behind her, giving her a gentle push.

When she saw me coming, she squealed and nearly jumped off the swing in mid-flight. "Momma!"

"Hope!" I yelled back, as if we hadn't seen each other just the night before.

I laughed as Mike caught the swing and helped her down. She ran over to me, and I lifted her into my arms. I nestled my face into her neck and gave her a kiss. My little miracle. "Mmm, you smell like lemon cookies."

She giggled as I put her back down. "Gamma gid me two!"

"She did?"

"Uh huh. It's my bird day!"

"Are you sure?"

"Yes!" She bounced up and down. "Uncle Mike gid me a pwesent!"

I glanced up at Mike, and he shrugged his broad shoulders. "It's her bird day. What can I say?"

I couldn't help but laugh. "So what did you get?"

She ran over to the tree and picked up a stuffed rabbit that had been leaning against the trunk. She held it in the air by its throat as she ran back to me. "See? See? It's a bunny!"

"I do see. What a perfect present!"

I met Mike's gaze as he glanced over at me. He was back in his dress blue uniform, reminding me it was his last day of leave before heading back to San Diego. "You look nice," I said. "I bet the young ladies at church were fervently praying for your attention this morning."

He shot me a crooked grin. "I didn't notice."

His eyes, blue like Jillian's, studied me in that way he had, with an easy-going confidence. I turned my attention back to Hope. "It's time to eat dinner. We best get everyone rounded up."

I took Hope's hand and we strolled past Mike around to the back of the house again. Because it was such a nice day, Mrs. Sawyer had set the picnic table with plates and silverware. As Hope and I came up the deck stairs, Mrs. Sawyer and Jillian placed the last of the serving bowls on the table.

"Now, where's Harold?" Mrs. Sawyer asked.

"I'm a-coming, Margaret!" Mr. Sawyer bellowed from across the yard. He was wrestling the meat onto a platter, his straw hat nearly falling off in the effort. He straightened himself and proudly walked his prize over to the table.

"Mr. Sawyer, that surely looks wonderful," I said. "Wherever did you find meat?"

He set the platter in the center of the table and beamed back at me. "I know a fella who owns a butcher shop, and he owed me a favor. Been waiting on a perfect shoulder roast for some time."

"This is too extravagant for Hope's birthday. You really shouldn't have."

"Oh, don't worry over it a bit," he said as we took our seats. "War's coming to an end soon. I'm sure the rationing will too."

"Not soon enough," Mrs. Sawyer said.

Mr. Sawyer took no notice of her comment. "Let's bow our heads. Lord, we thank You for this wonderful meal and all Your many blessings. We pray You'll watch over Mike as he returns to his squadron, and that You keep them safe as they face the enemy. Be with George as well, Lord. Keep him safe in Your hands. We pray that we will remain patient and faithful as we wait for his return in Your time. We pray for Matthew and Henry as well, that they are safe and will come home to their families. Give us strength to trust in You. It's in Jesus's name we pray. Amen."

We sat down and began filling our plates quietly. I figured we each had someone on our minds we wished was there.

Mike dipped a heaping spoonful of mashed potatoes onto his plate. "Mother, you worry too much. We got the Nazis on the run in Europe, the Japs on the defensive in the Pacific. Things will definitely be winding down this year. You'll see. The war will be over by summer, tops."

I glanced over at Jillian and gave her an encouraging smile. Her husband, George, was stationed in Europe and wouldn't be home for the birth of their first child. I could understand how hard that would be. I'd ached for Matthew to see his baby girl, and I'd spent many nights crying out to God for his safe return. At least Jillian knew her husband was alive.

I fixed Hope a plate of food, trying to keep my thoughts from wandering to Matthew. She looked up at me with her daddy's eyes, and like so many times before, I felt a stab of pain in my chest. It was the second birthday he would miss. Another year of Hope's life he'd never know.

How long, Lord? I thought. *How long will You keep us waiting? Is he even alive?*

***

Later that afternoon, as I sat on the deck watching Hope play with her bunny in the yard, Mike came out with two glasses of sweet tea. I took one eagerly as he sat in the chair next to mine.

"Thank you," I said.

"No problem. Everything all right? You've been a bit quiet this afternoon."

"I'm all right." I didn't know what to say. Mike had done all he could to find out where Matthew and Henry might be. Talking it over was pointless. Instead, I watched Hope pull up a handful of grass and form the stalks into a small pile.

She called over to me. "Momma! Look, I made bunny a bed."

"Very nice, sweetie," I said.

Mike didn't say anything else until I'd sipped on my tea for a while longer. I could tell he was working up to his goodbye. It was never easy on any of us. He'd come home on leave several times while his squadron was stationed in San Diego over the past two months for training. But this time they were shipping out for somewhere in the Pacific. He had no idea when he might return.

"Grace," he said quietly. And from that one word, I knew we were about to have a conversation I'd been dreading for some time. "I need to ask you something."

I pushed myself up from my chair and grabbed our empty glasses. "I'm going to take these inside. Can I get you anything else?"

He stood as well, gently taking the glasses from my hands. "There's no more time for putting this off. I'm leaving in a couple of hours. We need to talk about this."

"Talk about what?"

He set the glasses on the picnic table behind us. "Grace, it's been over two years, almost three. There's been no word on either of them."

"You can't be sure of that. Henry's mother, or maybe the Doyle family—"

"I checked. I called the Doyles myself, and I wrote a letter to Henry's mother."

"What?" My heart pounded. "You contacted my...I mean..." I had to take a deep breath. "You contacted Henry's mother *and* the Doyles?" What if he'd said something about me?

"Yes, a few months ago. I just didn't know what to tell you."

"What did you say? What did *they* say?"

He frowned and shook his head. "I told them I was a friend of Henry's and Matthew's. That I'd been stationed in the Philippines with them and wanted to know if there'd been any news on their location. Matthew's sister spoke to me on the phone." His eyes softened, and he rubbed his hand along my arm. "They received a telegram not long after we left Australia, Grace. The same one Colonel Dorsey gave you."

Hope bounded up the steps, shaking me out of my stupor. "Momma! Look! I'm a bunny!" She hopped back down the steps, rolling across the grass as she hit the bottom.

"Yes, honey. I see." My vision blurred. I lowered my voice when I spoke to Mike again. "And what about Henry?"

"His father wrote me back. He said they'd received a telegram stating Henry was missing in action. That was all they knew."

He offered me a handkerchief, and I wiped at my eyes and nose. "His father? I thought his father passed away."

"I don't know. His name was Asa Graves, so I just assumed."

"Why are you telling me this? It's nothing new."

"That's my point, Grace. There's nothing new. Matthew is...he's gone. You have to accept that. You can't waste your life waiting on a ghost to come back to life."

"I'm not wasting my life. I have Hope. She's all I need for now."

He turned his gaze on Hope, and we watched her hop across the grass with the stuffed bunny on one of her shoulders. "Listen, I love Hope. She's like a ray of joy that just bursts into your heart, no matter what you're feeling. She's wonderful. But you're using her as an excuse to keep from living your life again."

"You don't know what you're talking about. You aren't even here most of the time. You can't possibly know if I'm living my life or not. Besides, I work hard at my studies, and I have a daughter to take care of—"

"And you are amazing at it all," he said. "Mother brags on you all the time. I know you're working hard. But who do you trust? Who do you share your life with?"

I shook my head and turned away. "This is ridiculous. I thought you were trying to tell me goodbye, not how to live my life."

"I'm not trying to tell you how to live your life. I just want you to be happy."

"I am happy!" I said, a little too loudly.

Hope stopped her playing and looked over at us with a curious frown. I forced a smile and waved at her, and she resumed her game. I turned back to Mike, determined to keep my cool. But he looked at me with a deep sorrow in his eyes.

"Grace, I'm leaving, and I don't know what's going to happen out there. I don't have time for..." He swore under his breath and turned away for a moment before regaining his composure. He faced me with a searching gaze. "Is there any chance for us? I mean...do you care for me at all?"

"What? Of course I do. You know I do."

He let out a quiet moan. "That's not what I mean. Look, I'm just going to be straight with you. When I'm out there on the other side of the world, I'll be missing my family and thinking about home. But most of all, I'll be missing you and Hope. Most guys carry around pictures of their wives or girlfriends with them. You know what I have?"

I shook my head, unable to form any words.

"I have a picture of you and Hope, the one you sent me after she was born. I can't tell you how many guys say my wife and kid are beautiful. And all I can do is think about how much I wish that were the truth."

My throat ached, and I struggled to find words. "Mike, please try to understand. I'm married to Matthew." He threw his hands into the air, but I kept trying to make him see. "I can't just give up on him. What if he's out there right now, trying to get back to us?"

"All right," he replied, "I get it. I know you have to hang on to that possibility for now. But the war is coming to an end. MacArthur is taking back the Philippines as we speak. If he's there, if he's alive, then I'll be happy for you and Hope. But at some point, if he's not alive...then I hope you'll consider giving me a chance."

We stood there in awkward silence for a while, with Mike's confession still hanging in the air. I wanted to tell him how much he meant to me, how I'd appreciated his friendship and his love for us over the past three years. And maybe my feelings for him could one day grow, but I couldn't let go of Matthew. Not yet.

Mike shoved his hands into his pockets. "I should get going. Gotta give Mother at least a good ten-minute cry over me."

He looked down on me with gentle resignation, and I hated to send him off on such an awful parting. I slid my arms around his waist and laid my head against his chest. "Please be careful," I said. "I couldn't take it if anything bad happened to you too."

He hesitated, but wrapped his arms around me as well. "I'll do my best." Pulling me back, he kissed my forehead before calling Hope over and tossing her into the air as she squealed with laughter. Then he set her down and kneeled in front of her. "I have to get going, little bunny."

"When you coming back?" she asked.

"Don't know yet. Might be a few months."

"Where you going?"

"To the jungle. Gotta go fight some bad guys."

"Are there bunnies in the jungle?"

"If so, I'll catch you one and bring it back."

Hope's face lit up and her mouth dropped open. She looked up at me with wide eyes. "Can I have a weal bunny?"

My throat was so knotted up, I could barely answer. "We'll see."

Hope leaned forward and lowered her voice as she spoke to Mike again. "You bwing me bunny fwom the jungle. Momma will be okay."

Mike turned and looked at me over his shoulder, his mouth smiling, but his eyes still showing his sadness. "I'm sure your mother will be just fine." Turning back to Hope, he tapped his finger on her nose. "But you better keep an eye on her for me. She might need some hugs."

"Okay," Hope said seriously. "I have good hugs."

"Yes, you do. Can I get one now?"

She grinned and wrapped her arms tight around his neck. He held her close for a minute before giving her a tickle. She giggled and let go, nearly collapsing on the deck. Mike stood and looked back at me once more. "Goodbye, Grace. You take care, all right?"

"Be safe," I managed. "And stay out of trouble."

***

That night after her bath, Hope climbed into our shared bed with an exhausted smile. I put the package I'd brought home with me that afternoon in her lap. "You have one more birthday present. This one's from me."

She reached inside and pulled out the book I'd gotten her, gasping as she ran her hand over the rabbit on the cover. "What does it say?" she asked.

"It says, *The Velveteen Rabbit.*"

"Oh, can we wead it?"

"Of course, sweetie." I walked around to my side of the bed and climbed under the covers with her. Then I opened the book and read the story to her. She listened intently, and at the end, she pulled her stuffed bunny into her lap.

"I want to name him Belteen," she said.

"I like that," I said. "Maybe Velveteen will become real one day if you love him enough."

"I hope so," she said, turning onto her side and tucking the rabbit under her arm.

I leaned over and kissed her goodnight. "Happy birthday, sweetheart."

She was fading fast, but she looked up at me through heavy eyelids. "Tell me about Daddy again."

I pushed her hair off her forehead. "You're very tired tonight. You had a big day. I'll tell you tomorrow night."

"Does he miss me?"

"Yes," I whispered.

"Does he know it's my bird day?"

I shook my head. "We'll surprise him."

Her eyes drifted closed, and her breathing deepened. I ran my hand gently over her hair, praying that somehow Matthew was still out there, fighting to get back to us.

CHAPTER TWO

Matthew

January 8, 1945
Leper Colony, North of Manila, Philippines

As I paced around the cramped hut overlooking a steaming hot rice paddy, I deflected the looks of irritation from Bruno, who stood near the entrance with his arms folded across his broad chest. Every time I coughed or rubbed at the pain in my side, he'd clear his throat and raise his right eyebrow. I'd scowl at him and ask if he could see any of the men coming. He'd scowl right back, duck his head out of the opening, and come back to his stance with a grunt that I was supposed to interpret as a "no."

After almost half an hour of this routine, I lost the small amount of patience I'd been clinging to, and I threw one of the two bamboo chairs in the hut against the wall. Pain nearly split my midsection wide open, and I dropped to one knee.

Bruno was beside me in an instant, his large, heavy hand across my back, his deep voice in my ear. "You must be careful, Major. You are not yet healed."

I couldn't breathe, so I couldn't answer. It was a good thing, because I probably would've spewed venom at him. I was tired of his babysitting, and most of all I was tired of him being right. I knew I needed rest. I needed a lot of things that weren't possible right then. But what was possible was that my men would show up with the radio. After the nightmare I'd gone through to acquire that thing, it had better still work.

At last regaining my breath, I pushed myself up to standing. I shoved Bruno's hand away from my back. "I'm fine."

He glared at me with dark eyes that could see through my pretense. He'd been unimpressed by my rank since the moment we'd met, and he didn't hesitate to speak his mind. It was what had made him both a great doctor and an annoying companion. Still, when my mind was clear, I knew I wouldn't be alive if it weren't for Bruno.

I shouldn't be alive at all, I thought. I'd lost count of how many raids from the Japanese I'd survived, this latest one being the most costly yet. Only a third of my men had shown up at our new camp so far.

Raul Diego, who'd served as my bodyguard for nearly three years, pushed his way into the hut, followed by my second in command, Arnold Harris. Our radio operator, Kiko, followed him inside, placing the radio onto the table. Diego turned to me, reading Bruno's expression and mine.

"You all right, Major?" Diego asked in his thick Spanish accent. I nodded, but he turned to Bruno for confirmation. "Why is he not resting?"

Bruno huffed. "You think I not tell him? You try!"

Diego was nearly six inches shorter than I was, and it was almost amusing to watch him glare up at me. His size was deceptive, something I'd witnessed him using to his advantage while swinging his deadly bolo. I wasn't about to get lectured by my own men, so I changed the subject.

"What took so long? How many made it to camp? Is the radio damaged?"

Harris turned his head over his shoulder toward me. "The men don't want to come into camp. They say it's too close to the colony."

Bruno nodded. "They would rather fight the Kempeitai than risk touching a leper."

"Lucky for them the Kempeitai are just as afraid," I said. "That's what makes this location perfect." I didn't mention it was about the last place left on Luzon for us to hide out from the special group of Japanese soldiers organized from the infamous Kempeitai specifically to hunt down each member of my guerrilla organization. Not even the loss of their commander had slowed them down, and they'd been far more successful in the last few weeks. I was thankful for a place to regroup, even if it was among a colony of lepers.

I had to admit, I was also nervous about making my headquarters here. The only knowledge I had of the disease was from stories in the Bible. The doctor in the colony had assured me that it was not easily contagious, but all the same, the men preferred to make camp as far away as possible. Part of me had empathized with the poor souls I saw working in the gardens, their disfigured limbs wrapped in dirty bandages. I remembered how lonely I'd felt when I'd been isolated with tuberculosis. Everyone had been scared to be around me. Except for Ruby.

The thought of her flashed through my mind, as it did in the most inconvenient moments. But I quickly pushed it aside. I'd trained my mind so well over the past three years that I'd almost forgotten what she looked like. It was disconcerting at first, like losing her all over again, but allowing myself to dwell on hopes for the future made me weak, vulnerable. And that would put more than my own life at stake. Only the present mattered. Because with the Kempeitai hunting me down, if I lost focus for even a moment, there would be no future. I'd seen that too many times already.

"We're all set," Harris said. He stood and gestured for me to inspect the radio. Kiko scooted in front of it and began adjusting the dials.

I leaned onto the table and looked over his shoulder. "Is that from a bullet?" I asked, pointing at a rip in the metal housing.

"Yes, Major," Kiko said quietly. "Garzon passed it to me as he was hit."

No one breathed for a long moment as the news sank in. "How many men did we lose?" I asked, looking at Harris.

"Twenty-two enlisted," he answered. "Three officers. Garzon, Medrano, and Dayo."

I swore under my breath as I straightened. "Harris, you'll need to make a record of our losses."

"Yes, sir."

"All right," I said. "Let's get this piece of junk up and running again."

We'd been able to establish contact with MacArthur's headquarters in Australia in June of 1944. Up to that point, it had been a harrowing task to locate one. Losing the radio now would be devastating. I watched and waited, stood, leaned over Kiko as he tinkered with the nobs, stood again. Nothing was happening. Then the ground beneath me swayed. I didn't fall, but only because sure hands grasped my elbows.

"Major, you must rest," Bruno said from my right. "Your wound will get infected."

"Listen to him, Major," Diego said from my left. "We will alert you when we have established contact."

I jerked my elbows away. "I've had enough of you two babysitting me. Don't you have anything better to do?"

"No," Bruno said. "I did not work so hard to save your life time and again, only to have you die here in the leper colony."

I'd stopped admonishing him for refusing to address me properly. He wasn't military, and he wasn't going to give in. Still, I wasn't going to be treated like a child either. I was about to dismiss all three of them when the radio finally crackled to life. I'd never been so happy to hear static.

The mood in the hut lifted, and I clapped Kiko on the back. "Good job, Lieutenant. Inform me the moment we re-establish contact with MacArthur."

"Yes, sir," Kiko said.

I eyed Bruno and Diego with triumph, and then I ducked out of the opening into the fresh air. My body hurt all over, especially the incision in my side where Bruno had removed my appendix only a few weeks before. Despite the hot, humid air, I felt a chill run through me. Fever. Infection. A battle I'd been fighting so long, I couldn't remember what it felt like to be healthy. But I wasn't about to lose now with the American advance so imminent. I hadn't received official word, but it was the only explanation for the massive movement north by the Japanese, as well as the desperation in their latest attacks on our guerrilla forces.

I made my way to my personal quarters, a hut that was a bit larger than the others, but a hut all the same. I went over to the pallet made from blankets I'd been given by the doctor in the colony—they'd received a thorough cleansing by Bruno—and I laid down for a short rest. It seemed like I'd just closed my eyes when Diego shook me awake. No doubt, he'd been standing guard outside the entire time.

"Major, we've received a message from MacArthur."

I sat up and gave the earth a moment to stop swaying. Then I grabbed my pistol and followed Diego back to the communications hut, where Harris placed a piece of paper in my hand. I read it out loud.

MacArthur to Doyle. Start immediately. Destroy enemy communications, railroads, rolling stock and trucks, planes in concealed areas, ammunition, oil, and supply dumps. Unleash maximum possible violence against the enemy.

I looked around at the grinning faces of my most trusted men, knowing I was grinning as well. It was official. The Americans were coming.

January 31, 1945

North of Manila, Philippines

Over the past three weeks the Americans had swept through the southwestern side of Luzon, from Lingayen Gulf, taking back Clark Field and Bataan on their way toward Manila. Guerrilla units that had trained for two years, quietly awaiting their chance to exact revenge on the Japanese, unleashed a torrent of violence as soon as I passed on MacArthur's orders. Most of the Japanese forces had already moved to the mountains in the northeast section of Luzon, but the guerrillas and the invading Sixth Army wiped out pockets of soldiers with relative ease.

With the flurry of activity came a concurrent flurry of intelligence that needed to be relayed to MacArthur and his generals for their approaching assault on Manila. Our tiny communications hut near the leper colony was abuzz twenty-four hours a day, with couriers coming in and out of the camp at all hours. It was both invigorating and exhausting. I'd only dared hope these days would come, when I could finally fight back, and my American patriots would surround me with the strength I needed. But I was so malnourished, so sleep-deprived, and so ill; I could barely stand for more than a few minutes at a time without some form of medical intervention from Bruno.

One morning, just as the gray light of dawn crept into my quarters, I heard a commotion outside. I jumped to my feet, just as Diego, who'd been quicker than I, darted out of the door with a pistol in each hand. I grabbed my rifle from beside my pallet and went outside to find a group of my men huddled around a filthy, bloody figure on the ground.

Bruno and Diego scooped up the Filipino man, supporting him beneath his arms. Harris peppered him with questions, with Diego translating, but he seemed oblivious. His head lifted, looking around in a daze. "I...need...Major Doyle."

I recognized him. I couldn't remember his name, but I knew his face. He was a cousin to the Baon family from a barrio just outside of Manila. They'd become an integral part of my intelligence network, and had come to mean a great deal to me. With the most recent attack on our position, my thoughts immediately flew to the Baons' safety.

I strode over to meet the group as Bruno and Diego began to carry the battered man toward the camp. I came alongside them, my heart pumping hard against my chest. "What's happened?" I asked.

He looked sideways at me, blood mingling with mud and running down the side of his dark face. "Huks."

Diego met my gaze, and I nodded my acknowledgment. We'd been getting reports of the Huks taking advantage of the devastation the Japanese were leaving behind as they retreated. The native group of communist sympathizers moved in and seized the land, demanding allegiance and taking prisoners of anyone who resisted. Others who had supported us were simply killed. They were just as brutal as the Japanese, maybe worse in my book because they preyed on their fellow Filipinos.

Once the man was settled on a cot in the infirmary, Bruno went to work patching him up. I motioned for Harris and Diego to join me outside. Diego came at me with a look of warning. "Major," he said. "I know you must be concerned, but we can't—"

"I've gotten word from MacArthur that we're to be transferred under the command of Lieutenant General Walter Krueger of the Sixth Army. I plan to contact him today and let him know we're moving our headquarters."

"Moving headquarters?" Harris's eyes widened. "Where?"

"Meycauayan."

Diego dropped his head, shaking it with disbelief. "As I said, I know you are concerned for the Baon family. But if the Huks have taken over the barrio, we are walking into a bloodbath."

"I have to agree," Harris said. "Probably best we join up with the Americans and start taking the fight to the Japs. Let the Filipinos handle the Huks." I caught the look of surprise from Diego. I couldn't remember the last time the two of them had agreed about anything.

"General Beitler will be in Manila with the 37th Infantry within days," I said. "If we move to Meycauayan, we can clear the way for them. It will be all the easier for the Americans to take back Manila."

Diego knew when to press his case, and when to take orders. He nodded his head. "Yes, Major."

Harris was a different animal. "Major, with all due respect, I think we'd be making a mistake. I realize you have strong ties to the people in the area, especially the Baon family—"

"*Captain* Harris," I shot at him, "your opinion has been duly noted. We will be moving headquarters to Meycauayan today."

Harris narrowed his eyes, his freckled face turning just a slight shade of red. "Aye, aye, *Major* Doyle. I'll pass the word along to the Lieutenants. We'll set out after breakfast." He held my gaze a moment longer, an undercurrent of resentment radiating from him, before he snapped his body around and marched toward the rest of the camp.

"Best to watch your back with that one," Diego said. "He only looks out for himself."

I acknowledged the warning with a curt nod before making my way to the communications hut, where I ordered my message sent to Lieutenant Colonel Krueger informing him of our intentions. After that, I returned to my quarters to pack my few belongings. Within the hour, the entire camp of forty men had shoved down their breakfast and packed up for the journey south. It would be a long, dangerous hike.

**

We snaked along familiar paths and streams that I'd come to know well in my travels between our various camps and Manila. Every barrio we passed was deserted, many of them pillaged and burned. Rice paddies were left abandoned. Vegetable gardens, stripped of every source of food, lay trampled underfoot. Each time we passed through one, my mind grew more anxious, and I prayed for the safety of the people I'd come to care about so deeply.

After a long day of hiking, fueled by my worry, I nearly collapsed when we reached the Baon barrio, only a few kilometers north of Meycauayan. My men fanned out as soon as we reached the main path that spread through the barrio in three lanes. Diego, who had not left my side for a moment, sensed my exhaustion, and lightly gripped my elbow. He'd know where I wanted to go, and I let him support me as we made our way to the center of the barrio.

Like all the others, the little nipa palm shack was completely ransacked. Most of the huts were empty, and a few held only crying old women. The stench of death hung all around us. As Diego approached the Baon family's hut, he directed the three men in front of him to clear the surrounding area for any dangers. We stopped just outside the opening and called out for Dakila. There was no answer.

I stepped away from Diego's support, steeling myself for what I might find inside. Lowering my head, I entered the hut. I could smell the body before I saw it. Dakila Baon, chief of the barrio, my friend and most loyal supporter, lay on the ground unmoving. I fell to my knees beside him, placing my hand on his broad chest, and bowed my head.

"Thank you my friend, for being such a true companion. I will remember you always."

I heard shuffling behind me and jumped to my feet. I pulled my pistol from my waist as Diego stepped in front of me. But it was only Jabol, Dakila's son, who came into the hut. I dropped my weapon and embraced him like a brother while he quietly assured me he was all right.

When he stepped back, I asked him what had happened.

"The Japs came through first, setting fields on fire, slaughtering animals," he said. "They moved quickly, so there were no deaths. But then the Huks came, demanding everyone in the barrio pay them honor. They claimed the barrio as their own. Father stood up to them." Jabol stepped around me and looked down on his father with admiration. "He was the first of many to die."

I put a hand on Jabol's shoulder, trying to comfort him. "And Malaya?"

Jabol turned and found my gaze. "I am not sure. She was not here at the time."

Relief washed over me, and I turned my back to them to gather my emotions. Malaya, Jabol's sister, had given me strength when I'd had none. Without her, I'd be dead for sure. All I could do now was hope and pray she was safe.

CHAPTER THREE

Ruby

February 1, 1945

Houston, Texas

"And Gamma and me made a bed for Belteen," Hope said as she followed me around the table.

"Grandma and *I*," I said.

"Momma, you weren't there."

I set the last plate down and smiled at her. "No, sweetie. I meant that the proper way to say it is, 'Grandma and I made a bed for Velveteen.' Understand?"

She wrinkled her little nose and considered my correction. Then she shrugged and went right on with her story as if I hadn't interrupted her, following me around the table for the second time. I set the silverware in place and did my best to keep up.

"Gamma made a dress for Belteen, too. See?" She lifted the bunny into the air by its throat.

"I see."

"And Belteen took a nap wid me...I mean, Belteen took a nap wid I."
She stopped walking and looked up at me in the most serious fashion a
two-year-old could manage. "Momma, that don't sound wight."

I giggled as I set the last place at the table, then I bent down and
motioned for her to come to me, wrapping her in my arms. "It's a bit
confusing, I reckon. But you'll soon learn the right way to say it." I kissed
the top of her head. "You're right. It should be, 'Velveteen took a nap
with me.'"

I was about to give her a tickle, when a knock pounded on the front
door. My heart leapt into my chest at the same time as Mrs. Sawyer
came around the corner. Her expression reflected my own fear, and I
stood immediately.

Neither of us said anything. We didn't have to. She walked with
deliberate steps to the front door, her body stiff as she opened it.
Footsteps flew down the stairs, and I glanced over to see Jillian
descending with the baby in her arms.

"Is someone at the door?" she asked, her voice low but tense.

"Yes," I said. "Your mother is speaking with them."

Jillian came over beside me and we both kept an eye on Mrs.
Sawyer's back. Her posture relaxed, a signal that it wasn't a military
officer with a life-altering telegram in hand. My heart continued to
thunder a few moments more, as Mrs. Sawyer closed the door and came
toward us with a box in her hand.

"It's all right, Jillian," she said. "It's just a package for Grace from
Mike. You can go on back upstairs and finish getting the baby down for
his nap."

Jillian bounced little George, Jr. in her arms. Her eyes were
bloodshot from lack of sleep. She nodded and headed back up the stairs,
probably to join him in his nap.

Mrs. Sawyer brought the box from Mike over to the table, her face
still ashen. "I swear, I think I'd rather he not send any more packages if

it's going to give everyone a heart attack every time there's a knock at the door."

She dropped into a chair and pushed the box toward me. I felt like I should apologize, but I wasn't sure what for. I took the seat next to her and tore open the box. Inside I found a letter, two small jars of macadamia nuts, and a small box addressed to Hope all sitting atop some kind of garment on the bottom. I pulled the items out, unfolding a blue halter-top dress covered in white flowers.

"Momma, it's so pretty!" Hope said, running her hand along the fabric.

"It certainly is," I said. I glanced at Mrs. Sawyer. "He shouldn't have. I couldn't wear something like this."

Mrs. Sawyer smiled. "Hold it up, dear, and let me see it." I did so, and she nodded her head. "It would look wonderful on you. Just the style these days for girls your age."

Hope shook one of the jars of nuts. "What is this?"

"Gifts from Uncle Mike, sweetie," I said. I handed the smaller box to her. "This one's for you."

She pulled the top off and gasped. Inside was a matching set of a bracelet and necklace covered in tiny shells. "Momma, I got pretties too! Can I wear them?"

I helped her put the jewelry on, and Mrs. Sawyer and I admired them with the proper amount of excitement. "We'll have to write Uncle Mike a letter and thank him," I said.

Mrs. Sawyer stood, her usual joyful demeanor restored. "I best get back to the kitchen before I burn up supper. You girls enjoy your gifts."

Hope handed me a jar and asked me to open it. I twisted off the top and let her grab a few of the nuts, taking a small handful myself. "Why don't you go show Grandpa your pretties?"

Hope climbed down from her chair and ran down the hall toward Mr. Sawyer's study. I waited until I heard her excited voice talking up a storm before I opened the letter. I grinned at the sight of his sloppy handwriting. I'd teased him numerous times about not being able to read his letters, so he tried harder to be neat. Fortunately, I'd grown use to making out illegible handwriting while working at the hospital.

Dear Grace,

I hope that you and my little bunny are doing well. Tell Hope I'm searching all over Hawaii for a bunny to bring home. None are willing to cross the ocean as of yet, though. I'm sending her some genuine Hawaiian jewelry so she can play dress-up in style. I sent you something for playing dress-up too. I hope you'll put it on and go out on the town with Jillian. You girls need to have some fun.

On a more serious note, I'm sorry for leaving things between us a little strained. You know I just want you and Hope to be happy and to have the life you deserve. I think you know in your heart Matthew would want that for you both. Just think about it. Maybe once the war is over, we can finally make peace with everything that's happened.

We're shipping out soon, but I'll write again when I can. Take care of yourself, and give Hope a kiss for me.

Be seeing you soon,
Mike

After supper, I helped Mrs. Sawyer with the dishes while Mr. Sawyer took a turn reading *The Velveteen Rabbit* to Hope in the living room. His voice deepened as he acted out the part of the wise old skin horse, and I couldn't help but smile.

"I think he enjoys that story as much as she does," I said as I took a plate from Mrs. Sawyer and began drying it with the towel.

She smiled and paused, listening as well. "I think you're right." She went back to her washing, and I watched her for a moment, wondering how to broach the subject that had been on my mind all during supper.

"I hope you know how grateful I am," I said. "You all opened your home to us and welcomed Hope and me like we were family."

She gave me a warm smile as she handed me a plate and a glass to dry. "Don't even mention it, dear. We love having you both. Harold is just tickled to death over Hope."

I put the dishes in the cabinet, feeling my stomach knot. "The hospital has offered me a position once I finish my exams."

Mrs. Sawyer dropped her dishrag. "Oh, Grace! That's wonderful news!" She wrapped her dripping hands around my neck and we both laughed. "Sorry," she said, stepping back. "I'm just so proud of you."

"I couldn't have made it through the last couple of years without you taking care of Hope while I was working and studying." Mrs. Sawyer turned back to her washing, her smile still lingering, and I tried to find the right words. "But I was thinking that once I get started with the new position, I should look for a more permanent living situation."

This time when she let go of the rag, she removed her rubber gloves as well. "What's this? Why would you go and do a thing like that? You and Hope are welcome to stay here as long as you like. There's no need to think about placing any extra burdens on yourself."

"It's just..."

"Just what?" she asked, her eyes so warm and trusting.

"Well, with Jillian and the baby here until George comes home, I just figured you would want to spend more time with them. I don't want to be a burden. And now that I'll have a steady income, I can pay for a place for us to live."

"You have a place to live right here, for as long as you want." She lowered her chin and gave me the no-nonsense expression she usually reserved for Harold. "Does this have anything to do with Mike? He mentioned he thought he might've upset you before he left."

"No, it isn't Mike."

"I'm not blind, you know. I see you two together."

My defenses began to mount. "Mrs. Sawyer—"

"Oh, I know, I know. You can tell me all the same excuses you've been telling me for years. But at some point, you need to accept the truth God has given you about your situation. Holding on to hope is a good thing, until it becomes an excuse not to live your life or take chances on loving again."

"I understand—"

"Well, I certainly don't," she interrupted again. "You have people here who love you. Who accept you as part of the family. And my son, who loves you, and loves your little girl as if she were his own. You can't tell me you don't care for him as well. I have eyes. I see how you smile at each other. He brings out a joy in you that no one else seems to manage. Why can't you give him a chance? Give all of us a chance?"

I'd been doing my best to hold back tears, but they slid down my cheeks anyway. "I do love all of you," I managed. "I *really* do. I wish I could make you understand just how much. And Mike is...he's a wonderful friend, and I do care for him. But my heart still belongs to Matthew. It always has."

She pulled me back into her arms and patted my back. "Oh, Grace. I didn't mean to upset you. I shouldn't have said anything. I'm sorry, dear. Let's just forget all this nonsense for now, all right? You and Hope stay right here as long as you want. And we'll be whatever kind of family God intends for us to be."

I closed my eyes and prayed for wisdom. This lovely, kind, generous woman had no idea who was standing in her kitchen. How could I continue to live this lie?

***

"Momma," Hope said as she peered up at me from beneath the covers. "You been crying?"

I bent over and kissed her forehead. "Just a little. Nothing to worry over."

"You miss Daddy again."

"Yes. Very much."

"And Uncle Mike?"

"Yes."

"And Uncle Henwy?"

"Yes, sweetie."

She squeezed Velveteen up under her chin, and her eyes closed slowly before popping open again. "Pray, Momma. You tell God. He helps."

"You want to pray with me?" She nodded. I gently pushed her brown curls off her forehead and prayed. "Dear God, thank You for Grandma and Grandpa. Thank You for Aunt Jillian and Uncle Mike, for a warm home and good food."

"And Belteen," Hope said with her eyes closed.

"And Velveteen. Thank You, Lord, for Your goodness and mercy. We ask that you watch over Daddy and Uncle Henry. Please keep them safe and bring them home as soon as possible. Please be with Uncle Mike and Uncle George, and all the other men and women around the world who are away from their families. Please bring peace to the world. Thank You for Your blessings, and please forgive us for our sins. In Jesus's name we pray. Amen."

Hope's breathing was already deepening as I finished. I brushed my hand over her hair one last time. Then I dropped my head onto my hands as I continued to kneel by her bed.

Oh Lord, I come to You with such a heavy heart. You know the burdens I carry, despite my best efforts to give them over to You. I'll never understand Your ways, but I have promised to follow Your leading. Please guide me now. I feel such a strong desire to protect the Sawyers from the consequences of my past actions, and yet I know that Hope needs a family. I suppose I need one too. Am I being selfish? I know in my heart I'll someday have to face the conviction hanging over me, and I will face it with as much strength as You will give. But what about Hope? What about the Sawyers? Won't I just be hurting them by allowing them to believe I'm someone I'm not?

I reached for a handkerchief from the side table and wiped away the tears from my face. My heart filled with a longing for Matthew and Henry that physically ached in my chest. *Oh, Lord, please bring them back! If only they were here, I could figure all of this out. Please, can't You bring them home to us?*

The thoughts that often haunted me in my darkest moments once again whispered doubt and fear into my mind. Matthew was gone. Henry was gone. I was on my own. And one day, Mike and his family would find out everything as well. And then I'd truly be all alone in the world.

CHAPTER FOUR

Matthew

February 2, 1945
San Miguel, Philippines

Within two days of setting up our guerrilla headquarters at Meycauayan, I received an order to report to MacArthur's command post in San Miguel, a small town about ninety miles north of Manila. As Diego and I rode north in the jeep sent to retrieve me, I wondered what I might say to MacArthur when I finally met him face to face.

Before the war, I'd only held the general in moderate regard. During our desperate days on Bataan and Corregidor, my opinion took a nosedive when he left us to fend off the brutal bombardment of the Japanese. But the people of the Philippines held on to his promise to return like a life preserver and, over time, I'd come to greatly respect the man's determination to come back for us. It had become a faintly growing light at the end of a very dark tunnel.

When we arrived at the whitewashed building in San Miguel, Diego stepped out of the jeep and walked with me to the front door. "You want

49

me to come inside, Major?" he asked, eying the sentry at the door with suspicion.

"No. I'm fine. Relax for a bit, why don't ya?"

"What is this *relax* you speak of?" He offered me a tense smile with his salute.

I shook my head at him and returned the salute. I gave my name to the sentry, and he saluted as well before passing me in. The duty officer seated at the desk looked up at me and did a double take.

"May I ask whom you're here to see?" he said, looking at me as if I were lost.

"General MacArthur," I replied.

He looked me up and down with concern. I couldn't help but note that the young man filled out his crisp uniform quite nicely, as if he'd eaten a regular meal every day of his life. I could barely remember what it felt like to be satisfied after a meal. I must have looked like a threadbare scarecrow.

I was keenly aware that my faded fatigues and decaying boots spoke ill of my station, but there was nothing to be done about it. So I held my head as high as I could without feeling dizzy.

"You'll need to speak with Colonel Watson first," he said, pointing at a phone behind his desk. "You can call him from there."

I stepped over to the phone and lifted the handle to my ear. After a moment, a rigid voice came on the line. "Colonel Watson."

"Sir, my name's Major Matthew Doyle. I was ordered here to speak with—"

"Yes, yes. I've been expecting you. Come on up."

I headed up the stairs to his office, where a young lieutenant awaited me at the door. He opened it right away, and I stepped into what must have been the office of the previous business owner. Bookshelves were stocked full of items and boxes of papers were stacked along the wall to my left. Maps cluttered the desk and the wall off to my right.

Colonel Watson came out from behind the desk and gave my hand a rigorous shake. "Major Doyle, welcome. It's good to finally meet you."

He looked me over just as the duty officer had and appeared to come to the same unfavorable conclusion. "I apologize for the state of my appearance, sir," I said. "I haven't had a proper change of clothes in a couple of years."

Something shifted in his expression, and he pressed his mouth into a line before barking for the lieutenant to return. Then he looked at me and asked as if it were more of a command. "What can I get you while you wait for the general? Anything. You name it. A drink? A smoke? I can get you whatever you'd like."

My face warmed as I thought of the one thing I'd craved most often in my dreams. I felt like a kid hoping for a treat. "Sir, would it be possible to have a bit of ice cream?"

His stern mouth broke into a grin. "Of course! Lieutenant, get Major Doyle some ice cream!"

***

When Colonel Watson delivered me to General MacArthur's office, the general strode over to me, gave my hand a firm shake, and then patted my back so hard I almost coughed up the ice cream I'd inhaled earlier.

MacArthur was an imposing figure. Though he was an inch or two shorter than I, his broad shoulders dwarfed my emaciated frame, and his direct gaze commanded respect. His khaki uniform was perfectly pressed, leaving me feeling like a beggar in the presence of royalty. But he soon put me at ease and led me to the sofa near his desk where another officer stood waiting on me.

"This is General Dorsey," MacArthur said. "He's head of our intelligence here, so he'll be sitting in on our little meeting."

I acknowledged the recently promoted general and shook his extended hand. "It's good to finally meet you, Major," he said. "Your work here with the guerrillas has been invaluable in preserving the lives of Americans and Filipinos alike. Your country owes you a debt of gratitude."

"Thank you, General. But I was just doing my job."

MacArthur took the seat behind his desk and gestured for me to take a seat on the sofa with General Dorsey. "I want to especially thank you for your efforts to preserve the lives of the civilian population in your operations here. It's no secret that the people of the Philippines mean a great deal to me. Your efforts have gone a long way in making my return possible."

A twinge of guilt hit me as I thought of my failures to protect them more than my successes. We'd suffered so many losses over the past three years on these islands. I was eager to make sure their deaths were not in vain.

MacArthur launched into an in-depth interview over all the activities of the guerrillas of late. How many were there? Who could be trusted? Who were the commanders? How well were they trained? The questions went on and on for some time.

I answered him with as much detail as I could. "Sir, in the Luzon province, we have approximately 38,000 men and women and about 3,700 officers. They are eagerly awaiting your orders and will be loyal to the very end."

MacArthur cracked a pleased smile before digging into more questions, this time turning his attention to the prisoner-of-war camps and the position of the Japanese in Manila. I answered each question as thoroughly as I could, impressed by his understanding of the situation. All in all, the interview lasted nearly an hour.

When he was finally finished, MacArthur stood and came around his desk, once again extending his hand. "You've done a fine job, Major Doyle. Is there anything else I can do for you?"

I shook his hand and thanked him. "Actually, sir, I'm anxious to know how and when my troops will be incorporated into the regular army. They need to know that their service is appreciated and that they'll be treated as equals."

At this MacArthur frowned and glanced over at General Dorsey. "I understand your position," MacArthur said, "and I respect it immensely. I assure you that your men will be treated well."

"It's just...well, sir, if I may speak frankly, they've endured a great deal of hardship, all the while expecting to get their shot at fighting back."

"Surely you can't expect that these men are ready to fight in the regular American army?" General Dorsey spoke up.

The disbelief in his voice set me on edge. "I've trained them myself, and yes, they are ready. Even when they had every opportunity to attack the Japanese positions, they have followed the orders given to them to wait for reinforcements. They've seen their friends and families tortured and murdered, they've been hunted like animals, and many of them have given their own lives. They've done all this for the promise that when the opportunity comes, they will be able to fight for their own freedom."

"Perhaps their cause will best be served by allowing superior forces to do the job."

I stared at General Dorsey while doing everything I could to hold my tongue. *Superior forces?*

MacArthur cleared his throat. "I assure you, Major Doyle, if and when the opportunity presents itself, your forces will be called upon to fight. We'll need every fighting man available to beat back the Japanese. For now, I expect you and your men will continue to perform your duties admirably. The most important thing we need from you right now is information, which you have delivered with the highest professionalism. Again, I want to thank you for everything you've done." He gestured toward the door. "Please let Colonel Watson know of any of your needs for supplies for your men. If you have any trouble at all securing these, you let me know directly."

"Thank you, sir. One more thing, if I may, sir," I said, determined to get my boys the recognition they deserved. "I've promoted many men over the past three years, including several lieutenant colonels. I'd like to request that their commissions be honored. I'll also be recommending several for awards and medals."

MacArthur nodded. "You can vouch for these men?"

"Absolutely."

"Then I'll see to it."

General Dorsey followed me out into the hall afterward and walked with me toward Colonel Watson's office. "I wanted to speak with you privately for a moment, Major."

"Yes, sir," I said, still a little on edge from his comments. "What can I do for you?"

"Well, I wanted to let you know that early on in the war, when you were first left on Mindanao, we had some sketchy information on your whereabouts. We picked up Japanese communications that led us to believe you'd been in some skirmishes on Panay, and they were hunting you and some other Americans who had escaped from prison camps."

"That sounds about right," I said, remembering the weeks I'd trudged across the island north of Mindanao, hoping and praying to find anyone with a boat.

"We were getting spotty intelligence from the area that guerrilla units were forming, and in the best interest of protecting all of you, we made a decision to disseminate information to confuse the Japanese. We were hoping it would take them off your tail."

I stopped walking and faced the general. "Sir, what exactly are you getting at?"

"You and some other Americans in the area were officially declared dead. And your families were notified as such."

"You told my family I was dead?"

"Well, yes. We weren't sure you were even alive at the time. Like I said, the Jap communications we intercepted were spotty, and they've been known to put out false information. I personally spoke to your wife—"

"My wife? She thinks I'm dead too?"

A strange expression came over his face, almost a smile. "Well, I did my best to convince her, but I don't think she bought it. That's one determined young lady."

I couldn't believe what I was hearing. Mother and Mary must have been devastated. And Ruby. What must she have thought? "Sir, do you know where my wife is now?"

"I arranged for her transportation to Houston. I believe she had a family there she was going to stay with. I can contact her for you and let her know you've been located. There's no reason to protect your whereabouts anymore."

I could hardly process the information he'd given me. I hadn't let myself even imagine the outside world for so long. I didn't know what to do. Thoughts of home, thoughts of Ruby, made me weak. I had to stay strong, focused on the mission directly in front of me. My men needed me.

"Sir, I appreciate the information. I'm sure my wife and family would be relieved to know I'm alive. If you can arrange for that, I would be grateful."

"I'll take care of it myself, Major."

On the drive back to my headquarters at Meycauayan, I allowed myself only a few moments to think about Ruby. I pictured her standing beside me on our wedding day, holding her beneath me on our wedding night. My heart stirred, and I prayed she would forgive me for everything that had happened since.

***

I returned to headquarters to a group eager to take up arms against the Japanese. When I relayed the news to my staff that we would only be operating in a support role, the protests were loud and profane.

"What have we been doing this for if not to fight the dirty Japs when the time came?" Captain Harris yelled. "We've been sitting on the sidelines for three years!"

"We've hardly been sitting on the sidelines," I said, trying to keep calm. "Our work here has been instrumental in making the recapture of the Philippines even possible. MacArthur said so himself."

"Oh, he did? Well that's just great!" He paced around the hut we'd been using for meetings, his freckled face growing redder by the second as he continued to swear.

Others voiced their objections and complaints, but none as vehemently as Harris. Diego stood just off to my right, his arms crossed, his stance wide and ready to respond. We'd already had this discussion on the way back from San Miguel, so he had been prepared for the eruption.

Kiko stepped forward and raised his voice, his emotions thickening his Spanish accent. "Maybe we should return to our barrios. At least there we can help rebuild what's left of them. The Americans will never treat us as equals."

Diego stepped around me and pointed his finger back in my direction. "Major Doyle is American. He treats us like men. He treats us like brothers. We fight with him because he fights with us. With the Filipino man. We must stay with Major Doyle and do as he has ordered."

Harris huffed and stomped toward the entrance. "Well, I'm an American too, and I don't aim to sit around and watch the war like a spectator." He gestured around the room. "And any of you are welcome to join me." At that, he ducked and left the hut.

The remaining eight men looked around at each other and at me with anxious expressions. "I understand your frustrations," I said. "I really do. But I also believe MacArthur has a plan, and if we stick with him, we'll win this war, and you'll get your homes and your country back."

Diego nodded. "This is your country now too, hermano. I am with you."

A few of the others agreed with Diego, but Kiko couldn't be swayed. "Japanese must pay for what they've done to my people. I cannot stand around and do nothing." He stormed out of the hut as well.

Diego crossed himself and mouthed a prayer before turning to me. "What do we do now?"

"We wait for orders," I said.

***

By the time I reached my hut I was so exhausted that Diego and Bruno were supporting me by the elbows once again. I was looking forward to taking the sedatives Bruno had been feeding me for months, and shutting my mind off to the rest of the world for a few hours. But as I stepped through the small door, ready to collapse onto my pallet, I noticed a figure on the other side of the hut, half hidden in the shadowy corner. I froze and reached for my pistol.

Without hesitation, Diego maneuvered himself between the intruder and me. "Come out where I can see you," he demanded.

The small, graceful figure of Malaya Baon stepped into the patch of fading sunlight created by the window. My racing heart gave me a burst of adrenaline that made my head swim for a moment. Diego and I both lowered our weapons just as Bruno ducked inside as well.

I stared at Malaya, her fragrant, feminine presence a stark contrast to that of our sweaty, filthy aroma. "Malaya," I said, unable to hide the relief in my voice. "Thank God. Are you all right?"

"Yes," she said, glancing at Bruno and Diego. "I am sorry if I frightened you. Captain Harris said it would be all right to wait here."

"Of course. It's fine." I turned to Diego. "Thank you for your help in the meeting. I'm exhausted and would like to get some rest now. We'll discuss our options moving forward in the morning."

I meant the statement as a dismissal, but he looked between Malaya and me with concern. "Major, I can show Miss Baon to a place where she can rest for the night. Perhaps you can speak in the morning when you've had your rest. It has been a very long day."

"I appreciate your concern. But I'd like to speak to Miss Baon for a moment alone before retiring for the night."

Bruno frowned, his dark eyes narrowing. "You'll need these," he said, slamming two pills onto a nearby bamboo table.

"Thank you, Bruno," I said. "Goodnight."

He ducked out of the door, leaving only Diego to decide what he should do.

"Diego, it's fine. Really. Go on and get some rest."

Diego shot Malaya a final glance, shook his head, and mumbled to himself as he stomped out of the hut. Once alone, I went to her and gave her a hug, letting out a deep sigh of relief.

"I'm so sorry about your father," I said.

She held on to me, talking into my chest. "Jabol said you came to the barrio. I wanted to let you know that I am all right."

I stepped back to put some distance between us. "You can't go back into Manila. I spoke with MacArthur today. They're heading there soon, and the Japs are mining the city, digging in for a bloody battle. I don't want you mixed up in all that."

She managed a tired smile. "I can take care of myself. Do not worry for me, Major."

"Go home. Mourn your father. Comfort your family."

She wrapped her arms around her waist and looked up at me with large dark eyes. "And what about you?"

"Me?"

"Yes. You are ill. I can see it myself. Who will care for you?"

"I'm all right. I just need a bit of rest when this is all over."

She walked over to the table and picked up the pills Bruno had left behind. "And what are these? Sedatives?"

"Antibiotics."

She lifted an eyebrow. "If you are so tired, why do you need help to sleep?"

There was no getting anything past her. It was what made her such a good spy. "Too much on my mind, I suppose. There's still a lot of war to be fought."

Malaya dropped her gaze to the ground. "And then it will be time for you to return home to America. To your wife. Your family." Her eyes flickered up to mine. "Your real life."

"Yes. I suppose that time will come. But I can't think about that now. There's too much to do here, and the chances of surviving are grim at best. Like I said, there's still a lot of war left to be fought."

"Then you will need your rest," she said. "I will go now. Take care of yourself."

"Malaya, promise me you'll stay out of Manila until this is over."

"Is that an order, Major?"

"Does it need to be, Lieutenant?"

Her gaze was steady and true, as it always had been. "No. I will go home as you ask. Will I see you again? Or should I say goodbye now?"

"I'll try to come see you and Jabol as soon as I can. Just stay out of trouble."

She smiled then, the broad, beautiful smile that had convinced so many young Japanese soldiers to spill their secrets. "Then I will wait for you."

She swept out of the tiny room, leaving a ghost of her fragrance entwined with the dank staleness in the air. It reminded me of Ruby, and I fought to put my conflicting feelings out of my mind as I took my pills and lay down on the pallet. There was so much I still needed to do in the Philippines. How could I possibly leave these people—my people— behind?

CHAPTER FIVE

Matthew

April 17, 1945
Meycauayan, Philippines

Manila was secured on March 4, 1945, when the last Japanese stronghold of the city, Intramuros, was liberated. It was a significant, but costly victory. Manila was leveled, with only a single building here and there still standing in usable condition. But the Japanese had been driven from the city into the northern mountains of the Luzon province. With the Philippines soon safely in American hands again, the drive toward the islands of Japan would pick up speed.

As for the thousands of Filipino guerrilla forces across Luzon, MacArthur decided they would be incorporated into a Filipino Army. After being processed and trained, they would complete the liberation of their country by defeating the Japanese in the north. I spent March and April on the move between regiments across southern Luzon, overseeing the processing and training of the Filipinos.

Although food and medicine were no longer in short supply, my body struggled to keep up with the frenetic pace, and it refused to adjust to regular amounts of food. I couldn't seem to shake the dysentery and bouts of fever plaguing me during my travels. Bruno fed me a regular diet of various pills, including bromides to calm my nerves and sulfa tabs to fight infection. Somewhere in the back of my mind, I knew I was walking a tightrope with my health, but I kept thinking that if I could just make it through the next stop, I would walk back the meds as my body adjusted.

When I made it back to Meycauayan in mid-April, Bruno insisted I rest a few days before heading for another regimental inspection. I was so completely exhausted, I didn't argue. On the morning of April 17, I awoke feeling as close to rested as I had since escaping Mindanao. It was also my birthday.

I'd planned on keeping a low profile that day, trying to catch up on paperwork and seeing if I could get through the day with fewer pills propping me up. But word had gotten around somehow that it was my birthday, and when I stepped into the mess tent, I was greeted by a round of cheers and congratulations.

Diego came up beside me and clapped his hand on my back, nearly knocking me onto my face. "Feliz cumpleaños, Major! Today we celebrate!"

"No, no," I said. "Today we work. There's too much to be done."

But my protests were in vain. The cook presented me with a special breakfast of six pancakes stacked on top of one another, with a candle on top. The men broke out into a chorus of "Happy Birthday," and I humbly blew out the candle.

I was hoping that would be the end of it, but not long after breakfast, a group of survivors from the Baon barrio arrived, including Malaya and her brother, Jabol. Determined to celebrate despite their recent tragedy, they'd brought a feast with them, including a band. They brought native drums, kubings, which were small bamboo harps played against the lips by adjusting the shape of the mouth, and several kudyapi, which were larger stringed instruments held across the lap.

As soon as I saw the party, I knew my planned day of recovery was over. My head began to throb and I became breathless, aware of my heart rate speeding up. Making my excuses, I hunted Bruno down, and requested his help.

"Major," he said, frowning at me, "we need to talk about your medicine."

"Yes, I know. You can reduce the pills tomorrow. I just need to get through today."

"You should see army doctors now. They can treat you better."

"You're the one I trust," I replied, growing impatient.

I could see that statement amused him. "If you trust me, then you should listen. Your medicine is too high. You need to give your body time to adjust to all the changes naturally."

"Look, either give me the pills or don't. But I don't need a lecture right now."

He shrugged and reached for a bottle on the shelf behind him. "All right, then. Bromide for today."

He dropped the pills into my hand, which I could feel quivering as I held it out. I just had to make it through one more day. *Just one more day.*

I swallowed the pills and headed out of the medical tent, running into Jabol as I crossed the grounds. We shook hands again. "Major, it is good to see you looking well," Jabol said. "How old are you now? Should be about fifty, no?"

"Thirty-two, actually," I laughed. "Feels like fifty sometimes, though. Seems like I've been here forever."

We continued walking toward the center of camp where my men and our visitors were busy setting up for the party. Guys climbed trees to hang lanterns and colored streamers, and the women went about setting out all kinds of native food on large palm leaves.

"I don't want to seem ungrateful," I said, "but this is too much, Jabol."

"No, my friend. After all you have done for my people, this is not enough. We will show you today what you mean to us."

Malaya approached us from a cluster of palm trees where she'd been directing the men hanging lanterns. Her flowered halter dress hugged her tiny waist, the bright colors showing off her tanned skin. She smiled at me, sending a flutter through my chest I had to ignore. *Ruby.*

"Why are we hanging lanterns?" I asked. "It's broad daylight."

"Do you not remember how we celebrate, Major?" she asked. My mind went to another celebration over a year ago, and I could see from the twinkle in her eyes, that was exactly her intent. "It will be long after dark before it is over."

Before I could respond, a caravan of official vehicles pulled into camp. A young Filipino boy in uniform jumped out of the lead sedan and opened the back passenger door. Miguel Herrera stepped out with a broad smile and a booming voice.

"Ah, Major Doyle! It is so good to see you, my friend." He extended his hand and I took it with great joy.

"Señor Herrera, it is wonderful to see you as well," I said. "I was afraid for your safety with all the fighting in Manila."

His smile fell to a hard line. "It will take a long time for the people of Manila to recover from the great evil of Japan. But Filipinos are a proud people, and our hearts are strong. We will rebuild our treasured city." He turned to Malaya and embraced her. "Señorita, you are lovely as always. Are you taking care of the old man?"

Malaya's gaze flickered to mine. "When he will let me, Señor. He is a stubborn patient, as you know."

Herrera laughed as several others who'd been in the vehicles came up behind him. I recognized the three men and their wives from the covert meeting we'd had the previous fall, just before the Japanese had decimated my intelligence network in Manila.

I shook each of their hands and welcomed them to our headquarters. The three couples, the Vegas, the Gasparis, and the Moyas had all been instrumental in gathering intelligence on Japanese troop movements through their various businesses in Manila, all coordinated by Malaya.

The reunion was happy on the surface, but the absence of the friends we'd lost along the way brought a melancholy undercurrent to our conversation.

The party began around noon. We filled our stomachs with food and our hearts with merriment. The band played while we danced. The men of the barrio and my soldiers shared stories of how they'd tricked the Japanese and snuck into and out of Manila undetected. And there were many kind gifts offered in my honor, including paintings and carvings.

Late in the afternoon, two army jeeps arrived carrying four of the generals I'd been in communications with throughout the campaign to retake Luzon. I shook each of their hands and accepted their congratulations. Colonel Watson arrived shortly thereafter, bringing formal congratulations from MacArthur.

By the time I'd greeted everyone properly and shown them around the camp, my body was trembling from fatigue. I had no intention of losing control now, so I called Bruno into the medical tent again to request a little more help.

He furrowed his brow and studied me closely in the fading sunlight. "Major, this is no good."

"Tell me about it," I said. "I can't go around collapsing in front of all these generals now, can I? I swear, tomorrow I'll rest and everything will be fine."

He eyed me like he knew better. Malaya entered the tent, her face an expression of concern. "What is going on?" she asked. "Are you not well?"

"I'm fine," I said, gritting my teeth. "Just a little tired."

"Then perhaps you should rest," she said.

"Perhaps you should mind your own business, Lieutenant," I snapped.

She stared at me, unflinching. I didn't care what she thought at that moment, or Bruno for that matter. The pressure in my head was growing intense. "Look, my head's killing me; my stomach's in knots. Just give me something to get me through the next couple of hours."

Bruno grunted and handed me a couple of pills. Malaya shook her head as I swallowed them. "You are being foolish," she said. "You are going to kill yourself, and I cannot watch." She threw her hands up and walked out.

***

The party lasted long into the night, just as Malaya had said it would. I did my best to enjoy it. After all, it had been years since there'd been anything to celebrate. I smiled at everyone, even joined in the dancing now and again. But I could feel my body shutting down. I convinced myself that once I could go to sleep, I could rest and recover. I had it all under control, because that was how I'd operated for four years in a place where surrender was worse than death. I wasn't about to surrender now.

The next morning, I awoke with another splitting headache and trembling limbs. But this was much worse. I could barely sit up, let alone stand. When Diego caught sight of me, he immediately sent for Bruno, and the two of them did their best to get me on my feet.

The ground took a dip, and my legs shook uncontrollably. I fell into my friends' arms, and they laid me back down. Then the strangest things began to happen all at once. It was almost as if I split into two people. One of me lay on the pallet convulsing as if I were having some sort of seizure, unable to communicate anything.

The other me realized all this was happening, and seemed to be observing it from a distance. I wondered if this was some bizarre nervous breakdown, and I had the urge to laugh at myself. I was being ridiculous. I tried to tell them I just needed a moment to gather my wits.

"He needs army hospital," Bruno said.

"I will drive," Diego said. "Help me move him into the jeep."

Again I tried to tell them to give me a minute, but it came out in a garbled mess of syllables. They lifted me off the ground and loaded me into the back of a jeep. Malaya's voice came at me as if through a tunnel, asking what was wrong. Then she was beside me, lifting my head into her lap.

Diego started the jeep and we flew along the roads leading to Manila. I tried to process the sounds of honking and cursing as Diego dodged around the crowded streets. Malaya lowered her face near to mine, speaking softly to me the whole time.

"Just stay calm, Major," she said. "Everything will be all right."

I was shaking, my chest was tight, and everything about my body felt strangely detached. I seemed to float in and out of consciousness, because things moved in a disjointed fashion. I was in the jeep one moment, and in a hospital room a few moments later, with a doctor shining a bright light into my eyes. Then there was nothing but darkness.

CHAPTER SIX

Ruby

April 25, 1945
Houston, Texas

Wednesdays were one of my days off from the hospital, and now that I wasn't studying every available free moment, I spent those mornings with Hope at the park down the street from the Sawyers' house. I would push her on the swings for a while, then sit on a bench and watch her play in the sandbox with the other children at the park.

It was such a different life than I'd had as a child. No feeding chickens or milking cows, no sweeping or mopping porches, no tending to vegetables. I wouldn't change a thing about my childhood, but I was glad that Hope's life might be different. She wouldn't have to worry about where her next meal was coming from, or having to pick cotton until her fingers bled. After seeing so much heartache in my lifetime, I was determined to give my daughter a chance to just be a child. At least for the time being, anyway.

On this particular Wednesday morning, I sat on the bench contemplating what lay ahead for our little family as I answered the latest letter I'd received from Mike. There had been a subtle change in his words, a shift from the playful tone we'd always shared to a more introspective nature.

Dear Mike,

I was so sorry to read about the loss of the men in your squadron. I know all too well the weight of losing people close to you and the doubt of wondering what you could have done differently. You're a good man, with a kind, brave heart, and I'm certain you did everything you could to save them. I suppose all we can do is be thankful your plane was not shot down as well.

Throughout my time in the Philippines, I wondered how a loving God could allow so much suffering to take place. I've prayed continuously for an end to this nightmare of a war, but so far God has not granted that prayer. Still, I cling to the lessons of my father and uncle, who showed me what true faith is. No matter what evils are in the world, we serve a just, loving, all-powerful God. And somehow, in some unfathomable way, all of this is part of His plan for our good and His glory. Whenever I doubt that, all I have to do is look into the eyes of my daughter and know that sometimes, exquisite beauty is born from the most painful ashes.

I've been thinking about our last conversation before you shipped out, and all the kindness you've shown me. God gave me a great blessing when He brought you into my life. (Though I have to admit, I didn't think so at the time!) You've been a rock and a place of sanctuary when my heart was broken. As the time passes, and this war drags on, and no word comes of what happened to Matthew or Henry, I find myself facing an uncertain future. I'm so thankful to have a friend I can count on. There's still so much you do not know about me. But maybe, when the war is over, and you can return home, we can finally say all the things that need to be said.

I think of you every day and pray for your safety. The verses below kept me going during some of my worst experiences. I hope they'll offer you comfort and encouragement as well.

With Christ's love,
Grace

"One thing have I desired of the Lord, that will I seek after; that I may dwell in the house of the Lord all the days of my life, to behold the beauty of the Lord, and to enquire in his temple.

For in the time of trouble he shall hide me in his pavilion: in the secret of his tabernacle shall he hide me; he shall set me up upon a rock.

And now shall mine head be lifted up above mine enemies round about me: therefore will I offer in his tabernacle sacrifices of joy; I will sing, yea, I will sing praises unto the Lord." ~Psalm 27:4-6

I read over the letter once more, and sealed it in an envelope. As I addressed it to Mike, I wondered how long it would be before he actually received it. Weeks, at least. Maybe longer. Sometimes his letters arrived in bunches, sometimes out of order, sometimes several over the course of a couple of days. I imagined he received mine in much the same way.

I called Hope over to me, and she brought her most adorable pleading expression along. "Momma, can I play more?"

"I'm sorry, sweetie. If you want to get a book at the library, we have to go now. Grandma will have dinner ready soon."

She looked over her shoulder at the kids still enjoying the sandbox, before dropping her shoulders and taking my hand. "Yes, ma'am."

We walked around the corner and up the street a block to the library, where I turned in the previous week's adventures. *Pat the Bunny* and *Caps for Sale* would all return to their shelves for us to pick up again a few weeks down the road. Hope was nothing if not a creature of habit, and she loved to hear the same stories over and over. We'd read *The Velveteen Rabbit* so many times, I practically had it memorized.

We headed to the children's area, where Hope went straight to the sections for the books she wanted. "Momma, can we get *Rabbit Hill* this time?"

"Yes, of course."

"And *The Little House?*"

"Yes, sweetie. Whatever books you want." I lifted them from the shelves, knowing exactly where to find them. "That's two, so find one more."

She stood there thoughtfully looking around. "Can I have the one with the bull who doesn't wanna fight?"

"The Story of Ferdinand?"

She nodded and pointed to the section where I'd find it. We took the books to the front desk and checked out. As we left, I dropped my letter into the mailbox out front. Hope could never wait to get home before wanting a book, so I handed her *Rabbit Hill* to hug tightly to her chest as she hopped down the sidewalk beside me.

***

I'd just put Hope down for a nap that afternoon when there was a knock at the door. As usual, it sent my heart to racing. When I came out of our bedroom door, I met Jillian at the top of the stairs with the same tense expression on her face that I was sure was on mine. We descended the stairs together to find Mrs. Sawyer at the front door with a scrawny young man in a Western Union uniform. "Is there a Mrs. Grace Doyle at this residence?" he asked.

My heart thundered so loudly, I couldn't hear Mrs. Sawyer's answer. She put a hand on my back and gently pulled me beside her. The young man stretched out his hand, holding in it a small envelope. I took it, searching his face for some clue as to what news lay inside. But his face was blank.

"Th-thank you," I said.

I stepped backward, my knees buckling, and Mrs. Sawyer closed the door. She and Jillian escorted me to the sofa, where I sat and tried to catch my breath. A telegram about Mike would be addressed to his parents. Henry's would go to Mother. This could only be about Matthew. Would the army be so cruel as to inform me of his death twice?

"Are you all right, dear?" Mrs. Sawyer asked from beside me. Her hand circled my back. "Would you like some water?"

I shook my head.

"You want one of us to open it?"

"N-no, ma'am. I'll be all right." I should've been able to handle this better. The news couldn't be worse than I'd already received. Perhaps it was actually good news. That thought propelled me forward, and I tore the envelope open along its edge. With shaking hands, I pulled out the folded paper and read the message.

THE WAR DEPARTMENT REGRETS TO INFORM YOU THAT YOUR HUSBAND, MAJOR DOYLE, MATTHEW, HAS FALLEN ILL WHILE SERVING IN THE LUZON PROVINCE OF THE PHILIPPINES. HE WILL BE RETURNED TO THE UNITED STATES FOR TREATMENT. FURTHER DETAILS TO FOLLOW.

I stared at the telegram, at first unable to comprehend it. I handed it to Mrs. Sawyer and she read it as well, her eyes widening. "Oh, Grace," she said, covering her mouth with her hand.

"Is he...that means he's alive, right?" I searched her face for help in understanding.

"I think so," she said.

"Let me see," Jillian said, holding out her hand. She read the telegram and nodded. "I think you're right. This has to mean he's alive."

I couldn't dare to believe it just yet. "It could be a mistake. It could be someone else, and they just think it's Matthew. Or they looked up someone else's next of kin and somehow got my name instead."

"I don't think so, dear," Mrs. Sawyer said. "It clearly states the telegram is about Matthew Doyle."

"But he wasn't a major," I said. "He was a captain. And they already gave me a telegram just like this, except it said he was dead, that he was killed on Mindanao on May 5 of 1942. I mean, I didn't want to believe it. I forced myself to believe he was alive, but…"

My babbling trailed off with my thoughts. Could he really be alive? And coming home? I had to stand, but when I pushed up from the sofa, my head swam, and I sank back down.

"Jillian, get her some water," Mrs. Sawyer said.

I dropped my head into my hands, tears streaming down my face. He was alive. Matthew was alive!

CHAPTER SEVEN

Matthew

April 25, 1945
Manila, Philippines

The first few days in the hospital after my breakdown were fuzzy and disorienting. At first, I couldn't move much: my entire body had gone numb. No matter what my brain commanded my body to do, I couldn't seem to focus my nerves on any particular limb to move it.

Gradually, my thoughts became more coherent. I could control things again, a little at a time. After four days, I could sit up and feed myself. After six, I was up and walking. But my sense of self, of who I was at the center of my being, had been shaken severely.

Diego and Bruno visited me daily, but I soon ordered them to return to headquarters and get back to work. Malaya also visited, but was not deterred by my repeated requests for her to leave. Instead, she showed up each day at noon, helped me with eating my lunch until I was able to feed myself, and then, once I was able, walked with me around the hospital grounds.

On the eighth day, we ventured out into the city. The dead bodies no longer littered the streets, but the signs of near annihilation were everywhere. Crumbling buildings, debris, craters in both the ground and the sides of buildings—I'd never seen anything like it.

"I would never have imagined this kind of destruction was possible," I said. "I mean, I guess I could have imagined it, but that men would actually do this? It's unreal."

Malaya walked beside me, taking it all in. I wondered how it must feel to see this done to your homeland, to have your people slaughtered. How did you even begin to rebuild? "We should go back now," she said after a while. "I don't want to see anymore."

We turned around and headed back to my room at the hospital. My release was due soon, but I hadn't yet been informed where I would be heading.

"Malaya, I haven't told you enough how much I appreciate all you did for us."

"This is not necessary, Major."

"Yes, it is." I stopped walking and so did she. "If you hadn't put yourself in harm's way every single day, we might have lost even more lives. The Americans might not have even been able to come back."

She tilted her head. "The Americans? You speak as if you are not one of them."

"I think some part of me isn't anymore."

She stepped closer and started to put her hand on my chest before stopping herself. Instead, she looked up at me with sadness. "Major, you will always be welcome in the Philippines. You have a home here, if you ever want to return."

My pulse quickened. "Thank you, Lieutenant. That means more to me than you know."

I held her gaze a moment longer before breaking the trance and heading back to the hospital. My mind was flooded with conflicting emotions, and I was relieved when Malaya said goodbye to me in the lobby. I needed to think straight, to figure out what was happening to me, both physically and mentally.

When I returned to my room, General Dorsey, whom I'd first met in MacArthur's office, was waiting on me. He shook my hand and asked how I was doing.

My face flushed hot with embarrassment. Did the entire island know of my breakdown? "I'm all right, sir. Just got a little out of sorts is all."

"It's certainly to be expected, given everything you've been through."

"There are plenty of men who've been through worse, sir."

"Yes, well, I'm afraid there may be worse still. The Japanese are dug in to tiny islands all across the Pacific, like nests of ants. Gonna be a long, bloody march to Tokyo. Not sure too many folks really understand what's ahead."

"Sounds like you do," I said.

He studied me for a moment. "I'd bet my last dollar you know pretty well yourself."

I thought of all I'd seen over the past four years, of the torture and brutality the Japanese were capable of inflicting. Yes, I knew what still lay ahead. "Sir, if there's concern over my ability to continue in my duties, let me assure you, I am ready and able to fight every last Jap left on earth."

"Major Doyle, I have no doubt you'd perform your duties honorably until your dying breath."

Honorably, I thought. *Not quite.*

General Dorsey leaned against the windowsill and gestured toward me. "But by the looks of things, that dying breath might come pretty quick if you don't get serious treatment."

"Sir, I realize I'm not at a hundred percent, but I need to get back to my men. The Japanese are still on these islands, and I want to do everything I can to help the Filipino people reclaim their country." Without warning, my throat tightened, and I felt overwhelmed with desperation. "Sir," I continued. "I came close to death more times than I care to remember, and every time, I was saved by brave Filipinos who risked their lives for mine. I owe it to them to stay until the job is done."

General Dorsey straightened and patted me on the shoulder. "Major, your work here has been admirable and of the highest character. But it's over. Orders have already been sent through. You're heading back home for treatment, and after that, probably an honorable discharge. Be happy. You've earned it."

My heart rate sped up again, and the same sensations I'd felt during the breakdown returned. My hand trembled, so I squeezed it into a fist then released it. *Home.* What did that even mean anymore? My legs weakened, so I sat down on the edge of my bed.

"When?" I managed.

"Two days. You'll fly out to Hawaii, and then on to San Francisco before being admitted to the base hospital in San Antonio. Your wife has been contacted, and she'll meet you in San Francisco."

My wife.

I was going to see Ruby again. In two days. I couldn't even picture in my mind what that would be like.

General Dorsey took a seat across from me and began to speak about something else, an award or something, but I could barely focus on his words. My mind was searching for images of Ruby, memories I'd shut out so well I'd almost convinced myself they weren't real. I saw her standing in front of me, smiling as I'd said my vows. I felt her slight frame in my arms, beneath me as she'd told me how much she loved me. She was real. As strange as it seemed, I had to tell myself that again.

Ruby is real.

***

I still wasn't sleeping well, especially the night before I was to leave for the States. I'd spent the better part of four years sleeping on the ground, and adjusting to a mattress again felt foreign. The more I thought about going back, the more alien everything about America seemed.

The morning of my departure, I had my only bag packed with a spare uniform, my two pistols, a few of the birthday gifts I'd received, my official orders and some other papers, and a Bible I'd gotten from a missionary at the hospital.

A private carried my bag out to the car that was waiting to take me to Nichol's Field that morning. It was humiliating to be so weak, so vulnerable. The doctors in Manila had gotten my "nervous episodes" under control, but I was still dependent on heavy medication every day, and I tired out so easily I couldn't get around much.

I made my way down the steps and climbed into the car under my own steam, determined to do even the smallest tasks in my capability. Then we took the short trip over to the army air base.

When the car pulled up near the C-54 on which I was scheduled to fly, I stepped out to find a small party awaiting me. General Dorsey stood at the end of two columns of men from my unit. Several of the higher-ranking officers, including Diego and Bruno, stood near General Dorsey. My chest swelled to see them in crisp, clean uniforms, just as they deserved.

As my bag was loaded onto the plane, I headed over to the beginning of the columns, where the two lines gave me a proper salute. All of them except for Bruno, of course. He just stood there at the end of the column on my right, stiff as a board like the rest, hands to his sides, and a sour expression on his face. I could hope for nothing more fitting.

I walked between the columns of men who'd served me faithfully, who'd risked their lives for their fellow countrymen, and who had all lost some part of themselves in this war. I saluted each of them, working my way to the end where I finally faced my closest and most trusted brothers.

Bruno almost smiled at me. "I wish you safe travels and good health, Major."

I reached for his hand. "And I wish you joy and peace, my friend. Thank you for keeping me alive."

He shook my hand, his nearly swallowing mine. "You are welcome. In the future, you should try to listen to doctors more. You might feel better sooner."

I laughed and released his hand, stepping over to face Diego. "I owe my life to you more times than I can count. Thank you for your devotion."

"It is you whom we honor here today, Major. You are always welcome among our people. Your return will be highly celebrated some day."

My throat tightened, and I had to concentrate on keeping my limbs steady. They were already quivering from fatigue. I embraced Diego, catching sight of Malaya just behind him as I did so. Releasing him, I faced General Dorsey.

"Major Matthew Doyle," he said. "It is my honor to be able to present to you today the Silver Star for your gallantry on April 30, 1942, when despite great danger to yourself, you held off a Japanese patrol so that a plane full of your fellow servicemen and women could escape Mindanao for Australia."

He pinned the medal on the breast pocket of my uniform, then stepped back and gave me a salute. I saluted in return, doing my best to keep my arm from quivering.

"Thank you for your service," Dorsey said, extending his hand.

I shook it as firmly as I could. "Aye, aye, sir."

"I wish all the best to you and your wife, and I hope you have a speedy and full recovery."

I turned back to Diego and Malaya, who walked me to the ramp of the plane.

"Diego, you have served honorably," I said. "I'm relieving you of your duties."

He looked from me to Malaya, and back again. "Yes, Major. May God bless your journey."

As he headed back to the group of men gathering near the car, I took one look at Malaya and knew I had to make this farewell quick. My strength was failing, and I was determined to leave the Philippines with at least some dignity.

"Malaya, thank you for all you've done for me. None of this would have been possible without you."

"I wish you much joy and love, Major. You are a strong man, with a strong heart. You have given my people a chance to be free again. I will never forget you."

"Thank you," I said, grateful she'd left her true feelings unspoken. For all Malaya's care for me, I had never truly returned her affections. Although I'd pushed thoughts of Ruby aside out of necessity, I could never break my vows to her. "Take care of yourself."

"Goodbye, Major." A tear fell down her cheek before she could swipe it away. Abruptly she turned and walked over to join the group waiting to wave one last time.

I shuffled up to the top of the ramp, doing my best to hide how much effort it was taking. I waved one last time to the group of people who had become my family through so much turmoil. They waved in return, and I stepped into the plane.

A nurse traveling with me helped to seat me as comfortably as possible for the twenty-one hour flight to Honolulu. She gave me some medication to help me relax, and then took her own seat across the aisle. As the plane taxied and lifted into the air, I took one last look at the remains of the island that had held me captive for four years.

I wondered if Europe also looked this way, with huge craters and rubble scattered endlessly across the land. But as I watched the landscape shift from the destruction of Manila to the rolling green foothills in the east, I felt my chest grow heavy with regret. So much had happened out there, so much struggle, so much joy in small triumphs. And I'd never be the same again.

I thought of what lay ahead and what it would be like to see Ruby again. How would I ever share with her all that had happened over the past four years? How would I ever explain? I rested my head back against the seat, feeling the meds work their magic on my mind. I drifted toward the blackness of sleep, with only one thought in my mind. Would she ever forgive me?

CHAPTER EIGHT

Matthew

June, 1942
Northeast of Manila, Philippines

Time moved in fits and starts the first few days after Henry and his companions saved me. Because of the bullet wound to my leg, I couldn't keep up, so they took turns carrying me in a makeshift litter through the foothills. The rocking made me want to vomit, but luckily I was too weak to muster the energy for such activities.

After two days of traveling by night and resting during the day, we came across a small village of Filipinos who fed us and offered to guide us to a secret camp set up for straggling American soldiers. They provided two carabao and wooden carts in which we could conceal ourselves. This proved to be a blessing from God, since the caravan was stopped three times by Japanese patrols. Luckily, as our guides spoke no English, the Japanese must have assumed they wouldn't be hauling Americans and never looked under the rice straw concealing us.

The journey was hard on my body. Sometimes the fever hit me so hard, I was out of my head. I'd hear Kojima calling out my name in his fiery Japanese accent, telling me to surrender while I still could. Other times, I'd see Ruby moving through the jungle beside the cart, her gaze on me as she floated along. My whole body ached to reach out to her. But I couldn't have moved even if I'd wanted to.

We finally reached the small camp in the foothills of a large mountain. I was pulled off the cart and carried into a hut, where they placed me on a palette on the floor. I knew there were several men involved in my transportation, but I didn't have the mental capacity to distinguish any of them.

I lay in a state of feverish chills and nausea for several more days, mostly unaware of anything going on around me. I stumbled through visions that left me in pools of sweat and screaming for Ruby. In one such vision, I once again lay in the tiny fishing canoe of a Filipino family trying to help me escape Mindanao. I lay low in the boat, hidden within the foliage of the mangrove trees whose roots sprawled out into the water along the coastline. It was the first time I'd ever seen Kojima. He appeared slight in stature, and he carried a sharpened swagger stick instead of a samurai sword. He yelled at the father, beat the mother, and pointed his gun at the children. When the father shook his head, Kojima shot him on the spot. I was so weak, and so shocked, I couldn't move. I'd lain there for another day before the wife brought me food and a relative to act as my guide. I had no way of thanking her but to pray for her and her children before being paddled north into the Mindanao Sea.

Other times I dreamed of home, of the grassy slope behind my parents' house, the smell of the white ginger lilies my mother so carefully tended, of the cool dew on my bare feet in the early morning.

At some point, I awoke with a fuzzy sense of time and place, and I remembered where I was, or rather, where I was *not*. I rolled onto my side to see Henry seated on the other side of the hut, his back against the bamboo wall, his elbows propped on his knees. He puffed on a cigarette and smiled at me.

"Welcome back," he said. "How ya feeling?"

"Like I was dragged through the jungle with a rope tied around me, then beat half to death."

"That's not far from the way of things."

"Where are we?" I asked, pushing myself up on my elbow and looking around. Another man lay on a palette like mine a few feet away from me, his body swollen grotesquely with the obvious signs of beriberi. He too seemed to be mumbling through disturbing dreams. The door to the hut was open, and through it I could see more men outside milling around.

"It's a camp set up by a guy named Vasco Alapa and his family," Henry said. "They came over from Hawaii some years back and had a pretty wealthy sugar plantation going before the Japs overran everything. Alapa set this place up to give American soldiers on the run a place to recuperate."

"How safe are we here?"

"About as safe as anywhere else, I reckon. Seems to be about eighty men at any given time. Bound to get found out, though. Too many men moving in and out of this place for the Japs not to find us. We should make some plans to move out of here as soon as you're well enough."

"Where are the others?"

"The others?"

"The guys you were with when you found me."

"Oh, yes." He nodded and sucked deeply on the tiny butt left of the cigarette. "They left already. Bit jittery. They're trying to find a boat capable of getting them to Australia."

"Maybe that's what we should do."

"I don't know. From what I understand, the Japs have the Philippines blockaded. Sounds like a good way to get caught."

I tried to push myself up to a sitting position, but my body wasn't quite having it yet. My head swam, and the room spun for a second. I moaned and lay back on the palette.

"Yeah, you're gonna need a couple more days before you're up to snuff," Henry said. He pushed away from the wall and came over to my side. "Let me check your leg. It was festering a bit yesterday. A doc came by and treated it with some sulfa." He helped me roll onto my left side and pulled away my pants leg where someone had cut it open. "Does that hurt?" he asked, running a finger around the edge.

"Everything hurts," I said. "That don't feel any different than anywhere else."

"Looks a little better. You're still burning up, though. We should get some food and water in you. Sit tight, and I'll be right back."

He ducked out of the hut, leaving me to watch the goings on outside. Through the door, I could see four more huts like ours and about ten or twelve men sitting on stumps or logs around each hut. Every one of them was puffing on a cigarette. Most had some sort of bandaging somewhere on his body. All of them were emaciated.

Henry came back inside with a small bowl of rice and some water. I scarfed it down in five seconds. "Is that all there is?"

He shrugged. "For now. I can go out later and try to catch something. How ya feeling now?"

"My feet are killing me, like my shoes are two sizes too small. Can you take them off?"

Henry lifted an eyebrow. "They're already off."

I looked down at my feet and sure enough, all I had on them was a pair of socks with holes in the heels. "Well, that can't be good."

"Everybody's feet's in bad shape. Hardly anybody has on shoes. We should try to get some before we leave."

"You have a plan? Where are we going?"

He scooted across the floor and leaned back against the wall again. I noticed he was in only slightly better shape than I was. He was thinner than I'd ever seen him, and his eyes—Ruby's eyes—had dark circles beneath them. The last time I'd seen him was just after Janine's death. I wondered if he too had disturbing dreams. "I been doing a little scouting while you were writhing around," he said. "I think we should head further north into the mountains like the other fellas. Join up with the guerrillas. I say we give the Japs all they can handle until MacArthur comes back."

"I'm not sure how much I can give the Japs with the state I'm in, but I'll give it some thought."

Henry smiled at me, a haunted, grim sort of smile. "All right. I'll ask around and see what I can find out."

***

The next day, I was able to sit up and even walk around just outside the hut. Henry brought me a pair of uniform pants that weren't exactly clean, but at least hadn't been sliced up. I didn't want to think about where he'd gotten them. We walked through the camp together slowly due to the severity of my limp. I still couldn't get any shoes on my feet, so that only added to my discomfort.

I met many other American soldiers recovering from wounds and illnesses that ranged from concerning to downright deadly. Some seemed eager to recover and join in the effort to disrupt the Japanese operations. Others were so listless and defeated, all they wanted was to find a nice Filipino family to hide them until the war was over.

Henry and I went inside one hut about six down from ours. Inside, I met a short, but muscular former Filipino scout whom Henry introduced as Raul Diego. I shook his hand, making note of the strength in his grip.

"Diego says he'll go with us into the mountains and find the guerrillas," Henry said.

"Wait a minute," I said. "We haven't decided to do that yet."

"I think that's our best option."

"That may be true, but we should at least discuss it. There could be serious consequences."

"Fine," Henry said. "We'll discuss it. But for now, let's talk to Diego here and see what he knows."

I turned to Diego. "You know the area well?"

"Sí, Captain Doyle. I know very well. I was child in mountains."

"You speak Spanish?" I asked.

"Sí."

"I thought everyone spoke Tagalog," I said to Henry.

"Actually, Spanish is the official language. A lot of natives speak Tagalog still."

"I speak all," Diego said, his chest puffed out.

"You speak Japanese too?" I asked.

"No. But I can hear many Japanese words."

I glanced over at Henry, who was smiling at me as if to say, "See?"

"All right," I said. "We'll discuss what we should do. Either way, Diego might be able to get us to our destination. Are we sure we don't want to stay here for a while and see if we can join up with any other Americans?"

Henry shook his head. "Nah. There's some other bigwigs in camp making a hullabaloo about following rank protocol. Some sergeant wants to tell everyone what to do, but a lot of the guys ain't having it. Alapa wants to keep the camp a place to rest and heal, so the sergeant is trying to get men who are well enough to make a camp further east. I say we keep our party small for now and try to get deeper into the mountains. Less chance of getting caught. Then we can join up with the guerrillas."

I offered a hand to Diego, feeling my strength waning. "We'll talk more tomorrow."

"Sí, Captain," he said, saluting me instead.

"It's just Matthew," I said. "None of this Captain stuff."

Diego maintained a steady gaze up at me, and I could see he had much more inner strength than I did at that moment. "Captain Doyle,"

he said. "I must treat you with respect, sir. I will call you 'Captain' or 'sir.'"
He paused. "Sir."

Henry was obviously amused by this. "Yes, Captain Doyle. We must
treat you with respect."

I didn't have the energy to participate in any further discussion. I said
goodbye to Diego and headed back to my palette for some rest.

***

That night, I awoke with an urgent need to relieve myself, which I
suspected was due to an oncoming kidney infection. I slipped out as
quietly as I could and made my way into the cogon grass about thirty
yards from our hut. From this distance, I could see most of the camp in
the moonlight, noting that someone should let Alapa know that it
needed more camouflage. Sentries were posted at a fifty-yard perimeter
around the camp, with a few more lookouts spread around about a
kilometer out.

But they proved to be useless.

While I was relieving my infected kidneys, I heard shouts and then
the rat-a-tat of rapid gunfire. My heart lurched into my throat as I
dropped into the grass without thinking. There was more shouting,
more gunfire, and a blaze went up near the far side of camp.

I knew I had to run, but I couldn't just leave Henry behind. I crawled
through the grass as quickly as I could, reaching the edge of the small
field. There was another ten yards for me to cross in the open to get to
the hut, where my weapons lay as well.

I decided to make a run for it, but as I neared the hut, Henry came
barreling around the side, running right for me. He shouted for me to
run, waving his arms toward the direction I'd just come from. I turned
around, and by the time I got my feet moving in the right direction,
Henry was right behind me.

I managed to run for a short while, tripping three times and landing flat on my face. But I kept moving, afraid to stop and look back. We hurtled along a path that paralleled the stream near the camp, eventually breaking away from it to head up a steep slope.

"We need to get to higher elevation," Henry said. "Better cover up there."

I looked down and realized I was still shoeless, and my feet were throbbing from multiple lacerations. I began to drop behind, eventually unable to see Henry in front of me. "Hey," I said, trying to keep my voice low enough not to draw attention. "I can't...I'm too weak." I stopped altogether and dropped to my knees.

Henry came back through the palm trees and bent over, resting his hands on his knees. "If we can get just a little higher, there's a good place to spend the night. Come on. You can do it." He helped me get upright again, this time moving at a slower pace through the thickening foliage.

By the time we made it to the place he'd spoken of, he was practically carrying me. It was a ridge on the mountain, about a third of the way up. From the edge, we could look down and see the light of the fire still burning at the camp and hear the gunshots. But away from the ridge, near a steep incline of the mountain, there was a fairly shallow cave covered with vines. I had to admit, Henry had done some great reconnaissance.

"This will do," he said. "We'll hide out here until dark tomorrow. Get some rest."

My body was willing, but my mind raced through what had just happened. The adrenaline crash left me with a headache and knots in my stomach. My hamstring was on fire. All I could do was lie in the dark on the hard-packed earth and thank God once again for rescuing me in the nick of time.

***

The next morning, I awoke to a string of whistles that sounded like birds, but not quite. I leaned up on my elbow in time to see Henry crouched beside the entrance of the cave. He let out a string of whistles as well.

Deciding it was best to remain silent, I crawled over to the opposite side of the entrance from Henry. A few seconds later, more whistles came from outside, closer than before. Henry whistled in return.

A few seconds more, and a shiny blade eased through the vines. Henry looked ready to spring. Then Diego slid through the vines. Henry straightened, and his face broke into a smile. "I knew you'd find us."

"Camp is no more," Diego said, not returning the smile. "All gone or captured. Japanese all over."

"We need supplies," Henry said. "How many of them are there? Think we can sneak in and grab a few things?"

Diego held up a cloth sack he'd been carrying. "Already have supplies." He glanced over at me. "And shoes for you, Captain."

"Thanks," I said, gingerly sliding my right foot into a boot. It was two sizes too large, but with my feet still swollen, it would do.

Diego tossed a canteen of water at me and looked up at Henry. "We must go. Japanese all over area. Es muy peligroso."

"Listen, Diego," Henry said. "You can't be rattling off things in Spanish. Me no comprendo."

Diego sighed and tried again. "We must leave now. Japanese come this way soon."

"I understood that perfectly," I said.

"Me too," Henry said. "Guess we better get moving. Lead the way, Diego."

CHAPTER NINE

Ruby

May 1, 1945
Train to San Francisco

Another telegram from the army arrived, telling me that Matthew would fly in to Fairfield-Suisun Army Air Base outside of San Francisco on May 2. There'd been no mistake. He was alive, and he was coming home. I'd been waiting so long to receive word of this very thing, but now that it was true, now that we would be a family again, I felt like my world had been shaken once more. How sick was he? How long would he be in the hospital? Where would we live when he got out? How would we face my murder conviction? There were so many questions I had no idea how to answer.

I had only a few days to buy a train ticket, find a place to stay, and request leave from my job at the hospital. I was sure I would run into a roadblock at work, seeing as how I'd only been employed a few weeks, but my supervisor, Ms. Wharton, had a son in the service, and was sympathetic to my situation. She'd hugged me with tears in her eyes, telling me to take all the time I needed to bring my husband home.

Then I contacted Coach Frank Hudson in San Francisco to see if I could spend a night or two with him and his wife. He had coached Mike and Henry in the minor leagues, and had helped us out before. Once again, he came through when I needed him.

So on the morning of April 30, I boarded a train in Houston bound for California, the same train Henry and I'd taken just over eight years prior. My body and mind were exhausted, but come nightfall, I couldn't sleep. I lay in the lower bunk of the sleeping car watching the stars streak by the window, wondering what it would be like to see Matthew again. I played the scenario out in my mind, picturing us hugging each other until we couldn't breathe. Then my thoughts would wander to Hope. Because I had no way of knowing what awaited me with Matthew, I'd decided to leave her back in Houston in Mrs. Sawyer's capable hands. But I missed her warm, tiny body curled up beside me. What would she think of having her daddy home?

As the train rattled westwards, I gazed out at the night sky and imagined us all together as a family, playing at the park. She'd finally have her daddy to push her on the swings, and I could admire them laughing together.

Other thoughts played around the edges of my imagination as well: thoughts of injuries, illness, and the aftermath of war; thoughts of Henry still missing; thoughts of prison and the electric chair. I had to push those thoughts away, all of them. They served no purpose in the present. I would simply have to trust in God to help me face whatever lay ahead.

As I prayed for peace, God once again brought his beautiful Word to my mind, a passage from Philippians.

But this one thing I do, forgetting those things which are behind, and reaching forth unto those things which are before, I press toward the mark for the prize of the high calling of God in Christ Jesus. Let us therefore, as many as be perfect, be thus minded: and if in any thing ye be otherwise minded, God shall reveal even this unto you.

Coach Hudson picked me up at the train station late that evening, greeting me with his usual warm hug and cheerful demeanor. He was stocky, graying around the edges of the high-and-tight he still maintained from his days as a marine. I couldn't remember where he was from, somewhere in the Midwest, maybe Indiana, and he had a matter-of-fact approach to life, religion, and politics, though he rarely discussed any of them.

Coach Hudson had met his wife, Jun, while he was stationed in China in the early 30s. She was quiet and courteous, and she always wore a smile. She was so thoughtful that she seemed to know just what you needed before you even knew you needed it. Once when I was trying to help Henry with a paper for his degree, she'd shown up at our little shack of an apartment with a platter full of dumplings and kung pao chicken. It was my first experience with either dish, and I fell in love with both.

When we arrived at their home on the northern outskirts of San Francisco, Mrs. Hudson greeted me at the door, and immediately I smelled the food. "Oh, Mrs. Hudson, something smells wonderful!" I said. "I hope you didn't go to any trouble."

She dismissed the thought with a wave. "No trouble at all. Come settle your things and we will eat. You must be hungry."

She showed me to the guest room, and we spent the rest of the evening catching up and reminiscing over supper. Coach Hudson seemed particularly upset that Henry had been caught up in the terrible events in the Philippines. My best guess was that he'd been captured when Corregidor was surrendered and was currently in a POW camp somewhere in Japanese territory. "My aunt received a telegram telling her he was missing in action," I told him. "There's just so many different things that could mean."

Coach Hudson puffed out some smoke he'd inhaled from his cigar. "Henry's tough. He was a bit of a clown at times, but he set his mind on becoming a pilot, and he did it. If he sets his mind on surviving the Japs, he'll do that too."

"Well, knowing Matthew's alive gives me hope for Henry too."

Mrs. Hudson stood from her chair next to the fireplace and cleared her throat. "Can I get you something else?" She seemed tense from the conversation. I wondered how the war in the Pacific had affected her family and friends. Maybe she'd lost loved ones too.

"No, ma'am," I said. "But I would appreciate it if you would let me help with the dishes."

She wagged her finger at me. "No. This is not right. Where I come from, guest enjoy meal and company. That is all. You rest. Tomorrow is big day."

"Will you and Matthew be staying here tomorrow night?" Coach Hudson asked. "Or will you catch the train right away?"

"The train leaves in the afternoon, but I'm not sure how late we'll be getting back from the base. Would it be all right if we stay an extra night if we miss the train?"

"Of course," he said. "Our house is your house, Grace. You're always welcome here."

May 2, 1945

Fairfield-Suisun Army Air Base

I stepped out of Coach Hudson's green Chevrolet and took a moment to steady myself. My heart pounded and I couldn't seem to slow my breathing. When I slid my hands down my dress to straighten out the wrinkles, they were shaking.

I bent down and glanced in the rearview mirror, dabbing at the corner of my eyes. They were already damp and bloodshot. What would Matthew think when he saw me in such a state? I'd wanted to look nice for him, but my mascara was already starting to smear. Maybe makeup wasn't the best idea on such a day, but it was too late to do anything about it.

I fixed my hair and face as best I could, reapplying a slick of lipstick before I shook my head at my appearance. It would have to do. I straightened and met Coach Hudson's concerned gaze. "You all right?" he asked.

I nodded. "Just a bit anxious."

"Understandable."

It took me another moment to get my bearings. Henry had trained here, but it had been several years since I'd been to the base. I spotted the headquarters building off to my left, and headed there first to find out where I was supposed to wait for Matthew's plane.

After receiving some general directions to the waiting area from a gruff commander, I made my way over to the hangar, with Coach Hudson hanging back to give Matthew and me some space. I stood alongside five other women in my same condition, three with small children clinging to their legs. We managed tight smiles at one another, but there seemed to be an understanding among us that we needed to concentrate all our efforts on not falling to pieces. My thoughts drifted momentarily to Hope, and I knew I had done the right thing in leaving her in Texas.

"Is that the plane?" someone asked.

We all turned to the sky, peering at the dot approaching from the southwest. My heart renewed its thundering pace. My mind filled with the images I'd fought so long to forget: Matthew's eyes gazing down on me as he made me promise to get on the plane; a kiss before running down the dock toward the approaching Japanese. He'd turned to me one last time. *I'll be right behind you!* Even in that moment, had he known he wasn't coming back?

The plane carrying Matthew touched down on the runway. I knew I wouldn't be able to see him through the tiny windows along the sides, but I couldn't help myself from trying as it rolled past us. The entire group turned as one to watch it taxi over toward the hangar where we waited. Then the plane just sat there staring at us, almost as if to say, "Well, here I am. Now what?"

Within a few moments, a crew from the hangar pushed a rolling stairway up to the door. Our anxious group edged closer to the plane. The door swung open, and a tall figure in fatigues appeared at the top of the stairs. My heart skipped a beat before I realized it wasn't Matthew.

The young man, and several more after him, came down the stairs and were greeted by exuberant women and children. I could only glance at them for a moment, because my eyes were glued to the door of the plane. I made my way through the reunited families to the bottom of the stairway. What if there had been a mistake? What if Matthew wasn't on the plane? Or worse, what if he wasn't really alive?

My stomach swam with the thought. After every other woman in the group had found her soldier, I stood alone at the bottom of the stairs, waiting. And it felt as if I was right back in that plane on Mindanao, waiting and watching for Matthew to come running back to me. He hadn't come. And the thought that kept running through my mind over and over was, *He isn't coming this time either.* I was going to be sick.

Just as I was about to storm the plane to find him myself, there he was. He stepped through the door and looked around at the group below him until he found me. I covered my mouth to keep from screaming his name, and a sob burst out of me. He gripped the railing and took his time coming down the stairs, never taking his eyes off me. He didn't smile, but I could see there was a storm of emotion swirling through him, just as there was inside me.

When he reached the bottom, he barely got his hat off before I was in his arms, sobbing into his chest. He staggered back a step, but his arms were sure. Holding me fast to his thin frame, he mumbled reassuring words into my hair as he kissed the top of my head. "It's all right. Everything's all right now."

I couldn't let go of him, so I held on while the anger, hopelessness, and fear that I'd carried around with me for so long welled up and spilled forth. He held me close, still mumbling reassurances every minute or so. We must have stood like that for a long time, long enough for all the other families to abandon us.

I pulled my head back enough to look up into his dark eyes. His face was so gaunt and his cheekbones so pronounced, it took me a moment to find my words. He looked like he'd come from the very gates of hell. "Are...are you all right?"

He reached a hand to my face and cupped my cheek, looking me over as if he was unsure I was real. "I'll be fine. I just need some rest is all. And a few sturdy meals."

"I've missed you so much. There's so much to tell you."

He closed his eyes and touched his forehead to mine. "You're so beautiful. I'd almost forgotten."

A nurse cleared her throat beside us. "Major Doyle, I have your bag here."

Matthew kept his left arm tight around my waist as he reached for the bag with his right. "Thank you, Lieutenant." He took the bag from her hands and turned back to me. "You ready to get out of here?" He brought the bag toward his shoulder, but couldn't quite lift it.

"Let me take that," I said, stepping back with the bag. He released it and frowned.

"Reckon I'm in pretty bad shape."

"I'll get you all taken care of," I said, wiping my tears from my face. I must have looked terrible. We headed toward Coach Hudson standing patiently off to the side. "This is Frank Hudson. He was Henry's batting coach when he played ball. He drove me here today, and he's going to take us to the train station tomorrow."

Matthew extended his hand, and I saw it quivering just before Coach Hudson took it. "Thank you for helping us out," Matthew said.

"It's my pleasure, Major Doyle. You're a true hero. I'm here to help you and Grace out any way I can."

"Grace..." Matthew said quietly, shifting his glance to me. A dark expression came over his face, but it retreated just as quickly.

Coach Hudson took the bag from my hands. "I guess we should get going. I'm sure you'll want a hot meal and a comfortable bed to sleep on."

"I appreciate your hospitality, Mr. Hudson, but I don't want to be a burden. Perhaps it would be best if Ru—, if *Grace* and I stay in a hotel tonight."

"It's no burden, I assure you. Mrs. Hudson has a wonderful meal waiting on us. You can take a hot shower, relax, and get a good night's sleep without all the fuss of being surrounded by people."

"That sounds nice. I can't thank you enough," Matthew said, his mouth pressing into a line.

I was still having trouble finding my voice. I nodded my agreement as well, and we set off for the car.

***

The ride back to the Hudsons' home was somber and unsettling. Matthew stared out of the window most of the way. I sat beside him in the back of the car, clutching his hand in my own. I tried not to stare at him, but I couldn't help myself. He was so thin, frighteningly thin. And his skin was tanned like leather. His eyes had dark circles under them, and the whites had a sickly yellow tint. I kept wondering, who was this man beside me?

"The message I got from the army said you have to report to the base hospital in San Antonio," I said. "We should get you there as soon as possible."

He turned his gaze away from the window and on me. "Where are you living?"

"Houston, so I'll only be a short train ride away. I went through a nursing program there and got a job at the hospital."

"I thought you'd be in Australia, like we talked about."

"I was for a few months. But then MacArthur moved headquarters, and I couldn't go with them. I thought if they found you, they'd send you back to the States. And I wanted to be here in case that happened. And I needed to find a way to support myself—"

"Didn't you have my pay?"

"There was no record of our wedding. Sergeant Watters was missing in action, and Henry and Janine..." My thoughts trailed away, and I glanced down at our entwined hands. He no longer wore his wedding ring.

He leaned his head back against the seat. "So you had no money."

"It worked out, though. Mike's parents had a place for me, and—"

"Mike?" Matthew's head snapped up. "Who's Mike?"

"Mike Sawyer. He was the pilot of the PBY on Mindanao. He's friends with Henry. Taught me how to fly. Remember? He's been keeping tabs on everything for me. He writes to let me know what's happening, and he's done his best to find you and Henry—"

"So, you two are close, then." He turned his gaze back out the window, and an uncomfortable silence filled the car. "And you thought I was dead." He looked back at me again, a hint of an accusation in his gaze.

I had no idea how to answer. I hadn't actually thought of Mike in days. I would need to let him know that Matthew had been found and had come home to us. But that would have to wait.

"I...they told me you'd died, but I didn't believe it. That's why we kept searching for more information. I never believed you were really gone."

His mouth eased. Not quite a smile, but he seemed to relax. I wanted to talk to him, to share so many things on my heart and mind, but I had no idea where to start. I wanted to tell him about Hope, but I felt like we should be alone for that conversation. That would have to wait as well.

So we rode the rest of the way to the Hudsons' home with very little conversation. Every once in a while, Matthew would look over at me with this sad sort of smile and squeeze my hand. I'd squeeze his in return, and he would go back to looking out the window. All I could do was wonder what was on his mind.

We crossed the Golden Gate Bridge and headed through the city. The streets were crowded with vehicles and streetcars, slowing our progress. Finally, we reached the sloping street where the Hudsons lived and parked on the side of the hill.

When we stepped out of the car, Matthew stood and looked up and down the street. "Noisy, isn't it?"

"I suppose," I said.

"And crowded. Houses are on top of each other."

Coach Hudson took Matthew's bag out of the front seat and we all climbed the stairs to the front door. As we entered the foyer, Mrs. Hudson came out to greet us from the rear of the house where the kitchen was. Coach Hudson kissed her on the cheek and wrapped an arm over her shoulder, turning to Matthew to introduce her. "This is my wife, Jun," he said, smiling as she bowed her head slightly.

The color drained from Matthew's face and he stood frozen in place, staring at Mrs. Hudson with an intense gaze. "He—hello," he said. "Thank you for having me."

I squeezed his hand, and that seemed to bring him out of his shock. He smiled at us all, but again, I had the feeling it wasn't genuine. His eyes darted around the room, as if he were looking for an escape.

Mrs. Hudson's smile faltered as well. "I hope you like dumplings. I make chicken and carrots also."

"I'm sure it'll be just fine," he said.

"Come," she said, motioning for us to follow. "You must be very hungry."

Coach Hudson set Matthew's bag in the guest room, while we followed Mrs. Hudson into the dining room. Matthew and I took our seats next to each other. I slipped my hand into his again as Mrs. Hudson brought out platters filled with roasted chicken, carrots, dumplings, brown noodles, and rice.

"This looks wonderful," I said.

Coach Hudson joined us. "Shall we say grace?" Matthew's eyes flickered to mine before we bowed our heads. "Lord Almighty, we come to You with gratefulness in our hearts for bringing all of us to Your table. You have blessed us with our daily bread, as well as the joyful return of our dear brother, Matthew. We ask that You watch over Henry as well, and we pray that he will also return safely. May You continue to bless all those who are still serving overseas, as well as those here at home who are sacrificing so much. And may You bring peace to us all. It's in Christ's name we pray. Amen."

I let go of Matthew's hand and began to fill my plate, gushing over the food. Mrs. Hudson thanked me shyly, waiting until we were all served before serving herself. I took a quick glance at Matthew's plate. He'd taken a small amount of chicken and carrots. Nothing more.

"Aren't you hungry?" I asked him.

"Uh, well, of course. Just still adjusting to regular meals is all. Doctors said it's best to pace myself and eat small meals for now." He shot a quick glance at Mrs. Hudson. "Thank you. It's all very kind."

He took a bite of chicken, and even that he seemed to have to force down. I was shocked. He was obviously malnourished and grossly underweight. I recalled having a similar reaction when I first arrived in Australia. And yet, he seemed repulsed by the food before him. I had to wonder if it had something to do with the Asian nature of it all. It had taken well over a year for me to eat rice again after returning to the States. Even now, I barely touched the stuff.

"So, Grace tells us you've been on the Philippines all this time," Coach Hudson said. "What were you doing?"

"I commanded a large group of guerrillas in the central Luzon province. We mostly monitored the Jap movements and troop sizes to relay to MacArthur."

"I served in China myself, from thirty-two to thirty-four. Had a few run-ins with the Nips. Savages."

Matthew nodded, but then changed the subject. "This is a nice home you have here."

"Thank you. Built it myself several years back."

Every time Coach Hudson asked Matthew about his service, he expertly steered the conversation away. He continued to nibble on the chicken and carrots, but managed to put away several helpings by the time we'd come to the end of the meal. This confirmed my earlier suspicion about his aversion to the Asian dishes. I hoped Mrs. Hudson didn't pick up on it as well, but I was glad to see him get some food in his system.

***

Not long after supper, Matthew excused himself to the guest room for the night, and I followed suit. He still seemed uncomfortable, stealing long looks at Mrs. Hudson occasionally. Once we were alone, I asked him if he was all right.

"We should've stayed at a hotel," he said, looking around the room. He stood on one side of the bed, and I stood on the other. It wasn't late, but he looked exhausted.

"I'm sorry about that," I said. "I didn't think. Everything has been so topsy-turvy the past week. Let's just try to get some rest tonight. We'll have lots of time over the next few days to get things sorted out."

He nodded and rubbed his hands over his face. "I suppose."

When he dropped his hands, we stared at each other for a long while, and I became acutely aware of the fact that it was our first night together in three years. My *husband* was standing before me. How many times had I ached for this very night? And yet, I was paralyzed by the magnitude of it all.

"Do you want to go to bed?" I asked, my voice shaking slightly.

"I want to lie down," he said. His eyes moved over me, sending my heart racing. I broke eye contact and began turning down the bed for him. I started on my side, pulling down the comforter and sheets, then moved over to his side, still unable to look at him. I felt his eyes on my every move.

When I straightened and went to move past him, he put a hand on my hip and stopped me in front of him. His other hand slid around my neck, his thumb stroking my cheek. He looked at me as if he was trying to remember me. Tears I'd been trying to keep at bay broke loose.

"Why're you crying?" he asked.

"I don't know. It's just been so long. I was so afraid you were gone. I've been carrying this terrible hole in my chest around for so long, and now I don't know what to do."

He leaned down and kissed me, and that only shattered what was left of my control. I kissed his lips, his cheeks, his hands, crying the whole time. It was humiliating, but it was a release I needed. And he seemed to understand.

He kissed my cheeks too, and he held me as I cried. I didn't even realize he'd moved us to the bed. I lay cradled in his arms, still crying long into the night.

Matthew

May 2, 1945
San Francisco

Ruby finally fell asleep in my arms, but I couldn't find any sleep myself. The entire day had been so overwhelming, and my body was beyond the point of exhaustion. But I lay there throughout that first night thinking of how different everything around me was now. And how it felt all wrong.

It had started with all the traffic and the noise. It drowned out everything. I couldn't hear myself think. Then I'd seen Mrs. Hudson, and without a thought, my mind had gone on the defensive. I knew it was completely irrational—she wasn't even Japanese—but I couldn't help looking around for escape routes. Even as I lay safely in bed, with Ruby beside me, I had an uncontrollable sense that Mrs. Hudson was a threat I needed to be ready for. To top it off, the bed was so soft, I thought I might sink right through it.

So I lay there all night, replaying events in my mind, wondering what Diego was doing, how my men were fairing in their training. Who would lead them against the Japanese? Would they gain the freedom they'd been working so hard for? I began to wonder if the army would send me back once I was healthy again. What would that do to Ruby?

I thought back over everything we'd already been through. Could we face another obstacle? Would she be safe in Houston? What if the Sawyers discovered who she really was? There was so much still at stake. And at the end of all my troubling questions lay the one most troubling of all. Was this the life I really wanted?

CHAPTER TEN

Matthew

August, 1942

Luzon, Philippines

Diego was an expert guide, and I thanked God for him each day we climbed through the foothills of eastern Luzon, heading west toward the mountains north of Manila. Diego did indeed know the area well. He led us from one barrio to the next, entering first on his own to establish friendly relations, and then introducing us to the leaders of each barrio. We spent very few nights without some sort of shelter and a bit of food.

I learned more about Filipino culture during those days than I had in my entire seven months in the Philippines to date. Each barrio was set up as its own clan, with local leaders who may or may not welcome outsiders. Some barrios were better off than others, with a superior water supply and more crops. Some had been decimated by the Japanese and were trying to get back on their feet again.

Most welcomed us and offered to feed us regardless of their supply level. One such barrio leader, a man with three wives and thirteen children, had the last three chickens in the entire barrio killed in order to serve us a meal. He welcomed us into his humble home, a bamboo hut with thatched nipa palm leaves for the roof.

The one-room hut housed all seventeen members of his family, from infants to teens, all sleeping on the floor together. How they managed to adjust themselves to allow three more bodies inside was a mystery. I slept with my back pressed against the straw-covered wall while Henry slept on his back, head to toe beside me. Occasionally his feet would move toward my face, and I'd get hit by the most awful smell imaginable. It was the longest night of our journey so far. Still, the family had shared with us out of their meager stores, and it reminded me of when Jesus pointed out the poor widow who gave all that she'd had— only two copper coins—as her offering.

Lord, I prayed, *please bless this poor family out of Your abundance. Please take their generosity and multiply it back to them. Thank You for Your safekeeping thus far. Guide us and keep us from those who would harm us. Please be with Ruby, Lord, and please bring us home safely.*

***

The next day, we left the foothills behind as we entered into the floodplains of central Luzon. This felt like the most dangerous part of our trip so far, having lost the cover of the vegetation. We moved only at night, wading through rice paddies up to our thighs, praying the mosquitos would keep their malaria to themselves.

We headed west toward Mount Arayat, where Diego had been told we would find more Americans and Filipinos banding together. The only times we came across Japanese units was when we had to cross a road. We'd hunker down and study their pattern, waiting for a break in the line of armor, infantry, and equipment being moved in mass numbers.

It took us a couple more days to reach the barrio we'd been searching for. I realized we were heading back into the very landscape I'd traveled through six months prior when the Americans retreated to Bataan to make what turned out to be a futile stand.

As we approached the barrio from the south, we could hear music and children singing. Diego slowed our approach, sensing we were being watched. Within a few minutes, two armed Filipinos stepped in our path, commanding us to stop.

Diego spoke to them first in Spanish. I caught the words "Americanos" and "amigos." Then he addressed them in Tagalog, and they nodded, waving us forward.

"They say they will take us to American soldier in barrio," Diego said quietly.

"Do you trust them?" I asked.

"Sí, Captain."

I glanced over at Henry to my right. "What do you think?"

"Sí, Captain," he said, winking.

I couldn't muster a smile. My feet had gone numb from pain, my skin itched like it was covered in a million ants, and another fever had zapped me of nearly all my energy. I prayed this barrio would be our last stop for a while until I could recover more of my strength.

When we came to the outer edge of the group of huts, an older Filipino carrying a bolo approached us with an American enlisted soldier alongside him. The American was as skeletal as I was, and his tanned, leathery skin gave him the appearance of being in his forties. I was shocked to learn he was a corporal in his twenties. It made me wonder just how much of a toll this jungle life would take on my body as well.

Reaching his hand out to me, he was the first to speak to us. "Hello there! Welcome, welcome. I'm Corporal John Thatcher. Who might you fellas be?"

"I'm Captain Matthew Doyle with the engineering corps. This here's Lieutenant Henry Graves, a pilot, and our guide, Raul Diego."

Thatcher shook each of their hands and welcomed us. The older gentleman was the leader of the barrio. He only spoke some broken English, but he thanked us and promised to help the Americans in any way he could. As he barked commands in Tagalog, both men and women jumped into action.

"What are they doing?" I asked.

"They're preparing a meal and some medicines for you," Thatcher said. He gestured to a hut. "Come on inside."

The five of us spread out as much as possible, but the air inside the hut was hot and sticky. I took a seat on the ground and leaned against the wall for support. My whole body ached with exhaustion.

"So, we heard there are some Americans organizing in the area," I said. "That true?"

Thatcher passed a cigarette to Henry and then lit his own. "Yep. Colonel Charles Gandy is organizing the central Luzon area. If you're interested in volunteering, we can send you on to his base camp near Mount Pinatubo with a couple of Negrito guides to get you there."

"I'm in," Henry said.

"Now wait a minute," I said. "We haven't officially decided to join up with guerrillas. Let's think about this."

"What's there to think about?" Henry said. "We're soldiers in a war. The guerrillas give us the chance to keep fighting the enemy."

"Yes, but we're officers in an army that's technically surrendered. If we're caught still fighting, we're no longer considered combatants, we're rebels. The Geneva convention gives us no standing as prisoners of war."

"I'll shoot it to you straight," Thatcher said. "The Japs don't care about the Geneva convention. I saw 'em marching our boys to death after we surrendered Bataan. And I've heard what they're doing in these camps they're building. They're torture camps, is what they are. Dying would be better than getting caught."

I looked over at Diego sitting quietly to my right. "What do you think?"

"This my home, mi familia. I cannot flee. I must fight. But this not your home, Captain. You face great danger here. You must decide what is right."

I leaned my head against the wall and closed my eyes, wishing I could just go to sleep. Over the past several weeks, I'd somehow sailed and hiked my way from the coast of Mindanao, across more islands than I could count, and trudged almost completely across Luzon. By any reasonable estimate, I never should've made it. But the generosity of the Filipino people kept me alive at every turn, even when it came at great cost. How could I turn my back on them?

"All right," I said. "We'll send a message to this Colonel Gandy and find out what he wants us to do."

***

I was unable to do much of anything for the next few days on account of a raging fever and infection in my hamstring. So Henry wrote a message to Colonel Gandy offering our services and sent it by messenger. All we could do at that point was wait for an answer. In the meantime, two more Americans showed up at the barrio inquiring about guerrilla operations.

When they came into the hut where I'd been staying, I did my best to sit up and be friendly. "Hey there, fellas," I said, shaking hands with the tall, freckled one. "I'm Matthew Doyle. Where'd y'all come from?"

The freckled one chuckled. "Y'all? I haven't heard that in ages. I'm Sergeant Arnold Harris. This here's Corporal Ken Grimes. We were part of the 200th infantry before it got blown to smithereens."

"Wasn't the 200th at Clark Field?" Henry asked.

"Yeah, for a little while anyway." Harris plopped down onto the ground near Henry while Grimes stood near the door. He seemed on edge, his eyes darting around the hut constantly.

"Say, where're you from, Doyle?" Harris asked.

"Alabama. You?"

"New Mexico."

Henry laughed and shook his head. "I been through New Mexico a few times, and I don't reckon I ever saw a tall redhead in the desert. How did you keep from burning to a crisp? Out here, even?"

"Just lucky, I guess." Harris looked up at Grimes and tossed him a pack of cigarettes. "Hey, come on and have a smoke with us. Nothing's gonna happen here."

Grimes caught the pack and slid a cigarette out into his shaking hands. It took him four tries to get the lighter lit. He sucked on that cigarette like he was drowning, and that cigarette was a breath of oxygen.

"You fellas have a rough time of it?" I asked.

"More than some, not as bad as others," Harris answered. "Grimes here was caught up in that murderous march forced on our boys for a while. But he managed to escape by jumping into a ditch when the guards weren't looking. Saw some terrible stuff. Guys getting bayonetted, shot, run over." He took a long draw on his cigarette and appeared to consider his next words. "I aim to make them Nips pay for what they've done."

"We're joining up with the guerrillas forming under Colonel Gandy," Henry said. "Y'all should join 'em too."

"Just might do that," Harris said. "Providing I get to kill me some Nips."

"Amen to that," Henry said. "Every one of 'em ought to get sent straight to hell, and I can't wait to provide the transportation."

Henry and Harris continued plotting their revenge on the Japanese, while I listened with growing concern. Harris seemed to bring out the darker side of Henry, something I hadn't seen since just after Janine died on Corregidor. I hoped Harris and Grimes would go their own way soon. Antagonizing the Japanese with such a small group of guerrillas was surely risking capture or execution. And I tended to agree with Thatcher. Capture was the worst possible outcome.

***

Major Gandy responded to our letter by welcoming us into the guerrilla unit and ordering us to find a suitable location to establish a base camp for ourselves. By mid-September, and thanks to the help of willing Filipinos in the area, we'd built a headquarters in the Porac region, east of Bataan and in the foothills of Mount Pinatubo. Major Gandy informed us that I would head up the Porac region, and had authority to do whatever I deemed necessary to recruit, equip, and train cadres in the area.

After I got over the initial shock of being put in charge of something I had no idea how to accomplish, I consulted with Corporal Thatcher, Henry, and Diego to come up with a plan for recruiting local Filipinos into our forces. However, I soon learned that recruiting wasn't even an issue.

Once word got out, men and women from barrios all over the area came to us to volunteer, eager to inflict all manner of suffering upon the Japanese. Even those who were too old to fight volunteered to build structures and provide food. I commissioned Diego as a First Sergeant and put him in charge of organizing and training the soldiers. We had virtually no weapons, but I was amazed at what Diego could accomplish with bamboo poles and bolos. Dressed in their frayed, handmade clothing, the soldiers trained each day in the tactics for defending their homeland.

I put Henry in charge of "requisitions." He had a talent for finding the necessities to sustain us and bartering with the locals to obtain food and supplies. Fortunately most of the locals were already eager to help, but Henry had a knack for finding even the most obscure treasures, a lesson I'd learned early on in our days at Cabcaben. He still had never told me exactly how he'd acquired our wedding rings.

Among the local volunteers, I met a young Filipino named Garzon who'd been a student at the University of the Philippines in Manila before the war broke out. He showed up in our camp with a mimeograph machine, so I put him in charge of communications. He and his small staff were responsible for printing and distributing leaflets to combat the propaganda being pushed by the Japanese.

In the first part of October, Major Gandy sent for me to report to him with an update on our operations. I had intended to travel to his headquarters with the help of a local guide and a small band of soldiers, but Diego insisted on accompanying me as a bodyguard. He selected ten of the best men he'd trained so far, and the twelve of us set out trekking west along the river.

We were still at the tail end of typhoon season, so the riverbank and much of the land around it was so wet, our feet would sometimes sink into the mud up to our knees. It was tiring on my weakened body, and it was all I could do to keep up with Diego without feeling like death was at my door. It took us several hours to cover the few kilometers higher into the range of Mount Pinatubo.

When we arrived at Major Gandy's camp, I was surprised at how much it resembled a local barrio rather than a military camp. His staff and even some of the higher-ranking soldiers lived with their families or female companions. I was expecting a formal meeting with the major, but instead, I found myself seated at a festive dinner with him and his staff. Men and women, even some children, danced to music at the bonfire in the center of camp.

"This is not what I expected," I said to Major Gandy as we walked through the camp after our meal. Diego trailed along behind us at a conspicuous distance.

Gandy let out a hearty chuckle that matched his tall, broad frame. "I imagine it's somewhat less official than what you're used to. I've found that making our camp look as similar to the local barrios as possible gives us an added layer of protection. When Jap patrols are nearby, we can disappear for a while without raising suspicion."

"I see. Clever."

"Time will tell."

We made our way through groups of dancing couples and headed for his residence. He gestured for me to step inside first, and then he followed me into the nipa hut. Diego stationed himself beside the entrance.

"How are things going in Porac?" Gandy asked.

"Very well, sir, considering the challenges we've faced. We've established contact with eight other guerrilla cadres as far north as Mabalacat, and I've got people imbedded in a resistance network forming in Manila. We're beginning to get regular reports of Japanese troop strength and movement. Of course, we don't have a radio, so we can't actually do anything with the information yet."

Gandy pulled out a bamboo pipe and some tobacco from a desk drawer, then gestured to a large map unrolled on his desk. "That can be taken care of. We have a system of couriers in the southern islands gathering intelligence and sending it by boat to MacArthur in Australia. Thatcher has most of the Bataan region organized, and he's already established a flow of information. I'll get you the details, and you can send your couriers there. What about your organization size?"

"We have just over a thousand men and women altogether. About eighty percent of them are training to fight."

He puffed on the pipe as he lit it. Then he shook his head. "Keep training the men, but we won't be focusing our efforts on instigating skirmishes with the Japanese. MacArthur wants us to organize as much of the local population as possible, gather intelligence, and relay it to him. We are to be ready to support the American troops when they return, but we are not to engage the enemy ourselves. In fact, I'm going to need you to put out a fire that's brewing up near Fort Stotsenberg."

"Me, sir?"

"Yes. I've gotten reports of a group operating in the area that's making raids on Japanese patrols. They're poking at a hornet's nest, and attracting the attention of the Japanese generals. I need you to go up there and make contact with the leader. Name's Harris."

"Yes, sir. I met Sergeant Harris a while back. I can't say I'm surprised. He was itching to start striking back at the Japs."

"Well, he's an ignorant fool. He's going to get us all captured or killed. Get up there, and get him in line."

"Yes, sir."

He pulled his pipe out of his mouth, and his deep wrinkles sank into a frown. "Unfortunately, Harris may not be your toughest challenge." He pointed at Mount Arayat. "The Huks have completely taken over most of the surrounding areas here. I thought we'd be able to establish an alliance with them. After all, they seemed to hate the Japanese as much as we do. I met with their council a couple of weeks ago, and we signed an agreement that they would come under my command over Luzon. But then one of their leaders, some dirty communist by the name of Taruc, published a proclamation that the Huks were cooperating with us. They also included forged letters from several American leaders, including one from you, demanding all the Filipinos turn over their weapons to the Huks."

He reached into a drawer and pulled out copies of these forged letters, and to my surprise, I saw my signature at the bottom of one of them. "What does this mean?" I asked.

"It means we're fighting a war on two fronts. Not just against the Japs, but against the Huks as well. And they're both ruthless. So tread carefully, Captain Doyle."

CHAPTER ELEVEN

Matthew

May 3, 1945
San Francisco

The next morning, I couldn't get out of the Hudsons' house fast enough. I thanked them as much as I could for their hospitality, but I was desperate to escape. Ruby and I caught the train to Los Angeles, where we then caught another to San Antonio. It was easy to keep my thoughts away from the unknowns that lay ahead by focusing on the next thing to do. Get to the station, load the bags, find a seat, change trains, load the bags again, find a compartment to ourselves. But once we were settled for the long trek across the southwest, my thoughts began to swirl again. I couldn't stop thinking about my men back in the Philippines, and I couldn't stop the growing desire in my heart to return. I didn't want a discharge; I wanted to see my mission through.

I sat opposite Ruby, a small table between us, with my body still aching from exhaustion. My stomach was a mess from the food the night before, so I hadn't eaten much breakfast. I asked an attendant for some coffee and he brought it to our compartment. Sipping on it for a while, I stared out at the landscape flying past. After years of deprivation, I had forgotten how much I loved coffee, and it took some of the edge off my nerves.

Ruby made herself a cup as well, but it sat on the table in front of her, the cup rattling with a soft *ting* against the saucer. She sat with a stiff posture, alternately looking out the window and back at me with nervous energy.

"Something on your mind?" I asked.

"So much that I hardly know where to begin," she said. "You?" I nodded and took another gulp of coffee. She fidgeted with her hands in her lap. "How are you feeling?"

"Tired," I said. "A bit run-down, but not too bad."

She reached over and put her wrist on my forehead. "You're warm."

"I'm all right. Nothing to fret over."

"Did the doctors give you any medicine to take during the journey? You should definitely still be taking quinine and some basic—"

"Ruby," I interrupted. "Really. I'm all right."

She leaned back in her chair and returned to fidgeting with her hands. We seemed at a loss for words. "How about we discuss what comes next?" I offered. "I'll be in San Antonio for some time, weeks, maybe a couple of months. I figure once I'm well, we'll need to move to a less conspicuous place. Somewhere away from dense population."

"Move? But I have a job and..." She placed her hands on the table as if to steady herself. "Listen, there's something else we need to discuss first."

"I get it," I said, referring to her job. "But you can have my pay now. You don't have to work. We can find a more remote place, maybe even another country, where you can live and be safe—"

"Where *I* can live?" Her eyes widened. "What about you? What are you saying?"

"All I'm saying is that I don't know what's ahead for me after I'm well. I don't know where the army will station me. They could send me back to the Philippines or Japan—"

"Send you back?" Her voice rose an octave. "You just got home! How can they send you back?"

"I don't know that they will. I'm just saying we need to consider what's best for your safety."

She shook her head and let out a deep breath. "Matthew, you don't understand. I need to tell you something first."

"All right, so tell me." I set my cup of coffee down and gave her my full attention.

She leaned toward me and took my hands in hers. "When I escaped Mindanao with the other nurses, I didn't know it at the time, but I was pregnant."

It took me a moment to process what she'd just said. "Wh—what? You were pregnant?"

"Yes. That was another reason I didn't stay in Australia. The military was leaving, and I had no way to provide for myself and the baby."

Baby? A baby. She had a baby. "Wait a minute," I said. "You...*we* have a baby?"

She smiled, and her eyes filled with tears. "Yes. Her name is Hope. She's two now, and she's just the most beautiful little girl you've ever seen. She has your eyes."

I couldn't believe what I was hearing. I sat back against the seat, my head swimming. "We have a daughter," I said, more to myself than to her.

Ruby stood and pulled her suitcase down from the overhead compartment. She flipped it open and pulled out a picture in a frame, holding it out to me. "See?"

I took the picture from her and gazed down at what could have easily been a picture of Mary as a toddler. She had the same soft, brown eyes, the same wispy curls and pudgy cheeks, and a joy in her expression that melted my heart. I couldn't believe it. I ran my fingers over her smiling face. "Hope, you said?"

Ruby nodded. "When she was born, I was determined that if there was even the smallest chance that you were still alive, I was going to do everything I could to hold on to hope till you came back to us. She was my reminder to never give up."

I set the picture on the table and stood in front of Ruby, my chest nearly cracking open. I pulled her waist against me, kissing her deeply, drinking in everything about her I'd forced myself to forget. She slid her hands around my neck, heating my insides.

There was still so much I had to tell her, things I would rather bury deep in the past. But for now, nothing else mattered. I had Ruby in my arms again. There was no island in the Pacific, no Kojima, no death or suffering, no murder conviction, no one else in the whole wide world but us. And now our daughter, Hope. And I was going to keep it that way for as long as possible.

May 4, 1945
Douglas, Arizona

A train is no place to get reacquainted with your wife. Even though we had a compartment to ourselves, complete with two beds, we both felt it would be better to stop over for the night in Douglas. We departed the train the next day just before noon, after a night of intermittent sleep, both tired and starving.

The town was dry and windy, and a layer of dust coated every single car we walked past. We stepped into a small café and sat in a booth near the front windows, sliding our bags under the table. As soon as the waitress came over to us, I saw the pity in her eyes.

"Just coming home from the war, huh?" she asked.

I gave her a slight nod. "Yes, ma'am."

"France? Italy?" She took a pad and pencil out of her apron, asking such weighty questions with the nonchalance of someone who'd only read about war in the papers.

"Philippines."

She shook her head. "No good Japs. I hear we're whipping 'em good, though."

I glanced at Ruby, who was unable to hide her dismay at such forward questioning. She slid her hand across the table and covered mine. "So what's good to eat here?" she asked.

The waitress launched into a list of specials like an auctioneer. I caught "cheeseburger plate" in there and stopped her to order. I knew I'd pay for it later, but I'd been craving a cheeseburger so much I'd actually dreamed about it. My mouth began to water as Ruby ordered the same and two Coca-Colas.

As soon as the waitress left the table, I could think of nothing else but the food. I pictured it sitting on the plate in front of me, dripping with grease, a side of French fries drowned in ketchup. My stomach cramped. The sensation was so familiar; it made my palms start to sweat. *You're not in the jungle,* I told myself. I'd have to find a way to think about something else until the food arrived.

"So, tell me about Hope," I said. "What's she like?"

Ruby's face broke into a smile, and her eyes lit up. "She talks like she's ten, not two. And she knows everything about everything, and isn't afraid to tell you."

I couldn't help but smile along with her as she painted a picture of exactly what I would've imagined Ruby to be like as a child. Stubborn, but loving, and fiercely kind.

"She's head over heels for rabbits right now. Loves anything to do with them. I got her a book called *The Velveteen Rabbit* for her birthday back in January, and we have to read it every single night."

"I can't wait to read it with her," I said. Then a thought occurred to me. "Does she know where you are? What's going on, I mean? Does she know about me?"

"She knows all about you. We pray for you every night before she goes to sleep, and I've told her stories about you that I remember from when we were younger. But I didn't tell her why I was going on this trip. I wasn't sure what to expect, and I didn't want to get her hopes up if I was wrong."

"If you were wrong? About what?"

"I don't know. I guess I had a hard time believing it was real. I was afraid the army had made another mistake and sent the letter to the wrong wife."

The waitress appeared with our food, and for the next few minutes, every other thought vanished from my mind. I devoured each bite, barely tasting it, stuffing some fries down just behind. I washed it down with the Coke, and the sweet burn of the fizzy drink made me close my eyes in pleasure. When I opened them again, Ruby was watching me with a hint of both amusement and concern.

"I think people are beginning to stare," she said.

"Let them," I said, shoving another bite of the burger into my mouth. Then I licked the grease from my fingers.

Her cheeks flushed pink, but she continued to eat her own burger without saying anything else about it. Needless to say, I finished my plate well before she'd eaten even half of her food. I turned toward the counter to get the waitress's attention, but she was already coming toward me with another plate.

"On the house," she said, sliding it in front of me. "And thank you for your sacrifice. You're a true hero."

She walked away, leaving a cold weight in the pit of my stomach that had nothing to do with dysentery. *A true hero.* She was the second person in as many days to say that. Neither of them had any idea what they were talking about.

After that, my pace slowed down, and I didn't enjoy the taste nearly as much. I still finished off the second plate, but I turned down the waitress's offer for dessert. Besides, my stomach was already roiling with complaint over my binge. I might have a long evening ahead.

***

When Ruby and I checked in at a nearby hotel, it was still early in the evening, but already my energy was completely drained. I lay on the bed, fully dressed, trying to make sense of the new world I now lived in—a world in which I was a father.

Ruby came over to me and felt my forehead, and then she lifted my arm and checked my pulse at the wrist. Her soft hands on my worn, dry skin soothed the tension building up inside of me. "You're still warmer than you should be," she said. "I'll get you a cool rag."

I closed my eyes and listened to her moving around the room, turning on the water, flipping on a lamp. Everything was so different, so calm. It was too calm, and my mind and body had no idea how to process this new environment. I had to take a deep breath just get my heart rate to slow a bit.

One thing was clear: I would not be going back to the Philippines after my recovery. I would have to get a discharge from the army and move Ruby and Hope somewhere safe as soon as possible. Somewhere we could live in peace at last.

Ruby placed a cool rag over my forehead, before removing my boots and socks. She let out a small gasp, so I opened my eyes to see her standing at the foot of the bed with her hand over her mouth.

"Come on," I said. "You're a nurse. I know you saw worse than that on Bataan."

Her eyes grew moist, and her voice tight. "But this time they're yours." She reached for one of my feet, gently examining the sores. I held in a wince. "I'm going to walk over to the drug store and get some supplies."

I sat up and swung my legs over the side of the bed. "No, Ruby, come here." I held out my hand, and she moved onto the bed beside me. "I'll be at the hospital by tomorrow. My feet have made it this long. They'll make it one more day. Tonight, let's just talk and figure some things out."

"But you must be in so much pain."

"I barely feel it anymore."

She looked at me with wide eyes. "Well, that's not good either."

I couldn't help but laugh. "I'll be fine. I'm sure I'll be good as new soon."

She grew quiet for a moment, resting her head on my shoulder. "You know, it's all right if you're not."

"Not what?" I knew what she meant, but I couldn't acknowledge it.

"If you're not good as new. We've been through so much, both of us. It's all right if it takes some time to adjust."

I couldn't think about that right now, so instead I pulled her face to mine and kissed her, drowning out the voices in my head that whispered of chaos and destruction. I would drown them out. I would silence all the screaming of the dying, the whispers of the dead, and even the hopes of the living if I had to.

***

I was still so weak and ill that being intimate with Ruby was challenging at best, but I couldn't control my desperate need to touch her. Anywhere would do. Her arm, her face, her stomach, anything. I needed to know she was real, that I wasn't stuck in some drug-induced dream.

The strange thing was, as soon as I touched her, as soon as my mind knew she was real, I would be overwhelmed with a sense that everything I was trying to hold together would crack wide open. So I'd pull away just as quickly. She must have thought I'd lost my mind.

Even so, she was gentle with me, patient with my fumbling, faltering hands, my moments of pure exhaustion, and my involuntary wincing. She was just as amazing as I remembered.

Later that evening, I rolled up on my elbow and reached out for my wife. *My wife.* The concept was still so foreign. Her skin, warm and soft, was irresistible. I laid my head on her bare stomach, wondering what it would've been like to feel Hope moving inside of her.

But once again, the moment of closeness brought a torrent of conflicting emotions within me that had to be shut down. So I pulled away and went back to lying beside her. "We should make some plans," I said, focusing on things I knew I could control.

She ran her fingers lightly up my arm. "What kind of plans?"

"The kind you won't like."

"Why's that?"

"'Cause it's me telling you what I think you should do. I don't reckon you've grown any less stubborn in the past three years?"

"Not even one little bit," she said, her eyes dancing with humor.

"I'm serious, *Grace*. That is what I have to get used to calling you, right? And you do remember why I have to call you that, right?"

She nodded, her expression falling serious. "I remember everything."

"You can't just go about living a normal life like everyone else. Especially now that we have a daughter."

"Yes, I'm aware of our daughter. I've been taking care of her for more than two years."

"And I would bet my very life that you're the best mother in the whole world. Honestly, I've seen you care for people. I know all the love you have in your heart. But we need to figure out how to do things together. It can't just be your way all the time, and I know it can't just be mine either. I'm just asking you to listen to me and respect what I have to say."

She brought her hand to my bare chest, tracing the scar from my armpit along my collarbone. Her hand slid across my chest and down to the long scar to the left of my belly button. A memory flashed into my mind: my screaming, Malaya's voice trying to calm me. I shut that down too.

"Grace, are you listening to me?"

She looked up into my eyes again. "Yes. I'm listening. What do you think we should do?"

"I think we should get a house in a more remote location. I don't think you should work. I can provide for us. I'll work hard, and I'll give you and Hope the life you deserve. And no one will bother us. No one will find out who you really are. We'll just live out the rest of our lives in peace. Doesn't that sound nice? After everything we've been through?"

Tears formed around the edges of her eyes, making me feel like a total jerk. I didn't want to make her cry. There'd be plenty of that to come, I was sure. We were only just starting into difficult territory.

"Do we have to decide right now?" she asked. "I just started working at the hospital, and I love my job. It'll be a while before you're discharged, and we still need the money right now. We have some time to decide, right?"

I couldn't take the disappointment in her expression. "Of course, we have some time. I'll get everything with my pay straightened out while I'm in San Antonio. By the time I get out, we should have enough from my back pay to get a place of our own. We'll figure everything else out then."

She relaxed and laid her head on my shoulder. I closed my eyes and prayed for wisdom. *Lord, I know I haven't prayed like I should the past few years, and I've been angry at You for many things. I don't know how we get past that part, but I do know Ruby deserves so much better than me. Please help me be the husband and father she and Hope deserve. Help me find a way to tell her the truth. And please, Lord, let her forgive me.*

CHAPTER TWELVE

Ruby

May 5, 1945
Arizona

Matthew's frail, damaged body horrified me, but I did my best not to let that show. He was covered in scars, both from injury and illness. I saw signs of sores that had festered long before healing, maybe even a rudimentary surgery near his appendix that couldn't have taken place more than six months prior. There were lacerations on his chest, arms, and legs, what appeared to be bullet wounds in his arm, shoulder, and leg, and his bones looked as though they might pop right out of his skin. I only had to close my eyes and remember my time on Bataan to imagine what he must have gone through. I'd been there only a few months. What could it have been like for three years? I was afraid to ask.

I did my best to keep the conversation on happy things. The morning we spent in Douglas was nice, filled with food and stories about Hope. She was easy to talk about, and he seemed entranced with the idea of being her father. He even bought her a new stuffed bunny from a drugstore we passed on our way back to the train station.

We again settled into a private compartment on the train, but once the desert began flying by the window, turning orange with the sunset, Matthew grew distant and quiet. He sat on one side of the compartment nearest the window, staring out of it and saying nothing for nearly an hour, while I sat opposite. I watched him for a while, wondering if he would make eye contact with me, but it almost seemed as though he was in a different place altogether.

Eventually, I had to break the silence. "Is everything all right?" At first he didn't respond, so I tried again. "Matthew? Is everything all right?"

He dragged his eyes away from the window and looked at me like he was surprised to see me sitting across from him. "I'm sorry. I guess my mind wandered. Did you ask me something?"

I moved across the compartment to sit next to him, taking his hand in mine. It seemed important to establish a physical connection with him as often as possible. "I just wondered if you were all right. You haven't said anything since we pulled away from Douglas. Is something on your mind?"

He pulled his hand away and leaned forward onto his elbows where I couldn't see his expression. "I'm all right, I reckon. Just a lot to think about."

"I was thinking about what you said last night, about me quitting my job and moving. And I just think it would be better for us to stay where we are for now. Hope is happy there. I worry about taking her away from the only family she's known."

"*We're* her family," he said. "Just the three of us. That's all she needs."

I ran my hand over his back, struck by the tension in his sinewy muscles. "I know we're her family, but think of this from her perspective. She doesn't know you yet. You're a stranger to her. Sure, she'll be excited that you're home, but it may take her a while to feel comfortable around you. The Sawyers have been there for us since the day she was born. She calls them Grandma and Grandpa. She won't understand if we just cut them out of her life."

"She's two. She'll forget."

He pushed himself up to standing and moved toward the door. It hadn't escaped my notice that he couldn't seem to stay still for long. I would have to be patient, but I'd have to keep trying to reconnect with him. Something was eating away at him. In fact, it was probably much more than just *something*. This wasn't the time to push him too hard.

I decided to change the subject. "Well, I'm sure it'll all work out just fine. We'll figure everything out when you're better. Henry should be coming back soon too. I read in the paper that all the prisoner-of-war camps are being liberated in the Philippines. I don't know how we'll find out when Henry's coming home, but maybe you can reach out to Mother and Asa. Once Henry's back we can find a place where we can all live near each other."

The whole time I was talking, Matthew stood by the door, rubbing the back of his neck. I could tell he didn't like what I was saying, but he wasn't saying anything back to me. I kept right on talking, hoping he'd hear something he could agree with.

"Maybe we can even find a way to let Mother and Asa know the truth about me. I mean, we could all wind up back in Alabama. Wouldn't that be nice? You, me, and Hope living near our family? Maybe Henry with a little farm nearby? Of course, he never liked farming much. Maybe he can do something else. I bet he'd make a great baseball coach."

"Ruby, please stop." The ache in Matthew's voice made me pause. His face was sick with pain. "Just stop. Please."

"Stop...what?"

"Stop talking like we're all going to live happily ever after as one big fairy tale family. It's not going to happen."

"I'm just trying to hold on to my hope, that's all. I know it's a long shot. I know I'm probably dreaming, but what's wrong with that? Maybe

God will answer my prayers. He brought you home to us. Maybe He'll bring Henry home soon too. And then at some point we can figure out what to do about my conviction."

He turned away from me and leaned onto his hands against the door. I had no idea what was going on with him, but it was starting to scare me. Something in the pit of my stomach grew heavy and nauseous.

"Matthew, what's going on?"

He shook his head. "I don't even know how to begin to tell you."

"Just...tell me."

He said nothing, dropping his head below his shoulders.

"Please," I tried again, feeling the tremor in my voice. "Whatever it is, we'll face it together."

After another agonizing minute, he turned around and leaned his back against the door. He rubbed his hands over his face, and then seemed to steel himself, straightening up and looking directly at me.

"Ruby, I'm so sorry. I haven't been able to figure out a way to tell you this. But...Henry isn't coming back. He was killed by the Japanese."

My heart lurched. I couldn't have heard him right. "What? How? Wh—when?"

"I was with him, after I escaped Mindanao. We met up and joined the guerrillas together."

"No, no. He was on Corregidor when we left. He was captured when they surrendered. He was on Corregidor!" My mind couldn't understand, couldn't connect Henry to what Matthew was saying. My heart raced wildly in my chest.

"He escaped from Corregidor shortly after the Japanese captured it. He and a couple of other guys swam across Manila Bay before the Japanese were able to straighten out all the prisoners. By the time I ran into him, there were guerrilla units organizing all over Luzon, and we decided to join up."

I couldn't breathe. My chest felt like it was caving in. *No, Lord. Not Henry. He can't be gone. Matthew's wrong.* Like Colonel Dorsey had been wrong about Matthew. He had to be wrong.

"How...how can you be sure?" I choked out. "Colonel Dorsey said you were dead. He showed me the telegram. But you weren't. You're...you're alive."

He knelt in front of me, looking directly into my eyes. "Ruby, listen to what I'm saying. I was with Henry on Luzon. We joined up with the guerrillas together. I was there. I saw them kill him with my own eyes. He didn't make it."

A sob flew out of me, and I couldn't control myself. I reached for Matthew, wrapping my hands around his neck. "Please, no. You have to be wrong. Somehow...you have to be wrong. Please tell me you're just not sure. Maybe he was captured instead."

He shook his head. "I'm so sorry, baby. I'm so sorry. I tried so hard to save him." He came up onto the bench beside me and pulled me into his chest. "I'm so sorry."

I sobbed for a long time, begging him to tell me he was mistaken. But all he could do was say he was sorry, over and over. I cried like I hadn't cried in a long time, like I was ten years old again, and I was on my face in the woods, begging God to save Henry's life because I'd thrown that knife at him.

"He can't be gone," I said into Matthew's chest. "He just can't be."

Matthew held me against himself while I cried, but he didn't say anything else. All I could do was picture Henry and me playing together as kids, swimming and fishing, playing basketball, and walking home from the drugstore with ice cream melting down our hands. I remembered his first home run, how he'd strutted around the house for nearly half an hour before Daddy put a hoe in his hand and sent him out to the garden. I remembered his face, full of excitement and wonder, when he'd come back from his first time in an airplane. I'd wanted to jump right into an airplane with him. We'd talked all night about his plans, about how he might get through college and become a pilot. He'd worked so hard for that dream.

I couldn't stop crying for Henry. I couldn't make sense of a world without his smile and his laughter. I didn't want to doubt God, didn't want to let my thoughts stray toward anger, but why would He let this happen? First Daddy, then Joseph and Janine, and now Henry. I was so tired of losing my family. I didn't have the strength to face it again.

But like so many times before, the quiet voice in my heart spoke words of life:

Hast thou not known? Hast thou not heard, that the everlasting God, the Lord, the Creator of the ends of the earth, fainteth not, neither is weary? There is no searching of his understanding.

He giveth power to the faint; and to them that have no might he increaseth strength.

Even the youths shall faint and be weary, and the young men shall utterly fall:

But they that wait upon the Lord shall renew their strength; they shall mount up with wings as eagles; they shall run, and not be weary; and they shall walk, and not faint.

***

As we neared San Antonio, I tried my hardest to pull myself together. I went to the bathroom and wiped away the streaks on my face. I freshened up the best I could, but there wasn't much I could do about my pale skin and puffy, bloodshot eyes.

When I returned to the compartment, it was completely dark and Matthew was gone. I walked through a few of the other cars until I found him in the dining car seated alone at a table by the window. He held a drink in his hand that looked like whiskey, and he sipped on it as he stared out at the night sky.

I took the seat across the table from him. "I wondered where you'd gone."

He downed the rest of the drink and set his glass on the table, unable to hide the shaking in his hand. "I just needed to move around a bit."

A waiter came over and asked what I'd like. I ordered tea. Then he asked Matthew if he'd like another drink. Matthew slid the glass toward him and nodded. "Thanks," he mumbled.

When the waiter left, I leaned onto the table. "Since when do you drink whiskey?"

He shrugged. "I don't, usually. Tried it a few times when I was in college. Now seemed like a good time to try it again."

It seemed like the worst time, actually. But I decided to let it go. "I need to know something," I said. "I need you to tell me—"

"No," he said, glaring at me. "I know what you're going to say, and trust me, you do not want to know what happened."

"Yes, I do. I need to know. Was he...was he in pain?"

Matthew closed his eyes and rubbed his temples. "Don't do this to yourself."

"Do what to myself? I just want to know what happened to him. Was he alone? Did he suffer?"

The waiter returned with our drinks, and Matthew downed his in one long gulp. When he came up for air, his eyes were cold and hard. "Don't sit there and interrogate me about Henry. It's only going to cause you more pain. I won't be the cause of making you cry like that again. All you need to know is that he gave his life in service to his country. He's the real hero."

That wasn't enough. And even though something inside of me knew I shouldn't press him, a bigger part of me was desperate enough to try again. "Matthew, please. Just tell me something I can hold on to. It's so hard to accept. I need to know."

"I said no!" he bellowed, pushing away from the table and storming out of the dining car.

I sat in shock for a moment, unable to move. It seemed like everyone in the entire car froze along with me, staring at me as they whispered to one another. My face flushed hot, and I turned away from the stares. I took a sip of my tea, trying to calm my racing thoughts. Tears pricked my eyes again, but I was determined not to break down.

I finished my tea and paid the waiter. Then I slipped out of the dining car with my gaze on the floor. I found a passenger car that was mostly empty. Grabbing some tissue from the bathroom, I found a row to myself and leaned against the window.

I'd been so certain that all I needed was for Matthew to come home alive and well. That anything else, I could handle. I even thought I was prepared to face the possibility that either Matthew or Henry wouldn't make it off the island alive. Maybe even both of them. But the reality of it, the sock in the gut of actually hearing the words come out of Matthew's mouth, made me realize I was prepared for nothing—absolutely nothing—that lay ahead.

***

Just before dawn, I felt someone take the empty seat beside me. I'd dozed off. Even before I turned to him, I knew it was Matthew, and my emotions swelled.

"I'm sorry, baby," he said, as I buried my face in his chest once more. "I didn't mean to blow my cap like that."

The train's whistle and its squealing brakes announced our arrival in San Antonio. I pushed away from him and took the handkerchief he offered, dabbing at my eyes. I couldn't control my voice well enough to say anything, so I just nodded my acceptance of his apology.

As the train came to a stop, he stood in the aisle. "I reckon we should get our things." He held out his hand. "Come on."

I took his hand in mine, clinging to it as he led me back through the passenger cars, the dining car, and finally to the compartment where my small bag was located. I gathered my things in silence, stuffing my mirror and brush inside my purse.

"You ready?" he asked from the doorway.

I nodded. There was no hand extended this time.

I followed him off the train to where our bags sat waiting for us on the ground. When Matthew went to pick up his, I grasped it first. "Let me get that," I said.

"I can carry it," he said, setting his mouth in a hard line.

"No, you can't. And you shouldn't even try. We need to get you over to the hospital. You look like you could fall over at any moment." Part of me wondered if the alcohol was contributing to that state, but I kept my mouth shut on the subject.

He wasn't happy about it, but he didn't argue any further. We headed over to the counter and bought bus tickets for the ride to Brooke General Hospital. Then I carted the bags over to the bench where several others were waiting. That was when I noticed all the uniforms.

Soldiers in all sorts of conditions moved around the station in the gray light of approaching dawn, some in wheelchairs, some on crutches, most escorted by someone carrying their army-issued bag. Less than half appeared remotely well. I noticed Matthew looking around, catching the eye of a fellow soldier with a missing leg and giving him a curt nod.

I thanked God that at least Matthew's body was intact, even if his heart and mind were far from healed. *Lord, please heal his body and soul. Make him whole again. Give him Your peace. And please, help me find that peace as well.*

CHAPTER THIRTEEN

Matthew

May, 1945
San Antonio, Texas

Brooke General Hospital was located on three acres of flat emptiness that had been carved out of the even larger flat emptiness of Fort Sam Houston. Situated at the back of a long horseshoe curve, the main hospital building rose up out of the earth like a prison; it was missing only a fence with barbed wire running around it, as far I was concerned. Sure, there was a smattering of trees here and there, but mostly it was just wide open space. Made me feel exposed, like there was no place to hide.

Ruby stayed with me through my initial physical exam, my bath and shave, the meetings with doctors and nurses. I was diagnosed with malaria, amoebic dysentery, acute malnutrition, and general nervous collapse. I knew Ruby had questions, but she deferred to the staff and mostly just listened. She seemed particularly agitated when I explained the circumstances of my emergency appendectomy, but again, she said nothing. It was a long day for us both.

Afterward, she helped me get settled in my room. She put the picture of Hope on my windowsill, touching Hope's face and once again pointing out that the little girl had my eyes. I had a hard time looking at Ruby during all this, knowing I'd been a real jerk on the train. I wanted to apologize for so many things—things I hadn't even confessed yet—but I was afraid she'd go back to asking for details about Henry, and I couldn't go down that path with her. Besides, I was so tired; I could no longer control the tremors in my arms and legs.

Once I was settled into my bed and the nurse hooked me up to an IV, Ruby took a walk around the room to inspect it. After the nurse promised she'd return with supper soon and left us alone, she came beside me and took my hand.

"Looks like you're going to be in good hands here," she said. "Just make sure you do what you're told and don't get ornery." She tried to smile, but it didn't take.

"I'm not ornery," I said.

"Oh, yes you are. Especially when you're sick. I remember."

Our eyes met, and I remembered too. I remembered how she'd cared for me when I was sick with TB, so long ago. How she'd cleaned up after me as I'd coughed my very life out of my lungs. She'd never given up on me.

"Ruby, I love you very much. You know that, don't you?"

She nodded, her eyes filling with tears. I was exhausted, and I couldn't take her crying again. I glanced away and pulled my hand out from under hers. "Listen," I said. "Everything's going to be just fine. I'll be out of here in no time. We can put all the pain and suffering of the past behind us. And we can finally live our lives in peace."

"I need to contact Mother somehow. She should know—"

"The army will take care of notifying your mother. She's probably known for some time now. I reported...everything...back in March. In fact, I recommended Henry for a medal." I glanced up at her, but still couldn't hold her gaze.

She leaned over and kissed my cheek. "Thank you." Then she straightened and swiped at her eyes. "Do you think you might...someday...be able to tell me what happened?"

I dropped my head back onto the pillows supporting me. She was still as stubborn as ever, and I might have to eventually tell her everything. But not yet. "I don't know," I said.

She closed her eyes for a moment before letting out a shaky breath. "At least you're home. You're safe. And you'll be better soon."

"Absolutely."

"I should get going. The train leaves early in the morning, and I should get some rest. I need to get back to Hope and I really should report in at work—Ms. Wharton's been so generous with allowing me extra leave. But I'll be back as soon as I can, and I'll bring Hope with me."

That brought a genuine smile from both of us. "I can't wait to meet her," I said.

She leaned over and kissed me gently, her lips lingering on mine. Despite all the turmoil still stirring inside of me, she still stirred me as well, and in the best ways possible. I needed her, needed the peace and love that flowed out of her.

I reached up and slid my hand around her neck, holding her close for another moment. "I wish you didn't have to go," I said.

"I'll be back soon, I promise." She kissed me again before straightening. "I love you, Matthew Doyle."

"I love you too."

Ruby grabbed her bag from the corner and slipped out the door. As soon as she disappeared, my heart sped up a notch. My chest tightened, and a sharp pain shot out from the center of my chest into my left arm. The room swayed. I took a slow, deep breath and reasoned with my uncooperative body. *She isn't leaving for good. Just keep it together, and get out of here as soon as possible. And whatever you do, do not let them put you in the psych ward.*

***

My first two weeks in the hospital were focused mainly on getting acclimated to my surroundings and resting my weary body. The chloroquine they gave me helped bring my dysentery under control, as well as the malaria, which meant I was able to absorb more of the nutrients from my food.

The nurses soaked my feet twice a day in Listerine and vinegar, and they too gradually began to feel normal again. As my energy returned and my feet healed, I could walk around the hospital without tiring out too much. That was when I realized that I was one of the lucky ones.

There's no humane way to describe the evidence of inhumanity I witnessed, both in the jungles of the Philippines and in Brooke General Hospital. There just aren't words to explain how explosions and shrapnel, starvation and torture can ravage a man's body. I saw all of it. Arms and legs missing. Faces disfigured. Bodies burned and blistered.

But the worst part was the screaming. Some fellas cried out as their phantom missing limbs itched uncontrollably. Many screamed in the middle of the night, wrestling with demons in their sleep. A few were completely mad, sitting in a daze by a window one moment, shouting out maneuvers to their company the next. Yet along with this madness, the staff remained relentlessly positive. The nurses had a smile with every dose of medication; the doctors had an encouraging word for every setback. The army even brought in former patients to give us all pep talks about adjusting to life after war.

I wasn't buying it. Life might be difficult for the guys who lost a leg or an arm, but I was going to be just fine. I was determined to get well as quickly as possible and get out of that place. I listened carefully to everything the doctor said, followed every step of my regimen, and made sure I let every member of the staff know that I was improving each day.

About a week into my treatment, I received a letter from Ruby telling me all about her first conversation with Hope after my homecoming. They were both excited to come visit, and Hope had not stopped asking questions since Ruby had told her the news. "I'll have to bring her to you as soon as possible just to get some peace," she'd written. Included with the letter was a crayon drawing of what I assumed was Ruby, Hope, and myself holding hands in a grassy field, surrounded by butterflies and bunnies. It had both thrilled me and terrified me. Could I really be a father? Could I take care of them and protect them? I'd taped the drawing to the window beside the picture of Hope, and it reminded me every day of why I had to get well. And soon.

Every afternoon, Red Cross volunteers called Gray Ladies came through our ward passing out candy and light-hearted conversation. Most days, a young lady named Regina visited with me for a few minutes, asking about how I was feeling and encouraging me to keep my spirits up. She'd do her best to make small talk, asking about my home and family, but I wasn't much for conversation. Every day before she left, she would try to hand me some stationery to write letters, and I would pass.

"Don't you think your family wants to hear from you?" she asked in her Texan twang. "I'm sure they want to know how you're doing. When's the last time you wrote to them?"

I shrugged. "I'm not much for writing letters."

She gestured to the drawing on the window. "Well, someone is sending you letters. I'm guessing that's from your daughter. Why not write back?"

"I'm sure she'll come visit soon."

Regina reached behind me as I reclined in my bed, pulling out a pillow and fluffing it for me. "Well, what about your family back in Alabama? You mentioned a sister and some brothers a few days ago. Bet they'd like to hear from you." She placed the pillow back behind my head and gave me a sympathetic sigh. "If my brother was in the hospital, I'd want to know if he was all right."

"Thanks, but not today."

She threw her hands up in surrender. "All right. Can't say I didn't try. Now, you get some rest, Major Doyle. You're looking better every day. Bet you'll be out of here in no time."

She glided out of the doorway on her cloud of optimism, heading for the captain in the room next to mine. He'd been in a prison camp in the southern Philippine islands for over three years. In his sleep, he yelled out numbers in Japanese.

I thought about what Regina had said, suddenly overcome by a deep sense of loss. I wanted to reach out to Mary. I'd thought about it nearly every day since finding out I was returning to the States. But I just couldn't make it work in my mind. How could I protect Ruby and Hope if anyone discovered where we were?

I'd once told Ruby that running away would be easy. I'd begged her to do it, promising I wouldn't care if I never saw my family again. I'd been so naive. And now, I probably *would* never see my family again. Hope would never know her cousins or her Aunt Mary. Mother would never know her granddaughter. All for what? So my father could have his way? We'd all lost in the end. Every single one of us.

***

About a week later, I was playing checkers in my room with the captain from the next room over. We sat at the table near the window, soaking up sunshine and chatting about our experiences in the Philippines before the war. He was a few years younger than I was, and he'd lived the high life in Manila for a year before getting captured.

"Did you ever go to the Jai Alai club?" he asked, sliding a black checker forward.

"Once. Didn't stay long. You?"

"Yeah. That place was wild. The girls were too. Made quite a bit of money placing bets." He glanced out the window and seemed to contemplate something for a while. "I wonder if it's still there," he finally said.

"It isn't."

We both grew quiet and went back to moving our checker pieces. But the quiet only lasted for a few minutes. It was interrupted by a choked female voice.

"Matthew? Is that you?"

I glanced up to see a woman who could have easily been my mother standing in the doorway, clutching a handkerchief to her chest. Tears tinged black slid down her face. I knew it couldn't possibly be my mother, but the child inside me saw her nonetheless. Then reason returned.

"Mary?" I said, standing and taking a couple of steps toward her.

The captain stood and excused himself. "I'll let you two have some time. We'll pick this up later." He squeezed past Mary as she stepped into the room.

Tears came rolling down her pale face, and she rushed over to me, throwing her arms around my neck. I wrapped mine around her waist, holding her there while she mumbled both praises and curses. Finally, she stepped away from me and dabbed at her eyes with her handkerchief.

"What are you doing here?" I asked.

She threw her arms up in exasperation. "What am *I* doing here? I'm your sister. Remember me? The person who loves you? The person you haven't seen or spoken to in nearly nine years?"

I dropped my gaze and leaned onto the bedrail for support. This was the last thing I needed right now. "I'm so sorry. Really, I am. I was going to write—"

"Write? Was that all I was going to get from you? A note to say, 'Hi, sis. Just wanted to let you know that I'm actually not dead. I'm doing just swell.' Was that it?"

"No."

"Then what?"

"I don't know."

"Do you have any idea what our family has been through in the last nine years? Do you even care?"

I went around to the side of the bed and sat down, feeling my blood pressure rise. "Of course I care. Come on. Sit down, and let's talk. Tell me everything."

She dropped into a chair against the wall, dabbing at her eyes again and straightening her dress. She'd changed so much. Her hair swept back away from her face in soft blonde curls that barely touched her shoulders. And when she looked up at me, the playful brown eyes I'd always loved were filled with pain.

"Where have you been all this time?" she asked. "What's happened to you?"

"I was in the Philippines when the Japanese attacked. Did you get any of my letters before that?"

She nodded. "The last one I got was in the fall of '41. You said you'd just gotten there."

"Well, I've been there the whole time. I managed to escape into the jungle and operate as a guerrilla until the Americans returned and retook the islands."

"Are you all right? Why are you in the hospital? I mean, obviously you're not all right. Look at you. I've never seen you so skinny. Not since you had T.B."

"I'm all right. I'm recovering from malaria and malnutrition, but I'll be just fine."

She let out a long sigh and leaned her head against the wall. "I've been so scatterbrained. I just up and left the kids with Ellis and Esther and jumped on the first train to San Antonio. Andrew must think I've lost my mind. We all thought you had died. We had a funeral for you and everything."

"That must have been tough. I'm sorry you had to go through that." I hesitated, afraid of the answer to my next question. "How's...Mother?"

She shook her head, and her eyes filled with tears again. "Mother passed away shortly after we got your last letter."

My throat knotted, and shame heated my neck and face. I should've been there to say goodbye. She deserved better than that. I'd been a horrible son to her, but I'd drawn a line I couldn't have crossed. And there was nothing I could do about it now.

"I'm sorry I wasn't able to be there for you, Mary. I've been a lousy brother. I know that."

She leaned forward and looked up at me with a hopeful expression. "Can't we just put the past behind us now? You should come home and be with your family. Especially after everything you've been through. Everyone is so anxious to see that you're all right."

I started shaking my head before she even finished. "I can't do that. I'm not going back to Hanceville. I swore I'd never go back to that place, and I meant it."

She stood and came to the bedside, taking my hand in hers. "Please, Matthew. Just come home. It's time to forgive Father. He isn't the same man he was back then. When Mother died, and then you...he hasn't been well."

"I don't want to hear about Father. He's the reason all this happened to begin with."

"And he's paid for it, believe me. He had a stroke a few days after we got the telegram from the army about your death. He's been in a wheelchair ever since, and he can barely speak."

"Good. He deserves it."

Her eyes widened. "Matthew, that's horrible. How can you say such a thing?"

I dropped my head, unable to look at her anymore. If Father hadn't been so hell-bent on keeping me away from Ruby, we might never have been in the Philippines to begin with. Maybe we would've had a chance at being a family. But he destroyed all that. And everything that followed had nearly destroyed me.

"Maybe you should just go home," I said.

"Holding on to your anger won't bring Ruby back," she said. "You have to accept that she's gone. And you have to find a way to live again. God never meant for us to walk this life alone."

"I'm not alone." I realized as soon as I said it that I shouldn't have.

"What do you mean?"

Then it hit me. The picture and drawing in the windowsill. Ruby's letter on the bedside table. The proof was all around me. How could I have been so careless?

At that same moment, Mary's eyes fell on the picture in the window. She walked past the bed and gestured at it. "Who's that little girl? She looks familiar."

I slid off the bed and went over to the window, picking up the picture. "No one. It's just...just..." I couldn't think. My heart began to race, and my head swam from the rush.

"Is that..." she leaned over and looked at the drawing before I could grab it as well. "She has your eyes. Is that your daughter? Matthew, are you married?"

She reached for the picture, but I turned and held it out of reach. "Listen, you should probably go. I'm not feeling well."

Indeed, I wasn't. My head was throbbing and the same tingling sensations I'd felt back on Luzon began to spread through my limbs. Another breakdown.

"I'm not leaving until you tell me what's going on."

My hands began to shake. I had to get this under control. I couldn't end up in the psych ward. I took a deep breath, but it didn't help. My thoughts scattered, and I couldn't say what I wanted to.

Mary stepped closer and put a hand on my shoulder. "Are you all right? Do you want me to get the doctor?"

"No," I managed. I pushed past her and sat back down on the bed. "Just...need...rest."

I couldn't lift my legs onto the bed. I fell back against the pillows and lay there, shaking. Mary scrambled over to me, lifting my legs and situating me on the bed. Then she took off, hollering for a doctor.

Despite the tremors and dizziness, I could hang on to enough of myself to realize this was a bad situation. It was exactly what I'd been trying so hard to avoid. I had to make it stop. I closed my eyes, and pictured Ruby in my mind, holding her close. But the convulsions continued. I heard Mary yelling in the distance.

A moment later, a nurse grabbed my arm, taking my vitals and asking Mary to wait outside. Doctor Larson, who'd been treating me, came in as well, speaking calmly and asking me to answer various questions about my name and dates. I forced my brain to find one thing it could focus on. I looked down at the picture of Hope still gripped in my hand. Her wide brown eyes looked back at me, almost laughing with joy.

That joy seemed to spread for a moment, and I could finally hear Dr. Larson's question. "What day is it, Matthew?"

"Tuesday," I said.

"Good. How old are you?"

"Thirty-two."

"Good. Who's in the picture?"

"Hope."

***

Whatever the doctor gave me, it was enough to knock me out for a while. I awoke in the middle of the night, my bed soaked in sweat. I tried to stand, but I was so dizzy, I could only sit on the edge of my bed for a while. How had I let this happen again?

It had been a mistake to keep personal items around the room. I could correct that. And I'd have to make sure I called Ruby by the name Grace from now on, even in private. If one of the nurses overheard me calling her Ruby, and if Mary asked about my wife, it wouldn't be hard for her to figure out what had happened.

My heart began to race again. I had to get this under control, and soon. No more breakdowns. I had to keep calm. I had to have a plan. And I would have to get out of this hospital as soon as humanly possible. I would have to take Grace and Hope somewhere we could disappear for good.

***

As I'd expected, Mary returned the following morning. She came in quietly, with a cautious smile. "Morning. Is it all right if I come in?"

I had just finished my breakfast and was sitting up in bed. I motioned for her to come in. "I'm sorry about yesterday."

"No, I'm sorry. I pushed too hard. Believe me, I got a good scolding from the staff here. They wouldn't even let me see you last night."

"Well, I'm all right. No harm done."

Her eyes canvassed the room as she sat in the chair near the door. I'd removed the pictures, the drawing, and the letter, tucking them into my rucksack in the closet. "I'm heading back home today," she said. "I called Andrew last night from the hotel and told him you were here. He said he would let everyone in the family know."

"Look, I overreacted yesterday. I can explain everything." My stomach churned as I prepared the lie I had decided on in the middle of the night. "The little girl you saw is not my daughter. She's the daughter of a friend. I've known them for a long time. They heard I was in the hospital and sent those to cheer me up."

She furrowed her brow in contemplation. "Then why didn't you just tell me that? And why did you remove the picture?"

"Your visit was a bit of a shock, Mary. My body hasn't fully healed, and the shock was too much for me. Doctor Larson thinks it's best if my room is free of any kind of stimulation for the time being. No radio. No newspapers. He just wants me to relax."

"I see." She didn't seem convinced, but she didn't push. She swung her crossed leg a few times before changing the subject. "I also came to make sure you got your life insurance money. The army said you'd put it in my name, but I couldn't bring myself to spend any of it."

"You didn't have to give it back?"

"No, they said I could keep it. But I figured it's your money. You certainly earned it. I brought a check for the full amount." She reached into her purse and pulled out the check, then came over to my bed to hand it to me. "Matthew, I really do love you and want the best for you. I miss you so much. But I won't push you if you're not ready to come home."

"Thank you," I said. "For everything. For coming to see me, and for this. I just need some time."

"Just promise you won't completely disappear again like you did before. You can call us and write to us. Maybe Andrew and I can bring the children out for a visit when you're well. Just...please don't disappear."

I could barely look at her. My stomach rolled with nausea. "I'll do my best. That's all I can promise for now."

CHAPTER FOURTEEN

Ruby

June 7, 1945
San Antonio, Texas

I couldn't keep Hope from singing and skipping down the hospital hallway, no matter how many times I tugged on her hand. Most passers-by looked down at her and smiled, even the men who seemed to be suffering the most. Some stood in the doorways of their rooms and watched as we walked by, curious expressions on their battered faces.

I was regretting that I'd recently taught Hope to count because she was singing out the numbers of each room we passed. "What room is Daddy's?" she asked every five or six doors.

"It will be a three, then a two, and then a six," I'd repeat. Then she would go back to singing out the numbers on each door. Poor Velveteen was getting the worst of it. She slung him around by the arm as she skipped and hopped.

"Dree-two-two!" Hope squealed. "Momma, we're almost dere!" She pulled out of my hand and ran forward. Up ahead, Matthew stepped into

151

his doorway and looked on us with the same curious expression as all the others. Hope hadn't seen him yet, but he had definitely seen her.

He followed her hops and laughter all the way until she stood in front of him, trying to see around him to the number on his door. "Are you my daddy?" she asked.

He dropped to one knee. "Well, that depends. Are you Hope?"

She hopped up and down while nodding her head. "Yes, sir!"

"Then I'm your daddy."

Hope turned to me just as I caught up to them. She smiled and pointed at Matthew with Velveteen flopping in her hand. "I found him, Momma! Look!"

"I see," I said. "Why don't you give him one of your very best hugs?"

She stepped closer to him. "Do you want a hug?"

He nodded. She slipped her arms around his neck, and he wrapped his around her tiny waist. I thought my chest was going to explode right there in front of everyone. God had answered my most fervent prayer of the past three years. After all this time, she was finally hugging her daddy.

Matthew's eyes closed, and he held on to her for a while. "I'm so glad to finally meet you," he said. "You're even prettier than your picture."

She pulled back and grinned at him. Then she put her hands on his face, pushing the skin around just a bit. "Are you tired, Daddy?"

He took her hands and kissed them before standing up again. "Just a little, yes. But I'm so happy you're here. Come on inside so we can visit."

She took his hand and then reached for mine. My eyes met Matthew's, and we shared a smile. He looked healthier—he'd gained some weight, and his face didn't look quite so hollowed out—but something was off. His eyes still seemed dark and haunted. Hope was right. He looked tired.

We walked into his room, and Hope immediately climbed onto his bed. He stood back and watched her as she bounced. "You know, the nurses don't like it when we jump on the beds," he said.

She giggled and jumped again. "I have to hop—I'm a bunny!"

"I told you she loves bunnies," I said, coming up beside him and sliding my hand into his. "How are you feeling?"

He turned to me, taking my hand and kissing me on the cheek. "I'm doing well, actually. Hoping to get out of here soon. Just need to check a few things off the list is all."

"Like what?"

"Nothing major. They want me to go for a certain number of days without having a 'spell,' as they called it."

"What kind of spell?"

He let go of my hand and moved over to the table where he took a seat. "Oh, you know. Elevated blood pressure, which makes me dizzy. My hands shake a bit. Nothing that serious."

I walked over and took the other chair, studying him more closely. "That sounds serious enough. What's causing the spells?"

He waved a hand at me, dismissing the idea. "Hope, tell me, what's your favorite thing to do?"

She bounced onto her behind and scooted to the edge of the bed. "I like rabbits. I like to play. Do you like to play?"

"I used to, when I was little."

I wasn't going to let him change the subject. "Matthew, if you're having trouble with your blood pressure and dizzy spells, that could be something far more serious."

He ignored me and kept right on talking with Hope. "What's your favorite color?"

"Purple!"

"What's your favorite thing to eat?"

"Lemon cookies!"

"Matthew," I said. "You need to tell the doctors—"

He glanced at me and sighed. "Listen, I have a team of doctors and nurses looking after me. I don't want another nurse. I want a wife."

And I'd like a husband who'd tell me the truth, I wanted to say. But I held my tongue. I would have to keep reminding myself to be patient.

There was a knock at the door, and a young man in uniform stepped into the room at attention. "Major Doyle, sir."

Matthew stood and walked over to the young man. "Yes?"

"I've been sent to give you this letter and to inform you that you've been invited to participate in a war bond tour beginning in August. Congratulations, Major."

Matthew took the letter, mumbled, "Thank you, Corporal," and absently shook the soldier's hand. After the young man left, he returned to his seat at the table. Hope had climbed down from the bed and came over to Matthew. "What's dat?" she asked.

Matthew said nothing, so I answered instead. "The army wants Daddy to tell people about the bad guys he had to fight. They need to raise money to take care of the men and women still fighting. Daddy was very brave, and people want to hear his story."

"Oh!" she said. "Can I see?"

"There's nothing to see, sweetie. It's just a letter."

Matthew still hadn't said anything. He stared at the letter in his hand.

"Aren't you going to read it?" I asked.

"No," he said, tossing it onto the table. "I'm not interested in anything like that. We'll be long gone before then, anyway. Would you girls like to go for a walk? I could use some fresh air."

***

Once we were outside, Matthew took a deep breath and seemed to release some of the tension brought on by the letter. Hope ran into the grass with Velveteen, and together they searched for other bunnies to play with. Matthew and I strolled along the walkway beside her.

"That letter seemed to bother you," I said, taking his hand.

"I didn't do anything deserving of recognition," he said. "Besides, they already gave me a medal before I left Manila. I don't want anything more. There are a lot of other guys who deserve it more than I do. A lot of 'em in that hospital behind us."

I stopped. "You received a medal? Why didn't you say anything? What medal was it?"

He sighed and released my hand. "The Silver Star."

"Oh, Matthew, what an honor—"

"I don't want to talk about it," he interrupted. "Like I said. I don't deserve any recognition, especially a medal."

"What you did was very brave. Even just the part I saw on Mindanao. Running back to fight off the Japanese so we could get away. That deserves a medal."

He turned away from me and changed the subject. "I should be getting out of here soon. I want you to start looking for a house."

I decided not to pursue the conversation about the medal any further. "A house? How can we afford a house?"

"My pay should be straightened out any day now, and I'm getting my life insurance money."

"How did you manage that?"

Hope ran over and began bouncing in front of us. "Look, Momma, it's a worm!" She held out an earthworm as it wriggled in her fingers.

"Hope!" I said. "You go put that poor worm right back where you found it."

"But Momma, Belteen's hungry."

"No, ma'am. Velveteen does not eat real worms. We've talked about this already."

She dropped her shoulders and headed back into the grass, where she gently set the worm on the ground.

Matthew chuckled. "I would bet a thousand dollars she's just like her mother was at that age."

"Then Lord help us," I said.

156 | JENNIFER H. WESTALL

We stood and watched Hope for another minute before I remembered what we were talking about. "You said you get to keep your life insurance, but you didn't explain why *you* have it. I was told your life insurance was designated to go to Mary."

"It did. She returned it."

"So she knows you're alive? Have you talked to her? That would be wonderful! Maybe we can—"

"I'm not in contact with Mary," he interrupted. "I just wrote her to let her know I was all right, and she sent the check. That's it. No more contact."

"That doesn't seem like the Mary I knew. She adored you. I imagine she was thrilled to hear you were alive. Are you sure about this?"

His mouth hardened into a frown as he turned his gaze on me. "We can't afford to maintain contact with our families. We have to think about what's best for Hope. What do you think would happen if you were arrested again? And then I'd go to jail with you. What would happen to Hope?"

I couldn't respond. I'd gone through those same questions myself over and over. There were no good answers. But I also knew in my heart that God meant for me to face that conviction someday. "I understand how you feel. Really, I do. I just thought..."

"What? You thought we could tell our families about her?"

"I don't know. Maybe. Someday."

He sighed and shook his head. "You can't be that naive, Ru—." He threw his hands up. "Grace. *Grace.*" He looked at the sky and muttered something I couldn't understand before turning his gaze back to me. "Look, you have to be realistic. No one back home can know you're alive, or that I'm married. They can't know about Hope. That's just the way it has to be. That's why you have to find us a house out of the city. Some place quiet and secluded."

"And what about my job?"

"There's no way you can keep working. We can't take that risk. I'll work. I'll provide for our needs. You look after Hope."

"How are you going to do that without a job?"

His cheek bulged as he ground his teeth together. "I'll get a job. Just trust me, all right?"

"I do trust you. I've just heard talk from other wives and mothers of soldiers coming back. They've had a hard time finding jobs."

"We'll be fine," he insisted. "I can take care of us. I have an engineering degree, and I'm a major in the army. I'll get a job."

I sensed his frustration growing, and I could see the subtle throbbing of the vein in his neck. I couldn't be the cause of another spell with his blood pressure. I stepped close to him and put my hand on his chest. "We'll be all right. I know you'll take good care of us. All I'm saying is that we should wait until you have that job secured before we go buying a house. What's the harm in that?"

I came up on my tiptoes and kissed his cheek, but he pulled away and glanced around, clearly agitated. My stomach turned over, and my face flushed hot. Something had changed while I'd been in Houston.

Matthew called Hope over and ruffled her hair. "Come on. Daddy's had enough fresh air now." He shoved his hands back into his pockets and walked toward the back entrance of the hospital. I took Hope's hand and walked along beside him.

"All right, then," he said. "You win, just like you always do. I reckon you'll have to keep working for now, until I get out of here and get a job. Then we'll find a place where we can do our best to disappear."

Disappear. That word hung in my mind all the rest of the day as I watched Matthew. I sensed something had happened since I'd last seen him, but it was clear he wouldn't tell me what it was. He was eager to interact with Hope, almost to the exclusion of interacting with me. I couldn't exactly blame him. He'd just met his daughter for the first time, after all.

No, it wasn't that he focused his attention on Hope...it was the way he did it. Like he was building a wall between the two of us, and only letting Hope inside. But even with her, I noticed, he kept a safe distance.

I'd decided to do my best not to take it personally. Obviously something was troubling him deep in his heart. But when I thought of the word he'd used...*disappear*...there was something in that word that frightened me. I didn't want to disappear. So much of who we were had already disappeared. Our families, our friends, our home, were lost to us. And I was afraid that the Matthew I'd loved most of my life, was lost to me too, perhaps forever.

CHAPTER FIFTEEN

Ruby

July 15, 1945
Houston, Texas

For some reason, I was as nervous as a jitterbug the day I brought Matthew home to the Sawyers' house. We arrived on Sunday just after dinner, and I knew everyone would be lounging around after the big meal. I pushed open the front door and called out, "Hello? We're here!"

As we made our way through the foyer, Mrs. Sawyer came around the corner from the kitchen wearing her biggest smile. Matthew set his rucksack down to receive her hug, and his whole body tensed.

When Mrs. Sawyer pulled away, she beamed at both of us. "Well, look at you two. It does my heart so much good to know Hope's family is finally together." She leaned in to Matthew and reached out for his arm. "You know, that little girl stole my heart the moment she came into this world. She's a real treasure. You should be proud of the beautiful family you have."

Matthew's smile wasn't exactly easy, but I could see he appreciated her words. "Thank you, Mrs. Sawyer. I am proud of them."

"Well, come on in, and let's get you settled. I'm sure this isn't your ideal homecoming, but we want you to feel welcome here as long as you like." She gestured for us to follow, and Matthew once again picked up his rucksack. I took his hand and walked with him into the living room where Mr. Sawyer sat in his leather chair, his legs stretched onto the ottoman. Mrs. Sawyer dismissed his loud snoring with a wave. "He'll be awake in a little while, and we'll introduce you."

We made our way up the stairs and stopped for a moment outside Jillian's bedroom door. "My daughter, Jillian, and her baby are staying with us while her husband is away in Europe. George, Jr. is down for his nap right now." She turned to the door across the hall, still whispering. "And I'm afraid Hope is napping in your room. She wanted to stay awake until you arrived, but I told her she had to at least go to her room and look at her picture books for a while so Grandpa could relax. She fell asleep within five minutes."

She pushed the door open, and I stepped inside first. Hope was curled up on her side of the bed, a book splayed open on the floor. Matthew stepped inside behind me.

"I'll warm up some supper in about an hour," Mrs. Sawyer said as she gently closed the door. Matthew stood in the middle of the room like he was lost and had no idea what to do.

"I'll take that," I whispered, reaching for his rucksack. I set it down in the closet. When I turned around again, he was inspecting the room. "I know it's a tight space for all three of us," I said.

He shook his head. "It's fine. I've been in much tighter spots. It's not the space that makes it feel cramped. It's all the people in the space."

"Give it a little time. The Sawyers are wonderful people. And they mean so much to Hope and me."

"You've made that abundantly clear."

"Sorry. I'm just…afraid."

"Look, I told you. All we need to do is find a place out away from everyone, and we can live a fairly normal life. Just have to be careful is all."

"That's not what I mean. I'm not afraid of someone finding out who I am. I'm afraid of losing all contact with the people who make me who I am. I don't want a life in isolation away from the world."

Matthew's eyes darkened and he shifted his gaze to the window, walking over to it and turning his back to me. "The world's an evil place, Grace. It only wants to hurt you, to find your weakness and destroy you. We have to protect each other. To protect Hope."

"Daddy?"

Hope's sleepy voice sent Matthew turning on his heels and he gave her a hesitant smile. "I'm right here."

She rubbed her eyes with her fists. "Are you staying?"

"Yes, I'm home for good now."

She yawned and looked over at me. "Momma, can I play now?"

"Sure, sweetie," I said. "Let's go out back so we don't disturb George or Grandpa."

The three of us tiptoed back down the stairs, past Mr. Sawyer still snoring away, and out the back door to the deck. Once outside, though it was hot as a firecracker, Matthew's shoulders relaxed. Hope bounded off the deck into the grass, carrying Velveteen off to play. Matthew and I walked to the edge of the deck and watched her hop from shrub to shrub.

"She's full of energy," I said.

He nodded. "She's full of joy. She hasn't seen the evil that's in the world."

I glanced up at him. He stood there like a solid wall, and yet I was certain there were storms raging inside of him. "I know the world is full of evil, but it's full of love too. As horrible as everything was that we went through on Bataan, look at what beauty came from it. We have the most precious little girl anyone could ask for."

He considered this for a moment. "But was it worth it? Was it worth all the suffering? Was it worth losing so many lives?" He worked his jaw before continuing. "Was it worth losing Henry?"

The heavy ache in my chest I'd been carrying returned at the mention of Henry's name. I fought back my tears, 'cause I was sure they'd upset Matthew. "I don't think it's a bargain we can make—one person's life for another's. That's all in God's hands. He gives life. He calls us home on His terms. I can't understand it, and I can't reason my way out of my grief. I can't think of Henry's life measured against Hope's. But maybe...maybe Hope was God's gift to us to help us through the pain."

"Maybe. For you. I don't think there are any gifts for me. God's made it pretty clear that I ain't worthy of His presence."

"Well, of course not. None of us is worthy of it. But He gives us His presence all the same."

He faced me with despondent eyes. "Not to me, He doesn't."

Then it hit me why I kept sensing something dark stirring inside of him. Somehow, after everything God had done in his life, from healing to redemption to preserving his life in the Philippines, somehow, Matthew had lost his faith.

I wanted to ask him about it. I wanted to help him see God's love again. But he stepped off the deck and went to Hope, bending down and asking her about her pretend world. She lit up like a lightening bug; speaking so fast I could barely keep up.

"Dat is Belteen. See? He lives over dere. See? Dis is his house I made. And I put him to bed. He has to sleep now. Shhhh." She held her finger up to her lips.

Matthew followed her directions and crawled over to the bunny lying inside a small thicket of shrubs. He pointed at Velveteen and looked back at Hope. "Right here?" he whispered.

"Shhhh!" Hope gave him a stern warning. "You wake him up."

He crawled back over to Hope and sat cross-legged in front of her. "Then what can we do that won't wake him up?"

Hope looked back at me, then turned back to Matthew again. "Can I sit in your lap?"

The deep lines in his face smoothed just a bit, and he almost smiled. "Of course you can."

She looked at me again. "It's all right," I said.

She grinned and galloped over to Matthew, jumping and turning in the air. He startled and almost missed catching her. But just in time, his arms slid around her and pulled her safely into his lap. She squealed and giggled.

"I thought we were trying not to wake Velveteen," he said.

Her mouth made a big, silent "Oh!" Then she covered it with her hand, stifling more giggles.

He gave her a tickle, and she squirmed with laughter, still covering her mouth. Before long, her hand slid away, and her laughter filled the backyard. When Matthew took a moment to let her catch her breath, he glanced up at me and frowned.

"Grace, what's wrong?"

"Nothing," I said, realizing tears were sliding down my cheeks. "It's just...I've dreamed of this for a long time. Of you and Hope playing together. I can't seem to help myself."

"Momma," Hope said. "Are you sad?"

"No, sweetie."

She pushed herself out of Matthew's lap and came over to the deck steps. "Why are you cwying?"

I sat down on the steps and opened my arms to her. She came to me, and I pulled her onto my lap. "I'm not sad. These are happy tears. I'm so happy that Daddy's home and that you get to play with him."

"Should I cwy too?"

"No. You should laugh and play. Maybe we can even get Daddy to laugh a little." I glanced over at Matthew, still seated cross-legged in the grass. His mouth tipped into a half-hearted grin. Feeling mischievous, I leaned down and whispered into Hope's ear. "Let's go tickle him."

She grinned back at me. "Okay."

I helped her off my lap and stood beside her. "Ready?"

She nodded.

"What are you two up to?" Matthew said.

"One...two...three!"

We ran a few steps over to Matthew as he threw his hands up. Hope jumped onto his lap again, and I fell onto my knees beside him, reaching for his ribs. He fell backward, laughing and rolling from side to side. Hope's giggles and Matthew's laughter sent another wave of joyful tears.

"I think it's Mommy's turn now," Matthew said at last, pulling Hope away from him.

"Oh, no," I said, holding my hands up in surrender.

But before I could protest, Matthew launched himself at me. I screamed and tried to jump up, but he caught my waist and pulled me down on top of him. Hope bounced up and down beside us, laughing herself silly.

Matthew tickled me mercilessly, despite my screams and pleas for him to stop. He rolled me onto my back, pinning me beneath him. Finally, he stopped tickling me, and I took the moment to simply enjoy the laughter in his eyes as he looked down at me.

"Me next!" Hope yelled.

"My goodness!" Mrs. Sawyer called from the back deck. "You all seem to be having fun out here."

"Oh no! Sorry, Mrs. Sawyer, I hope we didn't wake up Mr. Sawyer and George—"

"—Gamma, do you want Daddy to tickle you too?"

Mrs. Sawyer smiled down at Hope. "No, dear. I think you should get all the tickles." She looked back to Matthew and me, now separated and sitting up. "Nothing to worry about. Everyone's awake and hungry.

Supper will be on the table in a few minutes. Come on in and wash up when you're ready."

As she went back into the house, Matthew met my gaze. The joy in his eyes had retreated, and he let out a somber sigh. "I think I'll pass on supper."

"What?" I asked. "Why? Aren't you hungry?"

He pushed himself up and offered me a hand up as well. He dusted himself off as he spoke. "I just don't want to be around a bunch of people I don't know."

"But if you give it a chance, you'll get to know them."

"Grace, this isn't my family. I don't feel comfortable here, and I don't want to sit around with a bunch of people trying to get to know me. This isn't our home."

He looked down at Hope, who was tugging on his pants. "Daddy, dis is home." She pointed to the house. "Right dere. See? Like Belteen has a home."

Matthew knelt down and pushed the curls from her cheeks, his frown softening. "I know it's your home, sweetie. It's just..." He looked up at me.

"She won't understand," I said softly.

He leaned over and kissed the top of her head. "I just got here. Understand?"

"Like when Belteen was new in the nursery." Hope looked up at me. "Right, Momma? 'Member? He didn't know the other toys."

"That's right," I said. "It took a little while for Velveteen to feel at home in the nursery with the little boy. It may take Daddy some time too."

She turned back to Matthew and placed her hands on the sides of his face. "Are you sad?"

"No. Of course not. How can I be sad when you're here?"

I walked over and took her hand. "Come on, sweetie. Let's go wash up for supper." Matthew stood and faced me, his expression somewhat softer. But I could see he hadn't changed his mind. "If you get hungry later, let me know. I'll fix something for you."

He nodded. "Thank you for understanding."

But I didn't understand. I took Hope inside for supper, wondering how I could help him get more comfortable with the Sawyers if he refused to be around them. I closed the back door and looked out the window as Matthew strolled around the backyard. I could only hope and pray that he would give the Sawyers a chance.

***

That night, no one got much sleep. We set up a small cot at the end of the bed for Hope, but when Matthew and I came upstairs later, she was curled up in her usual spot in the bed. Matthew lifted her and gently placed her back on the cot. We barely had time to remove our bed jackets and climb under the covers before Hope's little voice came from the end of the bed. "Can I sleep wid you, Momma?"

"No, sweetie. Not tonight. You sleep in your bed, and Mommy and Daddy will sleep in our bed."

She grew quiet, and I glanced over at Matthew. He shrugged, so I reached over and turned out the lamp. I rolled onto my side and faced Matthew. The moonlight coming in from the edge of the window was all that lay between us, but it felt like a canyon. He lay on his back, staring at the ceiling.

"Are you all right?" I whispered.

He turned his face to mine, and I could just make out his lifted brow. "Of course," he whispered back. "This is just a bit awkward, is all. It feels like I'm being watched or something."

I ran my hand down the length of his arm, taking his hand in mine. "I know this isn't ideal, but I'm so grateful you're here. We can face anything as long as we're together." Shuffling forward, I rested my head on his shoulder.

His lips touched my forehead, and I lifted my face to his. Just as our lips met, Hope's voice came from beside Matthew. "Can I sleep wid you, Momma?"

I started to tell her to get back in her bed, but Matthew interrupted. "It's fine, sweetie. Come on." He reached out and helped her climb over him into the spot between us. I slid over and made room.

Hope nestled against me, and soon her breathing deepened. I tried my best to fall asleep, but Hope shifted her head, sending it right into my chest. I felt more wiggling and glanced over at Matthew. He slid further away. And so it continued for nearly an hour—Hope shifting and squirming; Matthew and I doing our best to adjust. Finally, Matthew sighed and sat on the edge of the bed.

"Where are you going?" I whispered.

"The cot, I suppose."

"No, no," I said, sitting up as well. "I'll sleep on the cot. You need a bed."

"There's no way I'm letting my wife sleep on a cot. I been sleeping on a cot or on the ground for more than three years now. One more night ain't gonna hurt nothing. You lay back down."

He stood and walked around to the end of the bed. I swung my legs over the side, but he stopped me before I could go any further.

"Now, I mean it," he said. "I'll be fine right here. You and Hope been sleeping there in the bed for a long time. This is best for all of us. Don't fret over me."

He shifted the blanket around and lay down on the tiny cot. I was sure his legs were hanging off the end of it, but I knew better than to press the issue. I lay back down and shifted Hope to the spot Matthew had left. Closing my eyes, I prayed God would find some way to help me make Matthew more comfortable in the Sawyers' home. *Lord, thank you so much for providing for our needs. Please open Matthew's eyes and heart to all the love and peace in this home. Please help him find work, but also help him to see that we need family and friends. I know we aren't meant to live a lie. Please show Matthew that we can still lead a life of joy.*

I managed to sleep after that, but I awoke sometime during the night to more shuffling in the room. I opened my eyes, but I couldn't make out what was going on. I dozed back off, only to awaken again to moans and unintelligible words coming from the end of the bed. I slid out from under the covers and made my way over to where the cot had been. It was shoved against the closet now, and Matthew lay curled on the floor beneath a corner of the blanket.

I bent down beside him and straightened the blanket. That was when I felt the dampness all around him. His clothes were soaked through, and the sheet beneath him was damp as well. I felt his forehead, and he startled awake, yelling out as he grabbed my wrist. I yelped from the sudden pain.

"Matthew, it's me!"

He shot upright and searched the floor around him frantically. "Where is it? Where's my gun?"

"Shhh," I said, grabbing for his hands. "It's me, Ruby. Everything's all right."

He stopped and stared at me with wide eyes. Jumping to his feet, he whirled around in the room. "Where are we?"

I stood beside him. "Shhh," I insisted. "Hope's asleep in the bed. We're at the Sawyers' house."

His body relaxed, and he ran his hands over his face with a groan. "Sawyers. Right." I reached for his forehead, but he moved away. "I'm fine, really. Just...you startled me."

"Your clothes are soaked through. Let me fetch you something dry."

He grasped my shoulders and leaned down toward me. "I'll take care of it. You get back in bed. I'm fine. I'll put on some dry clothes and step out for a bit of fresh air. You get some sleep." When he released my shoulders, I could feel how tightly he'd grabbed them.

"Matthew, please let me—"

"Grace, I mean it." The sternness in his voice gave me pause.

"Momma?" Hope sat up and rubbed her eyes. "Momma?"

"I'm here."

"Get back in bed," Matthew said. "I'll be back in a few minutes."

I wanted to press him, wanted to somehow make him understand that he didn't have to shut me out. But there was probably a better time and place for such a conversation. I needed to get Hope back to sleep. So I climbed back into bed, as Matthew took some fresh pants and a T-shirt out the door with him.

I ran my hand over Hope's hair, smoothing it out of her face. She was already breathing heavily again. But I was wide awake, wondering what was plaguing Matthew's thoughts and dreams. My nursing experience had taught me his mind would need longer to heal than his body, but I'd hoped to be able to help him through that. But more and more I got the feeling that I was somehow part of the problem.

***

After tossing and turning for a couple more hours, I decided it was best to go ahead and get up. Dawn was beginning to lighten the horizon, but it was still mostly dark. I put on my robe and went in search of Matthew, who still hadn't returned to the bedroom. I crept down the stairs and through the living room, finding him seated in one of the metal lawn chairs on the deck. He appeared to be gazing up at the stars, or perhaps he'd dozed off. I couldn't tell from behind.

As I opened the door, the hinges creaked so loudly, Matthew jumped out of the chair. He spun round to face me, his chest rising in panic. "I reckon you're determined to give me a heart attack," he said, his shoulders falling as he relaxed.

"I'm so sorry," I said, closing the door behind me. "I didn't realize how loud those hinges were."

He ran a hand over his hair before dropping back into the chair. I moved behind him, placing my hands on his shoulders. They tightened beneath my touch. I kneaded the muscles in his neck and shoulders, searching for words that could calm him as well. "I was worried when you didn't come back to bed," I said at last.

"I was just as comfortable right here as I was up there. Figured it was easier to stay."

"I'll talk to Hope. I'll make her understand. She'll sleep on the cot tonight."

"We're just going to have to find our own place soon. I'll start hunting for a job today."

"There's no rush. I know the sleeping arrangements aren't ideal, but—"

"Let's not go through this again. I know you love the Sawyers. I know they're like family to you. But that don't change the fact that we need our own place."

I decided to drop it. Instead, I focused on kneading the tension out of his shoulders. He rolled his head from side to side. "That feels nice."

I continued a little longer before he took my hand in his. He pulled me around in front of him, staring up at me with those eyes that had undone me so long ago. How long had I loved him? Was it really *fourteen* years? We were just kids back then. *Lord, so much has changed. And so much hasn't.*

He sat up straighter, moving his hands to my hips. "You are...so beautiful."

My stomach flipped as he untied my robe and slipped his hands inside. My face flushed hot. "Matthew..."

He pulled me onto his lap, kissing my cheek, then my lips. Softly at first, but then with a hunger that awoke every nerve in my body. It was too much, too intense for the wide open outdoors. I pulled my lips back and glanced around. "People will be getting up soon," I said.

He kissed me again. "Let's go inside."

"Hope's in the bed."

"We don't need a bed." He slid me off his lap and stood, cupping my cheeks as he kissed me again and again. Then he took my hand and smiled. "Come on."

I followed him through the back door, my heart full from seeing him smile. I couldn't help grinning myself, feeling like a teen sneaking a boy into the house. As we neared the stairs, Matthew froze, and I nearly collided with his back. He turned his face to me and held a finger to his lips. Then he pointed around the stairs toward the door to the kitchen.

I peered around the banister and saw what had stopped him. The kitchen light shone beneath the crack of the door, and I heard the clang of a pan. Mrs. Sawyer was getting breakfast ready. Matthew gripped my hand again and tugged me up the stairs. We tiptoed as lightly as we could back into the bedroom, where Hope lay sprawled across the bed.

Matthew grabbed a pillow and went to the end where the blanket still lay on the floor. He knelt down and shuffled things around before standing up again and meeting my gaze with a mischievous grin. "You coming?"

I surveyed the makeshift nest. "Hmmm, I don't know." I glanced over at Hope, sure she would awaken at any moment.

He pulled my waist to his and whispered in my ear. "Come on, Grace. This may be the most privacy we get here. I'm not waiting until we have a house all to ourselves. There's no telling how long that could be."

"I know. It's just...it's almost time for her to wake up. If she sees us—"

He stepped back and dropped his hands with a loud sigh. "So then I guess we *are* waiting until we have a house of our own? Wonderful."

"I didn't mean that." I stepped closer to him, running my hands up his chest and coming up on my tiptoes. I kissed his chin and tried to get him to smile again. "I'm sure we can find some alone time. I'll ask Mrs. Sawyer to watch her."

"Yeah, sure. That's great. Just schedule some time for us, and let me know when it's okay to touch you again." He stepped past me and went

172 | JENNIFER H. WESTALL

out the door, not bothering to close it. His heavy footfalls sounded down the stairs and out the front door.

I dropped onto the side of the bed, wondering how things had turned so quickly. I hadn't meant to turn him down. I *wanted* him. I wanted him to touch me, to be close to me again. Why couldn't he understand that the floor of the bedroom, with our daughter sleeping in the bed nearby, was not the place to rebuild intimacy between us?

I glanced at the clock on the nightstand. It was just before six. A twinge of guilt hit as I realized I wouldn't have time for my quiet time. I glanced at Daddy's Bible on the nightstand, hoping God would understand today. I promised myself I would pray on the bus all the way to work. Given the situation with Matthew, that was probably a good idea.

***

When Hope and I came down the stairs an hour later, Matthew was seated at the table with plates of sausage, eggs, and sliced grapefruit already laid out. He held the newspaper open in front of him, and glanced over the top of it as Hope jumped from the bottom step.

"Daddy!"

He scooted the chair back from the table as she climbed up into his lap. "Well, good morning, little bunny! Did you sleep well?"

"Yes, sir," she said, bouncing up and down on his leg.

"You sure are a squirmy little bunny when you sleep. You kicked me clean outta the bed."

She giggled. "Where'd you sleep?"

"Well, I tell ya. I was just like Goldilocks looking for a bed. I tried your cot, but it was too small. So I tried the floor, but it was too hard. So I went outside and sat under the stars. And that was just right."

"I wanna sleep under the stars too!" she said.

"No, ma'am," I said. "You will sleep on your cot tonight so Daddy can get some rest in the bed." I walked over to them and held out my arms. "Come on. Let's get you in your seat so you can eat your breakfast."

Hope looked up at Matthew and put her hands on his cheeks. "Daddy, are you sad?"

"No, sweetie. How could I be sad when I'm with you? Now do what your mother says, and eat your breakfast."

She threw her arms around his neck and squeezed. "I give good hugs."

He patted her back and agreed. "Yes, you do."

As Hope climbed off his lap and into my arms, I swung her over to her high chair at the end of the table, placing some eggs on her plate. She protested momentarily until I reminded her the last time she had eggs, the yolk turned out to be just as tasty as the white, and it wasn't "yucky" at all. Mrs. Sawyer came out from the kitchen, rolling her eyes and smiling at Hope's protestations. She knew my two-year-old daughter's picky tendencies well, and brought with her a pitcher of milk and a plate of biscuits. She set them down next to the jars of jam and walked over to the stairs, calling Mr. Sawyer and Jillian down for breakfast.

Everyone took their seats within a few minutes, and after saying the blessing, we dug in. I kept sneaking glances at Matthew, wondering if he was still frustrated with me. The only thing he said directly to me was, "Thank you," when he took the plate of eggs from my hands. Once everyone had their plates filled, Mrs. Sawyer asked us if we'd had a good night's sleep.

"We were a bit restless," I admitted.

"I'm sure it will take time to adjust," she said, smiling over at Matthew. "I hope you weren't too uncomfortable."

He swallowed and glanced at me before answering. "No, ma'am."

"Daddy slept under the stars!" Hope announced.

Mrs. Sawyer set down her fork, looking horrified. "Oh, Matthew. Don't tell me you were forced to sleep outside."

"It was nothing to worry over," Matthew said between bites. "I've slept outside many nights. It was nice and cool."

"Sounds downright inviting," Mr. Sawyer said. "Don't mind catching a nap outdoors myself sometimes."

"But he's just home from the hospital," Mrs. Sawyer persisted. "He should have a proper place to sleep."

"George will be coming home soon," Jillian said. "At least, his last letter said he had enough points. It should be any time now. Then George, Jr. and I will be out of your hair, and Hope can have our room."

A warm flush crept up Matthew's neck as he gave Jillian and Mrs. Sawyer a tight-lipped smile. "There's no need to make a fuss over us, really."

"Well, maybe we can move some things around. Harold, you don't need that big study for your desk and books. We could move the furniture upstairs, and let them put a bed in there. Why, we could—"

"Margaret," Mr. Sawyer interrupted. "Now, we don't need to go turning the house upside down."

"That's right," Matthew said. "Please don't go rearranging everything for our sakes. We'll be getting a place of our own very soon. We might even be out of your hair by the end of the week."

"The end of the week?" Mrs. Sawyer gasped. "But that's so soon. You all need a chance to get your feet under you. And Hope needs some time to adjust—"

Mr. Sawyer laid a hand on her arm, interrupting her again. "Now, Margaret, that's none of our affair. They're grown adults and can decide what's best for their own family."

She turned her stricken gaze on me. "Grace, honey, you know you all are welcome to stay as long as you need to. We'll make whatever adjustments are necessary. Please don't be in such a rush."

I leaned toward her and put my hand over hers. "Don't worry. There's nothing concrete yet. I'm sure it will take longer than a week for us to get everything in order. There will be plenty of time for everyone to adjust."

She gazed over at Hope who, having forgotten her yolk aversion, was busy shoveling eggs into her mouth with her hand. Mrs. Sawyers' eyes welled up, even as she forced a smile. "It's just been so wonderful having you and Hope here. I can't imagine my days without her."

I glanced at Matthew. He'd set his fork down and was staring at his plate like he wanted to hit it. Letting out a sigh, he brought his gaze up to us. "Thank you for the lovely breakfast, Mrs. Sawyer. And I appreciate your hospitality. Please don't take my desire to leave as a sign of ingratitude. You and Mr. Sawyer have given my family a place to call home while I was away from them. And for that I will always be grateful. But I am anxious to provide them with the home they deserve. I hope you can understand."

"Of course we understand," Mr. Sawyer said. "And we'll do whatever we can to help. However, my understanding is that housing is quite difficult to come by at present. It might take longer than a week."

Mrs. Sawyer nodded her agreement, and we all went back to eating. Although, I noticed Matthew didn't eat another bite. He pushed his food around his plate for another few minutes before standing and thanking Mrs. Sawyer again for the meal. Then he disappeared up the stairs without making eye contact with me.

"I better get my things together for work," I said, excusing myself from the table and carrying my plate to the kitchen. I hurried up the stairs to our bedroom, hoping to speak to Matthew before I had to leave. He was standing at the window.

"Are we...all right?" I asked.

He turned to me, looking me up and down. "I can't get over you in that nurse's uniform. You look so different. So grown up."

"What is that supposed to mean?" I looked down at my white skirt, white pantyhose, and white shoes.

"I don't know. I suppose it means we aren't a couple of kids anymore." He shoved his hands in his pockets and rocked on his heels. "Look, I'm sorry about earlier. I reckon that wasn't the most romantic moment of my life."

"It's all right. I want to be with you...I just..."

"There's no need to rehash it. I'm going to check out some jobs I saw in the paper today. There's one for a construction company. Surely I qualify for that at least. And I'll see what I can find out about housing as well. Are you leaving for work?"

"Yes."

"Want me to walk you to the bus?"

"That would be nice."

He managed the beginning of a smile. "I'll just change my shirt and join you downstairs."

I took my cap off the hook beside the door and went to the bathroom mirror to make sure it was on properly, before heading downstairs to kiss Hope goodbye. Matthew came down wearing navy dress pants and a white button-down collared shirt. He'd shaved and combed his hair as well.

"My goodness," I said. "You clean up quick."

He smiled. "Military training, I suppose. It's downright dangerous to linger anywhere too long."

"Do you know where you're going? I'm sure the Sawyers have a map and bus schedule."

He pointed to his head. "Got everything I need up here. Studied the map and bus schedules this morning."

Hope and Mrs. Sawyer came out of the kitchen, where they'd been cleaning up. Hope ran over to me, and I bent down to give her a hug. I kissed her cheek and told her to mind Grandma.

"I will," she said, smacking her lips against my cheek.

"You'll be asleep when I come home tonight. I expect you to be a big girl and sleep on the cot, like I said."

Her lips dropped to a frown. "Yes, ma'am."

I kissed the top of her head as I straightened, noticing the look of concern on Matthew's face. "Tell Daddy bye."

She turned to Matthew with the same big eyes and frown. "Are you leaving too?"

"I'll be back before you know it," he said, kneeling down and spreading his arms. She walked into his embrace and leaned against his leg.

"Will you wead to me and Belteen tonight?"

"Velveteen and me," I said.

She let out a little sigh. "Will you wead to Belteen and *me?*"

"You can count on it," he said with a chuckle.

"Oh, tank you, Daddy!" Hope bounced up and down as she turned back to me. "Momma, Daddy's gonna wead to me and Bel...I mean Belteen and me!"

"I know," I said. "I bet Daddy's very good at reading stories. Now you go finish helping Grandma in the kitchen."

"Yes, ma'am!" she called, hopping toward the kitchen door.

Mrs. Sawyer waved goodbye, and Matthew and I headed out. When we were alone, he gave me that curious look again. "What time do you get home from work?"

"Around 8:30."

We made our way down the front steps and turned onto the sidewalk toward the bus stop. I reached for one of his hands, but he'd pushed them into his pockets again.

"That's pretty late for a young mother to be getting home from work," he said.

"I work twelve-hour shifts. Eight to eight. It's either work all day, or work all night."

"So when do you spend time with Hope?" There was a hint of an accusation in his voice that touched on my own guilt I'd felt at leaving her.

"I work four days a week. The other three I spend all day and evening with her. We go to the park, or the library, or for long walks. And the Sawyers have been wonderful with her."

"I'm sure they have. But you know you can't keep this up once we move."

My hackles went up before I could catch them. "Yes, you've made it perfectly clear that I have to stop working and stay home with Hope."

"I didn't realize it was such an inconvenience for you to be with our daughter."

I stopped walking and faced him. "What should I have done? You were gone, remember? You ran into the jungle instead of getting on that plane. The army told me you were dead, and it was up to me to provide for our daughter. I only did the best I knew how to do."

"Don't raise your voice at me," he commanded. "I won't stand here in the middle of the street and be disrespected by own wife. I was merely trying to have a civil conversation with you."

"No, you were reminding me of my place. You were reminding me that I belong at home with our daughter—"

"That *is* where you belong!"

The sudden intensity of the anger in his voice and face silenced me, and I took a step back from him. His chest heaved for a moment as he stared down at me like I was an insubordinate soldier.

"You are my husband," I said, deliberately softening my tone. "I love you, and I respect you. But you are not my commanding officer, and we are not in the army. I won't be ordered around. If you want to speak to me about my job, I suggest you cool off and try again tonight. Now, if you'll excuse me, I have a bus to catch."

I turned on my heels and headed for the bus stop without looking back.

CHAPTER SIXTEEN

Matthew

July 16, 1945
Houston, Texas

As I watched Ruby walk away, my frustration and anger only grew. How could she refuse to see the danger in continuing to work? Didn't she realize that every day she worked at that hospital, she was exposing herself to being discovered? How could she take that risk so lightly?

Sure, I was half-starved and being hunted like an animal, but at least when I was in the jungles of the Philippines, I could identify a threat, make a decision, and have my orders followed. It was maddening to be opposed by the very person I was supposed to protect.

I spent another hour walking around before I boarded a bus. The crowd and noise of a busy city did nothing to settle my raw nerves. I already hated Houston, and I had no desire to find a job in the city. But for the time being, that seemed to be my best option.

I spent the morning visiting construction companies, filling out applications and speaking with management. A couple seemed

179

promising. So when I returned to the Sawyers' house for lunch, my mood had improved considerably, and I was looking forward to spending a little time with Hope before heading back out.

But when I walked into the living room, I found Ruby seated on the sofa, her eyes bloodshot and damp.

"What's wrong?" I asked. "Is Hope all right?"

"She's fine," she said. "Mrs. Sawyer takes her to the park for a picnic on Mondays."

I went over to the sofa beside Ruby, afraid something terrible had happened. "Then what's going on?"

She sniffled into a handkerchief. "Well, you got what you wanted. The hospital told me today that they were letting me go. Apparently, everyone else shares your belief about where I belong."

"You were fired? I don't understand. Why?"

"Hospital policy. Nurses aren't allowed to be married. They allowed me to work there because technically I was a widow, but my supervisor told me this morning that since my husband was home, I should devote myself to taking care of my family."

I had no idea what to say. I had to admit, there was a large part of me that was relieved. But I hated seeing her so upset. "I'm sorry this happened."

She huffed and shook her head. "No, you're not. This is exactly what you wanted."

"That's not true. I didn't want this for you. Believe it or not, I want you to be happy."

She leaned her head back against the sofa, staring at the ceiling. "You know, I actually do want to spend more time with Hope. I love taking care of her. I love being her mother. Maybe I would have quit when you got a job. I just wanted it to be my choice. I wanted it to be because it was right for our family, not because someone else was telling me I had to do it."

"Especially if that someone was me."

"That's not fair."

"But it's true. You've never listened to me. In all the years I've known you, it's been one dismissal of me after another."

"Well, that's definitely not true." She glanced over at me and managed a small smile. "I agreed to marry you."

I slid over beside her and kissed her forehead. "Okay, so once."

"I let you pay my bond." She raised her hands and began ticking off her list on her fingers. "I got on the plane on Mindanao. I went to Australia—"

"Okay, okay. So you've listened to me all of about three times in your entire life."

She let out a short laugh. "I believe it was four."

I shook my head and kissed her lips. "And every single time it took all I had in me to convince you. You are so much trouble."

She placed her hand on my cheek. "Matthew, when it has truly mattered, when our lives depended on it, I have trusted you. I do trust you."

I kissed her again, this time lingering long enough for my chest to warm and my heart to speed up. "Did you say Hope and Mrs. Sawyer are at the park?"

She smiled. "Yes."

"What about the rest of the family?"

"Jillian takes the baby to the park with them."

"And Mr. Sawyer?"

She shrugged and smiled.

"So we're alone?"

"Mmm hmm," she said, kissing me again.

"Then what are we doing down here?" I took her hands and pulled her up from the couch, taking another moment to kiss her more before I led her up the stairs to our bedroom.

As I closed the door behind me, I took a long look at the beautiful woman standing beside the bed. It had been more than two months since we'd been alone together in the hotel. Every part of my body felt like it was on fire, and there was only one way to quench it.

I did my best not to rush things, to enjoy the relief of finally having her all to myself. But we had barely gotten undressed and in the bed, when I heard footsteps on the stairs. We froze, Ruby's eyes widening in horror as we heard Mrs. Sawyer talking to Hope.

"Yes, you can look at a picture book for a few minutes."

I rolled to the side and Ruby jerked the covers up over her chest. The door opened, and Mrs. Sawyer stepped inside. Her mouth dropped open, and she stuck her hand out to stop Hope from coming through the door.

"Oh my goodness!" Mrs. Sawyer exclaimed. "Excuse me!" She turned around and closed the door behind her.

Beside me, Ruby covered her face. "I cannot believe that just happened," she mumbled into her hands.

My heart continued to pound away. "It's all right. Bound to happen with all these people under one roof."

"It's humiliating!" She dropped her hands and looked at me in disbelief. "How can you be so casual about it?"

"This is nothing. The Filipinos out in the barrios don't even care to hide it. They all sleep in the same room together, mother and father and all the kids. We had to stay in these tiny huts with whole families sometimes. The parents just covered themselves and went right on with their business."

"With you in the hut with them?"

"Not usually, but sometimes."

After a moment, she laughed and rolled onto her side. "I suppose this explains why you were so eager to just drop onto the floor this morning."

"Maybe." I kissed her and pulled her back beneath me. "Now where were we?"

"Are you serious? With everyone in the house?"

"At least it's not the floor."

She chuckled and shook her head. "You must be desperate."

"You have no idea."

***

Mrs. Sawyer couldn't make eye contact with me that evening at supper. Ruby had explained why she was home, and most of our conversation at the table centered around the shameful policy of the hospital. Personally, I was rather happy about the incident in the bedroom. Maybe it would serve to highlight that we needed to find a place of our own as soon as possible.

Unfortunately, Mr. Sawyer had been right about the housing situation. I'd contacted a few realtors that afternoon, and there was nothing available near the city. Of course, that didn't bother me much. I preferred to find a place away from the masses. I'd build it myself if I needed to. But if I knew anything about Ruby, I was sure she'd want to stay close to the Sawyers. I wasn't looking forward to convincing her to move away.

Just as we were finishing the meal, there was a knock on the front door. Mrs. Sawyer nearly flew out of her chair. Before she even made it around the table, a male voice called from the foyer.

"Anyone home?"

Everyone's eyes widened, and there was a big commotion as a man in uniform stepped into the dining room. He dropped his bags and held his arms open, and Mrs. Sawyer rushed into them. It took me a moment, but just as his mother cried out his name, I recognized Mike.

Mr. Sawyer and Jillian hugged him next. Then Ruby stood and took her turn. Mike laughed as Mrs. Sawyer scolded him for not telling her he was coming home, before going over to Hope in her high chair and bending down in front of her. "How's the prettiest little bunny rabbit in all the world?" he asked.

She reached out her arms and he picked her up. "Uncle Mike, did you bwing me a pwesent?"

"I'm sure I have something in my bag for you. We'll find it in a little while."

Something about watching him hold my daughter while smiling at my wife sent an uneasy feeling skittering through me. I pushed my chair back from the table and stood, and he finally saw me. His eyes widened, and he set Hope back in her chair.

"Matthew? You're...you're alive! And here! Well, I'll be." He walked around the table and stuck out his hand, so I took it and gave it a firm shake. "It's great to see you."

"Good to see you too," I said. "How long you home for?"

"Just a few days." He glanced between me and Ruby. "Where were you all this time? I've been writing everyone I could think of trying to find you."

"Really?" I found that a bit disconcerting for some reason. "I was on Luzon with the guerrilla forces there."

Mrs. Sawyer set a plate and some utensils down at the table beside Jillian. "Come eat some supper," she said to Mike. "You're skinnier than a stick."

"Don't mind if I do," Mike said, grinning at everyone.

We all took our seats once more, and the others peppered him with questions. Seemed like the house was going to be even more crowded for a few days. He'd been discharged, which brought a "Hallelujah!" from Mrs. Sawyer.

"Will you be moving back home, then?" Jillian asked.

"Oh, well not anytime soon," he said. "I'll head back to San Francisco for a while. Some of the guys are getting jobs there. I'm probably too old to go back to baseball, but I still know people there."

I glanced at Ruby as Mike continued talking. She barely made eye contact with him. She mostly kept her gaze on her plate, but would look over at me and smile now and again. And while he was still telling the story of one of his missions, she stood and began clearing the table.

I picked up my plate and followed her into the kitchen. "Everything all right?" I asked, stacking my plate on top of the others.

"Of course," she said. "Why do you ask?"

"You seem a little uncomfortable."

She turned on the water and rinsed a plate, shrugging her shoulders. "No, not at all. I'm thrilled Mike's home. It's good to see the Sawyers so happy." She plugged up the sink and dropped in a bit of detergent.

I had no idea how to ask what I needed to know. "Look, I'm just going to ask you straight out. Was there ever anything...romantic between you and Mike?"

She scrubbed at the plate in her hand, but didn't look up. "No."

"'Cause if there was, you know, I mean...the army told you I was dead. I could understand if—"

"Nothing happened," she said, turning her gaze to mine. "He's been a good friend. That's all."

"I see."

The kitchen door opened, and Mrs. Sawyer stuck her head around it. "We're going out back for some dessert. Grace, can you two grab the ice cream and some bowls and bring them out to the table?"

"Yes, ma'am," Ruby answered.

The door closed. Another thought occurred to me. "Does Mike know who you really are?"

"No. I never told him."

"But he was there when Natalie threw her temper tantrum on Mindanao. He must have heard everything."

"He never said a word to me about it." She dried off her hands and opened the cabinets. "Look in the icebox over there and get the ice cream out, will you?"

I did as she asked, but I couldn't stop wondering why Mike wouldn't have ever brought up Natalie's accusations. Had he said anything to his family? I stood in front of the kitchen door, forcing Ruby to stop. "Do you really not understand how important this is?"

"Look, if he did hear Natalie, he probably just dismissed it. I was so focused on finding you that we never talked about much else while we were in Australia. And I've only seen him a few times since."

"I know you're not going to like this," I said. "But if Mike knows anything about who you are, and if he's ever said anything to his family, then we're going to have to cut ties with them."

"What? Cut ties with them? They're the closest thing we have to family! We aren't cutting ties with them."

"We can't be stupid about this. Just because they're kind to us doesn't mean we should risk your freedom. You have to think about all of us involved. If your true identity is ever discovered, then everyone who ever helped you will go down with you. Do you really want that for the Sawyers? You want them to go to prison for harboring a fugitive?"

She set the bowls down on the counter and closed her eyes. She was quiet for a minute before she turned to me and raised her chin. "Matthew, I won't live a lie for the rest of my life. I won't put you and Hope, and everyone I care about, through all this deception. It's not right."

My nerves tightened. "What are you saying?"

She took a deep breath and set the bowls on the counter. "I'm saying that I believe it's God's will for me to go back to Alabama and turn myself in."

I had to have misunderstood her. I set the ice cream down and tried again. "What did you just say?"

"I've prayed about this every day for over eight years. And God has shown me over and over that I was never meant to live a lie. It's why I lost my gift. It's why I've struggled to feel His presence. I can't keep lying."

The door swung open again, and this time Jillian came into the kitchen with her baby on her hip. She smiled curiously at us. "What are you two doing in here? Everyone's waiting on the ice cream outside."

"We'll be right there," Ruby said.

"All right." Jillian shrugged. "Need me to get anything?"

I took the ice cream and handed it to Jillian. "Actually, can you take this outside for me? I just remembered something I need to take care of."

"Sure," she said, lifting an eyebrow at Ruby before walking out.

"I can't do this right now," I said. "I can't even think about us going back to Alabama. You have lost your mind."

"Matthew—"

"No," I said, raising my hands to keep her from coming near. "Over all the years I've known you, you've said and done a lot of things I didn't understand. But I've always tried to support you, even when I thought you were being foolish. But this...this is insane. I can't even talk to you right now." I pushed the kitchen door open and headed past the dining room to the foyer.

Ruby followed me. "Where are you going?"

"Out."

"Matthew, please don't walk away."

I couldn't stay. I couldn't think. My chest tightened as I slammed the front door. I needed air. I needed to walk and make sense of the craziness in my wife's head. Better yet, I needed a drink.

***

I found a bar a few blocks from the house and took a seat near the back. I hadn't cared much for the whiskey on the train, so I opted for a beer instead. I was still fuming over Ruby's words, mostly because I knew in my heart that once she set her mind on something, there was no changing it. Didn't she understand she'd be dragging me into her plan as well? And what about Hope? Had she even thought about how our daughter would be affected if her mother were executed for murder?

I downed the first beer.

On the radio from behind the bar, Johnny Mercer told me I needed to "ac-cent-tchuate the positive and e-lim-minate the negative." So I ordered another beer. *That should help,* I thought. By the time Johnny was finished singing, I was finished with my second.

I ordered a third as a news report began. A fellow a few stools down from me yelled at the bartender to turn it up. The broadcaster jumped immediately into the progress of the US forces in bombarding the Japanese mainland. A round of cheers went up, and I raised my glass to the brave men continuing the war I'd left behind. Then I downed that drink as well.

By the time I returned to the Sawyers' house, everything was dark and quiet. As I made my way up the stairs, I had to hold onto the rail. I wasn't exactly drunk, but the alcohol had definitely made the world just a bit unsteady. But it had also eased the tension coursing through me, and that felt amazing. Maybe I'd be able to sleep through an entire night.

I entered the room as quietly as I could, kicking something near the bed. I froze, waiting for Ruby or Hope to stir, but neither of them moved. I removed my shoes and undressed to my shorts and undershirt, and tiptoed around the cot at the end of the bed. It was empty.

As my eyes adjusted to the dark room, I saw Hope curled up on my side of the bed. I debated on whether I should move her, but in the end, the prospect of a full night's sleep won out. I lifted her as gently as I could and tucked her under the covers on the cot.

Finally, I scooted beneath the blanket into the bed beside Ruby. Looking at her back, I wondered if I should wake her. Had she waited up for me long?

"You broke your promise," she said without rolling over.

"What? What promise?" I pulled on her shoulder until she was facing me.

"You promised Hope you would read to her. She was so disappointed."

Guilt washed over me. "I'm sorry. I'll make it up to her."

In the sliver of moonlight, I could see Ruby's nose wrinkle. "Have you been drinking?"

"Just a couple of beers to relax, that's all."

She put a hand on my cheek, studying me closely. "Matthew, we should talk about what I said earlier."

I leaned down and gave her a quick kiss. "Not tonight. I'm exhausted. We'll talk tomorrow, all right?"

"All right." She wasn't convinced, I could tell. But my eyes were so heavy, and the bed so soft. All I wanted to do was sleep for a few hours.

"Goodnight, Grace."

"Goodnight."

CHAPTER SEVENTEEN

Matthew

October, 1942

Luzon, Philippines

After my meeting with Gandy, a courier from Manila brought a leaflet to camp with a list of guerrilla commanders and rewards for their capture. I now, quite literally, had a price on my head. And my old pal Kojima was in charge of hunting down the guerrillas.

Diego put together a small unit of bodyguards to travel with me wherever I went, assigning himself as head babysitter. I was not accustomed to being escorted at every turn, and this led to several tense exchanges. We finally reached an agreement that satisfied neither one of us. One of the bodyguards would be by my side at all times, except for when I was sleeping in my own quarters. That, at least, I could still do on my own.

Soon after, Diego, Henry, seven of our best men and I set out for the mountains near Fort Stotsenberg, careful to avoid the heavily traveled roads. Gandy had given me an idea of where Harris might be located, and luckily it was near the village where Diego had lived as a small boy.

192 | JENNIFER H. WESTALL

He still had family in the area, and they were eager to help guide us to the camp.

As we approached the outskirts of Harris's camp, several Filipino men appeared, brandishing bolos. For a moment, tensions flared, and my men encircled me with their weapons at the ready. Diego fired off rapid explanations, and slowly, the weapons were lowered.

"Is that my good friends, Captain Doyle and Lieutenant Graves?" called out a voice from well beyond my line of sight into the jungle.

"Sergeant Harris?" I called back.

He came at us through the middle of the men, extending his hand to me first, then to Henry and Diego. "You boys look like you could use a good meal. Come on up to my headquarters, and I'll get you all taken care of."

"Not exactly a warm welcome you've got here," I said, nodding at his men.

"Well, what d'ya expect? Tea and cake? Between the Japs and the Huks, a man has to watch his back out here."

"All the more reason to unite with like-minded friends," I said.

He raised an eyebrow before gesturing down a path behind him. "This way, fellas. I've got something special for you."

We followed two of Harris's men along the winding path that snaked up ravines and crossed small streams, finding the camp within a few minutes. It reminded me of the children's stories I'd read of stranded travelers on deserted islands. A central hut was situated about fifteen feet up into the trees, with a ladder descending from its middle. Smaller huts were built into other trees surrounding it. There was even a pulley system, which I imagined brought water buckets up to the huts.

"Interesting base camp you have here," I said.

Harris beamed like a proud father. "We're still working on some things, but it's home for now. Come on up, and I'll show you around."

I glanced at Diego and signaled for him to stay on the ground with the other men. Only Henry and I followed Harris up the ladder. Inside, it wasn't much different from the other huts built all over the island. I walked over to a small window and glanced down on the men. Diego looked up at me, and I waved to show we were fine.

"You said you had something interesting to show me," I said, taking a seat on a stool. Henry continued to stroll around the hut, examining every inch.

Harris grinned and went over to a bamboo desk to my left, unrolling a medium-sized map. He waved me over, so I stood and joined him. Henry came up on his other side.

"We've gotten a report from our contacts north of here that there's a good-sized convoy heading toward Manila, and it's coming through Fort Stotsenberg tomorrow. From what we've gathered, it seems to be the perfect size for an ambush. Not too large; not too small."

"An ambush? You're going to attack a Japanese convoy? Why?"

"Why not?" Harris stepped back and crossed his arms over his chest. "I figure it's time to start giving the Japs some payback. And like I said, it's not too large for us to handle. But now, if you and your boys come in with us—"

"Out of the question," I said.

"Hold on a minute," Henry said. "Let's hear him out. Maybe he's on to something."

I should've known better than to bring Henry along. It figured he'd want to jump on Harris's bandwagon. "Now look here," I said. "Major Gandy sent me up here to make contact and explain what we're supposed to be doing. He's eager to unite all the different units on Luzon."

"Yeah, yeah," Harris said. "I know all about what Gandy wants. He wants to sit back on his hands and wait for MacArthur to come back and save us all. Well, how did that work out for all of us making a stand on Bataan? While we were starving to death and getting shot to pieces, ole Dugout Doug was sneaking off to the safety of Australia. I don't put any stock in waiting around for his return."

"The man's got a point," Henry said.

I shot him a look meant to silence him. "I ain't arguing for MacArthur. I feel much the same as you. But I'm an army man and an engineer, and I was taught the right way to do things. And that's working together as a team, with an agreed leader and goal. Now maybe you're right about some things, but Gandy has good points too. And he's the superior officer. We owe him our allegiance."

"I don't owe him anything," Harris said. "I do owe the Japs a good whippin', though."

"Again, I ain't disagreeing with you. I'm eager to whip 'em. But we have to think about more than just our own desire for vengeance."

Harris looked between Henry and me before throwing his hands up. "Look, you fellas are welcome to stay as long as you like. Eat, get some sleep, and think about things. But come first light, my men and I are heading out to ambush the convoy. You can come along, or you can stay behind. Your choice."

Henry looked over at me, and I could see from his expression that he was itching to join Harris. He couldn't hardly stand still. But I was responsible now for a whole camp of men, including Henry, and I wasn't about to put them in harm's way for no good reason.

"Thanks for the hospitality," I said. "But we'll be heading back to our camp in the morning."

Henry's expression fell. "Come on, Matt."

"No. It's my call, and we ain't going."

"Suit yourselves," Harris said. "Come on down and eat, then we'll get you boys settled somewhere for the night."

"I'm going," Henry said.

I stared him down, and the air in the hut filled with tension. Harris didn't even try to hide his amusement. "Well, I'll let you two work this out. Come on down when you're ready." He slid down the ladder, leaving me alone with Henry.

It was all I could do to keep my cool. "How could you undermine me like that in front of him?" I demanded.

"Undermine you? I think that rank is going to your head. You may be above me in the army, but you ain't no better than me. And you sure ain't gonna tell me what to do in the middle of the jungle."

"I certainly will tell you what to do. I'm your commanding officer, whether you like it or not. And you are going back to base camp with us in the morning. You got that, Lieutenant Graves?"

His expression hardened, and he took a step toward me. He lowered his voice as he spoke. "Those dirty Nips killed my wife. I ain't gonna just stand by and do nothing about it. And if they'd killed Ruby, you wouldn't either."

"Henry, I know—"

"We done had this conversation, and I ain't having it again. I told you, I plan on killing every last one of 'em if I have to."

I could see there wasn't any chance of reasoning with him. That darkness I'd seen in him on Corregidor overshadowed everything. I had to try something different.

"Henry, you know I love Ruby with all my heart. If something happened to you, she'd never forgive me. You're her rock. She needs you. And it's my job to make sure you get through this war alive."

That seemed to make an impact. He blinked a couple of times and let out a deep sigh. He walked over to the window and leaned on his elbow. "I ain't no rock. All I ever did was run away when she needed me. I ran out on the family after Daddy died. Couldn't get back to Ruby during the trial. Even dragged her into running away here." He turned and faced me with a somber expression. "I thought marrying Janine would change things. I was finally going to quit running. But...it just wasn't meant to turn out that way."

"Killing Japs ain't gonna bring Janine back. It's just another way for you to keep running. Don't you see that?"

There was a long pause, while Henry considered my words. "Maybe. Maybe you're right."

"Don't go down Harris's path. It'll only lead to death. Just come back with us in the morning." I shoved my finger into his chest and smiled. "That's an order."

He grinned and gave me a flimsy salute. "Sí, Captain."

***

I startled awake, unsure of where I was. Had I been dreaming? I sat up and looked around the hut, seeing only dark shapes of the bodies of my men.

Next to me, Diego stirred and sat up also. "Qué pasa?" he asked, his voice low but tense.

"I'm not sure," I said, reaching for my pistol on the floor beside me. I stood and glanced around again. Then it dawned on me. "Where's Henry?"

"No sé, Captain."

"English, Diego. English."

"I do not know where Lieutenant Graves has gone, sir."

My chest grew heavy with dread. "Let's wake the men up and get ready to move out. I'm pretty sure I can guess where he went."

We were alert and moving out within ten minutes. I explained to Diego what I remembered from the map Harris had shown me the night before, and he led us through the jungle at a pace I struggled to match. I noticed I was the only one having difficulty navigating the hills and ravines while roots grabbed at my ankles from below and thick leaves and vines swatted my face. The only thing keeping me from falling behind was the intermittent stopping to clear the thick vegetation. I had to wonder why Gandy had put me in charge when more than half the time I felt lost and overwhelmed.

After about an hour of fighting through the damp morning mist, we came out onto a ridge above the road that led south to Fort Stotsenberg. Diego paused for a moment. "Captain, you said ambush will take place in the middle of the curve shaped like snake, yes?" he asked me.

"Yes. Which way do we need to go?"

He looked down at the road again. "East."

A string of gunfire in the distance interrupted us. "How far?" I asked.

"Not far now. We must hurry."

It was all I could do to keep the men in front of me within sight as we ran. I thought my chest was going to explode, and my hamstring pulsed with stabbing pains. But I thought of having to tell Ruby that I hadn't been able to keep Henry safe, and I forced my legs to keep moving.

As we neared the gunfire, we had to take a slower, more deliberate approach. We rounded a curve along the ridge, and I got my first view of the scene of the ambush. Five trucks were stopped in a line on the road just as they were coming out of a curve. Japanese soldiers were stationed around the trucks at various points—behind open doors, lying beneath truck beds, crouched behind tires. As they fired into the surrounding foliage, I could just make out a few sparks of return gunfire.

"Captain," Diego said. "What are your orders?"

The only way to ensure Henry made it out of this alive was to join the ambush. I surveyed the layout quickly. Harris's attack was coming from four points, two squads in front and two at the rear of the convoy. Several Japanese soldiers gathered at the back of the third truck, preparing to make an assault on one of the rear positions.

"There," I said, pointing this out to Diego. "We need to hit the middle. We'll split up and come in from the sides. Once they hit the ditch, they'll be sitting ducks."

Diego took half our platoon and slipped down the ravine toward the middle of the convoy. I signaled for the rest to fall in behind me, and we swung a wider path as we descended toward the road. Shouts in both Japanese and English echoed in every direction.

Reaching the bottom of the ravine, we dropped to our bellies, crawling through the grass parallel to the road. On my left, I caught sight of Harris with four of his men, bunkered down behind a thicket of dense palm trees. They fired several shots at the trucks, hitting metal and earth, but no Japanese.

I whistled and caught Harris's attention. I signaled that I was moving to his right, and he acknowledged. We crawled toward another group of trees. These were less dense, and bullets whizzed and popped above our heads.

We made it to the trees, spread out and lay flat to the ground, firing at the advancing Japs I'd seen gathering behind the third truck. They ran straight toward us in formation, with the outside men providing cover. With my heart in my mouth, I aimed my pistol at the first face I could make out. I fired over and over, dropping one, then two, then a third. More of them fell, but the group kept coming.

A flash of metal swung through the air, and I saw Diego just off to my right. He seemed to come out of nowhere, and he slashed through one Japanese soldier after another. The last of the surging group fell, but Diego continued his assault on the remaining soldiers barricaded around the trucks. Several more Filipinos and Americans joined him, finishing off the last of the resistance.

As I emerged from my cover, I met Diego near the third truck. His chest heaved, and he was covered in blood. Harris came from the front of the trucks, checking the cabs as he passed. He stopped at the second truck, firing a single shot into the cab before continuing over to us. "Secure those trucks at the end!" he yelled to the men at the back of the convoy.

After three more shots, someone called, "All clear!"

Harris strode up to me with a huge smile on his face. "Decided to get in on the action after all, I see."

"Where's Henry?" I asked.

"Lieutenant Graves led one of the rear assaults. I'm sure he'll be along in a moment."

I stepped between the trucks, keeping my hand tight around my pistol, and headed for the back of the convoy, determined to give Henry a piece of my mind.

"Medic!" someone yelled ahead of me. "Get Sanders over here, now!"

I broke into a jog, veering left into the ditch. Four men stood around another on the ground. I pushed through the group to see a young Filipino struggling to get his breath. The medic dropped beside him and tried to staunch the bleeding from the wound in his neck. I turned away, intent on finding Henry.

At long last, I saw him jump down from the back of the last truck. He saw me coming and crossed his arms over his chest as I approached.

"You've got some nerve," I started.

"Now hold your horses before you go getting all riled up," Henry said.

"You put our entire team in danger!"

"No, you put them in danger by coming out here."

"We only came out here to get you!" When I reached him, it was all I could do to keep from punching his lights out right there.

"I didn't ask you to come after me. I'm a grown man, and I can decide which battles I fight."

"What about our conversation last night? I gave you a direct order, and you agreed."

"You don't order me around."

"Out here, yes I do! I swear, you are just like Ruby. You get some fool idea in your head and can't nobody talk any sense into your brain. I've had it with you Graves people making me crazy! If you want to fight the Japanese so bad, and you're so determined to die, then you can just stay here with Harris."

He threw up his hands. "Fine! I will."

"Great! That will be one less headache for me."

We stared at each other for a long moment, until I felt someone come up behind me. I turned to see Diego approaching, still brandishing his bloody bolo.

"We need to move out, Captain," he said. "More Japanese will come soon."

"Get the men together," I said. "Henry's not coming with us."

Diego shook his head at Henry. "This place is no good for you, Lieutenant. Come back with us."

"Diego, look," Henry said. "You've been a true friend through all this, and I'm grateful. But I told Harris—"

"Never mind Sergeant Harris. You and Captain Doyle are friends, yes?" Diego asked. "You knew each other before the war?"

"Yes, but—"

"You...uh, like brothers, yes?"

Henry gave me a sideways glance before huffing and turning his back on us. Behind me, Harris ordered the remaining men to load up with as many supplies as they could and fall in at the back of the convoy.

Henry stopped short as he reached the back of the truck. Without warning, he let out a loud, guttural moan and lashed out, kicking the bumper. "I hate this godforsaken place!" he cried.

I jogged up to him with Diego close behind. Henry spun round, pressing his hands against the sides of his head. His frustration was etched across his face, his eyes simultaneously wild and pleading. "This jungle is going to drive me crazy. All I wanted was to fly my plane, swing a bat at some baseballs, and have a few laughs with my wife at the end of the day. Why is that so hard?" He threw his hands in the air. "What am I doing here? What are we even fighting about, Matt?"

"I don't know, all right?" I said. "I can't explain any of this. Who can make sense of any of it? All we can do is get through today. And then get through the next day, and the next, and the next. One day. That's all we have. You gotta hang in there, and get through today for me.

Understand? Eventually those days are gonna add up to us getting outta here."

His eyes searched mine, before he gestured over my shoulder. "Tell that to that poor soul."

I turned and watched as Sanders stood, shaking his head at the group. Harris yelled at them to get moving. Two men picked up the limp body and carried it into the jungle while the rest fell in with loaded-down rucksacks. My squad stood about ten yards beyond them, awaiting orders.

I put a hand on Henry's shoulder. "Look, Henry. This ain't the way to get home. All this is gonna do is bring the Japs roaring to our doorsteps. We gotta be smart about this. But we gotta stick together. Whaddaya say?"

Henry looked between Diego and me, then down at his feet in silence. "I reckon you two wouldn't make it more than a day without me," he mumbled at long last. "Guess I'll put up with ya a bit longer." A slow smile spread across his face. "But that doesn't mean I'm gonna take orders from you when I don't agree."

"All right, then," I said, "I reckon that's the best I could hope for here. Diego, let's get outta here while we still can. I'd say Harris's cooperation is a no-go."

"Sí, Captain." Diego turned and jogged over to our men, barking at them in Spanish. They fell in behind him, and we headed back up to the top of the ridge.

CHAPTER EIGHTEEN

Ruby

July 16, 1945
Houston, Texas

I lay in the bed praying over Matthew as his breathing deepened. The smell of alcohol swam around me, making me nauseous. I couldn't believe he'd gone out drinking. What had he been thinking?

Maybe I shouldn't have mentioned going back to Alabama. I'd expected resistance from him, and I'd planned to talk to him when it seemed like a good time. But it was never a good time. And then I went and just blurted it out. Typical Ruby.

Lord, please soften Matthew's heart to Your will. He's in so much turmoil. I can sense the war still raging inside of him. Help me to be a comfort to him so he doesn't have to turn to alcohol. Give me wisdom, and give us strength. Lord, You are a righteous and just God. I know in my heart You desire obedience over sacrifice. My spirit is willing, but my flesh is weak. If there's any other way, please show me. But if Your desire for us is to return home and face the consequences of our actions, I pray you would reveal that to Matthew. I fear that path, Lord, and I don't think I have the strength to carry us both.

My eyes grew heavy, and I drifted off to sleep with images of courtrooms and jail cells haunting me. I couldn't have been asleep long when I jolted awake from a lurch beside me. The room was pitch black. I could barely make out Matthew's shape sprawled out beside me. He must have startled in his sleep.

I sat up and moved his arm closer to his side. He was drenched in sweat again. I set his arm down, but he flung it back at me, catching me across the face.

"Get down!" he yelled.

I fell back and tumbled off the bed, my head colliding with the corner of the nightstand. I yelped as pain streaked through my head.

"They're flanking you on the right!" Matthew yelled again. "I need cover on the right!"

I sat on the floor holding my throbbing head. Hope called out to me. "Momma?"

"I'm here, baby," I said, moving to the cot.

Matthew thrashed around again, screaming incoherently, as if he were in pain. Hope took my hand and climbed off her cot. "Momma? Momma?" Her voice shook with fear.

"It's all right. Daddy's having a bad dream." I picked her up and reached for the lamp on the nightstand. It fell over, crashing to the ground.

Matthew shot up on the other side of the bed. "Diego! Diego, get in here!"

I managed to grasp the lamp and turn it on just as the door swung open behind me. Matthew stood on the other side of the bed, his pistol raised at the open door.

"Oh my heavens!" Mrs. Sawyer screamed.

"Matthew!" I cried, barely able to breathe. "It's just us." I kept my arms wrapped tightly around Hope as she whimpered in my arms. "It's us. You're home. Put the gun down."

His eyes were wild and unseeing. He dropped to a crouch behind the bed, his arms straightened across the top of it, the gun still pointed at the door. "Diego! Bruno!"

I heard shuffling behind me. "Get out of here, Mother," Mike commanded. "Grace, come on outta here."

I slid across the floor, handing Hope to Mike. He took her out the door as she screamed for me. Hope's wailing must have penetrated Matthew's consciousness because he dropped the gun onto the bed and blinked. Slowly, he straightened, looking at me and then the door with confusion.

"What's...what's going on?" he asked.

In the hallway I could hear Mrs. Sawyer trying to comfort Hope and explain to Mr. Sawyer. George, Jr. wailed from the other room. "Matthew?" I asked, standing as well. "Are you all right?"

He rubbed his hands over his face. His hair was drenched, and his undershirt clung to his chest. "I think so. Was I...did I just point a gun at you all?"

"You certainly did," Mike said, coming into the room. He took me by the shoulders and looked me over. "You all right, Grace?"

"I hit my head, but I'm sure it's all right." I went out into the hallway and scooped Hope into my arms.

"Momma," she sobbed. "What's wrong with Daddy?"

"It was a bad dream, that's all." I tucked her under my chin and brought her to the door. "See? Daddy's fine now."

She pressed her body into my chest and gripped my arms even tighter. "No!"

Matthew came around the bed and reached for her back. "Oh, no, sweetie. It's okay now. I'm so sorry I frightened you."

She turned her face into my neck, refusing to even look at him. Matthew continued rubbing her back, his tortured gaze meeting mine. "I am so sorry, Grace. I don't know what happened."

Mr. Sawyer approached, still tying his robe. "Son, I think everyone here is sympathetic to what you're going through. But it's probably best to lock that gun up somewhere."

"Yes, sir," Matthew said. "I assure you, it isn't loaded. I can't explain what happened."

Mr. Sawyer put his arm around Mrs. Sawyer's shoulder. "Well, all the same. I'd appreciate it if you locked it up somewhere while you're staying here. I think that's best for everyone's state of mind."

"Yes, sir."

Mrs. Sawyer looked over my shoulder and smiled at Hope, pushing her hair away from her face. "It's all right, sweetheart. You're safe now." Then she glanced at Matthew warily. "Grace, honey, you want me to take her downstairs and get her some warm milk?"

"If you don't mind," I said. I pried Hope loose and handed her to Mrs. Sawyer. "I need to get the bedroom back in order."

Mrs. Sawyer took Hope downstairs. Across the hall, Jillian paced her bedroom and bounced George, Jr. in her arms. "You all right?" she asked.

"Yes, we're all fine," I said. "Sorry we woke everyone."

Matthew's face reddened, and he went back into our room and sat on the edge of the bed. Mr. Sawyer announced he was going back to bed. Mike looked from me to Matthew and back to me again.

"There's a safe in Dad's office," he said. "Want me to take the gun?"

"Yes, please," I said.

He stepped over to the bed with his hand out. Matthew held the gun for a moment, looking it over. Then he looked up at Mike. "It wasn't even loaded. I just keep it beside me out of habit."

"Then it shouldn't be a big deal to put it away, right?" Mike said.

"It shouldn't be. But it is. I don't know."

Mike sighed and dropped his hand. "Look, I get it. I've been in some pretty sticky situations. It's hard to set aside all your training and experience. But you don't need that here. You're not at war anymore."

Matthew looked over the gun once more before handing it over to Mike. "I guess you're right. Sure don't feel that way sometimes."

Mike took the gun out of the room. Matthew propped his head in his hands. I sat down beside him and rubbed my hand over his back. His muscles were tight with tension.

He dropped his hands and shook his head. "I don't understand what happened. I was dreaming, I know that. But they've never been so...so vivid.

"Must have been a pretty intense dream. Were you in a battle?"

"Yeah. Felt like I was right there, back in that ambush. So strange."

"I'm sure it's a common reaction. I had some awful dreams after leaving the Philippines."

"Bet you've never pointed a gun at anyone while you were dreaming." He glanced at me with a small smile.

"Um, no," I said, smiling back.

"Poor Hope. She's probably terrified of me now."

"She'll be all right. It's you I'm worried about. Obviously everything you went through is still weighing heavily on your mind. Are you...Have you prayed about it?"

He stood and went to the dresser, pulling out a clean white T-shirt. He stripped the soaked undershirt off and pulled the T-shirt over his head. I couldn't help but notice the scars again. There was so much evidence of his suffering. I wanted to find some way to heal his pain, just as God had healed his tuberculosis. But in many ways, this was so much worse than tuberculosis.

He faced me, but he didn't meet my gaze. "I uh, I don't pray much anymore. Doesn't seem to be much point in it. God knows who I am, what I've done, and what I need. He works things out as they should be, no matter what I pray for. So what's the point in asking? He doesn't answer my prayers. Well, I suppose He does, it's just more of a no than anything."

I stood and crossed the room, sliding my arms around his waist. "The purpose of praying isn't to get God to do your will." I laid my head against his chest, listening to the thump-thump of his heart. "We pray because we love Him. We pray because He tells us to bring our cares to Him. We pray because no one on Earth is able to understand our pain like Jesus does. He feels your anguish, even when you don't have the words to express it. Prayer doesn't change God; it changes you."

His arms tightened around me, and we held each other for a long moment. But then he dropped his arms and stepped away from me. "I appreciate what you're saying. You just don't get it. You've always had this connection with God that I can't understand. He doesn't talk to me the way he talks to you. When I pray, I get nothing in return. Just a silent room that feels empty."

"Matthew—"

"No, no. I don't want to talk about this anymore. I need to get some air. I'm going outside for a bit. Just put Hope in the bed with you if she's scared. I don't think I'll be going back to sleep."

He left before I could say anything else.

Matthew

Outside, the air was still and muggy, not exactly the refreshment I was looking for. But it was better than being cooped up in the bedroom with Ruby picking at the wounds I'd so carefully covered. I took a seat in a lawn chair and propped my feet on another, dropped my head back, and closed my eyes.

The door creaked behind me. No doubt it was Ruby coming to save me from myself. I didn't move. Just waited to hear her voice. But it wasn't her voice I heard.

"Mind if I join you?" Mike said from beside me.

I opened my eyes and sat up. "Sure. Have a seat."

He took the chair across from me where I'd propped my feet and held out a pack of cigarettes. "Want one?"

"No thanks. I don't smoke."

"That's right. I knew that, I think."

He lit his cigarette and took a drag, blowing the smoke to the side. I could sense he wanted to say something to me, but he didn't. He just sat there quietly smoking and looking up into the sky. Silence was fine and dandy with me, so I slid back down a bit and rested my head on the back of the chair, closing my eyes once again.

We sat like that for several minutes. Maybe even half an hour. I tried to clear out the images of my dream, focusing on making them as small as possible in my mind. I shrunk them down until they were as small as the head of a pin. That's how I dealt with these things in the jungle, anyway. It worked. Well, it worked long enough to get me through the next conflict. But here, there was no enemy I could see, no target at which to aim my gun.

"You're not the only one, you know?" Mike broke the silence. I sat up as he lit another cigarette. Reckoned he was ready to talk.

"How's that?" I asked.

"You're not the only one having nightmares. I've seen it a lot. Even had a few myself."

"Have you awakened to find yourself pointing a gun at your friends and family?"

"Not exactly," he said, chuckling a bit. "But I have fallen out of my cot a few times trying to dodge incoming fire from zeros flying right at me."

I shared his chuckle. "Guess that's all over now. Just can't seem to get it out of my head."

"Yeah, coming back is hard. The people you care about have all stayed the same. They've gone about their lives at the factory or on the farm. They've watched some newsreels and think they know what war is like. But no one really gets it."

"Grace does."

He met my gaze. "Yeah. You're right about that." He sucked on his cigarette for a moment before continuing. "She was pretty shaken up when we got to Australia. I thought she was going to shoot me between the eyes if I didn't refuel and fly her straight back to Mindanao."

"That sounds about right." A sudden ache for a beer came over me. "I'm gonna grab a beer. Want one?"

"Sure."

I went to the kitchen and pulled out the six-pack of Budweiser. It only had four in it, but that would be plenty for the two of us. On my way back outside, I passed Mrs. Sawyer rocking Hope in the living room. She lifted her brow, but didn't say anything.

I sat back down and handed a beer to Mike, then opened mine and took a long gulp. I needed to ask Mike some questions, but before I could handle the answers, I needed to swallow a little courage. So I finished the first beer before I began.

"Listen, Mike. I want you to know I appreciate everything you did to get Grace to safety. Not to mention finding her a place to live where she and Hope would be accepted and loved." I popped open a second beer and took another swallow. "But I have to ask you something, and I need you to tell me the truth."

Mike took a big gulp of his beer as well. "If you're wondering if anything ever happened between me and Grace, I can assure you that you've got nothing to worry about." He leaned forward onto his elbows. "She was always thinking of you. Always doing everything she could to find out where you were. Even after Dorsey tried to convince her you were dead, she never gave up hope that you and Henry would come home safe someday."

Henry's name dug a hole in my chest. I took another swig of beer, feeling its effects relaxing the tension in my neck. Maybe this would be easier than telling Ruby.

"I guess Grace hasn't had a chance to tell you yet. Henry died in the Philippines."

Mike dropped his head into his free hand and swore under his breath. He stood and paced the deck. "Are you sure?"

"I was there when it happened."

He swore again and dropped back into the chair, where he downed the rest of his beer. "How did it happen?"

I shook my head. "We were running a guerrilla operation in northern Luzon. Japs ambushed us at a barrio. Killed almost a third of my men, including Henry."

"Does Grace know?"

I nodded.

"She must be devastated. You and Henry were her entire world. Well, until Hope was born." He let out another slew of curses, got up and went back to pacing. I was surprised to see such a strong reaction from him.

"I take it you and Henry were close," I said.

"Yeah, well, we played ball together for a few years. Joined up about the same time and all. Then we both wound up stationed in the Philippines. He was one of the best friends I ever had."

"Me too."

We both grew quiet, and I thought about all the times Henry had saved me, or lifted my spirits, or just made life in the jungle bearable. That hole in my chest grew, so I tried to fill it with the rest of the beer in my hand.

"Well, I don't mean to be insensitive," I said. "But...how well do you know Grace? I mean, has she told you much about her past?"

He stopped pacing and set his empty bottle on the railing nearby. "I know who she is," he said quietly. "I've known for a long time."

I was afraid of that. But I also didn't want to give away more information than he already knew. "What do you mean you know who she is?"

"Henry told me, back when they first came to San Francisco. We were out one night having a good time, and I guess he had too much to drink. He told me all about how his sister, Ruby, had been convicted of a murder she didn't do. Said the police believed she was dead, and they were starting a new life."

Now it was my turn to pace. "I don't believe this. After all his...he's the one who spilled it. Perfect. So now you know." I was already planning our departure. We would have to leave first thing in the morning. Fleeing with a two-year-old wouldn't be easy.

"Look," Mike said. "Henry didn't even remember telling me."

"Well, isn't that a relief! I wonder how many more people he told."

"What I'm trying to say is that her secret is safe with me. I haven't told a soul."

"Not even your parents?"

"Especially not my parents. I haven't even told Grace that I know. I would never hurt her. She means the world to me."

I stopped pacing at the way he'd said her name. "Wait a minute. She means the world to you? Do you have feelings for her?"

"I already told you, nothing happened."

"But not because you didn't want it to. Admit it. I can see it. I can hear it in the way you talk about her. You fell in love with her."

"I think she's wonderful. She's smart; she's kind; she's—"

"—beautiful."

"Yes. Inside and out. She's amazing. But she's not mine. She never was. And I know that."

This guy was killing me. Could he be any more noble? He probably thought of himself as Lancelot, and Ruby was his Guinevere. I wondered just how close they had become in the years I'd been missing. But I snapped my mind back to the pressing matter.

"Tomorrow, we're packing up and leaving," I said.

"Where are you going?"

"Somewhere remote. Somewhere far from here, hopefully, where no one will know who she is."

"I've already told you, you have nothing to fear from me. Don't uproot her and Hope. I swear, Matthew. You can trust me."

"Trust you? With her life? Did Henry tell you what her sentence was?" I didn't wait for his reply. "It was the electric chair. The *electric chair*. Can you imagine her getting electrocuted?"

"No, of course not."

"Then you understand why we have to be careful. Leaving here ain't about whether or not I trust you. It's about doing everything I can to ensure she and Hope are safe."

He held up his hands in surrender. "All right. I get it. I'd probably do the same in your shoes. Just don't rush into anything. You're all safe here. There's no hurry."

I went back to where I'd been sitting and popped open the last beer. Walking to the edge of the deck, I stared out over the rows of backyards surrounding me. There were too many people. And they were too close. At first light, I was heading out to find a home for the three of us. Maybe Mike was right. Maybe we could trust him. But it wasn't worth the risk. Especially with Ruby so willing to walk right into the fire and turn herself in. Was I the only one who saw the danger ahead?

***

I spent the next couple of weeks searching for both a job and a house. The two promising positions had come to nothing—returning GIs were swarming the job market, and even with preferential status, I was having a hard time finding anything in the construction or engineering field. I even branched out and began looking for positions that had nothing to do with my training.

It just didn't make any sense. There were job openings. I saw them in the paper every day. I saw posters in windows that advertised openings. And other GI's were getting hired. I knew this because I tended to be the very next person to inquire after a job once it was filled. I can't say how many times I walked into a place, sat down to fill out an application, and some person from management would walk out and announce the position had been filled. I started to get a sense that this was no coincidence, like some force was working against me.

I couldn't say the same thing for house hunting. There just weren't any houses to be had. The very few on the market were priced so high, there was no way I could afford them. Not even with the GI Bill helping out.

Now, don't get me wrong. The GI Bill was a great help to most of us coming back from the war. Just not for me. The benefits helped many of my fellow soldiers go to college and get degrees, but I already had mine. I had the degree, I'd worked in the Corps of Engineers, and I had leadership experience. By all accounts, I should've been all set to re-enter society.

But as Ruby would've pointed out if I'd brought it up, God often has different ideas for us than we have for ourselves. By the last Friday in July, I felt like I'd been banging my head against the same wall for days on end. To make matters worse, Hope hadn't come near me in nearly two weeks. She cried anytime Ruby put her down on the cot to sleep, so I wound up sleeping on the sofa downstairs. Once Mike returned to San Francisco, I moved to the sleeper sofa in Mr. Sawyer's office. Being awakened each morning by his cheerful whistle only made me more anxious to find a home.

As I sat on the bus that afternoon, heading back to the Sawyers' from another long, fruitless day, I stared through the rain cascading down the window as the city rushed past. I couldn't take care of them. No matter what I did, no matter how hard I tried, I couldn't shake the feeling that Ruby and Hope were slipping through my fingers. And every time I thought about it, my chest would tighten, and all the symptoms from my breakdown would flood my mind. Was I really so fragile? Why couldn't I just toughen up and handle this?

The bus stopped to let passengers on and off, and I caught sight of a church on the corner. Ruby's words came to me. *Prayer doesn't change God; it changes you.* I felt drawn to the church, and at the same time, I resisted it. If God hadn't answered my prayers in the jungle, when lives depended on it, when I needed Him the most, why would He answer my prayers now?

Still, the pull on my heart was something I hadn't felt for a very long time, not since I'd joined up with the guerrillas. Maybe I should just check out the church. I exited the bus and pulled my jacket up over my head. Rain poured down as the people around me dodged the puddles on the sidewalk.

I made my way to the end of the block and jogged up the steps to the front doors. I tugged on the one in the middle, slowly opening it to the large foyer. I stepped inside and shook off the rain, half expecting someone to come over and tell me I couldn't be there. But the place remained quiet.

I ventured over to the open door leading down the middle aisle of the sanctuary. I wasn't alone: a few souls were scattered in the pews, most with their heads bowed. I felt like I was trespassing somewhere sacred. My heart was full of anger and bitterness. How could I bring those feelings to God? What could I even say to Him? How was I supposed to praise Him, or thank Him, or enjoy His presence in any way? I was lost. And I was certain there was no place for me in that sanctuary.

I turned around and headed back out into the rain, determined I was going to find a way to take care of my family, with or without God's help. I would make it happen, somehow.

***

By the time I made it back to the Sawyers' house, I was soaked down to my underwear. I took a quick shower and put on some dry clothes before heading downstairs to find the rest of the family. I found Mrs. Sawyer in the kitchen preparing supper, and the smell made my mouth water.

"Have you seen R—" I stopped myself, irritated that I had to constantly remember to call my wife by her *other* name.

Mrs. Sawyer had the oven open, and she was leaning over a large pan of roasting vegetables. She flipped the last of them over and slid the pan back into the oven. "I'm sorry, Matthew, what did you ask me?"

"I was looking for Grace. Do you know where she is?"

"The girls took Hope and George, Jr. out shopping. Of course, that was before all this rain started. I expect they'll be home any time now."

"All right. Thank you. Supper smells delicious." I turned to leave, but Mrs. Sawyer stopped me.

"Oh, wait a minute. I nearly forgot. You got some mail today. Come on in here, and I'll give it to you."

I followed her over to the console table in the foyer, where she handed me several envelopes bundled together with a rubber band. The top letter was addressed to me, with a return address for Mary. My heart sped up. How would Mary know where to find me?

"Thank you," I mumbled to Mrs. Sawyer as I took the letters upstairs to our bedroom.

Once I was alone, I pulled off the rubber band and examined the envelopes more closely. The top letter was dated only a couple of weeks ago, and she had addressed it to me at the hospital. That gave me a moment's relief. At least she didn't know where we were staying.

I flipped through the other envelopes, a collection of letters from Mary dating back to just before the fall of the Philippines in 1941. There were six all together. I sat on the edge of the bed staring at them, wondering if I should even read them. After all, I'd decided the best thing to do was to cut off contact with my family.

The first five were between December 1941 and August 1942. I figured those would be the most difficult to read. They would be full of worry and fear, and most likely my mother's passing. I couldn't bring myself to read those just yet.

So I opened the most recent letter and began reading.

Dear Matthew,

Seeing you alive and (mostly) well was the most wonderful blessing I could have asked for. I've prayed for you every day since you left home, and even though you haven't come back to us, I'll take your safe return to the States as answer to my prayers.

I assume you won't be in the hospital forever, so when you're released, please send me your new address so that we can keep in touch. I don't ever want to lose you again. You mean so much to me.

I've told everyone that you're alive. Of course, they all want to see you for themselves. I'm not pressuring you. I just wanted you to know that you are loved dearly and missed. You should have seen the joy in Father's eyes when I told him...

I stopped reading the letter at that point. Just sensing the pain and hope behind Mary's words was difficult enough. I wasn't about to read anything having to do with Father. I skimmed over phrases.

...eager to welcome you home...

...Father's doctor says...

...he regrets everything...

I got past the paragraphs about Father and picked up my reading there.

Your nieces are desperate to meet their uncle, about whom they've heard countless stories. Their favorite is the time you took me on the Ferris wheel at the county fair. Do you remember? I was only seven, and you had just turned eleven. You were so mad that Mother had forced you to ride the Ferris wheel with me when you wanted to ride with your friends. So you put me in the seat, slammed the bar shut, and sent me off on my own! I was terrified! I could hear you and your friends laughing in the chair behind me, but I was too scared to turn around. The worst part was when the wheel stopped, and I was swinging so high above the ground, I could have sworn I could see clear to Atlanta!

I was finally unloaded from that torture, and I took off to tattle tale on you. But I was so scared and angry, I got confused and lost. I sat down on the ground and cried because I just knew I'd never see my family again. Do you remember what happened next? You found me. Do you remember what you did? You took me over to the games and shot basketballs at the hoops until you won me the prize I wanted.

I'll never forget that day, not because you were mean to me (that wouldn't be the last time), but because I realized that even when I didn't like you much, you would be there for me if I truly needed you. I grew up believing that with all my heart. Don't you see? By leaving everyone behind, you've left yourself behind too. Come home, Matthew. Come home, and find yourself again.

With all my love,
Mary

I folded the letter back in its envelope, took the bundle of letters over to the closet, and put them at the bottom of my rucksack. That was where they would have to stay. There was no way to make Mary understand. There was too much at stake. I'd already been responsible for so many deaths. I couldn't be responsible for Ruby's too.

I closed the closet door just as Ruby came into the room. She smiled at me, uncovering her head and laying the scarf on the bed. "How was your day?" she asked.

"Not so good. Same as the day before. And the day before that."

She came over to me and slid her arms around my waist, stretching up on her tiptoes to kiss me. "Something will come along. We just have to be patient."

I let the warmth of her spread through me, and I kissed her in return. I had no desire to talk. I needed to work off my anxiety. "How long do we have before supper?" I asked.

"About fifteen minutes or so."

"And where's Hope?"

"Downstairs playing with Mr. Sawyer in his study."

I pulled her tight against me, and kissed her neck as I moved her to the bed. I shut out all thoughts of jobs and nonexistent houses, of family and Alabama. I didn't need to return to Hanceville in order to find myself. I only needed to hold Ruby in my arms.

CHAPTER NINETEEN

Ruby

August 6, 1945
Houston, Texas

Matthew grew more and more restless as the days passed with no job prospects and no home for us to move into. Seemed like the more I tried to reassure him, the tenser he became. And even though I didn't say anything out loud, I knew in my heart that God was working on him, preparing him to accept the path that would lead us back to Alabama, and to our salvation.

I prayed every morning and every night that God would open Matthew's heart. I prayed for strength to follow God's path, even when I was afraid. I thought back on all the times God had called me to a place of great danger, to serve others in need, and how He'd protected and sustained me through those times. I needed to hang on to those memories with all my might, 'cause I knew when the time came, fear would shake my faith.

The first week of August brought a welcome distraction from our anxieties. Jillian had received word that George was coming home from

Europe. This brought on a great flurry of excitement in the Sawyers' home. Even Matthew seemed pleased once he learned that George's return meant Jillian and the baby would be moving back across town to their apartment.

Mr. Sawyer picked George up from the train station on Sunday, and on Monday we celebrated like it was Christmas. George doted on Jillian and the baby, unable to contain his pride. It took some convincing to get Matthew to forgo job and house hunting for a day, but he eventually gave in. Mr. Sawyer grilled hamburgers and hotdogs, while Jillian and I helped Mrs. Sawyer with all the fixin's. It was quite a spread!

Once things were taken care of in the kitchen, I sat on the back deck, watching Hope play and listening to the radio we'd set up. Matthew and I had found a small skin horse in a little shop a few days prior. It looked almost exactly like the old skin horse in *The Velveteen Rabbit*, and Hope had been beside herself when we gave it to her. She'd even given Matthew a hug—a major step forward given that she'd done all she could to avoid him since his nightmare.

Hope lay on her stomach in the grass just below the deck where I sat. She manipulated Velveteen and Skin Horse as they spoke to each other. "What is *weal*?" Hope said, bobbing the rabbit's little head.

"When somebody loves you a loooonnnggg time," said Skin Horse.

"Does it hurt?"

"Sometimes. But dat's ahwight. You don't mind much."

I couldn't help but smile as she acted out the scene, amazed she knew it so well. Though I shouldn't be surprised since she must have heard it a thousand times.

"See?" Hope said, turning Skin Horse sideways. "You hafta be loved for a long time, so your hair falls out, and your eyes get woose, and you get wough spots. But it doesn't matter 'cause you can't be ugly anymore when you're weal."

"Are you weal?" the bunny asked with amazement.

"Uh huh." She turned Skin Horse back to face Velveteen, bringing them close together and lowering her voice to a near whisper. "The boy's uncle made me weal a long time ago. And once you're weal, it lasts forever."

"Oh, dat sounds nice! I wish I was weal."

"Don't worry, Belteen. Hope loves you. She will make you weal."

My heart swelled listening to such gentle love pouring out of her. I knew I didn't deserve her, and yet I was so grateful for her. I looked over at Matthew on the other side of the yard. He caught the football George had just thrown at him, clutched it near his head, and threw it back. I was doubly blessed for sure.

I stood and walked to the other side of the deck, leaning onto the railing and looking down at Matthew. He smiled up at me before turning his attention to another pass from George.

"You have a nice arm," George said. "You play in high school?"

Matthew threw the ball back and shrugged. "A little."

"He's being modest," I called to George as he caught the ball. "He played at Alabama for a little while."

George dropped the ball to his side, and his eyes widened. "Really? You played at Alabama?"

"I wouldn't go so far as to say that," Matthew said. "I walked on for a few weeks and practiced with the team when I was a freshman. Never saw the field, though."

"Still, that's impressive." George threw the ball again.

"They were taking just about anybody. Besides, I had to quit the team and focus on my grades."

Mr. Sawyer turned from the grill and watched them pass a few more times. "Looks like Bama will be a strong team again this year," he said. "But I think my Longhorns will be better."

George tossed the ball at Mr. Sawyer. "Look out, old man!"

Mr. Sawyer caught the ball with ease, winking at Matthew. "George hates the Longhorns. Poor kid grew up with a father who went to A & M. Never stood a chance."

Matthew laughed. A real laugh that sounded just like the old Matthew I knew when I was young. He looked happy and relaxed, and I thanked the Lord for giving him these moments of peace and joy. I prayed they would bloom to even more moments, and that soon the pain of the past would be a distant memory. The three men threw the ball around a little longer before Mr. Sawyer went back to the grill.

"Want a drink?" George asked, setting the ball down and trotting up the steps of the deck.

"Sure," Matthew called back.

George smiled at me as he passed by, his deep dimples creasing his cheeks. He stopped near the door where Jillian sat rocking George, Jr. and leaned down to give her a kiss, asking if she wanted anything from inside.

She beamed at him. "Some lemonade would be nice."

George glanced over at me as he pulled open the back door. "Grace, would you like some too?"

"Why, that would be lovely, thank you."

"Coming right up."

I marveled at how happy George seemed, especially in contrast to Matthew's solemn disposition when he'd first returned. Had their experiences been so different? I wasn't exactly sure what George had done in Europe, but from what Jillian had told me, his letters had mentioned missions. He had to have been in combat.

Matthew came up behind me and slid his arm over my shoulder. He leaned toward me and spoke into my ear. "You having a good time?"

"Yes," I replied. But the scent of alcohol on his breath hit me at the same time. My optimism faltered. No wonder he seemed more relaxed. As much as I hated the idea of him drinking, I decided that having the old Matthew back was enough for the time being.

He kissed my forehead and walked across the deck to where Hope was still playing with her toys. "How's Velveteen and Skin Horse getting along?" he asked.

"Great!" Hope answered, her distrust all forgotten. "Do you want to play too?"

"Absolutely!" He went down the steps and lay down in the grass next to her.

She handed him the skin horse. "You be Skin Horse."

"Does he have a name?"

By this time I'd crossed the deck and was watching from above them. "Of course he has a name," Hope said with a giggle. "It's Skin Horse!"

"Oh!" Matthew said, glancing up at me and winking. My stomach did the same flip it used to do when I was a young girl, and he'd smile at me while we worked in the soup kitchen.

Just then, Mrs. Sawyer and George came out of the back door carrying plates of food. "Dinner's ready," she called. "I hope you have those hamburgers and hot dogs ready!"

Mr. Sawyer came up the steps carrying a large plate of patties and hot dogs. "Don't start yapping at me. I got 'em right here."

I turned back to Hope and Matthew. "Come on, you two. It's time to eat."

Matthew jumped up and held out a hand to Hope. "Come on, honey bunny."

She giggled and took his hand, popping up as he pulled her and lifting her arms to him. "Cawwy me?"

Matthew stared down at her for a moment, an easy smile spreading over his features. Lifting her into his arms, he carried her up the steps, placed her in the high chair on my right and took the chair on my left. Mrs. Sawyer took George, Jr. over to the playpen and set him inside. We all filled our plates.

After Mr. Sawyer blessed the food, we dug in. I noticed Matthew was drinking another beer with his meal, which made me uneasy. But

George was drinking one too. I had to wonder if his happiness was as fragile as Matthew's; a cover-up for the turmoil simmering beneath the surface.

I forced myself not to dwell on those thoughts. I listened as Mr. Sawyer, George, and Matthew continued to talk football. I cut up carrots for Hope, and shared baby stories with Jillian and Mrs. Sawyer. It was a perfect day. I should've known it couldn't last. After all, I was still Grace Doyle to the Sawyers. I was still living a lie. But those few hours of joy were precious oxygen to my spirit, and by all appearances, to Matthew's as well.

Near the end of our meal, during a lull in conversation, the music on the radio was interrupted for a news announcement. Every one of us froze.

"The White House has just made an important announcement on the war. And to bring you this story, we interrupt our program to take you to Washington."

Another voice took over. "I have just returned from the White House where it has just been announced that the United States is now using an atomic bomb, the most powerful explosive yet developed. At the White House, Eben Ayers, Presidential Press Secretary, released a statement by the President of the United States on the atomic bomb. Here is President Truman's statement..."

"The world will note that the first atomic bomb was dropped on Hiroshima, a military base. We won the race of discovery against the Germans. We have used it in order to shorten the agony of war, in order to save the lives of thousands and thousands of young Americans. We shall continue to use it until we completely destroy Japan's power to make war."

When the music started back up, we all looked at each other in astonishment. "What is an atomic bomb?" Mrs. Sawyer asked.

Mr. Sawyer looked from George to Matthew, who both seemed baffled. "Whatever it is, it sounds ominous."

"Maybe the dirty, no-good Japs are finally getting what they deserve," Matthew muttered.

Everyone stared at him, but he kept his eyes on his plate as he lifted a bite of potato salad to his mouth. And just like that, our wonderful day together as a family slipped away.

***

The rest of the week was filled with one story after another about the devastation in Japan. It was sickening. Some newspapers even speculated that the atomic bomb would destroy the world. I marveled at the amount of destruction one bomb could cause. And I mourned the loss of life as, three days later, another bomb was dropped on Nagasaki.

Mr. and Mrs. Sawyer discussed the bombings at length during supper each evening. Like myself, Mrs. Sawyer was horrified by the death toll being reported. But Mr. Sawyer extolled the possibilities of harnessing such a powerful energy source.

For his part, Matthew stayed quiet during these discussions. In fact, after the initial news of the Hiroshima bombing, he said nothing more about any aspect of the war. It pained me to see him withdraw again, especially after those precious hours on Monday when we'd been so happy. It was as if God had given us a glimpse of what was possible, and then yanked it out from under us.

George and Jillian moved back into their apartment across town, so Hope was now sleeping in the bedroom across the hall from us. Matthew and I were finally able to sleep in a bed together all night, which I had thought would be a nice change. But each night, he'd toss and turn violently, and sometimes yell out in his sleep. He'd sweat so much, I had to change the sheets every day. At some point during the night, he would awaken from his nightmares, go out to the back deck, and sit in the lawn chair until morning. Then he'd shower and dress, and head back out to find a job and a house. In the evening he'd return, smelling of alcohol and cigarettes.

I was losing him in some horribly intangible, indefinable way that I had no idea how to fight. I was losing him. So I prayed. I prayed from morning till night. Most nights, I woke up with him during his nightmares, and I prayed until I fell back asleep. But it seemed to be doing no good.

The only small ray of hope I held on to was that Matthew finally agreed to attend church with us the following Sunday. Although Mr. Sawyer was a believer, he refused to participate in "organized religion." So Mrs. Sawyer and I took Hope with us to an old Methodist church a few blocks from their house every Sunday. And when I had to work, she took Hope along with her.

Given the circumstances, I was surprised Matthew wanted to go. But I prayed this would be the opportunity for us to connect on a deeper level again. I prayed God would begin to heal Matthew's heart. When he came into the bedroom in his best shirt and tie, I admired him from head to toe.

"It means so much to me that you're coming with us today," I said.

"I reckon if my family's in church, then I should be too. Right?"

That wasn't exactly the enthusiasm I was hoping for, but I'd take it. "You've been different this week. Quiet, more so than usual. And you seem...distant."

He tugged on his tie, straightening the knot. "I'm sorry if I've concerned you, but I assure you, I'm just fine. There's a lot going on in the world. A lot to think about. I reckon that's all. I've just been thinking."

I went to him and slid my hands along his chest, smoothing out his shirt. "Do you remember the first time you took me to church with you?"

His mouth twitched and almost smiled. "Yes."

"You were so handsome that day. I was so frightened of you, and so drawn to you at the same time."

"You were beautiful," he said. "When I got out of my car, and I saw you in that dress, I thought you were the most beautiful girl I'd ever seen." He kissed me, gently pressing his lips to mine. "I loved you, you know? I loved you then, even though I couldn't admit it." He slid his hand around my neck, caressing my cheek with his thumb, and he pressed his forehead to mine. "Ruby," he said.

"Yes?"

"I just wanted to say it."

"Say what?"

"Your real name."

***

Matthew reached for my hand as we sat down in the church pew. He didn't hold it long, maybe only five minutes or so. But I treasured it in my heart. Hope sat in his lap for the first few hymns, leaning in to his chest as if that was where she'd always been. Hope loved the music, but was never able to sit still during a sermon, so we always sat near the back, where I could easily slip out and return with little disruption. As the congregation stood for the penultimate hymn, I took her to the nursery, leaving her with a hug and a kiss.

When I returned to the service, the final notes were sounding, and I took my seat next to Matthew. Reverend Young, who was normally vibrant as he took the pulpit, approached it with a troubled frown. He gripped the sides of the wooden pulpit and looked out at the congregation, saying nothing for what seemed like a full minute.

"My brothers and sisters in Christ," he began, pausing before continuing. "The events of this week have been both troubling and encouraging, both dreadful and hopeful. Like many of you, I have read with great sorrow of the devastation in Japan. The loss of life is shocking. And in my spirit, I have mourned over the innocent victims whose lives were cut short. I have prayed for their souls, and for the souls of those who survived."

I glanced sideways at Matthew. His arms were folded over his chest, and he frowned up at Reverend Young as he continued.

"In fact, I have mourned many lives over these past few years, some of them your own sons, brothers, husbands, and friends, whose lives have been cut short or forever altered by this terrible war. I've felt your pain, but more importantly, God has felt your pain. As difficult as it is to see at times, He is ever present in our sorrows, and He shows us the light to lead us out of the darkness.

"We have been living in times of great darkness. And none of us knows what will become of this terrible new weapon that has been unleashed. But time and again, as I bowed my head before the Lord this week, He brought me to the Scriptures I'd like to share with you today from Paul's second letter to the Corinthians. I'll be reading from Chapter Four if you'd like to follow along."

I opened my Bible and turned to the correct place, moving the Bible toward Matthew so he could look on with me. But he remained stiff, not even glancing down at the book.

Reverend Young took a deep breath and began. "For God, who commanded the light to shine out of darkness, hath shined in our hearts, to give the light of the knowledge of the glory of God in the face of Jesus Christ. But we have this treasure in earthen vessels, that the excellency of the power may be of God, and not of us. We are troubled on every side, yet not distressed; we are perplexed, but not in despair; persecuted, but not forsaken; cast down, but not destroyed; always bearing about in the body the dying of the Lord Jesus, that the life also of Jesus might be made manifest in our body. For we which live are always delivered unto death for Jesus' sake, that the life also of Jesus might be made manifest in our mortal flesh. So then death worketh in us, but life in you."

Reverend Young closed his Bible and looked out on the congregation as though he was once again considering the meaning of these verses. "Yes, we are living in times of great darkness, but it is in the darkness that the light shines the brightest. Let us not lose hope. Let us not grow weary of praying for our enemies. God hears our prayers. He sustains us in our times of trouble. And He will guide us through these uncertain times as well. Please join me in praying for the people of Japan, as well as all the soldiers on both sides of this conflict, who have been injured or killed. Let us pray."

As the congregation bowed their heads, Matthew mumbled something and stood. He slid past me and disappeared out the back of the sanctuary. Organ music filled the room. I tried to bow my head and pray, but I was worried about Matthew. So I scooted close to Mrs. Sawyer and asked her to fetch Hope from the nursery. Then I slipped out the back.

After a few minutes of searching, I found Matthew pacing the sidewalk on the west side of the church. His pacing led him in my direction, and he put up his hands to stop me before I could say a word. "I don't want to hear it right now," he said.

"Matthew—" I tried.

"I mean it, Grace. I don't want a sermon from you too. The first one was bad enough." He turned his back to me and walked several paces away. I waited for him to turn again. As he did, he met my gaze, threw his hands out and heaved a frustrated sigh. "I don't understand," he said.

"Understand what?"

"How can he pray for those people after everything they've done?"

"You mean the Japanese?"

"Yes! I mean the soulless animals who have tortured people in ways that were once unimaginable to me. Did you know that when they caught guerrilla operatives, they would shove nails under their fingernails? Then they would hold them down, force a hose down their throats, and fill their bellies with water until their stomach expanded.

And then the real fun began! They'd take turns jumping up and down on their stomachs!"

"Matthew, please, stop."

"That wasn't even the worst of it. That was the gentler torture they used on women. After they raped them, of course. I don't even have the words to describe what they did to the men. Maybe I should go back in that church and tell all those people in there exactly who they're praying for!"

He kept on pacing, back and forth, his face growing red. I walked up to him and put my hands on his chest, looking up into his fiery eyes. "I know what they did, Matthew. Remember? I was there too. I saw it with my own eyes. You're right. Many Japanese soldiers did unspeakable things. And they will answer for their actions."

His chest heaved against my hands, and I could feel his heart racing. "Then how can you pray for them?"

"God tells us to pray for our enemies."

He stepped back and looked at me like I was crazy. "What good does that do? Praying for them don't undo all the evil they've brought on countless innocent people. I'm sorry, but if they're suffering right now, it's because they brought it on themselves. I don't feel one lick of sympathy for 'em."

"You're right," I said, trying to keep my voice calm. "Praying for them doesn't change the past. It won't bring back the friends we've lost. It won't bring back Janine or Henry, or anyone else. It's like I said before. Prayer doesn't change God, it changes us."

"Yeah, yeah. I know." He walked away from me again, but this time, he stopped with his back to me. "I just can't get there in my mind. I can't forget what they did." He turned and faced me. "I can't let go of it yet. I don't know if I ever will."

"Matthew, don't harden your heart. Find something, even the smallest thing you can pray for. Maybe…for the children who are orphans now. Surely they don't deserve this. Pray that God will change the hearts of the Japanese people, and they'll come to know Jesus. Ask God to give you the forgiveness you can't find inside yourself. There has to be some small place you can start. Don't let this bitterness sink so deep inside you that it kills every ounce of hope and love you have. Because it's a poison, and that's exactly what it will do if you continue to let it fester in your heart."

He shook his head and looked away, up at the sky, saying nothing for a few moments. I followed his gaze. Dark clouds were rolling in, as if summoned by his anger.

I didn't know what else to say, so I prayed God would grant me wisdom, and I tried one last time to get through to him. "You've held on to so much anger for so long, that it's swallowing you. Finding some way to forgive the people who've hurt you is the only way you're ever going to find peace. And if you can't, eventually, it will consume you, and you will be all alone."

At last Matthew looked away from the storm clouds. He walked back to me, his expression softening. Taking my hands in his, he kissed the back of my palms. "I'll try, all right? I can't promise anything, but I'll try."

He pulled me into his arms, holding me close for a few moments. Behind me, I heard the growing hubbub as churchgoers filled the sidewalks. I didn't want to move. I only wanted to stand there a while longer, trying to absorb Matthew's pain. But a rumble of thunder warned us of an approaching storm.

I released him and took his hand. "We better find Mrs. Sawyer and Hope so we can beat this rain home."

Matthew walked alongside me to the front of the church, and together we searched the crowd exiting the sanctuary. Soon, we saw Mrs. Sawyer come out holding Hope's hand. I waved them over to us.

"We better get moving," Mrs. Sawyer said. "There's trouble brewing."

Hope reached for my hand, and then took Matthew's hand too. "Swing me!" she said.

"We have to hurry today," I said to her. "We'll swing you next time."

Matthew picked her up, and we walked as quickly as we could without leaving Mrs. Sawyer behind. Just as we reached Alabama Street, the clouds opened, and the rain came down in sheets. There was only one block to go, so we began running.

I did my best to stay with Mrs. Sawyer while Matthew ran ahead with Hope. Mrs. Sawyer yelped as she nearly slipped.

I reached out and caught her, steadying her before we continued. "Be careful!" I said. "We're almost there."

She laughed and spread her arms. "Oh, it's all right. I won't melt!"

I took her arm and helped her across the last intersection. We passed the last two houses and turned onto the Sawyers' walkway. That was when I noticed Matthew standing in front of me like a statue, still a good thirty feet from the porch. He still held Hope in his arms, but he stared at the Sawyers' house like he didn't even notice the rain pelting him.

"What are you doing?" I asked him. "Let's get inside!"

He held his arm out to the side, blocking me from moving past him. Then he handed Hope to me. "Turn around!" he shouted.

"What?"

"Grace! Listen to me! Take Hope, turn around, and go back to the church. Do it now! Do not stop for anything or anyone. Go!"

The command in his voice left no room for questions. My gut told me to trust him, so I grabbed Hope from him. Beside me, Mrs. Sawyer looked at us like we'd lost our minds. I had no time to explain. "I...uh...I have to go back to the church," I said.

"The church?" She splashed over to Matthew as rain continued to pour down all our faces. "What is going on here? And whose car is that in my driveway?"

I looked to my left and saw the black Ford that didn't belong there. Dread slid down my throat, filling my stomach. Matthew looked over his shoulder, then back down at me. "Go to the church. I'll come get you when it's safe."

I nodded, taking a quick glance over his shoulder. At the top of the stairs, two men awaited our approach. One was standing. The other was seated in a wheelchair.

CHAPTER TWENTY

Matthew

August 12, 1945
Houston, Texas

Mrs. Sawyer was aghast. She turned indignant eyes to me and raised her voice. "What on earth do you mean by sending them back to the church? They're going to catch their death in this weather!"

"I don't have time to explain," I said, as Ruby and Hope hurried down the sidewalk and turned the corner. "I'll go get them with the car as soon as I can."

We continued up the walkway, and I took Mrs. Sawyer's elbow as we climbed the front steps to the porch. She straightened and began wiping the water from her cloak. "Gracious! What a mess I'm in." She unbuttoned and removed her cloak.

I stared at the two men waiting at the door. The one standing was a complete stranger. He was shorter than I was, but I could see that he was well built underneath his dark suit. He couldn't have been much older than I was, maybe even a bit younger.

But it was the man in the wheelchair who held my attention. Although it had been nearly nine years since I last saw him, my father looked like he'd aged twenty. His expression was still as hard as ever, but the right side seemed slack, as if it might slide right off his skull any moment. As he looked up at me, his mouth twitched, and the left side slid up into a hideous half-smile.

Mrs. Sawyer finished removing her headscarf. "Well now, how can I help you gentlemen today?"

The stranger was the first to speak. "Yes ma'am. I'm Daniel Fisher, and this is my employer, Mr. Patrick Doyle."

I had no intention of allowing Mrs. Sawyer to know any more about my life than necessary, so I interrupted. "Mrs. Sawyer, this gentleman is my father. If you'll excuse us for a few minutes, I'll speak with him and be right inside to dry off."

"Your father?" she exclaimed. "Well then, please, come inside out of this weather!"

"He won't be staying long," I said, glaring down at him.

"Matthew, that's just silly." She wasn't giving up. "I won't hear of it. Now come inside, dry off, and take the car to go get Grace and Hope. I'll get a nice dinner on the table so you all can visit."

I pushed open the front door. "Mrs. Sawyer, can I speak to you inside for just a moment?"

She hesitated, a flustered expression creasing her forehead. "All right." She stepped through the front door and hung her cloak and scarf on the coatrack while questioning me. "What in the world is going on? Why would you send your own father away? And why did you send Grace and Hope back to the church?"

"Listen, I don't want to go into detail about my childhood and everything that man has put me through, so please just trust me on this. He is evil. He's done despicable things that have nearly wrecked our lives. I want nothing to do with him, and if you knew him, you'd feel the same way."

She glanced at the front door behind me, and then rubbed her hand down my shoulder. "Oh, Matthew. I'm sorry for your pain. I really am. I don't want to interfere. But maybe you should at least talk to him and find out why he's here? I'll go upstairs and dry off. Why don't you take your father and his friend to Mr. Sawyer's study where you can speak in private? I promise you won't be disturbed."

"Thank you," I said, genuinely moved by her concern. "I won't be long. I'll hear what he has to say, then I'll go fetch Grace and Hope from the church."

"There's no need. I'll ask Mr. Sawyer to drive me to the church with some dry clothes for them. We'll bring them home in say, half an hour?"

I couldn't imagine needing more than five minutes to tell Father to get out of my life for good. "That would be very helpful. Thank you."

She gave me a sad smile. "You know, parents are human. We make mistakes, but we love our children fiercely. You may understand your father much better as you grow into a father yourself. It's never an easy job." As she walked over to the stairs, she called over her shoulder, "Stay there for a moment and I'll bring you a towel."

After changing into dry clothes, I led my unwelcome visitors to the study. Mr. Fisher wheeled Father to the center of the room, and stood just behind and to the right of him. I looked down at Father without an ounce of sympathy. He too deserved every drop of his suffering.

"You have five minutes," I said. "Then I want you to leave and never come back."

It was Mr. Fisher who spoke up. "Matthew, your father wants to begin by letting you know how deeply he regrets his actions during Miss Graves's trial."

"Wait a minute," I interrupted. "Who exactly are you? And why can't my father speak for himself?"

"I'm Daniel Fisher. You know my great-uncle, Dr. Melvin Fisher. He treated you when you had T.B."

"I see. And Mr. Fisher, you're here because...?"

"Please, call me Daniel. I'm employed by your father to be his full-time assistant. Your father's stroke several years back left him with limited speech and mobility. I help him communicate with others, and I've been working with him physically to help restore better movement for him."

"So he's told you what to say to me?"

"He has a small chalkboard that he can write symbols on for me to communicate for him. We've worked out a good system over the years."

"Can he understand me?"

"Yes. He can understand language and even form words in his head. He just can't move his mouth to form the words he wants to say."

I glanced down at Father, whose ghastly expression must have been some form of hope and sorrow. "Listen," I said directly to Father. "What you did to me, to Ruby and her family, is unforgivable. I said it before I left, and I'll say it again now. I do not want to have anything to do with you ever again. If you think I'll have some sympathy for you now because you're stuck in a wheelchair, then you're delusional. I'm glad you regret what you did, but it won't change anything. It won't change the path my life took because of you. It won't erase the years I spent fighting for my life, running from deranged Japanese soldiers who wanted to capture me and torture me until my dying breath. It won't erase my nightmares. Nothing you can say or do will change anything. So take your wheelchair and your assistant, and get out of my life for good."

I turned and opened the door to the study just as an awful noise came out of Father, a garbled sound of agony. Despite my hatred of him, it stopped me. I turned back to him, and he made a hand signal to Daniel. He pulled out a chalkboard from the back of the wheelchair and handed it to Father. Father scribbled something with his left hand, and then Daniel looked up at me and translated.

"He says you're right. He knows you can't forgive him." He looked back down while Father scribbled some more. "He just wanted to see you with his own eyes." He glanced down and back up again. "His heart was filled with joy when he learned you were alive."

I didn't know what to say. Seeing Father, a man who'd once commanded respect and fear from others, reduced to a garbling cripple was disconcerting. Some small part of me did feel something for him still. But it wasn't enough.

"All right," I said. "I've heard you out. Now it's time for you to go."

Daniel stared at me wide-eyed. "Are you really going to just turn him away? Do you know what he's been through? To what lengths he's gone to find you?"

"You don't know anything about me or what he's done. Don't stand there and lecture me."

"I apologize if I'm overstepping my bounds here, but Mr. Doyle has agonized over losing you for years. He only wants to do what he can to make your life better from this point forward."

"Wonderful," I said. "That's quite simple. All he has to do is leave me alone." I gestured to the door. "And he can begin that right now."

Father scribbled something again. Daniel reached for a satchel tucked in beside Father that I hadn't noticed until then. He pulled out a folder and handed it to me. "These are documents your father wants you to look through. Take your time. You can even consult a lawyer if you wish. We'll be staying at the Shamrock downtown for several days. Once you've looked through these, give me a call so we can discuss how you wish to proceed."

I raised a hand in protest, refusing to take the folder. "I don't want anything to do with him. Nothing in that folder interests me."

"I believe you'll change your mind once you see what's in there."

I glanced at the clock on the wall. Soon the Sawyers would return with Ruby and Hope. I decided it would be most expedient to take the folder, though I had no intention of looking at it. "Fine. I'll take it. But don't be surprised if you don't hear from me."

I took the folder from him and to my relief, Daniel stepped behind the wheelchair and pushed Father out of the study. I walked behind them around the stairs and to the front door, opening it for them. I didn't bother looking at Father as his chair rolled past me. Nor did I bother helping Daniel carry him down the stairs. He placed Father in the passenger seat of the car and came back for the wheelchair. As he reached for the chair, he paused and looked up at me.

"Matthew, your father has told me about what he did, how he's hurt you, and how much he regrets interfering in your life. It may seem impossible, but those papers come as close as a man can possibly get to changing the past. Give him a chance."

He folded the chair and lifted it, carrying it out to the Ford and placing it into the trunk. I watched to make sure the car left, and closed the door. I walked into the living room and tossed the folder onto the coffee table. Grabbing two beers from the kitchen fridge, I dropped onto the sofa and started on the first. What was I going to do now?

***

By the time the Sawyers arrived home with Ruby and Hope, I'd been through both beers, and another for good measure, and a couple of possible scenarios of where we could go and how we might get there. The closest, and maybe easiest place to go, would be Mexico. That was my first option. But we could also go back to California. The location was less important than putting distance between us and Father, and making sure he could never track us down again.

Ruby carried Hope up to her bedroom and laid her down for a nap. I followed and gave Hope a kiss on the forehead. Then I took Ruby's hand and led her into our bedroom across the hall. She sat down on the edge of the bed, surprisingly calm.

"That was my father," I started.

"Yes, I thought so." She glanced at the folder I'd brought upstairs with me. "Did he give you that?"

"Yes."

"What is it?"

"I don't know. It doesn't matter. He's here, and he's staying at the Shamrock for a few days. We have to get out of here. There's no telling what he'll do if he sees you." I tossed the folder onto the bedside table and began pacing the tiny room.

"Do you think he did?" she asked.

"No. Well, he didn't say anything. And surely he would have if he'd seen you."

"What did he want?"

"He wanted to apologize for everything, and to give me that folder. Actually, his assistant did all the talking for him. Father had a stroke a few years ago. Left him unable to talk and in the wheelchair."

"That's terrible."

I stopped pacing and nearly laughed. "Figures you'd feel bad for him. You do remember what he did to you?"

"Yes."

"He's the reason you were convicted for a murder you didn't commit."

"I know."

"Well, he's not the only one to blame for that. You should've told the truth from the very beginning instead of trying to protect that colored boy."

She stood and placed herself in my path. I recognized the fire in her eyes, and knew I was about to catch her wrath. "Are you going to continue to throw that at me every time you're scared? I know what I did, and I accepted the consequences. And I would do exactly the same thing all over again. The only person in this room who did something wrong was you! If you'd listened to me...if you'd just had faith and some patience—"

"This is my fault? Is that what you're saying?"

"'Let's run away together,' you said. 'I don't care if I never see my family again.' Those were your words, not mine. This is exactly the life you begged for, exactly the life you created for yourself when you set in motion that whole fiasco with my uncles. I told you it wouldn't work. That if you sacrificed your faith to be with me, it wouldn't be worth the cost."

"Yes, I know!" I said, more loudly than I'd meant to. My heart raced, thumping against my chest, and the room took a dip. "You are all-knowing Ruby, the one who knows best about everything!" Tiny stars flashed in the edges of my vision. "I am so tired of disappointing you! I will never be the man you want me to be!"

"Have you been drinking again?"

"Are you calling me a drunk now? Let's just add that to my endless list of failures!"

At that, something inside me exploded, shattering my thoughts. I turned away from her, picked up the first thing I could lay my hands on and threw it against the wall. I could barely see now. I heard another crash. And then a scream.

I knew in some tiny corner of my mind I had lost control, and that I had to stop. But I felt so small, and so separate from the body that was destroying the room. At some point I staggered, and my vision cleared enough for me to see the bed. I sat down, my limbs shaking uncontrollably.

Then everything went black.

CHAPTER TWENTY-ONE

Matthew

January, 1943
Luzon Province, Philippines

By January of '43, I'd been shoring up our network of spies for months, and was pleased with our progress so far. We'd established a solid line of communication, with security checks and policies to ensure no one ever revealed their true identities. The best intelligence had started to come in from Manila, with reports of the size and routes of Japanese forces, both in the Philippines and throughout the Pacific.

We still weren't sure if our information was getting to MacArthur, but we kept sending it down to Thatcher, now promoted to Corporal, and his region of control on the southern tip of Bataan. We had runners moving in and out of our headquarters in all directions, like a giant spiderweb. And it was running more smoothly than I had imagined it could.

Harris was still a source of grief. His ambushes along the roads north of Fort Stotsenberg kept the Japanese angry enough to raise the price on our heads. But it also kept some of the pressure off the Porac region.

Thus, we were able to thrive virtually undetected. At least for a few months, anyway.

One morning in late February, a messenger arrived from Thatcher. The young man handed me a small note.

GANDY CAPTURED. TORTURED. KILLED.
LOCATIONS MAY BE COMPROMISED.
MEET AT FLORIDABLANCA ON 27 FEB.

I shared the news with Henry and Diego. I'd met Thatcher at a small barrio several kilometers west of Floridablanca a few times before. I assumed that was where he intended for us to meet again. It was quite a hike, but we could do it in a day if we needed to. First though, I had to decide whether we should relocate.

"Captain, we can be ready to move in two hours," Diego said. "Just give the order."

"Yes," I replied, "That's probably best, but where's the best place to move to?"

"Closer to Manila," Diego said. "Best intelligence comes from there."

Henry took out his cigarette and looked at Diego like he was nuts. "So, closer to the Japanese? Of course! That makes perfect sense. I mean, we have been making it too difficult for them to catch us."

Diego was unfazed. "Captain, Japanese are all over the island. No matter which direction we move, we will be closer to them."

"Can't argue with that," I said. "Then it's settled. We'll move south. Diego, put together a scout squad to find a good spot for us. Henry, give the order to the other Lieutenants to start packing up. I want to be out of here in hours, not days. As soon as we establish a new headquarters, I'll go to Floridablanca to meet with Thatcher."

"Sí, Captain," Diego said, turning and leaving the hut.

Henry grinned. "Sí, Captain." He gave me a salute and left as well.

By nightfall, we'd established a new headquarters about three kilometers south of our old location. By doing so, we'd actually cut my travel to Floridablanca a bit. As the men went about building the bamboo and nipa huts, Diego organized a small squad to travel with us. With some hesitation, I left Henry in charge of finishing the camp construction.

We arrived at the barrio the following morning, having slept only a couple of hours the night before. Corporal Thatcher hadn't arrived yet, so I took the opportunity to find a secluded spot at the small creek nearby for a bath. Although, it wasn't entirely private. Diego insisted on keeping watch over me every minute of the day, but at least he turned his back while I bathed.

When I returned, Thatcher had arrived with his squad. He was even thinner and more haggard than when I'd seen him months before near Mount Arayat. I had to wonder if I too was showing the same wear and tear. With the generous hospitality of the barrio's chief, we went into his hut and sat down. After some of the local women gave us some meat I couldn't identify and small cups filled with drinks that stank to high heaven, we were finally alone.

"We took a big hit by losing Major Gandy," Thatcher said.

"He was a good man. It's a shame." I had no desire to hear the details of his torture at the hands of the Japanese, so I moved on quickly. "Who do you think will replace him?"

"You," Thatcher said.

"Me? No. Who was his second in command?"

"You were."

"No. In his headquarters. Who was second?"

Thatcher leaned forward and almost smiled. "Listen, the fact that you don't want the job probably means you're the best person for it." He took a sip of the awful-smelling drink and wrinkled his nose. "Besides, you're the next highest ranking officer in the entire area as far as I know." He set down his cup and his expression sobered. "And most of his men were captured or killed anyway."

"Perfect."

Thatcher leaned over and tried the meat. Deciding it tasted better than the drink, he grabbed a handful and shoved it into his mouth. Once he'd finished swallowing, he smiled at me. "Can't afford to be picky out here. Better get some food in your system while you can."

There was no arguing with that. So I wolfed down the mystery meat as well. When we'd finished all the food and forced down a bit of drink, we turned back to business. "Doesn't someone need to make this official if I'm taking over?" I asked.

"Already done. I hereby promote you to Major."

"You don't have the authority to do that."

"Who's around to complain or dispute it?"

"Good point," I said, laughing in spite of myself. "Maybe I'll get a raise."

We had a good chuckle and then set about planning the next phase of our operation. We both agreed I needed to re-establish communication with the various cadres across Luzon. This would involve a lengthy journey across many kilometers of jungle and mountain terrain. We mapped out the locations we knew of, and Thatcher agreed to visit the cadres closest to his location in the Bataan region, while I would visit the cadres around the central region of Luzon. It was a trip that could take months to complete, but it was necessary if we were going to maintain control of our growing force.

As we were coming to the end of our discussion, a rush of people into the hut interrupted us. Thatcher and I jumped up as the chief and Diego flew over to us. "Captain, we must go now!" Diego said. "Japanese coming."

The chief spoke rapid Spanish to Diego, who then translated. "He says they will search his hut. You must get to a safe place. We will follow him."

We ran out after the chief to the outer ring of huts. He pointed to one of them, again spewing Spanish at Diego. "He says to get into this hut and stay quiet, no matter what happens."

We piled into the hut, Thatcher, Diego, our two squads, and myself, all nine of us. We stood shoulder to shoulder, with Diego in front, and the rest of the men surrounding Thatcher and me. Every one of us had his gun at the ready, and I prayed we weren't in for a bloodbath. Through the slats in the bamboo, I could see the people of the barrio scurrying off to hide.

Within moments, a Japanese patrol entered the barrio opposite from our position. They marched to the center of the barrio and the leader of the patrol barked orders. I immediately recognized Kojima's voice.

"Dis barrio giving help to Americans!" he yelled, waving around what looked like a swagger stick that had been sharpened on the end. "All men and women to come outside!"

The Filipinos moved uncertainly, huddled in groups. It wasn't fast enough for Kojima. He whipped the swagger stick down onto the back of the nearest Filipino, a woman who hadn't moved yet. She lurched forward, screaming. This only seemed to enrage Kojima. He brought the stick down on her five more times. My heart thundered, and everything within me wanted to give that animal just what he deserved.

He yelled something in Japanese, and three of his men jumped out of line, came over and scooped the woman up. They dragged her into the nearest hut and disappeared. Kojima continued shouting, now in English. "Ahr people in barrio rine up here!" He dragged the swagger stick across the ground. His soldiers went through the huts nearby, chasing any stragglers into the center of the barrio. The Filipinos formed a line where he'd indicated, many of them women holding their young children. My stomach churned, knowing there was nothing I could do to help these people.

Kojima yelled out more commands in Japanese, and two of his men from the back of the formation brought someone forward whose head was covered in a burlap sack with small holes cut out for the eyes. All I could tell was that it was a male.

"Now," Kojima continued. "Whoever dis man point to must come wid us for questions." He turned to the man in the sack. "Now! Who is helping Americans?"

The man stood there for a few seconds, unmoving. Kojima walked over and stood beside him. "Again! Who is helping Americans?"

When the man didn't respond immediately, Kojima brought his wrath down on the man's head and back, sending him to his knees. When he ran out of energy, the man remained on his knees, his head drooped forward.

"Get up!" Kojima yelled. "Who help Americans?"

The man pushed himself back to his feet. He brought his arm up and pointed to a young man across from him. Kojima ordered him to step forward.

"Who else help Americans?" Kojima demanded again.

The man moved his arm slowly, pointing out another young man. This process continued for several minutes. Anytime the man wearing the sack tried to stop, he was beaten again. When ten people had been pointed out, Kojima seemed to be satisfied. Those unfortunate souls were rounded up, tied together with the man who'd identified them, and placed at the back of the patrol formation. He barked another order in Japanese, and the three soldiers who'd taken the woman into the hut reappeared. She didn't follow.

Kojima made a final speech to the barrio as he marched back and forth, proclaiming how fortunate the rest of them were to live under the care of the Japanese Empire. He warned them of the evil Americans who would make them slaves and eat their children. Then he told them that if any Americans came to the barrio, they were to report it immediately or face harsh punishment for the good of their people.

Finally, he gave the order to march, and the patrol left the way they'd come. The people of the barrio stood frozen in shock for several minutes, watching their loved ones get carted off. Several of the men inside the hut with me began mumbling curses in Spanish, but we didn't dare leave the hut until the chief himself came to let us out.

I glanced over at Thatcher, who shook his head in disgust. "Well, at least none of them gave us up," he said.

"Doesn't say much for the guy with sack on his head," I said.

Diego looked over his shoulder at me. "Captain, he has no choice. Japanese will kill his family if he does not do as they wish. He points at the strongest, in the hopes they can survive Japanese interrogation."

Everyone in the hut fell silent. My sorrow for the Filipino people swelled as I thought of all the sacrifices they continuously made to help us. I remembered the family on Mindanao, whose father was slaughtered as I lay in the boat off shore. They'd never even hinted at my presence.

Lord, I thank you for giving these people such courage, and yet I can't help but wonder why they're made to suffer. How long will You allow this to go on? Where are You in the midst of this hell?

CHAPTER TWENTY-TWO

Ruby

August 12, 1945
Houston, Texas

"**M**omma, can I sit in your lap?" Hope looked up at me with large, frightened eyes as she gripped Velveteen.

"Of course." I pulled her into my lap, keeping my ears trained on the doctor and nurses in the room just behind where we sat. The hospital hallway was mostly empty, so I could hear them discussing Matthew's vital signs. I slipped my arms under Hope's, pulling her tight against my chest. For the hundredth time in the past couple of hours, I prayed for Matthew to be all right.

"Momma, does your head hurt?" Hope turned her face to me and brought a tiny hand up to the bandage on my forehead above my right eye.

"No, sweetie. I'm fine. It's just a little cut." I glanced at Mrs. Sawyer seated beside me. Her eyebrows lifted, but she said nothing.

"Is Daddy all wight?"

"I think so."

"Can we go home now?"

"Not yet."

"I want Skin Horse."

Mr. Sawyer, seated across from us, leaned forward. "Why don't we take her home? We'll feed her, read with her, and get her ready for bed. You can stay here and keep an eye on things as long as you need to."

I lowered my head and spoke into Hope's ear. "Would you like to go home with Grandma and Grandpa while I stay with Daddy?"

"Yes ma'am," she said, nodding. She slid off my lap and went to Mr. Sawyer. He stood and picked her up.

"Come on, Margaret. Let's get Hope home."

Mrs. Sawyer let out a deep sigh and turned to me. "At some point, Grace, you need to explain to us what's actually going on. I don't want to stick my nose in where it doesn't belong, but I think..." She looked up at Mr. Sawyer. "We think, for everyone's safety, Matthew needs to get help."

Mr. Sawyer cleared his throat. "I'll just take Hope and get the car."

"I'll be along in a few minutes," Mrs. Sawyer said.

When Hope and Mr. Sawyer were out of earshot, she continued. "I know you love Matthew, and you want to take care of him, but—"

"Mrs. Sawyer," I interrupted, placing my hand over hers on the armrest. "I know you care about me and my family. Thank you. You mean the world to me. And I understand you're concerned about Matthew. I am too. I don't intend to just sit back and let things continue as they have. You're right. He needs help. The kind of help he can't get from me. But we have many issues all jumbled into one big mess right now, and I'm not sure which thread to begin with to unwind it all. I just need to think things through and spend some time in prayer."

She tilted her head and gave me a sad smile. "Like I said, I don't want to interfere, but I want you to know you can depend on us for support. We can even take care of Hope for a while if you need us to. Just know that we're here, and that we love you."

I leaned my head onto her shoulder, unable to stop the tears that spilled out of my eyes. I hadn't quite processed everything that had happened in the past couple of hours. She put an arm around my shoulder and let me cry awhile. The doctor came out of Matthew's room, and I straightened, wiping the tears from my face.

"Grace? Why don't you come on in?" he said.

Mrs. Sawyer and I stood, and she gave me another hug. "You call if you need us," she said.

"I will. Thank you."

I turned to follow Dr. Keagan into Matthew's room. I hadn't known Dr. Keagan well when I worked at the hospital, but he had an excellent reputation. He was old enough to have gained valuable experience, but not so old he was stuck in his ways.

Matthew looked up at me with a pained expression. "Did I do that to you?" he asked, his voice rough and full of emotion.

I took his hand and tried to smile. "Don't worry about it right now. I'm just fine. Let's hear what Dr. Keagan has to say, and then we can talk."

"I'm so sorry," he said.

Dr. Keagan cleared his throat. "Major Doyle, I understand you had a couple of episodes of..." He glanced down at the clipboard in his hands. "...headaches, high blood pressure, blurred vision, tremors, etc. at the base hospital in San Antonio, along with another serious episode in the Philippines before you were sent home."

"Yes, sir," Matthew answered.

"And while in the Philippines, you suffered from malaria, malnutrition, foot ulcers, and had your appendix removed?"

"Yes, sir."

"In Manila, you were diagnosed with combat exhaustion with anxiety state. You were treated mainly with rest along with medication for the malaria. All of this sound familiar?"

"Yes, sir."

Dr. Keagan frowned and looked at both of us over the rim of his glasses. "I believe the shock of all you've been through has greatly affected you, both physically and mentally. I don't think I need to tell you that this is serious, especially when you seem to be losing control of your actions and threatening the well-being of others around you."

Matthew looked up at the ceiling, the muscles in his jaw working as he closed his eyes. When he opened them again, they were damp. "I didn't mean to," he said.

"I understand," Dr. Keagan said. "I'm going to refer you back to Brooke General in San Antonio—"

"Doc, no," Matthew said. "Don't send me back there. They'll just put me in the ward with all the crazy guys. I'm not crazy."

"Matthew," I said, leaning toward him and squeezing his hand. "No one thinks you're crazy. But you should be treated by doctors who specialize in the care you need."

He glanced up at the bandage on my head, touching it gently. "I'm so sorry I lost control. I was just so...so overwhelmed at that moment. I won't let it happen again. I swear. I *swear*, Ruby."

I kissed his cheek and wiped the corner of his eye. "I know. We'll get through this." Straightening, I spoke to Dr. Keagan. "So, is there any way you can treat him here?"

He pressed his lips into a line, considering the request. "I suppose I could contact his doctor at Brooke and coordinate something. But I still believe it would be best for him to receive care directly from the doctors treating combat exhaustion."

Matthew let out a sigh of relief. "Thank you so much, Doc. I promise I'll do everything you say, and I won't be any trouble."

Dr. Keagan didn't look convinced. "The most common treatment for anxiety state right now is narcosis therapy. I'll speak to your other doctor, and we'll decide how we want to proceed. I'll be back shortly. For now, rest and do your best to stay calm. No stress." He gave me a pointed look as he left.

I sat down on the edge of the bed, leaning over Matthew and touching his cheek. "See? It's going to be all right."

"Ruby, I can't believe...I'm so sorry I hurt you. Are you sure you're all right? Is Hope all right? Where is she?"

"Shhh." I kissed his lips to quiet his panic. "You have to stay calm or Dr. Keagan will kick me out of here."

He touched my bandage again. "How bad is it?"

"Not bad at all. Only needed five stitches. That's not even worth the trouble."

He didn't smile. "Where's Hope? Is she all right? Did I scare her again?"

"She's fine too. The Sawyers took her home. She's concerned about you, but missed everything that happened. She just knows you weren't feeling well and that I got a boo-boo."

"The Sawyers must think I'm nuts."

"No, they think you've been through a traumatic experience and are doing your best to deal with it."

He shook his head. "I wouldn't blame them if they did think I'm nuts."

"You're not nuts. You've just got to find a better way to face the demons haunting you."

"Demons," he muttered. "That may be the most accurate description of them."

"Of what?"

"The nightmares. The flashes of memories in the middle of the day, when I'm not even asleep. I see things, and sometimes I can't tell if they're real or just in my mind. I can't make them stop." He dropped his gaze, and his voice cracked. "It's like Henry's ghost is with me all the time."

The empty space between my heart and my stomach that ached every time I thought of Henry hurt now for the pain I saw in Matthew's eyes.

"I let you down," he said. "So many times, over and over and over. From the first time I saw you, through every challenge you've faced, I've failed you."

"That's not true!"

"Yes, it is. Do I need to list them?"

"No, please—"

"Chester attacking you—"

"You found me—"

"Walking away from our friendship after the tornado—"

"You came back—"

"Betraying your trust—"

"You stood by me—"

"When I told Mr. Oliver your secret, and let's not forget nearly killing you in Cold Spring. And worst of all...Henry. It was my fau—"

I put my hand over his mouth, and he finally stopped. "This isn't helping." I took my hand away and gazed into his eyes. "You are a strong, kind, honorable man who's had my heart for so long, I can't remember when it wasn't yours. You haven't let me down. You've been my friend, my confidant, my love, and my partner. You've put up with my temper and my stubbornness, and you never seem to mind when I correct your grammar. And now, I get to share a beautiful little girl with you. We both have faults. But despite that, God has blessed us beyond what we could ever deserve. You just have to be willing to see it. The nightmares, they're just a symptom of all the guilt and shame you've put on yourself. They're all lies from the enemy. And they thrive in the darkness that's got ahold of you. The only way to beat the darkness is to come into the light."

"You always did explain things to me in a way that needed simplifying for my mere human brain. Sweetheart, the rest of us don't speak Angel."

He managed a smile then, and I smiled back. "Boy, they must have given you a lot of drugs if you think I'm an angel."

He turned his head toward the window. The light streaming in had turned a deep orange beneath the retreating clouds. "What are we going to do?" he asked.

"We're going to stop running."

***

"You'll have to keep your head still till I finish," I said, holding a large cup of bath water over Hope's head.

She tilted her chin up, and I poured the water over her soapy hair. "Momma, where did you sleep last night?"

"At the hospital with Daddy."

"Oh." She turned her head to me. "When's Daddy coming home?"

"Keep your head straight for me." I poured another cup. "He'll be home in a few days."

"Why does he hafta stay?"

"The doctor is going to put Daddy to sleep for a while so he can get better. It's called narcosis therapy."

"Nah-co-kiss?"

"It's a big word. Sounds a little scary, huh?"

She pushed her boat around the water, getting up on her knees now that I was finished with her hair. "Uh-huh."

"Daddy hasn't been sleeping well, so they are going to help him sleep. That's all."

I wished it were as simple as my explanation. If only he just needed more sleep. I'd listened as Dr. Keagan explained what they were doing, giving Matthew doses of sodium amytal to put him into a deep sleep that would last around eight hours. Then he'd be fed, visit the bathroom, and get another dose right away. He'd be in a near constant state of sleep for at least two days. And when he woke up, he *might* be better. He might not. But what did that mean for us?

After this latest breakdown, which I attributed to Mr. Doyle appearing on the doorstep, it was clearer to me than ever that our life of deception and hiding had to stop. The only way to truly help Matthew heal was to give him the chance to live a peaceful, honest, hard-working life. And that meant going back to Alabama.

I pulled the plug from the tub, despite Hope's protests. Then I took the towel off the rack and wrapped her up in a big hug. "Come on, you little bunny rabbit. Time for bed." I carried her into her room, helped her into her pajamas, brushed her hair, and waited for her to climb under the covers. Together, we pulled them up to her chin, leaving her arms out just the way she liked it.

"Momma, I pway for Daddy tonight."

"You want to say your own prayer?" She nodded. I sat down beside her and took her hands in mine. "All right. Go ahead."

She closed her eyes. "God? Tank you for your bessings. Tank you for my momma and for bwinging Daddy home. Pease help Daddy feel better. And bess Belteen and Skin Horse and Sugar Pie and Aunt Jiwian and Uncle George and Baby George and Gamma and Gampa and Uncle Mike. And God? Pease help me make Daddy weal. Amen."

I'd started to reach for her lamp, but I stopped. "Hope, sweetie, what did you ask God to help you with for Daddy?"

"To make Daddy weal. You know. Like Belteen and Skin Horse."

I had no idea how to make sense of that. "Daddy is real, sweetie."

"No, not yet. He is still scared and alone, like when Belteen first come to da nursewy."

"What do you mean? How do you know he's scared?"

She looked at me just as seriously as any two-and-half-year-old could. "Cuz da bad men are still twying to get him."

My throat knotted. I held my arms open. "Come here, sweetie." She climbed over the covers and sat on my lap. I held her close under my chin, wishing she didn't have to see her father suffer. "Listen, Daddy has dreams about the bad men chasing him, but they aren't really chasing him anymore. He's safe. And you're safe."

She sat there quietly for a few moments, processing this. Then she scooted away from me, took Velveteen and Skin Horse out from under the covers, and sat cross-legged on the bed. "Momma, look at Belteen. He has scars and wough spots, and he's dirty. See? I love him a long time. I made him weal."

"I see. But Daddy isn't real?"

"Not yet." She put the toys back beside her pillow and went back to sitting. "He needs us to love him a little more."

I looked at this amazing sparkle of light that had landed in my life when I'd needed her most. And I wondered what miracles she would witness in her lifetime. Was that what Asa had seen in me?

I took her hands in mine. "I think you might be right about that. Let's make sure we love Daddy as long as it takes for him to become real."

"I will."

"Now, get in bed, and get some sleep." I held the covers back as she crawled back under them, then I leaned over and kissed her on the forehead. "I love you."

"I love you too, Momma."

I left her room and went immediately to my bed, dropping to my knees. *Lord, You are so merciful to me, a sinner who does not deserve it. Thank You for carrying me through my times of trouble, for being a hedge of protection when my life and my faith were in doubt. You are my Redeemer, my Rock, my only breath. Whatever lies ahead, don't let me forget all that You've already done. Keep Your faithfulness ever before me, reminding me daily of Your provision. And Lord, I ask You to work in Matthew's mind, soul, and body as he sleeps. Heal the pain and darkness clouding his mind. Show him Your love. Show him how to surrender everything to You. Walk with him through this valley. And I thank You for sharing Your precious little one with me, so that I can watch her grow in her faith, and share Your love with others.*

Bless her heart, keep her from evil, and may Your light shine through her. In Christ's name I pray, Amen.

After finishing my prayer, I sat on my knees a while longer, enjoying the quiet presence that had come over me. Once again, I was reassured that going home to Alabama was the Lord's plan for me, and for the first time, I was sure that the journey was at hand.

Was my faith strong enough to walk through that fire?

My grace is sufficient for thee...

Could Matthew handle the stress?

When you are weak, I am strong...

Who would take care of Hope?

She is My workmanship, created in Christ Jesus unto good works, which I have ordained that she should walk in them...

Every doubt that came to the surface was met by Scripture brought to my mind. I thanked God again for His tender mercies, and for once again coming close to me in my time of need. I was certain I would face opposition, that even Matthew may refuse to accept God's call. But as for me, it was time to climb out of the boat again.

***

I didn't expect the opposition to come so soon. I went downstairs to get a book to read from the study, and instead I found Mike sitting on the living room sofa with his mother. I stared at him in shock. "What are you doing here?"

He stood and walked over to me, hugging me close. "I heard there was another ruckus. Just wanted to check on you."

"You got here awfully fast from San Francisco."

"I flew my new plane."

I stepped back, my mouth dropping open. "You got a new one? That's wonderful!"

He stared at the bandage on my forehead. "Are you all right?"

"Of course. You know me. I can take a lot worse than this."

He brought his gaze down to mine, growing serious. "But you shouldn't have to."

"Mike—"

Mrs. Sawyer cleared her throat and stood from the sofa. "I think I'll head off to my bedroom to read for a bit and fall asleep." She stopped beside Mike and patted him on the arm. "It's good to have you home for a day or two."

"Goodnight, Mother."

"Goodnight, Mrs. Sawyer."

We stood in awkward silence as she went up the stairs. "Don't forget the lights, Mike," she called down.

"Yes, ma'am." Once she was gone, concern wrinkled his brow. "What exactly happened?"

I sat down on the sofa, curling my legs beneath me. "I don't want to talk about it. Everyone's making a big deal out of it—"

"It is a big deal," he said, taking the spot beside me. "He lost control, and you were the one who got hurt."

"I know it's a big deal. Matthew's state of mind is...troubled. He has a lot going on. *We* have a lot going on. He needs my support right now."

Mike leaned forward onto his knees and shook his head. "I'm worried about you, Grace. And Hope too. What if it had been her?"

I couldn't even think about that. I closed my eyes and shut out the image that flew into my mind. "It wasn't that bad."

"You keep talking about this time. I'm talking about the next time. Or the next. When is it enough? When does it cross the line?"

"I don't know. I can't give you the answer you want."

"Maybe you need to consider divorce."

"What? Are you serious?"

"Yes. You have to think about Hope's and your safety."

I couldn't listen to this anymore. I pushed away from the sofa and headed to the kitchen.

"Where are you going?" he called after me.

"This is me controlling my temper. I'm getting some water."

Grabbing a glass from the kitchen cabinet, I began filling it at the tap. About halfway through, Mike joined me.

"You know I'm right," he said.

"No, you're not." I turned off the water and leaned against the sink. "You're letting your feelings get in the way here."

"My feelings?"

"Yes, your feelings for me. You want me to leave Matthew and be with you."

He crossed his arms and leaned against the counter, while I took a sip of my water. "So? What if I do? That doesn't mean I'm wrong."

"You don't think trying to steal another man's wife is wrong?"

He threw his hands up and groaned. "I'm not trying to steal you! Good grief. I'm trying to protect you. That's exactly what Henry would've wanted me to do."

"What does Henry have to do with any of this? And he would not have wanted you to tell me to leave my husband and break up his niece's family." I took another sip of water as my words sunk in. "You realize that's what you're suggesting. For Hope to lose her father. Because that's exactly what would happen. Matthew would..."

"He'd what? Go nuts? I think he's already there."

"No, he isn't. You just don't understand."

"I don't understand? Are you kidding? I've been through my own problems, Grace. I've seen what happens to guys like Matthew who've been destroyed by the war. He isn't going to get better. He's going to keep drinking and keep losing control until he seriously hurts himself or someone else."

"He's getting treatment," I insisted. "Again, you don't understand everything that he's dealing with."

I pushed the kitchen door open and went back to the sofa, setting my water on the coffee table. In the kitchen, I could hear Mike getting a glass of water too. He came out a few minutes later, but he remained standing in front of me with his arms crossed.

"Grace, I need to tell you something," he said. "I, um, I actually *do* know everything."

"What do you mean?"

"Henry told me. A long time ago. Back before we went to Manila." He glanced at the stairs and lowered his voice. "I know who you really are. I know you were convicted of murder, and that everyone thinks you're dead. I know your real name is Ruby."

"I see." I took another sip of my water, waiting for him to explain more. I was surprised. Not by his admission, but by the fact that it hadn't terrified me. Every time I'd faced someone else learning of my past, I'd been terrified. But not tonight.

"I guess I should've told you before, back when we were in Australia," he said. "I just wasn't sure I should. I mean, even Henry didn't remember that he'd told me."

"What do you mean he didn't remember?"

"He was drunk when it happened."

A laugh burst out of me. "Wait a minute. Henry told you I was a convicted murderer, and you just took it in stride and never brought it up again?"

He had a chuckle as well and relaxed his arms. "I don't know. By then I knew you two pretty well. He told me you didn't really do it, that you were defending yourself. He made you sound like an angel." He gazed down at me, his smile fading. "And then I saw it for myself. You really are an angel. I knew there was no way you could ever kill someone."

I finished off the water in my glass, unable to bear the emotions in his expression. I didn't want to hurt him. I owed him so much, and I loved him about as much as anyone could love a true friend. But I loved Matthew infinitely more.

Setting my glass down, I steeled myself. "Mike, I love Matthew with all my heart. I won't divorce him. And I'm not an option for you. I never was. You must know that. As much time as you spent with me, comforting me, keeping me from losing my mind, providing a home for my daughter. You had to know."

He walked around the coffee table and fell into the leather chair. Resting his elbows on his knees, he stared at the floor between his feet for several moments before making eye contact again. "Yeah. I know. I've always known. I guess I just...hoped. Sheesh. I make it sound like I wished Matthew was dead. I never wanted that."

"I know you didn't."

He leaned back and stared at the ceiling. I waited for something to come to my mind, some words of comfort I could offer him. I wanted him to know that we would be all right, that he didn't have to worry about our future. But I was at a loss.

After an uncomfortable silence, Mike raised his head and looked at me. "So now what are you going to do?"

"I'm going back to Alabama to turn myself in."

He dropped his head back, shaking it in disbelief. Then he chuckled to himself. "Of course you are."

CHAPTER TWENTY-THREE

Matthew

August 17, 1945
Houston, Texas

I awakened just as the sun peeked up over the trees outside the hospital window. I felt more rested than I had in years, and strangely, I couldn't remember dreaming about anything. My roommate, an older gentleman whom I'd met only briefly before my treatments began, snored softly in the other bed.

A nurse came into the room a few minutes later, bringing two trays of food. She smiled as she set mine on the bed table. "How are you feeling this morning, Major Doyle?"

"Good," I said. "Refreshed."

"That's good to hear." She went to the other side and placed my roommate's tray on his bed table. "Mr. Gardner, your breakfast is here." He snorted, still half asleep. She turned her attention back to me, taking a pillow from the chair next to my bed. "Sit up a bit, and I'll get you situated."

I followed orders, and soon she had me propped against the pillows so I could sit up and eat. Breakfast consisted of eggs, a bit of sausage, two biscuits, and some gravy. I devoured the food and the large glass of orange juice like I was back in the jungle, finishing before she'd gotten Mr. Gardner fully awake and propped up.

She stopped by my bed, her blue eyes widening. "My, my. Someone's hungry this morning."

"Yes, ma'am."

The nurse swung the bed table away from me and offered her arm. "You need help getting to the bathroom?"

"I think I can manage."

"All right, then. I'll be back in a little while to check on y'all. Be sure to eat all your breakfast, Mr. Gardner." He grunted and took a bite of eggs, a few pieces falling onto his chest.

My bladder was about ready to explode, so I swung my legs over the side of the bed. My head swam, but it leveled out quickly. I tried to remember how long I'd been asleep. I vaguely recalled awakening previously to eat and go to the bathroom, but I had no idea how many times. How many days had I missed?

I pushed myself up from the bed and stretched my arms over my head. Bending over, I touched my toes, rocking my torso back and forth. I wasn't especially stiff. Couldn't have been asleep for too long.

After using the bathroom, I decided to take a short walk down the hall to see what was what. As I passed a waiting room, I saw several people with newspapers opened, and I moved closer to read the large headline.

JAPS END TWO-DAY PEACE STALL

Peace? Could it be possible I'd missed the end of the war? I picked up a paper that had been left in an empty chair, scanning the front-page headlines. Sure enough, Japan had surrendered while I was sleeping. The war was over.

I took the paper with me back to my room and sat in the chair beside my bed. I read the article in detail, soaking up the humbling of the once mighty empire with a deep satisfaction. Maybe now the world could somehow find its way back to normal. Maybe I could, as well.

I'd finished reading the paper, had a check-up from another nurse, and returned to lounging in my bed, when Ruby came into the room. Her face brightened, and my heart sped up. But then I saw the small row of stitches on her forehead, and I remembered what I'd done. Shame heated my face as she came over and kissed me.

I pulled her back a bit by the shoulders and examined her forehead more closely. "Is your head all right? You should have the doctor take a look at it while you're here."

She waved a hand in dismissal. "Forget about it. It's fine. I'll get them to take the stitches out soon, and I'll be good as new. Stop fretting over it."

Easier said than done. "How's Hope? Did she come with you?"

"She's just fine. Mrs. Sawyer is taking her to the library this morning. I'll bring her by later this afternoon. I wanted to see how you're feeling and make sure you're awake."

"I feel good, actually. More rested than I've felt in a long time."

She studied me, I suppose a habit from years of taking care of sick people, including me. Still, it always made me uneasy. "Has Dr. Keagan come by to speak with you yet?" she asked.

I started to say no, but the doctor stepped into the room as if he'd heard his name. "Good morning, Major Doyle," he said. "Grace, how are you?"

"Good," she said, stepping away from the bed.

"I see you're awake and already moving around," he said to me.

"Yep. As right as rain."

He flipped through the papers on his clipboard. "Your vitals look good. You seem to have handled the therapy well. It may take some time to know if it's had a positive effect on your mental state and quality of sleep. I'd like to keep you here another couple of days to observe your sleep without medication."

"Two more days in the hospital?" I said, glancing at Ruby. "Doc, that alone might drive me crazy. I'm fine, I tell ya. I just need to sleep in my own bed. Grace can keep an eye on me."

He turned his attention to my wife. "I'd feel better keeping him at least one more night."

Ruby dropped her chin and looked at me like I was a misbehaving child. "You promised you'd do everything Dr. Keagan said."

I'd already been stuck in the hospital for nearly a week. Most likely, Father had left town by now. But I didn't want to take that risk. I needed to get out of the hospital and get my family out of town. But Ruby was right. I'd given my word, and the last thing I wanted was for Dr. Keagan to change his mind and send me back to Brooke.

"All right," I said. "Keep me as long as you need to. Just not a second longer, okay?"

Dr. Keagan grinned. "I knew she'd get through to you. I promise we'll have you out of here lickety-split."

As he headed out the door, Ruby pulled the curtain across the room that separated us from Mr. Gardner. She came over and sat next to me on the bed, pulling her purse onto her lap. "We need to talk over a few things," she said.

"That sounds serious."

"It is." She inhaled and set her expression to that look that meant there was no compromising. "First of all, you can't drink anymore. I don't mean to make that sound like an order, but I reckon by all accounts, it is an order. I've done some reading, and I've seen it myself: drinking makes it harder for you to sleep, not better. Besides, I think you're getting to the point of using the drink to try to reduce your stress. But all it's doing is making things worse."

I'd been thinking the same thing myself, so it was easy to agree with her on that point. "All right. I won't drink anymore."

Her mouth dropped open slightly. "You mean it?"

"I swear."

"Well, all right then. That was easy."

"What's the second of all?"

I could tell right away the "second of all" was not going to be nearly as easy to face. Ruby set her purse on the chair beside my bed. "I don't want to do anything to upset you. I just want to talk. I have something for you to think about, that's all."

My chest tightened, so I took a slow, deep breath. "All right. I'm listening."

"If you feel like you're going to get upset, just say so. I'll stop, and we can talk more later."

"Just get on with what you need to say."

She closed her eyes for a moment, then opened them and looked directly into mine. "I've been thinking and praying on things for a long time now. And ever since Henry and I ran away from Alabama, I've been afraid. I've run nearly halfway around the world and back trying to live between truth and lies. And so have you. You've been fighting and running for your life for years, and even though the war's over, you're ready to keep on running." She paused, twisting her hands together.

I knew what she was summoning the courage to say. She'd already told me once. "So you want to go back, right? Is that what you're trying to say?"

She nodded. "Don't you see? It's all this lying and running and hiding that's weighing on your mind, not to mention all the trauma you've already been through. Medicine and sleep can only do so much for you. At some point, we have to face what we did."

"You didn't do anything wrong. Why are you so determined to be punished for something you didn't do?"

"Believe me, I don't want to be punished. But it's all this lying. It's just not right. I feel it in my soul. I know it in my heart. I have to go back and face my accusers. I have to go back and deal with the consequences of my actions with honesty and courage."

"So you're going to tell the truth? You're going to tell them you didn't kill Chester? That Samuel did it?"

Her face grew pale, and she shook her head. "I don't...I don't know. I was so sure I was doing the right thing by protecting him. I couldn't let him die when he was just protecting himself. And I wouldn't go back and do anything different. No, I don't think I can tell them the whole truth."

I dropped my head back against my pillows, staring at the white ceiling. "Ruby, I can't just stand by and watch you walk to your death. That would be like...like..." I brought my head up and looked into her eyes. "Like surrendering to the Japs. They'd do their best to sweet-talk you into it. And some days, I'd be so miserable, I'd consider it. Especially after losing Henry. At least then, it would be over. But that was the lie. That was the trick of it all. Surrendering wasn't giving up the fight so you could rest and wait to be rescued. Surrendering was worse than fighting to the death. Surrendering meant unimaginable torture. Don't you see? If you go back to Alabama and turn yourself in, and I have to stand by again and watch as one person after another lies about you, or twists the truth to make you into a monster...If I have to watch you go to the electric chair...If I have to explain to our daughter why Mommy's not there..." My voice cracked.

Ruby took my hands in hers. "Matthew—"

"No, listen to me. That would be worse than anything the Japs could've done to me. I'd rather die than surrender to that torture. I can't do it. I can't go down that path with you." I met her gaze, unable to bear the tears that spilled down her cheeks.

"What are you saying?" she asked, her voice shaking as well.

"If you go back to Alabama, and you turn yourself in, I can't go with you. I'll take Hope, and she and I'll go somewhere else. I'll raise her myself. I won't let her suffer through a trial. I won't let her watch her mother die."

Ruby's tears came in earnest now, dripping onto our hands. She bent over them, kissing my hands and laying her head on my legs. My eyes pricked, and I felt my own tears slide as well. I put my hand on her head, stroking her hair. How could I face the rest of my life without Ruby? How could she even think about leaving Hope behind?

I pulled gently on Ruby's arms until she came up beside me. Wrapping my arms around her, I held her close, and she laid her head on my chest. I thought of how hard I'd tried to save her that day in Cold Spring, how I'd fought the freezing water until I nearly drowned myself. I thought of our time together in the Bataan jungle, when I'd fought untiringly to get her to safety. I'd killed those animals in her tent as they'd tried to rape her. I'd charged into a patrol of Japanese soldiers on Mindanao so the plane could take off. And I'd do it again and again to save her if I had to.

But I couldn't save her from herself.

Ruby

I came home from the hospital in a state. As sure as I was of God's leading me back to Alabama, my heart hurt so badly I could barely stand. I must have looked a fright to everyone on the bus. When I got back to the Sawyers' house, I went straight to my room and collapsed on the bed.

I muffled my cries into my pillow, letting the fear and heartache flow out of me. Once I began to calm down, I asked God to give me peace and clarity. Maybe I was wrong about what He wanted me to do. How could I know for sure? Could I really risk losing Matthew and Hope without a sure sign from God that it was the right path? How could He want me to do something that would break up our family?

"Lord," I cried. "Your word says 'What God hath joined together, let not man put asunder.' So how can Your plan be to tear us apart?"

I pulled my knees to my chest, hugging them as my body shook. I pictured Hope and Matthew living on without me, and I thought my very soul would split in two. Was I really to choose between my family and God?

In my worst days of missing Matthew, of wondering if I'd ever truly be whole again without him, I'd often found comfort in the very book of the Bible that bore his name. It spoke to me so clearly. And now, as I sought desperately to understand what I was to do, I turned to Matthew once again. I took Daddy's Bible from the bedside table and scanned the worn pages, my eyes running over stories and lessons I'd practically memorized. At last I came to Chapter Ten, where Jesus sent out the disciples to preach and heal among the Israelites. My gaze fell on his instructions, about how to handle the rejection they would face, the accusations of evil intentions. I couldn't help but think of my own trial nearly nine years before, of the accusation laid against me. Was I to face that again? Would the Lord allow me to be put to death for a murder I hadn't committed?

Slowly, I soaked in the verses:

Fear them not therefore: for there is nothing covered, that shall not be revealed; and hid, that shall not be known. What I tell you in darkness, that speak ye in light: and what ye hear in the ear, that preach ye upon the housetops. And fear not them which kill the body, but are not able to kill the soul: but rather fear him which is able to destroy both soul and body in hell.

Are not two sparrows sold for a farthing? and one of them shall not fall on the ground without your Father. But the very hairs of your head are all numbered. Fear ye not therefore, ye are of more value than many sparrows. Whosoever therefore shall confess me before men, him will I confess also before my Father which is in heaven. But whosoever shall deny me before men, him will I also deny before my Father which is in heaven.

Think not that I am come to send peace on earth: I came not to send peace, but a sword. For I am come to set a man at variance against his father, and the daughter against her mother, and the daughter in law against her mother in law. And a man's foes shall be they of his own household. He that loveth father or mother more than me is not worthy of me: and he that loveth son or daughter more than me is not worthy of me. And he that taketh not his cross, and followeth after me, is not worthy of me. He that findeth his life shall lose it: and he that loseth his life for my sake shall find it.

I closed the Bible and held it against my heart. It wasn't the answer I'd hoped for, but even Jesus had prayed for his Father to find some other way for His will to be accomplished. In the end, Jesus had accepted the Father's will over his own. And I would also.

I just couldn't understand why God wouldn't reveal the same path to Matthew that he'd revealed to me. Didn't the same Bible command me to submit to my husband? How could I reconcile those verses? How could I submit to my husband, when my husband wasn't seeking God?

Lord, I beg you to make things clear. Show me what to do. Work in Matthew's heart to reveal to him the faith he needs. I plead for Your mercy for my doubt. Give me strength, and please, give me peace.

Matthew

My sleep did not improve, but I neglected to say anything about it to Dr. Keagan. Whenever I managed to doze off for periods of time, I'd awaken shivering in soaked sheets, with all sorts of nightmares fading from my mind. At least I didn't raise any ruckus during those times I slept for a couple of hours here and there.

I was released from the hospital late Saturday afternoon with instructions to return for a follow-up visit with Dr. Keagan in a week.

By the time we got back to the Sawyers' house, it was time for supper, baths, reading with Hope, and then bed. Ruby was quiet, saying no more than what was necessary to get through the evening. I couldn't exactly find words myself, so we retreated into our own worlds.

"I think I'll sleep in tomorrow," I said after she'd climbed in bed and turned out the light. "You and Hope go on to church with Mrs. Sawyer."

She was quiet for what felt like a whole minute, and I thought I heard her breath shaking. "All right," she whispered.

I turned over and did my best to fall asleep. But like the other nights, all I could do was think about a life without Ruby. I wavered between anger and heartache, resolve to leave, and doubts. I longed for a drink to numb the conflicting emotions running riot in my head, and cursed myself for becoming so dependent on alcohol. I was the worst kind of husband, I was sure of that.

I tried to pray. I closed my eyes, and I begged God to hear me, to speak to me like He spoke to Ruby. But it wasn't long before my prayers became more of a shouting match in my own head. At the end, I was left with the same gut-wrenching question. How could I leave Ruby to face what lay ahead all alone?

And then finally, sleep came, and I had the most wonderful dream. Gone were the images of Kojima and his patrol closing in on me, my boots sinking further into the mud with every step. There was no gunfire, no screaming, no cries for mercy in a language I couldn't understand. There was just Ruby and me, lying together on an old army blanket spread over the jungle floor.

Above us, palm leaves wave in the breeze. Before us, a clear blue sky stretches over Manila Bay. Ruby lies on her back beside me in her white camisole, her bare shoulder nearly irresistible.

"I can't believe this is real," I say. "After all the time I spent dreaming of you, you're really mine."

She presses her hand against my cheek. "I don't deserve you. Not after everything I did. I should've never left."

I press my finger to her lips. "Shh. None of that matters now. All that matters is that we're together." I lean down and murmur into her ear. "And you know what the best part is?"

"What?"

"Now you have to do what I say."

"Excuse me?" Her grin betrays her attempt at anger.

"It's in the Bible. God says so. You have to submit to me."

"I see." She narrows her eyes. "I should've known you had an ulterior motive. Well, you can forget that." She moves to stand, but I roll her onto her back and gently pin her beneath me. She twists and giggles.

"Oh, no you don't," I say, kissing her to quiet her protests. "You're mine forever now. Don't you know that?"

She sobers. "You promise?"

"I already did. Do you want to hear it again?" She nods. I grin and begin kissing her shoulder, her neck, her chest, as I repeat my vows. "I, Matthew...take thee, Ruby...to be my wife...forever...and ever...and ever...

I stirred, the dream fading away, my heart still full of joy. I tried to go back to sleep. If only I could make the dream come back. But it wouldn't stay. And the morning sun streamed through the window, reminding me of the reality I would face soon enough. But something about the dream stuck with me.

I remembered that day so well. After our wedding, we'd gone up on the ridge to be alone, to make love for the first time, and I'd joked about her submitting to me. But I hadn't really been joking. I'd been counting on her rigid sense of right and wrong, her certainty of the inerrancy of Scripture, to work in my favor. Maybe God had sent that dream to me for a reason.

I got out of bed and went to the bedside table. I opened the top drawer, but it was empty. Ruby must have taken her Bible with her to church. I remembered the Bible I'd received from the missionary in the Manila hospital. Digging through my rucksack in the closet, I came across everything I'd thrown in there over the past several months: the letters from Mary, the picture of Hope and her drawing, and finally, the Bible. I pulled out the drawing Hope had made of all of us together and stared at it with determination. I had to find a way to make Ruby see. This was my hope. I'd find that Scripture again. Was it Galatians? Maybe Ephesians?

I took the Bible over to the bed and began my search, combing through verse after verse that held no meaning at the moment. After a half hour, I found it in Ephesians 5:22-24.

Wives, submit yourselves unto your own husbands, as unto the Lord. For the husband is the head of the wife, even as Christ is the head of the church: and he is the saviour of the body. Therefore as the church is subject unto Christ, so let the wives be to their own husbands in every thing.

In everything. That was it. I just had to convince her that God wasn't really telling her to go back to Alabama. That the blatant words of Scripture outweighed some vague notion in her head that God *wanted* her to do something crazy.

But before I could enjoy even a moment of relief, my eyes fell on the verses that followed.

Husbands, love your wives, even as Christ also loved the church, and gave himself for it; That he might sanctify and cleanse it with the washing of water by the word, That he might present it to himself a glorious church, not having spot, or wrinkle, or any such thing; but that it should be holy and without blemish. So ought men to love their wives as their own bodies. He that loveth his wife loveth himself.

A new thought began to work its way into my mind, one not of my own making. An admonition. An accusation. *Love Ruby more than yourself.*

"I do," I said out loud before I realized it.

Love Ruby...and give yourself up for her.

Give myself up? What was that supposed to mean? That sounded like surrendering, and I'd already explained to Ruby, and therefore to God, exactly how I felt about surrendering. I wouldn't just go marching back to Alabama and surrender. And I couldn't give my blessing to Ruby doing it either.

In my frustration, I tossed the Bible onto the bedside table with too much force. It slid across the top and fell behind the table. "Great," I muttered. "Throwing the Bible around. Just strike me down right now."

I bent over to pick it up, but as I did so, I noticed a folder lodged between the table and the wall. It was the folder Mr. Fisher had given me from Father, and a few of the papers had slid out. It must have fallen back there during my breakdown.

I set the Bible carefully on the table before picking up the folder and papers. I laid the folder on the bed, and looked over the papers that had spilled out. A deed to some land in Cullman in my name. I had no interest in that, especially if it came from one of Father's shady deals.

The next page was something I didn't understand. It had to be out of order. The letterhead was from an attorney I didn't know, and it seemed to be the continuation of a letter. My instincts told me to toss the whole thing, but the third paper caught my attention. It had Ruby's name on it. And it looked like an official court document. An affidavit, maybe. My heart raced, shooting my blood pressure up and blurring my vision for a moment. I set the paper down and calmed myself before trying again.

This time I read every word carefully. The document appeared to be a request to vacate Ruby's conviction on the basis of corruption on the part of the solicitor, Mr. Charles Garrett, and two members of the jury, Richard Moore and Jim Davis. Who was Jim Davis? I didn't have the

280 | JENNIFER H. WESTALL

whole thing. I rifled through the folder, searching for the rest of it. In the end, I found the missing papers and learned that Jim Davis was a juror in Ruby's trial, but I couldn't find anything definitive that explained everything in language I could understand.

I'd have to talk to Father, which was the last thing I wanted to do. I put the papers back in the folder, and considered everything that had happened in the past week. Maybe God was speaking to me after all. Maybe Ruby was right, and we could put the past to rest. Maybe we really could have a future filled with peace. I just had to agree to go back to Hanceville, Alabama.

CHAPTER TWENTY-FOUR

Ruby

September 12, 1945
Birmingham, Alabama

Matthew grew more anxious the closer our train drew to Birmingham. As the whistle blew, and the screeching of the wheels signaled our imminent arrival, he stood from the bench across from me and leaned against the large window spanning our compartment. He peered in both directions, as if he expected us to be boarded immediately, followed by my arrest.

I couldn't blame him. I was anxious as well. But I was also full of so many other emotions competing with the anxiety. Matthew and I had come to an agreement about the path forward, that God did indeed seem to be pointing us home. Matthew didn't elaborate too much on how he'd come to this conclusion, only that he'd prayed over it and had read Scripture that had changed his mind. I was too relieved to pressure him for more of an explanation. I'd prayed for God to change his heart, and He had answered my prayers. In this case, I was not inclined to look a gift horse in the mouth.

Hope scooted along the bench we shared and climbed into my lap. "Momma, are we there?"

After hearing this question for nearly the thousandth time in the past two days, I was finally able to answer yes. She bounced out of my lap and went to Matthew, holding her arms up toward him.

"Can I see, Daddy?" He didn't seem to hear her, so she tugged on his pants. "Daddy, can I see?"

He glanced down as if he'd just remembered she was there. "Oh, sure sweetie," he said, lifting her into his arms.

The picture of him holding our daughter sent a wave of doubt through me once again. What was I about to put them through? I reminded myself that we were in God's hands, and that whatever lay ahead was part of His plans for our good and His glory. I just needed to keep reminding myself of that, over and over, until it stuck.

"Okay, sweetie," Matthew said. "Hop down." He set Hope on the bench beside me and squatted in front of her. "Remember what we talked about. You stay with Mommy while I take care of our things. Do not let go of Mommy's hand."

"Yes, sir." She popped her thumb into her mouth.

"Do you have Velveteen and Skin Horse?"

She nodded.

"Where are they?" She looked around on the bench, not seeing them. "You need to find them and get ready to get off the train."

Hope slid off the bench and crawled on the ground looking for her animals. Matthew sat on the bench across from me, leaning onto his elbows. He lowered his voice as he spoke to me.

"When we get off the train, take Hope to the restaurant and get a bite to eat or something. I'll get our bags unloaded and wait for Asa."

I reached over and took his hands, trying to smile. "I know what the plan is. We've been over this. Everything is going to be all right."

He grimaced. "I just need you to understand that we are not waltzing into Cullman and turning ourselves in with no plan in place. We're going to take the time we need to talk with Asa and your mother, explain everything to them, get a lawyer who can make sense of the mess we're in, and then—and only then—will we go to the authorities."

By this point I was fairly certain Matthew was in this for the long haul, so I ventured to ask what had been bothering me the entire trip. "Why are you doing this? What made you change your mind?"

"I told you why. I'm not going to let you face this alone. And I'm not convinced everything is going to work out the way you think it will. You may still need to disappear again. That's why we have to talk to a lawyer first."

"Oh," I said, unable to hide my disappointment. "I thought you'd accepted that God wanted us to come back. I thought you had decided to trust Him."

"Look, I'm not saying I don't trust Him. It's myself I don't trust. I've been wrong about so many things already. I just want to have a backup plan. You're probably right. Maybe He is leading us back here, and He's going to make everything work out great. You're the one who's always so sure about these things."

I leaned back in my seat and turned my gaze out the window. A backup plan had nothing to do with trust. For me, there was no backup plan. But now wasn't the time to debate it. I was about to face Asa and explain to him why I'd let him believe I was dead for so long. And then I'd have to face Mother.

Fear, excitement, longing, and sadness swirled around inside me, making me nauseous. The train came to a stop, and Hope climbed back into my lap with Velveteen and Skin Horse in her arms. Matthew went out into the passageway and asked a porter about helping with our bags. I hugged Hope close to me, and said another prayer.

Stepping off the train, we made our way into the huge central waiting area, beneath a beautiful domed skylight. I hadn't noticed it when Henry and I had come through Birmingham, our heads down, my heart racing with fear of being discovered. I was still afraid. I couldn't seem to chase all my doubts away, but this time I forced myself to see the beauty around me.

Matthew pointed out to the porter where he wanted him to take our luggage, and then came over to me for a quick kiss. "I'll come and get you both after I speak with Asa. I'm sure he's going to be in shock for a bit. I'm not sure how long we'll be."

"It's all right. Take the time you need." I tugged on Hope's hand. "Come on, sweetie. Let's go get something to eat while we wait."

***

Hope and I had finished a second plate of fried green tomatoes when Matthew came to get us. I tried to read his expression to know how Asa had taken the news, but he looked just the same as he had for weeks now. Determined.

He slid into the booth across from Hope and me, keeping his voice low. "Asa's waiting out by his truck. We already took all the luggage out and loaded it. We're ready to go."

"How did he take it?" I asked.

"I can't rightly say. He was most certainly shocked, but he took it in stride after I explained it all to him a second time through. Poor fella. Maybe I should've explained it in the letter I sent, but I just didn't want to take the risk of putting anything in writing. Honestly, I expected him to already know everything. I figured Henry might've told him too, since he was so freely telling his friends."

I let that last comment slide. "Do they know about Henry?"

Matthew nodded, his eyes flitting to the waiting area. "They got a telegram back in April."

At least we wouldn't have to break that news. I turned my attention to Hope. "Get Velveteen and Skin Horse, and let's go meet your Uncle Asa."

When we made it to the row of cars where Asa was waiting, I couldn't contain myself. I dropped Matthew's hand and took off running toward him. I must have looked like a little girl, and I suppose for a few moments, I felt like one.

Asa, still tall and thin with a full head of gray hair, pushed away from the back of his truck and came to meet me. He threw his arms around me, and I soaked up the joy of feeling the familiar love of both him and Daddy all wrapped into one big hug.

"Oh, Lord have mercy," he said, holding me tight as we rocked from side to side. "It's true."

"I've missed you so much," I managed through my tears.

"Praise the Lord. God is so good." He pulled my shoulders back and studied me with a huge smile. "Let me look at you." His eyes teared up. "I never wanted to believe you were gone. I just...I'm so happy to see you." He pulled me back into his embrace.

"Asa, you haven't changed a bit," I said.

He released me, and I turned to see Matthew carrying Hope toward us. She looked at Asa and me with a curious smile, her hand shading her eyes in the sunlight.

"This must be your sweet angel," Asa said. "She's just as beautiful as her momma."

I held out my arms, and she climbed into them. "Hope, this is your Great-Uncle Asa."

"Hello," Hope said in a tiny voice.

Asa bent down a bit and stuck out his hand. "Well, Miss Hope, you have made this one of the happiest days of my whole life. Did you know that?"

"Weally?" She looked at me like she wasn't too sure, before shaking his hand.

"Yes, ma'am. In fact, I think you're going to spread so much happiness today, we just may have to name this day after you from now on."

She giggled and buried her head in my neck. "How are we going to tell Mother?" I asked.

Asa chuckled and lifted an eyebrow. "Well, I reckon we have just over an hour to figure that out."

The ride to Hanceville was crowded, but I didn't mind. I squeezed into the cab between Asa and Matthew, while Hope sat in Matthew's lap. Asa asked one question after another about what we'd been up to, what happened to us on the Philippines, and how Matthew had survived for the three years he'd been trapped there.

There was enough subject matter for a year's worth of conversations, so we barely scratched the surface of our experiences. Matthew let me do most of the talking, and when he did talk about the Philippines, I noticed he didn't mention Henry. As happy as Asa and I were to be together, Matthew still seemed anxious. He spent most of the ride looking out the window or fussing over Hope squirming in his lap. There wasn't a thing I could do about it, so I kept my attention on Asa, asking him all about the goings on around Hanceville.

"We see James and his family twice a year," Asa said. "They come over around Christmas, and the kids come to stay a couple of weeks with us in the summer. They got four young-uns now. Abner's going on twelve—"

"Twelve?" I exclaimed. "Oh my. I won't even recognize him."

"Percy'll be turning nine next month. Now he's a handful, that boy."

Percy, I thought. They'd named him after Emma Rae's father. I'd only seen him once, the day I'd helped Emma Rae give birth to him. The day Chester Calhoun had died. A shiver ran up my arms.

Asa kept on talking, telling me about the twin girls born two years after Percy. "Ellen and Jennifer are quite a pair. They're right pretty, and boy don't they know it."

"They only come around for Christmas and a couple of weeks during the summer? I suppose James hasn't softened any toward Mother."

Asa frowned and shook his head. "No, I reckon he's softened as much as he's ever going to. He's respectful when they visit, but he calls her Elizabeth. Breaks her heart, but she tries to understand. He don't hardly speak to me a'tall. I figure he spoke to a few family members and found out about my part in his mother's death, and that was that."

"I'm so sorry," I said.

"Well, you can't go back and undo the past. You can just do your best to learn from it, try to make things as right as you can, and move forward with an aim to be better. Took me a long, long time to learn that lesson, but I'm grateful for it. Carrying around bitterness and regret in your heart is like drinking a little poison every day."

I couldn't help but glance over at Matthew. He didn't say anything to acknowledge Asa's words, but I saw the muscles in his jaw working. I realized that maybe I wasn't the only one God was trying to get back to Alabama. Maybe there was healing for Matthew here too.

***

Asa slowed down as we turned onto the dirt driveway. "All right," he said. "Let me go in and prepare her. She's going to be shocked, and she'll probably come flying out of the house as soon as I tell her. But if you just walk in there she might faint dead away."

"Should we stay in the truck?" Matthew asked.

"I'll park down by the barn so you can get out and stretch your legs. She won't think to look for you."

"She knows I'm with you, right?" Matthew said.

Asa cringed a bit and glanced at Matthew. "Well, not exactly. See, when I saw your letter, I was pretty shocked. The last I'd heard, you were killed in action. I wasn't sure what was going on, and I didn't want to upset Lizzy. So once I read you were just needing a lift somewhere, I figured it was best not to say anything. She ain't even expecting you."

"Wow," Matthew said, turning his face to the window. "That's going to be one heckuva surprise."

We drove past the house and my chest warmed at the sight of the familiar farm. Asa pulled the truck into the barn. Hope tugged on my sleeve. "Momma, where are we?"

"This is where Uncle Asa and your Grandmother Graves live. Remember, I've told you about her before. You're going to meet her today."

"I have anudder Gamma?" Her eyes opened wide.

Matthew let out a sigh and rubbed the back of his neck. Beads of perspiration rolled down his forehead. He pushed Hope into my arms and opened the door. "I gotta get some air."

Asa closed his door, and I helped Hope climb out after Matthew. She took off running toward the entrance, and I yelled for Matthew to grab her. He lifted her up into the air, and she giggled.

"Daddy, thwow me up!"

"Not right now, sweetie." He brought her back to the truck and pulled down the gate. "You wait here until Asa comes out to tell us to come inside."

I'd climbed out of the truck and joined Hope on the tailgate. I soaked in the aroma of cows and pigs, grass and lavender. My stomach twisted with excitement. Part of me couldn't wait to hug Mother and tell her how much I'd missed her. But part of me was afraid she was going to be mad at me for lying all these years.

Matthew leaned against the tailgate and let out another sigh. I couldn't stand it anymore. "Is something bothering you?" I asked.

He crossed his arms and looked out over the fields. "I just hope you're staying realistic, is all. It don't do any good to get excited about seeing your brother or his kids. This isn't a family reunion. I mean, I know you're happy to see your mother and Asa. I am too. But we need to be careful and take this one step at a time."

"Listen, I'm seeing my mother today for the first time in nine years. I'm happy about it. And I'm not going to let you spoil it for me."

"I ain't trying to spoil—"

Just then, Mother came flying out of the front door, just like Asa said she would, and ran faster than I'd ever seen her move down to the barn. I jumped off the tailgate and took off running too. We about crashed into each other in the middle, and by the time we were finished with our ruckus, we were both crying and laughing. We probably stood there hugging each other for a solid ten minutes before either of us let go. And that was only to take a good look at each other before we went back to hugging and crying and laughing again.

Once we'd settled down, Mother looked toward the barn. "Where's my grandbaby?"

Matthew carried Hope out of the barn, walking up to us like he was nervous. "Mrs. Graves, this is Hope. Hope, this is your Grandma Graves."

Mother held her hands beneath her chin, tears still streaming down her face. She smiled at Hope, beaming as she looked between us. "Hi Hope. It's wonderful to meet you."

Hope regarded her grandmother for a moment, her face pinched into a thoughtful expression. Then she opened her little arms and reached for Mother, who scooped her away from Matthew. Mother held on to Hope, her eyes closed in pure joy, and Hope squeezed her arms around Mother's neck.

"I give good hugs," Hope said.

"You surely do," Mother whispered, a fresh set of tears rolling down her cheeks. "You surely do."

***

While Matthew and Asa fetched our luggage, Mother showed me all the changes they'd made to the house, but it was the changes in Mother I noticed first. Her hair was completely gray now, and worry lines creased her forehead and cheeks. I couldn't help wondering how much of that I'd caused.

She showed us the addition off the dog run of two bedrooms, just like our old house in town where'd we'd lived until Daddy passed away. Matthew set our luggage in one of the bedrooms, and Mother showed us the main part of the house.

It was mostly as I remembered it, with a bedroom off the back of the living room, and a kitchen and dining area connected to the living room. Asa had added an indoor bathroom just off their bedroom, with a large clawfoot tub. Mother was especially fond of that.

Arranged across the mantle on the fireplace were several photos, including one of me just after I'd graduated high school, and one of Henry in his pilot's uniform. As I drew closer, I realized a Silver Star was displayed next to my brother's picture. It must have been awarded posthumously on Matthew's recommendation and sent on to his next of kin. Taking care not to disturb the medal, I picked up Henry's photo and ran my fingers over his smile. He looked so handsome, so young and lighthearted. My chest ached with pride and loss.

Mother came up beside me, looking at the photo. "Henry sent that to us just after he was stationed in Manila. He wrote me a nice letter telling me how much he loved it there, and what a great time he was having."

"He did love it there for a while," I said, passing her the picture.

Across the living room, Matthew's frown deepened. He cleared his throat. "Mrs. Graves, I...I don't know how to tell you how sorry I am about Henry. He was a good man, and a good friend. I owe my life to him."

Mother set the photograph back on the mantle. "So you were with Henry in the Philippines?"

"I didn't get much of a chance to explain things," Asa said. "Soon as she heard you all were alive, she took off. She doesn't know about you three being together over there."

I picked up Hope, who'd been tugging on my dress hem. "Why don't I get Hope down for a nap, and we can talk for a while? Matthew and I will explain everything."

She nodded and wiped her eyes with a handkerchief. "You can put her down in our bed if you like. She may be more comfortable there for now."

I retrieved Velveteen and Skin Horse from our luggage, as well as a picture book she could look at. I brought Hope into the bedroom and did my best to get her to settle down. But she had so many questions; I thought she'd never go to sleep. After about twenty fruitless minutes, I handed her the picture book. "Look, sweetie, you don't have to fall asleep, but you do have to stay in the bed and rest until I come back to get you. Understand?"

She sighed and pushed the book away. "I want to play with Belteen."

"You can hold Belteen and Skin Horse, but you cannot get off this bed."

"Yes, ma'am."

I kissed her forehead. "I'll be back in a little while. I love you."

"I love you too, Momma."

I closed the door behind me and joined the others at the table. Mother dabbed at her red-rimmed eyes, and Matthew looked pale. "I've been telling your mother about our time on Bataan and Corregidor," he explained. "I just finished telling her about your escape from Mindanao."

Mother looked across the table at Matthew and clasped her hand over his arm. "I cannot thank you enough for what you did to get Ruby to safety."

Matthew dropped his gaze, looking almost ashamed. "You don't have to thank me."

Mother stood and wrapped me in a hug again. "And you! You must have been so frightened, all alone in Australia. And pregnant too. You've all been through so much."

"I don't think we're in the clear yet," Matthew said. "Ruby's determined to turn herself in."

"What?" Mother said, stepping back and looking like she was getting ready to scold me. "Turn yourself in?"

"Ruby, you can't be serious," Asa said from the other side of the table. "That's why you came back here?"

"I can't live this lie anymore," I said, searching their eyes for understanding. "It's a burden my conscience can't bear. And I don't want to live a life always looking over my shoulder. It's hurting us." I met Matthew's gaze. "All of us."

"But why would you want to do this now? Why not wait until Hope is older?" Mother slipped back into her chair like she was exhausted. "She's so young. She needs her mother at this age."

"I've prayed about this for years now, ever since Henry and I left. I knew it was wrong to run away back then. I've just been too scared to face it. But God has shown me that I can trust Him. I can trust Him to provide for my family just as He always has."

Asa turned to Matthew with wide eyes. "And you agreed to this?"

"Agreed? Not exactly. But it was either support her decision, or let her come back here alone. I couldn't do that. So we're here to see what we can work out. No one can know that Ruby's here until we put a plan in place to handle what's ahead. Can we agree to that?"

Mother and Asa nodded. The room fell silent, and I wondered if they were all remembering the last time we'd faced my legal troubles. Maybe they were wondering, like me, if they could face that trauma again. I'd been so determined to set my life back on the right path; I hadn't really considered that it would affect more lives than just Matthew's, Hope's, and mine.

"Well," Asa said, standing up and rubbing his hands together. "Don't know about y'all, but I do my best thinking and planning on a full stomach. How about we get some food on the table?"

"That's a good idea," Mother said.

CHAPTER TWENTY-FIVE

Matthew

September 12, 1945
Hanceville, Alabama

I had rarely seen Ruby look so happy as she did helping her mother prepare supper that afternoon. She was home, and I saw the Ruby I'd known before. The Ruby whose sense of peace and understanding baffled me. The Ruby I'd fallen in love with. Coming back here was good for her. I could see that with my own eyes. And somehow I'd have to find a way to make it last.

Asa and I went out onto the porch to talk until the food was ready, which gave me a chance to ask some questions I needed answering before I confronted Father about the documents I'd found.

"We'll need to get in touch with Mr. Oliver as soon as we can," I said, surveying the farm from a wooden rocking chair.

Asa pulled a long piece of straw he'd been chewing on out of his mouth. "I'm afraid we can't. Mr. Oliver passed away a couple of years back."

That would be a blow. We'd have to bring a new lawyer up to speed. All the same, it might work in our favor to have a different lawyer. As hard as he'd worked, Mr. Oliver had fumbled the ball as far as I was concerned.

"I reckon we'll have to get a new lawyer," Asa continued. "I believe the fella that took over his cases has done a fine job. We can start with him. Name's Pierce, I believe. Stanley Pierce."

"Do you know if there were ever any motions filed about Ruby's case in the years after she disappeared?"

"I believe there was something a few years back. I didn't pay much attention 'cause it didn't seem to matter. The solicitor got in some trouble. Corruption or something. The court reviewed all the cases he tried within a certain time frame, which would've included Ruby's trial. But at the time, with everyone believing she was dead, I'm not sure if the judge reviewed it. Come to think of it, they did overturn a few of his convictions."

"That's promising. I'll go into town tomorrow and set up a meeting with Mr. Pierce."

"Listen, son, not to get too personal, but starting this whole business again might get expensive. You have a plan for coming up with the money?"

"I have enough to get us started. But not much more than that. I haven't been able to get a job since coming back from the war. I'll have to find work around here if I can."

He gestured toward the barn. "You can always help me if you want. I could use the extra help, and the money isn't bad. Don't know if it would be enough, but I'm willing to share the work and the profits if you're interested."

"What do you do?"

"Well, generally speaking," he said, "I shoe horses and mules for most folks in the community, repair their plows, do some minor carpentry work here and there. I could use someone who's a quick study and knows his way around tools. Lately, I've been getting more work than I can handle."

I couldn't believe it. I'd just spent weeks upon weeks looking for a job, and after no more than an hour at the Graves' farm, God plops one into my lap. I'd never imagined myself as a blacksmith, but something about this opportunity felt right. "I'd love to work with you," I said.

Asa stuck out his hand, and we shook on it. "Well then! I reckon it's a deal."

My heart flooded with warmth and gratitude. And the slightest hint of genuine hope that we really were right where we were supposed to be.

***

The next morning I drove Asa's truck into Cullman, thankful Mr. Pierce's office was several blocks away from Father's store. I was surprised at how little the city had changed, and yet how foreign it felt to walk along the sidewalk of the streets where I'd grown up. I realized that I was the one who'd changed. And even though the city wasn't large by any stretch of the imagination, somehow, it felt smaller.

I walked into the office of Mr. Stanley Pierce about ten minutes before nine that morning. A gray-haired woman in tiny spectacles sat at a desk off to the right. She greeted me with a smile as soon as I entered. "What can I help you with, young man?"

"I'd like to speak with Mr. Pierce, please," I said.

She dropped her gaze to a large calendar on one side of her desk, running her finger along it as she bent close to read it. "Let me see. I believe I can squeeze you in, but let me check with him first. Have a seat, and I'll be right back."

I took a seat across from the desk and waited. Nothing about this place spoke of success. The furniture was dated and worn, and cracks spread across the checkered linoleum floor. The walls were dark and bare, with only the windows in the front of the building to brighten it up. I had a feeling I'd be looking for another lawyer before dinner.

"Mr. Pierce will see you now," the receptionist said, breaking my train of thought. "Come this way, please."

I followed her into an office that was only slightly larger than the foyer where I'd been sitting. A young man who, judging from the freckles and auburn curls, couldn't be much older than thirty, stood up from behind the desk and extended his hand. "Stanley Pierce. Pleased to meet you."

"Matthew Doyle."

"This is my secretary and legal assistant, Lilah Pierce." Mrs. Pierce gave him a scowl. "She's also my mother."

"It's nice to meet you both," I said, trying to hide my dismay. There was no way this was going to work. This kid couldn't have tried more than five cases in his lifetime.

"Please, have a seat," he said. "Would you like some coffee?"

"Yes, please."

Mrs. Pierce stepped out of the office, and Stanley took his seat as well. "What can I do for you?"

"Uh, well, I'm not sure yet. I may be in need of your services, but I'd like to ask you a few questions first."

"Shoot." Stanley sat back in his chair and propped his feet up on the desk.

"Well, uh...all right, first of all, how long have you been in practice?"

"Five years. I know I look young and inexperienced, but I spent four years before that working at a firm in Atlanta. I assure you, Mr. Doyle, I'm qualified to represent you in a criminal case."

I let out a nervous chuckle. "Well, this one's a humdinger. Just to be sure, if I explain the circumstances to you, you won't share that information with anyone, correct?"

"Of course. Even if you choose someone else to represent you, I won't disclose anything we talk about here."

I still wasn't comfortable about all this. I gestured to the degree hanging on the wall behind him. "I see you went to school at Mercer. You from Georgia?"

"Originally, yes." Removing his feet from the desk, Stanley leaned forward with a friendly smile. "Can I make a suggestion? Why don't you explain your circumstances to me, and I'll tell you how I would handle it and what my fee would be. Then you can decide if I'm the right man for the job. How's that?"

"Sounds fair."

Mrs. Pierce reappeared and handed me a cup of coffee. "Cream and sugar?" she asked.

"Yes, ma'am."

She disappeared again, leaving me holding the warm mug in my hands. Stanley looked at me expectantly, so I decided to do my best to explain. "All right. I'm not the one needing representation. It would be for my wife. She was convicted of murder and sentenced to the electric chair back in 1936."

Just as I took a breath to continue, Mrs. Pierce returned with two cubes of sugar and poured a bit of cream into my cup. She dropped a small spoon into it and promptly left again. I stirred my coffee, trying to think straight.

"I see," Stanley prompted. "Are you looking to make an appeal?"

"Well, it gets complicated. You see, my wife, who wasn't my wife at the time, was being transported to Wetumpka, when there was...an incident."

"An incident?"

"Yes. Her uncles staged an escape attempt, and she had no knowledge of it. During the confusion, the car she was in crashed into a deep spring. Her body was never recovered, and she was presumed dead."

Stanley sat back and held his fingertips together over his chest. I could tell he needed a moment to process everything, so I paused. "This is beginning to sound familiar," he said.

298 | JENNIFER H. WESTALL

"I'm told you took over the cases for Mr. Oliver. She was one of his clients."

"Yes. I remember reading a summary of the case a few years back when I first took over his files. I believe the last name was...Graves." He paused and his eyebrows shot up. "But you said she wasn't your wife then."

"Yes."

"And she is your wife now...so..."

"Yes."

"Ah, so she isn't as dead as everyone thought?"

"No. She isn't."

The lawyer tapped his index fingers together. After a long moment, he sat up and leaned onto his desk again. "So what is it you're after?"

"First of all, she did not kill anyone. She's innocent, and I want a lawyer who's going to operate from that standpoint. Second of all, I have documents in my possession that seem to imply there have been motions filed to overturn her conviction. I'd like you to look over the papers, tell me what they mean, and find out what is going on in her case before we make any decisions about her turning herself in."

"I'm presuming that folder you're holding on to contains the documents in question?"

I placed the folder on the desk. "Yes. I received these from my father a few weeks ago. He played a role in Ruby's conviction. I don't trust him. I want to know if these documents are legitimate and what exactly they mean."

Stanley picked up the folder and flipped through the papers. "All right. Tell you what I need to do. I'll dig out everything I already have on your wife's case, contact the county clerk and request details on everything that's happened involving the case, and I'll look over these documents as well. I'll need a few days. When I'm ready, we'll meet again, and if you decide to go with another lawyer, you're welcome to take everything I've collected with you."

"Sounds fair."

"Mother!" Stanley called. "Set up an appointment for this gentleman on Wednesday or Thursday."

Lilah Pierce called her assent from her desk.

"I think I'll be able to make sense of everything for you, Matthew, but it'll be better if I paint the whole picture for you when you come back next week, so you can decide how you want to proceed." He pushed away from his desk and extended his hand again. "You can trust me to keep all this information confidential."

I stared at his outstretched hand, my gut uneasy. I stood and extended to my full height as I looked down on him. This kid had better not be lying. I took his hand, gripping it tightly in mine. "Just so we're clear: I want nothing, absolutely nothing, to do with my father. And if you have anything to do with him, I won't be able to trust you either. I do not want him to know anything about my presence here. Not until I'm ready. Understand?"

Stanley swallowed hard, but met my gaze. "I understand."

I released his hand and headed out to the foyer, stopping only to make an appointment for the following Wednesday morning. When I pushed the door open, I glanced back over my shoulder. Stanley stood in his office doorway, watching.

I was going to have to stay on my guard. There'd be no unpacking for us just yet.

CHAPTER TWENTY-SIX

Matthew

March, 1943
Luzon Province, Philippines

For the past two months, we'd been working our way north across the Luzon Province, cutting a main path from Floridablanca, up through Fort Stotsenberg, with a destination of Lingayen Gulf. From the main path, we often took detours east or west, contacting every guerrilla cadre already in our network, and recruiting from barrios we discovered along the way. We avoided the Huks by sending out local scouts ahead of us to report on any tricky situations in our path. It made for slow progress, but this also allowed us to avoid Japanese patrols.

We were nearing Tarlac when I got word that Harris and his cadre were camped only a few kilometers west of us. I debated on whether I should make contact, especially since I was wary of Harris's influence over Henry. But I wanted another shot at bringing Harris into our fold. So we made the trek west and found him camped within a small, abandoned barrio.

After sharing some of our provisions with his men, Harris and I sat alone by a small fire in a dilapidated hut, while he complained about the lack of support for his efforts. He'd conducted several more raids since we'd seen him last, and he'd lost over half his men to death or capture.

"I need supplies, and I need more men," he summarized. "That's just all there is to it."

I'd listened without interrupting, but I'd seen who Harris truly was, and what he was about. I already knew how this conversation was going to go. "I can't send you more supplies. We don't have enough for ourselves. I've told you over and over that these ambush tactics aren't going to benefit the war effort in the long run. All they're going to do is get you and your men killed, and threaten the intelligence efforts of the rest of our network. We're building a strong system across the Philippines, and we're getting good information out to MacArthur about the Japanese troop levels and movements. I'm telling you, staying underground, keeping ourselves hidden, and gathering information is our most valuable contribution. It's also the best way to get out of here alive."

Harris shook his head. "We've had this conversation. I'm not going to just sit around on my behind like some scaredy-cat waiting for MacArthur's gang to rescue me. Maybe you can do that. Maybe you can just give up, but I have to fight. And I'll fight until those dirty Nips kill me."

"I'm not giving up either. I'm fighting just as much as you are, but I'm fighting to get home. You're just fighting out of anger. What good does it do to die out here in the jungle? Just think about it. If you join our organization, you can come to our camp. This place isn't a camp. It's a cemetery. Come back with us to Floridablanca."

"And get ordered around by you every day? No, thank you. Out here, I run my own ship. It may be a sinking ship, but it's mine."

"All right, look. I'll put you in charge of something. Maybe it'll be a smaller ship, but it won't be sinking, and it'll be yours."

He perked up at that. "Like what?"

"I need someone to go into a particularly dangerous section of Manila. It's so dangerous, even the Japs don't go in there. So it's a perfect place to establish an underground intelligence hub. But it's also a perfect place to get killed."

"Sounds like my kinda place," he said, grinning. "What's the catch?"

"The catch is that I'm in charge. You gotta run this operation the way it's designed. You can't go off on your own program. I need to be able to count on you."

"So it's still technically your ship, I'm just borrowing it."

"If that's the way you want to see it."

He considered his options, but not for long. "It's a deal. But one last thing. I want a promotion to Captain."

"Done."

***

Captain Harris and I nailed down the details of the arrangement. He and his men would join us on our journey north and return to Floridablanca with us. He cozied up to Henry pretty quickly, bragging about his dangerous assignment. Of course, Henry wanted to join in on the fun. I squashed that immediately. Not only could I not afford to lose Henry from a personal standpoint, he was my most valuable scavenger out in the jungle. He kept us from starving.

Two nights into our journey north, I was awakened by Diego's intense voice. "Major, we have a problem."

Shaking my hazy dream from my mind, I grabbed my pistol and followed Diego to the position one of our night sentries had taken about fifty yards away from camp. Several of my men had already gathered there, including Harris. I pushed through the circle to find a small Filipino woman seated with her hands tied behind her back and a bandana around her mouth.

"What's going on here?" I demanded. This had to be the work of Harris or one of his men.

But Sanchez stepped forward, one of Diego's best guards, who'd been on my personal detail several times. "Major, she...ah..." he glanced at Diego. "Ah...espiar."

Diego rattled off questions in Spanish, and Sanchez answered quickly. Then Diego turned to me. "He says she is spy. He caught her watching us."

I took another look at the woman, realizing she wasn't much more than a girl. "Get that off her mouth," I said. "And find out what language she speaks."

Diego questioned her, but she said nothing. Her dark eyes darted from mine back to Diego's, before she dropped her gaze to the ground. After several minutes of getting nowhere, I told the crowd to go back to camp and get some sleep. Most of them cleared out, except for Diego and Harris.

I went around in front of the woman and knelt down, trying to get her to look at me. "Diego, ask her again what language she speaks."

He tried both Spanish and Tagalog. She looked up at me and mumbled something I didn't understand. "Tagalog, Major," Diego said.

"Tell her we're not going to hurt her. I just need to know where she came from and what she's doing out here."

He translated. She shook her head.

"Tell her we'll have to kill her if she doesn't talk," Harris growled.

I glared up at him, knowing it wasn't necessary to tell Diego to say any such thing. "Diego, tell her again. We're not interested in hurting her. If she'll tell us where she's from, we'll help her get home."

Diego stared down at me in surprise. "Ah, Major. We do not know if she is spy. We should not promise what we cannot keep."

I stood just as Henry came out of the shadows from the direction of camp. "What's going on?" he asked.

Harris struck a match and lit his cigarette, talking out of the side of his mouth. "Caught a spy. Just trying to get some answers from her."

"Her?" Henry stopped when he saw her seated on the ground, her hands still tied behind her back. "That little thing is a spy?"

"You'd be surprised," Harris said.

"We don't know if she's a spy," I said. "We're trying to ask some questions now."

"You can't just turn her loose," Harris drawled, blowing a puff of smoke out of his mouth. "She knows where we are. If she runs to a Jap patrol and reports us, we're dead. We don't have enough men to defend our position from a raid."

I hated to admit it, but he was right on that point. But still, we weren't in a position to maintain a prisoner. "Then what do you suggest?" I asked.

"Kill her," Harris said, without hesitation.

"What?" I gaped at him, surprised by both the suggestion and his flippant attitude about it. "We can't kill her."

"Why not?"

"For several reasons. First of all, it's a war crime. Second of all, it's just morally wrong. I ain't having that on my conscience."

"That's only two reasons. Besides, you'd rather have the blood of our men on your conscience?"

Harris was insufferable. I couldn't have this conversation with him. I turned to Henry and Diego. "Come on, now. I'm not the only one here who has a shred of decency left, am I?"

Henry and Diego stared back at me, then looked at each other. Diego spoke first. "Major, this is difficult decision."

"Yeah," Henry chimed in. "I don't know. Harris might be right."

"You can't be serious." I paced back and forth, unable to comprehend the choice before me. Coming to a stop, I looked at Diego and Henry directly. "All right, then. Which one of you wants to pull the trigger?"

They both dropped their gazes.

306 | JENNIFER H. WESTALL

"I'll do it," Harris said.

I wasn't surprised. "No one is doing anything of the sort," I asserted. "Harris, go back to camp and get some rest. Henry, go find some food to give her. Diego, we'll sit out here all night if we have to until she talks."

Henry shrugged. "All right. But come tomorrow, we're going to have to move out. Better figure out what you're gonna do."

"Just get her something to eat, and she'll start talking as soon as she realizes she's not in danger."

Henry looked skeptical, but he followed orders. We spent the next several hours feeding her and trying to encourage her to break her silence. The most she would do was nod or shake her head. "Are you from a barrio nearby?" Nod. "Are you helping the Japanese?" Shake. "Are you helping the Americans?" Shake. "Where is your home?" Nothing.

By the time dawn approached, we were exhausted and getting nowhere. Harris approached again, this time with some dried meat and rice for breakfast. If I had to eat another grain of rice, I was sure I would vomit. I took some meat from Harris.

"What did you find out?" he asked, lighting up another cigarette and handing one to Henry.

"Nothing, really," I said. "Just that she isn't helping the Japs or the Americans, and she lives in a barrio nearby, but won't tell us where."

Harris leaned against a palm tree, looking out over the jungle. "I tell ya, I got a bad feeling about this. I've seen this kind of thing before. Most of the locals will help you out in a heartbeat, but there's a few that are either loyal to the Nips or need the reward so bad they're willing to rat you out. Some of them actually believe the Nips will go easy on them if they turn us in."

"Well, I'm not willing to trade my soul to the devil on the off chance she's a snitch," I said.

Henry, who'd been sprawled against a tree sucking on his cigarette, waved his hand around in the air. "Look at this place. We're stuck here in the jungle, going on, what? Well over a year now? And there's no sign of the Americans coming back for us. We're on our own out here. And it's kill or be killed. The way I figure it, I still owe them a few more head shots before we're even."

"Henry, my friend," Diego said as he leaned against the tree to my left. "You must not despair. The time will come for your victory, not your revenge."

Henry shook his head in disgust. "Revenge is my victory."

I looked over to my right at the young Filipino woman sleeping on the ground. She'd closed her eyes nearly an hour ago. "We can deal with vengeance or victory tomorrow. Today we need to decide what to do about her."

"Well, I'm with Harris," Henry said, pushing himself up to standing. "I know it don't feel right, but it ain't worth risking all our lives."

"Agreed," Harris chimed in.

"We don't even know if she's a snitch," I said.

"Don't matter," Harris said. "Sanchez said she was snooping around. What else would she be doing out here in the middle of nowhere? Have you searched her?"

"No."

Harris went over to her and pulled her up to sitting. She jolted awake, letting out a scream. He planted his hand firmly on her mouth. I jumped up and pushed him away from her. "Hey, take it easy."

"She's going to tell the entire Jap force where we are."

"Look, I'll take care of this. You just back off." I went back to the girl and held my palms in the air. "Diego, tell her I'm not going to hurt her. I just need to search her to make sure she doesn't have any weapons."

Diego translated. I helped her up to her feet, and patted her legs up and down. I stuck a hand in her pockets, my cheeks warming. I'd never put my hands on a woman without her permission before, and everything about this felt wrong.

Kneeling down, I patted my hands along the lower part of her legs, feeling nothing. Then I stood and turned her around. I ran my hands down her back. When I turned to her front, I realized I'd have to touch her in areas that I just couldn't bring myself to do. So I turned away and declared her clean.

Harris groaned. "Oh, come on. You can't worry about being a gentleman out here. You're a soldier in a war." He walked over to her and pulled the collar of her shirt away from her chest, sticking his hand inside.

"Harris, that's not necessary," I said.

"Well, looky what we have here." He pulled out a small folded piece of paper and held it up between his fingers. "Not a spy, huh?"

"Let me see that," I said, snatching it from him. I unfolded the paper, unable to read the markings written on it. They appeared to be some kind of shorthand. There was also a crude map drawn in the corner. My stomach sank as I handed the paper to Diego.

"She's a snitch," Harris said. "I told ya. You gotta kill her. She'll report our position."

I walked a few paces away, needing to think this through. "There's gotta be another way." I turned back and tried to find help in Diego's eyes, but he shook his head.

"Major, I know this is difficult decision, but if she is spy, then you cannot let her go."

"So even you agree with them now?" My head was about to explode. "I am not about to kill a girl, no matter if she's a snitch or not! I won't do it."

Henry walked over to me and put a hand on my shoulder. "Matt, you don't have to do it yourself."

"I won't order someone else to do it. That's just as good as doing it myself."

"You heard Diego. We can't just let her go."

I shook off his hand and walked back to the girl. She stared back at me in defiance. "You speak English?" Nothing. "You know what we're talking about, don't you?" Nothing.

Anger swelled in my chest, and I shouted curses to the sky. I turned back to the three of them. "I will not kill her."

They looked at each other without saying a word.

"I'll come up with a solution," I said. "Just give me a few minutes."

I paced back and forth, weighing my options. Killing her was off the table. Releasing her wouldn't work. Taking her with us was out. I could think of only one possibility, and it still put all of my men at risk. But it was the only option my conscience could live with.

"All right, here's what we're going to do," I said. "Harris, go back to camp and get the men started on packing up. We're moving out now. We'll discuss which direction after I rejoin you. Diego and Henry, we're going to blindfold her and walk her at least two kilometers from here. Then you'll tie her loose enough to be able to work herself free after some time, and we'll be long gone by then."

None of them looked enthusiastic about this plan. Harris threw his hands up and mumbled that we'd regret this. Diego gave me his usual, "Sí, Major."

Henry said nothing, but he went to work blindfolding the young woman. After Harris was gone, I walked over to him to help. "I don't know what else to do," I said. "Henry, I can't kill her."

"I know," he said. "Honestly, I couldn't either. We'll just have to be on our guard more so than usual until we get out of the area."

CHAPTER TWENTY-SEVEN

Ruby

September, 1945

Hanceville, Alabama

I spent the next several days soaking up every second of my time with Mother, Asa, Matthew, and Hope. Hope was enthralled with the animals around the farm. Each morning, Matthew would carry her on his shoulders down to the pens and let her do some chores before breakfast. She tossed feed to the chickens, helped dump the slop for the pigs, and insisted on petting the mules. She even tried to milk the cow, but preferred standing by Asa and receiving a few squirts in her mouth instead.

When they returned, Mother and I would have breakfast on the table, and Hope would entertain us with stories of what the animals had been doing all night while we slept. The pigs were especially mischievous, digging holes under the fence and holding parties for the mice. And each morning Hope would ask, "Momma, can I go out tonight and see them?"

"No, sweetie," I'd say. "If they know you're there, they'll just act like regular animals, and then they won't get to have their fun."

She'd frown and think this over. "All right, then."

After breakfast, Matthew spent the rest of the morning with Asa in his workshop. Hope would trudge around with me, her shoulders slumped, as I tried to get her to help with washing floors and windows, preparing food for dinner, and doing the laundry. She was definitely not enthusiastic about doing the "girls' jobs," as she called them. I couldn't blame her, and I remembered how much I'd hated those chores when I was a little girl too.

Just after midday, Hope would go out on the porch and play, waiting for Matthew and Asa to come to the house for dinner. I would sit in the rocking chair and watch her play with Velveteen and Skin Horse, while she kept one eye on the barn the entire time.

One afternoon after we'd been there about four days, she came over and climbed up into my lap. "Momma, I tink Daddy is becoming weal here," she said.

I rested my chin on her head. "What makes you think that?"

"He's getting very dirty."

I couldn't help but chuckle. "You're right about that. He is getting very dirty."

"And he smells bad too."

"We should tell him to take a bath tonight."

At that moment, Matthew and Asa came out of the barn, and Hope jumped from my lap. She leapt off the porch, stumbling, but catching herself, and took off running across the yard toward them. As soon as he saw her coming, Matthew's face broke into a wide smile, and my heart nearly burst with joy. This was how we were always meant to be.

***

That evening, after Hope was tucked into bed, Matthew came into our bedroom newly shaven and smelling as fresh as spring. He held his arms out to his sides and did a slow turn.

"Well, what do you think?"

I closed the book I'd been reading and climbed out of the bed. I walked over to him and inspected him from head to foot. "My goodness. A haircut and everything."

"Your mother cut my hair while you were reading to Hope."

"What's the occasion?"

"A little bunny told me earlier that you wanted me to take a bath because I smell bad."

We shared a laugh, and he pulled me close. I pushed up on my tiptoes and kissed him. "Thank you," I said. "Not for the bath, even though that's nice. But thank you for coming here with me. This is the happiest I've been...well, I suppose it's the happiest I've ever been."

"Do you realize you spent most of your early years dreaming of getting out of this town and finding adventure? And here you are, content to live the quiet life."

"I think we've both had enough adventure to last ten lifetimes. All I want now is to be at peace. I want you to be at peace."

"You think that's still possible? There's so much we don't know about your future."

"We're not guaranteed tomorrow anyway." I slid his shirt over his head and ran my hands over his chest. "Let's just enjoy tonight."

He bent down and lifted me into his arms, carrying me over to the bed. "I think we can manage that, at least for one night."

***

The next day, I once again did my best to convince Hope that sweeping the floors was a good thing. She twisted her sweet little face into a thoughtful expression. "Momma, dey just get dirty again."

I could see the smile on Mother's face as she cleaned the breakfast dishes. No doubt she enjoyed watching me deal with a little version of myself. "I know it will get dirty again. But dirt doesn't belong inside the house. It should stay outside. So we have to sweep it up and take it back out. Now, hold the dustpan for me."

Hope did her best to hold the dustpan, for about five seconds. Then she dropped it and pointed to her feet. "Momma, it's my shoes!"

"What's your shoes?"

"Where the dirt is! It's on my shoes." She plopped down on the floor and stuck her foot in the air. "See?"

"I do see. What are we going to do about it? I think we have to throw them out!" I swooped her up in my arms, and she squealed with laughter. "Out they go!" I shouted, as I marched her to the front door. I swung it open and carried her onto the porch, walked over to the edge, and pretended I was about to toss her into the yard.

She gripped my arms, laughing and screaming at the same time. "No, Momma! I'm not dirty!"

I stopped swinging her and plopped into the rocking chair, cradling her in my arms. I tickled her once more, just to have that sweet laugh fill my soul. Then I hugged her close. "I would never throw you out," I said.

"I know." She wrapped her arms around my neck. "We're just having fun."

While I continued hugging her, I caught sight of the dust kicking up behind a car coming down the long driveway. I jumped up from the rocking chair and hurried inside with Hope.

"Mother," I called. "Someone's here."

Mother rushed to the living room and peered out the window. "I don't recognize the car."

"I'll take Hope to the bedroom."

"I'll go fetch Asa."

I carried Hope into Mother and Asa's bedroom, closing the door behind me. I sat Hope on the bed and handed her the picture book she'd been looking at before her nap. "Here, sweetie. I need you to sit quietly and look at your book for a while."

"But I'm not tired."

"I know, but we need to sit here quietly, please. It's very important. Do this for Mommy."

Her brow furrowed, but she agreed and opened the book. I went to the end of the bed and tried to keep my nerves calm, praying it was nothing. Just a neighbor passing by, or someone needing Asa's services. I was both surprised and disappointed that fear had come over me so quickly. Hadn't I come here to stop all this hiding? I was such a coward.

Matthew

Asa was just letting me rasp the last hoof of the mule he'd been shoeing that morning when Mrs. Graves hurried into the barn with a worried expression. I dropped the mule's hoof and the rasp, my heart immediately racing.

"Where's Ruby and Hope?" I demanded before she could utter a word.

"In the house," she said. "They're fine. There's a man here that says he needs to see Matthew."

"Who is it?" Asa asked.

"He says his name is Stanley Pierce. You went to see him last week?"

I leaned against the nearest post and let out a slow breath, trying to bring my heart rate under control. I could already feel the effects sparking in my vision. "Yes, I went to see him on Thursday about Ruby's case. I'm supposed to meet with him at his office tomorrow morning. Why would he come out here?"

"Maybe he has news," Asa said. He bent over and picked up the rasp I'd dropped. "Let's not jump to conclusions."

"I don't like it," I said. "I don't trust this guy yet. Especially now. I never told him where he could find me."

Asa dropped the rasp into his toolbox. "Well, let's go hear what he has to say."

I took another deep breath, and my heart slowed just a bit. The last thing I needed was another breakdown right now. I walked around Asa and Mrs. Graves as we approached the front of the house. Stanley, who'd been leaning against the hood of the car, came to me with an outstretched hand and a smile.

"Morning folks!" he said.

I shook his hand firmly. "I thought I was coming to meet with you tomorrow morning."

"Yes, well, I got some answers to your questions and figured it would be more discreet if I came to you instead of you coming into town again."

"How did you know where to find me?"

He let out a chuckle. "Oh, that wasn't too hard. I figured you'd be staying with Ruby's folks. Now, shall we get down to business? We have a lot to discuss."

Mrs. Graves went up the steps and opened the front door. "I'll put on some more coffee."

"Wonderful," Stanley said. "I'll just grab my files and we'll get started."

I glanced at Asa, who also looked unnerved by this kid. He wasn't even wearing a tie. What kind of lawyer was he?

As Stanley spread his folders on the table, and Mrs. Graves went to work at the stove, I went into the bedroom to retrieve Ruby. As her terrified eyes met mine, I tried to put her at ease. "It's the lawyer I went to see last week. He has some information about your case."

She let out a sigh of relief and dropped onto the edge of the bed. Hope stood up and hopped a couple of times toward me. "Daddy, you're done already?"

"No, sweetie. But Mommy and I need to talk to someone for a few minutes. Can you stay in here with your book?"

She jumped off the bed at me, forcing me to catch her. "I don't wanna look at my book. I wanna play with you."

"I can't right now. You'll have to wait in here a little longer."

Her little pout turned into a frown. Ruby stood and took Hope from my arms. "I thought you were going to meet him at his office tomorrow."

"So did I. Listen, I'm not sure about this fella. He seems a bit...inexperienced. Maybe you should stay in here."

"Why?"

"I don't know. Just in case we have to make a run for it. The fewer people who see you, the better."

She put Hope on the bed and came over to me, placing her hands on my chest. "Look, we're both a bit jumpy. But let's not overreact. We just have to trust that God is still in control. We are not making a run for it anymore. Just breathe. Everything will be fine." She took my hand and turned back to Hope. "Mommy and Daddy won't be long. Stay in here."

Hope rested her chin in her hands and whined. "Yes, ma'am."

Ruby and I walked out of the bedroom together and over to the table, where Stanley had already taken a seat. The lawyer stood and stuck out his hand. "You must be Ruby."

She shook it and gave him a tight smile. "And you must be Mr. Pierce."

"Please, call me Stanley."

Ruby shot me a quick glance that said everything I'd already been thinking about this guy. I took the seat next to her at the table, noticing the four piles of folders. "So let's have it," I said. "Start at the beginning and spell everything out."

Stanley pulled the chair away from the table and stood in its place. He pointed to the first stack of folders. "First of all, we'll start with Ruby's current situation. These folders contain everything to do with her case. In 1940, Solicitor Charles Garrett and the Sheriff's department were investigated on corruption charges. The result of this investigation was that every conviction between the years 1935 and 1939 was re-evaluated. Almost all of the convictions were vacated, including Ruby's."

"What does that mean exactly?" I asked.

"It means that, officially, Ruby's trial never happened. The new solicitor, Mr. Norton, didn't see the need to retry the case with no defendant present. So, as of right now, she hasn't been convicted of anything."

"That's wonderful," Mrs. Graves said from the kitchen. She walked toward us with her hands clasped at her chest. "You mean Ruby's free?"

"Not exactly," Stanley said. "She was indicted and arrested. Technically speaking, she's still under that indictment. Mr. Norton can, and most likely will, retry the case once her presence has been established. He was put in place because of his reputation for riding out corruption. He's fair, but he'll be eager to make sure there isn't one hint of anything improper."

"Still," Asa said. "That means we have a shot at Ruby being exonerated. Praise the Lord."

I wasn't so optimistic. "So what you're saying is that we have to go through that whole trial again?"

"I wish it were that simple," Stanley said. "Let me continue. Not only is Ruby still under indictment for the murder charge, she could also be charged with a whole list of other crimes involving her escape and flight from justice."

"But if her conviction never happened, then what followed wouldn't have happened," Mrs. Graves said, taking a seat beside Asa.

"It doesn't work that way. At the time, the state had legally imprisoned Ruby, and she *illegally* fled." Stanley set down the first group of folders and picked up the second group. "Now let's talk about what happened during the escape. There's a lot of missing information on that event, and a lot of rumor. It was one of the key events investigated in the corruption scandal. Here's what I know. During the transfer of Miss Graves to the State Penitentiary in Wetumpka, where she would await her execution, the Sheriff and Deputy stopped the car to help what appeared to be a couple of men who'd been in a car accident. Instead, it was an ambush by several men, who Sheriff Peterson claimed were Ruby's uncles, the Kellum brothers. The exact number of assailants was unknown, but Sheriff Peterson and Deputy Frost reported seeing at least three different individuals. In 1939, state officials raided a moonshine operation in Rickwood Caverns belonging to the Kellum brothers. Roy and Eddie Kellum were killed in a shootout."

Ruby covered her mouth and shook her head. "Oh, Mother. I'm so sorry."

Mrs. Graves muttered something about foolishness and went back to the kitchen.

Stanley barely paused before continuing. "Thomas was also killed in a shootout with police in 1940. Another Kellum brother, uh, Franklin...was arrested in 1942 on unrelated charges. Apparently he was questioned about the incident involving Ruby, but he never offered up any information. He's currently in prison, and could still be called on to testify."

Ruby looked at me with damp eyes. We'd only known her uncles for a short time, but I knew she'd grown to care deeply for them. Of course, given their lawless lifestyle, it was no surprise that three out of four of them had ended up dead.

As Mrs. Graves brought cups of coffee to the table, Stanley turned his attention to me. "Now, Matthew, according to your statement at the time, you were traveling to Wetumpka several minutes behind the sheriff because you...let me see..." He shuffled through the papers in the folder, stopping to read from one. "You were so distraught over Ruby's sentence, you weren't thinking clearly. Despite being told by the sheriff to wait a couple of days, you decided to drive to Wetumpka to see if you could see Ruby after she was transferred there. You came upon the scene of the ambush, thought Ruby's life was in danger, and so decided to get her out of there for her own safety, fully intending to return her to custody. The roads were particularly dangerous due to all the rain, and the car slipped into the river, ending up in Cold Spring. You did everything you could to find Ruby, but never saw her or any evidence that she survived the crash." Stanley looked up at me with raised eyebrows. "Did I get it all right?"

I nodded. "That was the statement I signed."

"Indeed. But given your subsequent marriage, I highly doubt any judge is going to believe you had no idea Ruby was alive. Mr. Norton definitely won't. You may be charged with making a false report."

"But he didn't," Ruby started.

Stanley held up a hand to stop her. "You can explain what actually happened later." He picked up the coffee and took a swig before reaching for the third stack of folders. Actually, it was a single folder that appeared to have only a couple of sheets of paper in it. "For now, as you can see, there's very little information here that shows anything about your lives between December of 1936 and now. This will have to be filled in by you two if you decide to allow me to represent you. All I have is a document from the War Department stating that Captain Matthew Doyle was killed in action in the Philippines in June of 1942. That is, obviously, not the case. So we have two people believed to be dead by most of the people who ever knew them, but who are actually alive and well."

Stanley set the single folder down and then reached for the final folder, this one containing several documents. "Now we get to the information your father delivered to you a few weeks ago. I've looked through all the papers in here. A few have nothing to do with your legal situation. They're simply Mr. Doyle's will, some financial documents leaving you money at his death, along with some property near Smith Lake. However, there are also documents here that could be useful in moving forward with Ruby's case, as well as yours if you're charged with anything."

My head was spinning at this point. What a convoluted mess we'd gotten ourselves into. I needed to think, so I stood and paced between the kitchen and the table. Ruby, who'd been sitting there with her head down most of the time, finally spoke up. "You mean Matthew might be charged too? With what?"

Stanley began ticking off possibilities on his fingers. "Obstruction of justice, conspiracy to aid an escape, harboring a fugitive, aiding and abetting, just to name a few. It depends on how far Mr. Norton is willing to go to show there is no corruption in his administration."

Ruby stood and came to me, wrapping her arms around my waist. "Matthew, I'm so sorry."

I held on to her and let her cry. "It isn't your fault. It's mine. It's all mine."

"But what if...what if we both go to prison? What will happen to Hope?"

I couldn't give her an answer, at least not a good one. So I turned my attention back to Stanley as I held Ruby in my arms. "All right. So explain what my father has to do with all this."

"Well, essentially, he started the process to get Ruby's conviction vacated. He's the one who turned over the evidence against Garrett and the Sheriff's Department in 1943. Indirectly, of course. His stroke left him nearly incapacitated. His lawyer filed the court documents you saw, one of them being the motion to vacate Ruby's conviction."

"Why would he do that?" I wondered out loud. "He was the one who worked so hard to get Ruby convicted in the first place."

"Maybe he had a change of heart," Stanley said, closing the folder in his hands. "So, I've presented my findings to you. I know it's a lot to take in. My recommendation at this point would be for Ruby to turn herself in, show the court she's willingly doing so, and we'll find out exactly where the solicitor stands on charges for the both of you. From there, we can put together a plan to fight whatever he comes up with. In all honesty, it won't be easy. We'll just have to take things one step at a time. That is, if you want me to represent you."

I wasn't ready to commit to anything. My head could barely wrap around everything he'd said. "I'll contact you in a day or two and let you know."

Stanley nodded and began stacking his folders. "All right. Just don't take too long. The sooner you take action, the better it will look in the eyes of the court."

He took another gulp of coffee, gathered his things, and shook hands with all of us. Then he promptly headed out the door and drove away. I was pretty sure that was exactly what we needed to do as well.

***

After Stanley left, we sat around the table in silence, each trying to process everything he'd said. The enormity of all that had happened in our lives because of one horrible day at the Calhoun farm was nearly incomprehensible. How would we even begin to unravel this mess?

"Momma?" Hope's small voice came from the crack in the bedroom door. "Can I come out now?" She opened the door and squeezed her knees together while wiggling back and forth. "I have to go tee-tee."

"I'll be right there," Ruby said. She gave my arm a pat and took Hope to the bathroom, closing the door behind them.

Asa and Mrs. Graves took a collective breath, as if we were all waiting for Ruby to leave the room. "What do you think?" Mrs. Graves asked me.

I couldn't stand to look into their hopeful expressions. I dropped my head into my hands. "I don't know yet. I just don't know."

"Maybe she could get a fair trial this time," Asa said. "And Mr. Pierce could make sure those lesser charges are included as options. Maybe she could even take a plea deal."

My skin felt like it was crawling with ants. I stood and paced the area again. "She'd still be going to jail for something she didn't do. Even the escape wasn't her idea. She begged me to stop and take her back."

Asa and Mrs. Graves exchanged a look. I wondered how many conversations they'd had over the years about my foolish actions that day. I'd give almost anything to be able to go back and do things differently.

"What do you two think we should do?" I asked.

Mrs. Graves stood and came over to me, taking ahold of my shoulders. "No one can make this decision for you and Ruby. But I promise you, no matter what, you all have a home here if needs be. Whether it's Ruby and Hope, or you and Hope, or...God forbid...just Hope. We'll be here. Don't worry about what will happen to her."

Ruby came out of the bathroom carrying Hope in her arms. She stopped by the table and met my gaze. "Uncle Asa, do you mind taking Hope down to visit the animals for a while?"

He jumped up from his seat and reached for Hope. "Don't mind a'tall. Come on, honey."

Hope scrambled into Asa's arms. "Can I pet the chickens?"

"Yes, ma'am," Asa said, pushing the front door open.

Ruby watched them through the window for a moment before turning to me. "Can we take a walk?"

"Sure." I went to the front door and held it open for her. We strolled in silence for a while over to the path that led down to the stream. All around us, the crickets and birds chirped away, as if urging us on.

"So, do you want to go first or should I?" I asked.

She took my hand and leaned her head against my arm. "I just don't know what to think. I was so certain about what I needed to do until today. It's not just my own life that's affected by our decision. I mean, I knew that already, but I thought...I thought the worst thing that could happen would be for me to go to prison, and you and Hope would go on without me. I never imagined she might have to live without us both."

I stopped walking and pulled her against me. "She doesn't have to live without either one of us. You heard what Mr. Pierce said. Your conviction's already been overturned. You're not a convicted criminal. If we disappear, we can still raise Hope together."

"And what would her life be like?" She stepped back and looked up at me with tears threatening the corners of her eyes. "Being here these past few days, seeing how happy she is, and how close you are to being happy too, has shown me what's possible for us. This is home. I feel it. Don't you?"

I realized we were almost right back where we were nine years ago, the night before she testified. Here we were, standing on the same path, having nearly the same discussion. Run away, or stay and fight? And once again, my instincts told me to run. But look what had come of that. I didn't want to make the same mistakes again.

"Yes, there is something special about this place," I said. "But home, for me, is with you and Hope. Both of you. No matter where that is."

Her mouth tipped into a half-hearted grin. "Even at the Sawyers' house?"

"Even at the Sawyers' house."

She turned and paced a bit, something I'd rarely seen her do. Hands on her hips, she looked back toward the farm with a furrowed brow. Was she wavering? Was it possible she'd agree to leave and forget about turning herself in?

"Look," I said, "I don't want to go on the run again any more than you do. But how is peace possible with what's hanging over our heads?"

She stopped pacing and smoothed her hands through her hair. "We just have to keep our eyes on the Lord. We're not doing that right now. We're looking at the problem, not the Savior. God is faithful. If we keep our eyes on Him, listen to His still, small voice, and follow where He leads, then the destination will be joy and peace, no matter what the circumstances look like."

"You're doing it again."

She tilted her head. "Doing what?"

I stepped over to her and slid my hands around her waist. "Speaking that foreign language of yours. You have to speak Human to me, love."

She put her hand on my face, looking into my eyes with so much love it actually hurt. "I can't be the Holy Spirit for you. God has placed you here in this moment, as my husband and friend, to lead our family. Take your eyes off me. Take your eyes off Hope. And put them on Jesus. Focus on Him, on getting your path straight to Him. And Hope and I will follow you."

A wave of emotions swelled up inside me, and I thought my knees might buckle. "I don't know how. I've tried. And I've failed so many times already. I can't bear to let you down again."

"That's what I'm talking about, right there. You're still looking at me. Close your eyes."

I closed my eyes, dropping my head down until my forehead rested on hers.

"Clear your mind," she continued. "Shut out every thought, even my voice. Even my presence. Feel God inside of you. Dig down deep into your heart. The pain that's there. The fear, the doubt, the regret. All of it. Can you feel it?"

I nodded, because my throat felt like it was sealed shut. I thought of every failure haunting me, the images coming to mind from the depths of my soul. I saw Ruby healing Hannah, and the doubt that had flooded me that day. I saw Ruby looking into my eyes and telling me she loved me, and I'd turned her away. I saw her kneeling in front of me in her jail cell...*Don't lose your faith for me.*

Ruby...sinking away from me in Cold Spring.

Ruby...sick and wasting away on Bataan.

Henry...

Oh, God. Henry...

CHAPTER TWENTY-EIGHT

Matthew

March, 1943
Luzon Province, Philippines

Japanese patrols were everywhere and the people of the small barrio we'd settled in for a short rest clearly didn't want us there. Many had argued in heated Tagalog with their chief. Several had left. Diego translated the conflict for me, and I promised the chief we would be gone after a few hours of sleep.

But I couldn't rest.

I leaned against the bamboo wall, unable to even close my eyes. Henry and Diego lay on the floor in the hut with me, but from the shifting of their bodies, I suspected they weren't asleep either. Ever since we'd left that girl tied to the tree two days before, I'd been filled with an urgent desire to get as far away as possible. But with the increasing threat of Japanese patrols, we'd been traveling only at night. I'd never been able to sleep well during the day. Too hot, too bright. Too much to think about.

Since I couldn't sleep, I tried to pray. *Lord, I pray I did the right thing. Give us Your protection. Confuse the enemy. If she did report us, I pray You'll lead them in the wrong direction. Give me wisdom, and the strength to do what's right.*

The rat-a-tat of machine gun fire startled me from my prayer. I jumped up with Henry and Diego, seizing my pistol from beside me. Diego cracked the door open to look outside. From behind him, I could see Filipinos rushing across the barrio—men, women, children—running for their lives.

"Diego, tell our men to stay in their huts and hide the best they can."

He sprinted to the two nearest huts where the rest of the men were sleeping. I closed the door and turned to Henry beside me. "Do a quick recon and see if there's an escape route. Hurry."

Henry darted out of the door, heading the opposite direction to Diego. I closed the door and paced, thinking of my prayer. This wasn't the answer I'd had in mind. Diego returned, followed by Harris.

"Japanese patrol," Diego said. "About twenty men. Coming this way. Filipinos are trying to leave."

"We should go too," Harris said.

"I just sent Henry to scout the route." I cracked the door again, peering into the jungle. I couldn't see anything yet. But I also knew that by the time I could see anything, it would be too late. Where was Henry?

"There's no time," Harris said. "We have to go now."

I paced again. Diego watched me, unmoving. I had to decide whether to make a run for it, or stay and hide. It may not even matter. Either way, we might have to fight our way out.

"Major!" Harris shouted. "We need to move out."

"Not until I know which way they're coming from!" I said. "I won't march us right into their hands!"

I went to the door again and cracked it open, praying I'd see Henry coming back. Instead, I watched in horror as the Japs jogged into formation in a circle around the barrio. Kojima marched into the clearing in the center, a small squad behind him. With a sick sensation in my stomach, I watched as the girl I'd left tied up in the jungle came from the back of the squad and spoke to Kojima. She pointed to various huts, including ours.

Harris, peering through a crack in the bamboo wall, cursed and turned away in disgust. "What did I tell you? You should've killed her when you had the chance."

I closed the door again. It was too late to escape undetected. Maybe we could hide, like we'd done before. But the people in this barrio didn't seem nearly as willing to protect us. I had no time.

"All right, listen. We lay low as long as possible. If the Filipinos turn us over, we open fire and scatter. Whatever you do, *do not* surrender. We fire every last bullet we have and keep fighting until we die if necessary. But hopefully, God willing, it won't come to that."

I went to the crack in the bamboo Harris had spied through a moment before. Kojima was barking orders about turning in the Americans. This time he was promising reward rather than threatening death. We were done for.

The people left in the barrio huddled in their huts while Kojima kept on talking. "Japan is your friend. Japan will honor you for loyalty. Show us Americans, and all Filipino can leave. No punishment. All Filipino walk away."

A nervous family inched their way out of their hut. Three of the men from Kojima's squad ran over to them and ushered them out of the hut. Then they went inside as the family scurried away.

"See?" Kojima yelled. "Filipino can go free. If stay, you will die with Americans."

I backed away from the wall, my heart pounding. We were going to die here. This was it. And it was all my fault. I couldn't kill a spy simply because she was a girl. And my weakness was going to kill us all.

330 | JENNIFER H. WESTALL

I met Diego's gaze. "Get over here behind the door. When they come in, you ambush them from the left. I'll take them from the right. Harris, you hit them with everything you got from the far wall."

Harris pulled the few pieces of bamboo furniture in the hut toward the back wall, piling them into a barrier. Bamboo wouldn't provide much protection, but every second he had to fire would count.

I set up on the opposite side of the door from Diego. "Are you ready?"

"Sí, Major."

Harris checked his sub-machine gun and ducked behind the barrier. "Ready."

I peered through the crack. The Filipinos were filing out of the barrio. When the last of them had fled, a thick, dreadful silence followed. The only good thing to come of this, was that maybe...*maybe*...Henry had escaped.

Kojima turned in a circle. "Major Doyle! You surrounded all side! Dis time, you cannot escape. Come out. Your men will be spared."

"That's a lie," Harris muttered. "You go out there, and we're all dead."

"I stay in here, and we're all dead," I said.

"Yes, but we take as many of them with us as we can."

Kojima had no patience to wait for me to decide. "I see you are coward, Major Doyle! You will die coward!"

Three of Kojima's men ran forward with torches, lighting the palm roofs of the huts nearest them on fire. He was going to burn us out. *Oh Lord, where are you? What do I do? Give us your protection!*

The men walked from hut to hut, lighting them on fire. We were only five huts away. *Jesus, save us!*

Then I heard a shout. "I'm here! Stop!"

I looked out of the crack again. Kojima turned as an American soldier walked out of a row of huts, his hands in the air. My heart nearly stopped. It was Henry.

"I'm Major Doyle," he called. "I'm turning myself over. Let the others in the village go."

Kojima pointed his swagger stick at Henry. "Bring him here!"

Two men ran over to Henry, grabbing him by the arms and forcing him to the ground. They kicked him in the sides and head, before dragging him over to Kojima. My fury ignited. I was not going to just stand there and let Henry die. I had to do something.

They dropped Henry in front of Kojima. "Stand up!"

Henry pushed himself up to his feet. Blood ran down his face.

"I have to do something," I said to Diego.

Harris came at me. "If he wants to sacrifice himself for the rest of us, then so be it. We need to get out of here."

For all his bravado, Harris was a coward and was showing his true colors when it really counted. Henry was the true hero here. I shoved Harris back. "Fine! You run! But he's my brother, and I won't stand here and let him die in my place!"

I went to the door, and Diego put a hand on my chest. "Major, I will go with you." I nodded.

Diego flung open the door and walked out ahead of me. As I stormed into the clearing, Kojima's back was to me as he brought his swagger stick down on Henry again and again. I rushed forward, pointing my pistol and firing a single shot into Kojima's back. He dropped to the ground, and everything went completely silent for a split second.

Then chaos erupted.

Bullets and men came from everywhere. I dropped to the ground, crawling toward Henry. The ground exploded all around me. I heard Diego yelling, so I looked to my right. He was swinging his bolo into one Jap after another, like a man possessed. More of my men ran by, stopping to duck behind trees and fire at anything that moved.

I saw Henry, crumpled on the ground a few feet away. I pushed up and ran for him, a bullet catching me in the arm. Ignoring the sharp pain, I dropped down and wrapped my arms under his, pulling him across the ground. Bullets flew everywhere, and all I could do was pray God would keep them from hitting us. But another bullet caught my shoulder, and I fell to the ground with the force. I rolled, and spotted a patch of trees several yards away. I had to get there. I grabbed Henry again, pulling with every ounce of strength I had. We were almost there. Bullets hit the dirt around us. I fired off my pistol in the direction of the Japs.

I pulled Henry the rest of the way to the trees and dropped him to the ground, kneeling beside him to examine his wounds. He was bleeding from the head, and his nose was shattered. I checked his chest. Two bullet wounds.

I shook him. "Henry!"

Nothing.

"Henry!"

His eyes twitched. Opened. I ripped off my shirt and tore it into shreds. The barrio was ablaze. Bullets still whizzed in all directions. Men shouted. But I could only see Henry. My friend. My brother.

I wrapped a strip from my shirt around his head, and ripped open his bloody T-shirt. The holes in his chest bubbled up blood. "Oh God, please help me."

I tore my shirt again and pressed down on the wounds. Henry's hand suddenly covered mine. His eyes gazed up at mine, filled with that steady Graves peace I'd never understood.

"It's all right," he said.

But it wasn't all right. I couldn't lose Henry. Not Henry. *God, not Henry!*

Ruby. Ruby could do this. She could heal him. How had she done it? What had she prayed? I closed my eyes, and I tried to still my racing mind. *Lord, whatever she prayed in these moments, just give me the words. Give me the faith. Heal Henry! Please heal Henry!*

I placed my hands over his chest. How had Ruby done it? I tried to remember my own healing. She'd rubbed my back. And God had come over me. How had she healed Hannah? She'd prayed. Were her hands on Hannah? What about Sheriff Peterson and John Frost? What had she done?

"Lord, I don't know the words! I don't know the words!" I pressed down harder on Henry's chest. "Lord, You can heal him if You want to. I don't know the words, but You are able. You are able."

Henry squeezed my hand again. "Matthew...it's...all right." His eyes closed and opened slowly.

"No," I said, unable to focus through my blurry vision. "No. It's not all right. I'm so sorry."

His eyes closed again. I panicked. I spread my hands over him. "Lord, heal him before it's too late! You've done it before! Please! I *know* You can heal him!" My voice rose until I was yelling at the top of my lungs. "You can heal him! You can heal him! Just do it!"

But nothing happened. No presence rushed in. No help. No healing. Just Henry's spirit drifting away.

I sat back on the ground and groaned. Henry was gone. And I was never getting off this island alive.

CHAPTER TWENTY-NINE

Matthew

September, 1945

Hanceville, Alabama

I sank to my knees from the weight of the memory of Henry's death, and all the anger I'd felt since, that God had ignored my pleas. How could I trust in a God who didn't seem to hear me? How could I ever know what He wanted from me?

Ruby dropped to her knees by my side, and I buried my head in her lap, unable to speak the pain coursing through me. She cradled my head, stroking my hair like I was a child, and it seemed like a long while before I could finally find my words.

"Why didn't He answer me?" I asked. "I begged God to heal Henry. I knew He could do it. I've seen Him work through you. I tried to remember what you did, what you said when you prayed…but it was like…I was all alone, and God never heard me. He just stood by and let Henry slip away."

At first, Ruby said nothing. She only caressed my head as I did everything I could to hold myself together. Her hands were soothing, comforting the rage that often sent my heart rate and blood pressure racing. I breathed in her peace, and somehow, the breakdown I was anticipating never came.

"Do you remember when my daddy died?" she asked. "You were so sick, and so was he. I prayed for God to heal both of you. I begged and pleaded. I thought if I just had the right kind of faith, if I believed strongly enough, with no doubt in my heart, that God would heal you both. But then, Daddy died, and it nearly crushed my faith. I remember thinking that there was no way I could serve a God who demanded such perfection before He would save me from so much pain."

She grew quiet for a while, stroking more of the anger from my mind with her fingers. I did remember when she lost her father. At the time, I'd thought about how unfair it was that someone like Ruby, so full of faith, should lose a kind father who loved her so much, when my loathsome father was walking around as healthy as could be.

"But over the years since Daddy's death, God has shown me His faithfulness and love over and over. He brought Asa into my life, and the gift of healing, and you...the greatest earthly love I could've ever imagined...and He brought me through war, hunger, violence, and all the fear that came with it. And He gave me our daughter to get me through those awful days when I thought I might never see you again. And none of those things might've ever happened if Daddy had lived."

She paused again, and I thought about all the awful things that had come from my terrible decisions. But for the first time, I also considered all the good. I had memories I'd shared with Ruby that nothing could ever replace. And Hope. I had Hope.

"Don't you see?" she said, lifting my head until our eyes met. "It's not that I'd trade Daddy for any of those things. I can't think on things from my earthly perspective like that. God sees this huge tapestry of intertwining lives, people who need each other and need Him in ways only He can weave together. That's what gives me peace. Knowing He loves me, even when I take my eyes off Him and stumble. He lifts me up again. Even my sin, my poor decisions, my heartache and loss, are all woven into the beautiful tapestry of my life. And my life is interwoven with yours, and ours is interwoven with Hope's and Henry's, Asa's and your father's. We're all woven into this massive tapestry that somehow radiates God's glory and love. Even the death of His own son is woven in.

"Don't you think the disciples thought that was the worst possible thing that could've happened? Don't you think Peter agonized over his denial of his friend and Lord? But that horrible, gut-wrenching day that Jesus died was the very day that made it possible for us to be with Him forever. That's what I mean when I tell you to keep your eyes on Him, and not on me. Not on Hope. Not on anything this world throws at us. Because the story didn't end with His death. Jesus lives."

She was right, like always. I knew she was right. I'd been fighting so long to keep everything under control, to stay ahead of disaster, that I'd actually walked right into it time after time. I couldn't keep living this way. But what now?

I stood and pulled Ruby up with me. "I think...I *know* things have to change. I have to change. I'm not exactly sure where to start, but I think it's this decision on whether to stay and face the charges against us, or leave and try to start over. I just...I need to pray."

She came up on her tiptoes and kissed me. "I'll be waiting at the house for you. Take your time. Listen to the still, small voice. And know that I love you. Whatever God says, wherever He leads you, I'll follow."

She turned and headed back down the path, leaving me in the immense quiet of the woods. I thought back over every decision I'd made since meeting Ruby, and how each one had been an attempt to keep control. *Just like Father.* He'd once told me I was more like him than I knew. And he was right.

"Lord," I said, speaking softly to the quiet woods. "I've been so wrong. I've spent a lifetime looking at all the wrong things, trying to fix what was wrong, or trying to save Ruby or Henry, when I'm not the Savior. I can't do it anymore. I can't keep running, but it's all I've known. Tell me what to do."

Surrender.

"God, how do I surrender? Everything I know tells me surrendering is worse than dying. Better to fight to the end and die on my own terms, than to surrender. I don't know if I can."

The birds and crickets continued their song, and for several minutes, nothing more came to me. I'd never known how to hear God. I'd always just listened to Ruby. She was the one who knew Him. She was the one who led me...*She's been leading me.*

"Lord, teach me to me lead my family. Show me how to follow You. What do you want me to do?"

Surrender.

I walked further down the path, continuing to pray. I wanted something more, something I could see or touch. Some sign that I was supposed to walk Ruby into the sheriff's office and turn her over to the very people who were prepared to kill her nine years previously. Surrender? With no plan? No way to escape if she wound up right where she'd left off?

Surrender.

If we left town and went to Mexico, we could live together in peace. No one chasing us down. No need to lie about our names. Who would care? But would Ruby ever look at me the same? Would I ever be able to please God? What kind of husband would I be? What kind of father? Did I want to keep fighting and fighting to stay one step ahead, when all I'd ever done was make one wrong turn after another?

I turned around and walked the other way, still arguing with myself. I prayed for God to still the anxious thoughts in my mind. Where was that still, small voice Ruby spoke of?

Surrender.

Was that it? Just the one word? I stopped walking and closed my eyes, pushing every thought out of my mind. I was done fighting. I was done trying to control everything around me. I knew what I was supposed to do.

When I opened my eyes, Ruby walked toward me from down the path. "I couldn't go far," she said.

"It's all right. I'm glad you're here."

"Have you made a decision?"

I nodded and pulled her into my arms. "You've been right all along. It's time to surrender. Not just to the authorities. It's time for me to surrender everything I have to God. Even you."

Ruby

Two days later, I did my best to explain to Hope where I was going. But how do you tell someone who isn't yet three years old that her mother is going to jail and may not be coming back? I had no words for that.

In the end, I spent the morning playing with her down at the barn, watching her care for the animals she'd come to love. I hugged her close while Asa sat in his truck, and I did my best not to cry.

"Mommy has to go someplace for a while, sweetie. I may be gone for several days. Maybe a little longer."

"Who will take care of me?" she asked, sitting in my lap on the front porch.

"Daddy will be here to take care of you, and so will Grandma and Uncle Asa. Remember when Mommy would go into work sometimes at the hospital, and Grandma would give you supper and your bath...and she'd read to you and put you to bed?"

She nodded.

"Well, it will be like that for a while. And I need you to be a good girl and do what Grandma says. You mind her and Daddy, and Uncle Asa too."

"Can I go wid you?"

"No. You have to stay here and help take care of your animals. They would miss you if you left. You have to feed them and play with them every day."

She squirmed in my lap until she was on her knees facing me. She put her hands on my cheeks and studied my eyes. "Momma, are you sad?"

"Yes, sweetie." I took her hands in mine. "I'm going to miss you. But I'm going to pray that I'll see you real soon." It was all I could do to hold back my tears. I was determined not to scare her.

"Maybe you should just stay here."

"I wish I could, but I can't."

She scrunched up her face, thinking this through. I looked over her head at Matthew leaning against the truck. His hands were shoved into his pockets, and he kept his eyes on the ground. Mother stood at the front door behind the screen, trying to hide her sniffles.

I couldn't take it much longer, so I pulled Hope into a hug. "No matter what, you make sure you know how much Mommy loves you. All right?"

"All right, Momma. You make sure you know Hope loves you."

My throat closed up. I couldn't remember why I was doing this. Was it really so important to turn myself in now? Why couldn't I wait until she was older? Did it have to be so soon?

Lord, give me strength. Help me keep my eyes on You.

I waved Mother over, and she scooped up Hope from my lap. "Come on. Let's go check on the chickens and see if any of those eggs have hatched yet."

I stood and hugged Mother's neck. She whispered in my ear. "God bless you and keep you. I love you. Don't worry about Hope. She'll be just fine."

I watched Mother and Hope walk down to the chicken coop behind the barn until they disappeared, and then I released the tears I could no longer hold back. Matthew came over to me as I walked down the steps, wrapping his arm over my shoulder.

We climbed inside the truck, and I laid my head on Matthew's chest. None of us spoke a word from the time we pulled out of the driveway until we pulled into a parking spot behind the courthouse and jail. We sat in silence, unwilling to move.

Matthew gripped my hand. "We'll wait until you're ready."

I leaned my head against his shoulder and ran my free hand up and down his arm a few times. We'd spent nearly the entire night before just clinging to each other in the bed. I couldn't hold on to him tight enough. But it was time to let go.

"I'm ready," I said.

We all three stepped out of the truck. Across the parking lot, Stanley got out of his black Chevy sedan and headed for us. He had on a suit and tie, and his expression was serious. He shook Matthew's hand and then Asa's before turning to me. "Big day. You ready to go shock everybody?"

"I don't know about that. There's no way to prepare for this moment. I suppose I'll just have to get it over with."

We crossed the lot, with my hand still clutching Matthew's. Stanley walked in front of us, stopping as we reached the door. "All right. I'm going to go inside and speak with the sheriff so he won't be quite so shocked when you walk in. I'll come and get you in a few minutes."

Stanley disappeared into the brick building, leaving me to wonder once again if this was really the right thing to do. Matthew stepped over to the wall, pulling me into his arms. I stood there with him and rested my head against his chest.

"Last chance," he said. "We're sure we want to do this?"

I couldn't speak, so I just nodded. His chest rose with his deep sigh and we stood together in silence again. There are no words for the moment right before you jump off a cliff. All I could do was hope Jesus was at the bottom to catch me.

The door opened, and Stanley motioned us inside. Matthew took my hand again, leading me into the foyer of the sheriff's office. It looked exactly the same as it had nine years ago. The cold cement walls and the sharp odor of concrete made my stomach swim. Every nerve in my body protested at being back in this place.

I followed Matthew over to the desk where the sheriff sat, in the same place it had been before. Only this time, it wasn't Sheriff Peterson siting there. Instead, John Frost stood behind the desk, his mouth agape when he saw me.

"I...I thought you was playing a joke on me..." He turned wide blue eyes to Stanley. Then he stared back at me. "Ruby? You're...you're alive?"

I nodded. "I know this must seem a bit...um, shocking. But here I am. I'm turning myself in."

John blinked, but he didn't move. He looked from me to Matthew, and then at Stanley again. "You weren't joking."

"No, Sheriff Frost. I wasn't." I took a quick glance at Stanley. He almost seemed to be enjoying this. "Now, I believe the correct procedure here would be for you to book Mrs. Doyle and place her in a cell."

"Mrs. Doyle?" John said.

Matthew cleared his throat. "We married a few years back."

John rubbed the back of his neck and shook his head. "All right. Well, yes...we need to get you booked." He came around his desk and went to a filing cabinet, where he pulled out some papers. He dropped two of them on the floor, and I noticed his hands shaking as he picked them up.

I dropped Matthew's hand and went to John as he stood. "Listen," I said quietly. "It's all right. I won't be any trouble. I know this is confusing and all, but I'm here to make things right, not cause a stir."

He put the papers back in order, refusing to look me directly in the eye. Instead, he looked over my shoulder at Stanley. "I'll have to get Mr. Norton down here."

I reached out for his arm, and when my hand touched him, John pulled it away quickly. Our eyes met then, and he looked at me like Matthew had that day he'd seen Hannah healed. Like I was some kind of witch. Then he darted back to his desk and started explaining the booking procedure.

I'd expected some surprise and lots of questions—those were sure to come soon—but the look on John's face was more than surprise. It was fear.

Matthew

Hope talked continuously through supper, though the rest of us only half-listened as she told us about the adventures the animals had been on that day. I was numb all over, and I couldn't get more than a few bites of food down my throat. It was tight with emotion, and sore from my efforts to control them.

What have I done?

The question repeated itself over and over in my mind. Ruby was back in jail, and this time was so much worse than the last. There would be no bond, I was sure of that. And John had informed us of the strict visitation policy now in place, most likely due to my actions nine years ago. I would only be able to see Ruby on Tuesday and Sunday afternoons. Unless, of course, they decided to arrest me too. Mr. Norton would be informing Stanley of the charges we both might be facing in the next few days.

"Hope, eat your okra," Mrs. Graves said.

"I don't like oh-ka, Gamma." She pushed the slimy green vegetable across her plate. I couldn't blame her. I'd never liked the stuff either. I especially didn't want any now.

"We don't waste food," Mrs. Graves said. "Take a bite."

Hope stabbed a piece of okra with her fork and took the smallest bite possible. She scrunched up her face and shook her head. "I don't like it."

Mrs. Graves gave up. I reckoned none of us had the heart to make her miserable over something as insignificant as okra. I pushed my creamed corn and sweet potatoes around on my plate too. "Sweetie," I said, "why don't we go take a walk for a bit while Grandma cleans up?"

"Can I see the chickens?"

I stood and went around behind her chair, lifting her into my arms. "The chickens will be going to bed soon. Just like you. But we'll take a quick peek in on them."

I could barely look at Mrs. Graves and Asa, so it was a relief to get out of the house for a bit. I set Hope down so she could run off the last of her energy. We made our way along the worn path beside the pasture fence. She chased the fireflies, jumping for them as they darted out of reach. I watched her with a deep sense of loss, wondering how badly Ruby and I had just altered her whole life.

What if it was all for nothing? What if I'd just thought I'd heard God's voice directing me? *Lord, I hate to doubt you so quickly, but I could sure use some reassurance here.*

Hope and I reached the chicken coop, and I picked her up so she could watch them peck around in the dirt for a while. When they started flying up into the trees to roost for the night, I said, "Looks like the chickens are going to bed. I think it's your turn too."

"Will you wead to me?"

"Of course." I carried her back to the house and set her on the front porch. "All right, now go let Grandma get you ready for bed, and we'll read."

"I don't want to go to bed." She dropped her chin and looked at me with large, pitiful eyes that tugged on my heart. "I wanna wait for Momma."

I sat on the edge of the cement porch, exhausted and out of words. "Mommy won't be back tonight, remember? She said she would be gone for a few days. So you can't wait for her to come back. You have to go to sleep."

"I don't wanna go to sleep," she said, more insistent this time.

"I know. And I understand. But sometimes we have to do things we don't want to do. And tonight, we both have to go to sleep without Mommy."

She seemed to be grasping for the first time that Ruby wouldn't be coming home tonight. Her eyes filled with tears. "I don't wanna go to sleep!"

"Hope—"

"Go get her!"

"I can't."

"I want Momma!"

She was sobbing now, and my chest nearly cracked wide open. I had to make her stop, but I knew nothing I could say would bring Ruby home. I tried to take Hope's hands, but she pulled them away. She rubbed her eyes and sobbed even louder.

"I want Momma!"

Mrs. Graves came out onto the porch, stricken with worry. "What's going on?"

"She wants Ruby."

Hope ran over to Mrs. Graves and clung to her skirt. "Can you go get Momma?"

Mrs. Graves met my gaze, and I could see the same heartbreak in her expression that was tearing me up inside. What could I do? Mrs. Graves picked her up, shushing her as she swayed back and forth. But Hope was inconsolable.

"Momma...has to...wead to me," she gasped.

"Hope," Mrs. Graves said. "You have to calm down. Mommy can't come home tonight. You're going to have to let us take care of you."

"I want Momma!"

Mrs. Graves went in the front door, but I could still hear Hope sobbing for Ruby. I climbed into the rocking chair, resting my head in my hands. Hope's cries only grew louder. What could I do? I couldn't make Ruby appear. I gripped the sides of my head, pressing with all my might. I ached for a drink to numb the pain, but I'd promised Ruby before I'd left the hospital that I'd never revisit that path, and there was no way I was going to let her down again.

"I want Momma! Go get Momma!"

I couldn't take it. I couldn't handle breaking Hope's heart. What was I doing? Could I somehow still get Ruby and make a run for it? Why would God have me put my daughter through this pain, when she had no ability to understand it? I had to have misunderstood. That made much more sense than believing in a God who could be so cruel.

"Lord, what do I do?"

Surrender.

I pushed up from the rocking chair and paced the front porch. There was that word again. That was all fine and good when it came to walking alongside Ruby. Surrender meant going back to jail. But how did it help me with Hope? Was I supposed to surrender to the pain? Give in and crumble? What did it mean to surrender after we'd already physically surrendered everything?

Her cries continued to escalate. I had to do something, but I had no idea what. This was Ruby's area of expertise. I still barely knew my own daughter. But I had decided to lead my family, and I couldn't let someone else take care of Hope. I had to learn to do it myself.

I swung open the front door and ran through the house to Mrs. Graves' bedroom. She held Hope in her lap on the bed, trying to rock her. Hope's face was red and streaked with tears.

I went to her and lifted her into my arms, pressing her against me. "Hope, I'm right here. I know you're scared. I am too. But I'm right here with you, baby. I'm right here with you."

"I want Momma," she cried, but with a little less force than before.

"I know. I want Mommy too. It's all right to be sad. But God is with Mommy, and He's with us. We're not alone. Mommy's not alone. You're never alone, little bunny."

I swayed her in my arms, feeling her tense body relax. She still whimpered, and her tears fell down my neck onto my shirt. Mrs. Graves came over and wiped her nose with a handkerchief, rubbing her hand over Hope's back.

"When...is...Momma...coming home?" Hope asked between gasps of air.

I had no answer. I met Mrs. Graves' worried expression. "As soon as she possibly can," I said.

"But Daddy...Momma has...to wead to me...and I hafta...help her...sweep tomorrow."

"I'll read to you," I said. "I'll read to you as much as you want. We'll read about Velveteen and Skin Horse, and we'll sweep, and we'll play with the animals, and we'll stay so busy that Mommy will be back before we know it."

She lifted her head off my chest. "Can we go to the pigs' party at night?"

I tried to smile. "Yes, sweetheart. We'll go to the pigs' party."

I hugged her close for a few more minutes before her breathing returned to normal. My back ached from walking the floor with her in my arms, but I wouldn't trade that pain for anything in the world. Once Hope was finally settled down, I turned to Mrs. Graves. "All right. Show me what to do to get her ready for bed."

"I can do that," she said.

"No. She's my daughter. And it's my job to take care of her. I want to do it. Just...just show me what I need to do."

Mrs. Graves walked me through every step of preparing Hope for bed, from bathing her to dressing her, brushing her hair, and finally settling into the sofa to read *The Velveteen Rabbit.* Hope held on to her stuffed animals and snuggled into me as we opened the book. It was all I could do to keep my voice steady.

"There was once a velveteen rabbit, and in the beginning he was really splendid. He was fat and bunchy, as a rabbit should be; his coat was spotted brown and white, he had real thread whiskers, and his ears were lined with pink sateen..."

Hope yawned, and her body relaxed against me as I read about the toys in the nursery snubbing the plain little rabbit. Across the room, Mrs. Graves sat knitting in her chair beside Asa, who puffed on a pipe while he read to himself.

"...Even Timothy, the jointed wooden lion, who was made by the disabled soldiers, and should have had broader views, put on airs and pretended he was connected with Government. Between them all the poor little Rabbit was made to feel himself very insignificant and commonplace, and the only person who was kind to him at all was the Skin Horse."

"Daddy," Hope interrupted me. "What's...dis...dis-abled sholders?"

"Soldiers. They're men who fought in a war and got hurt."

"Like you? Momma said you were a sholder and you had to get better."

"Well, not exactly like me. I was sick when I came back, and I did have to get better. But I'm not disabled. Some brave men get hurt very badly in war. They might only have one arm or leg. They might have lost their sight. Some..." I had to clear my throat. "Some, like your Uncle Henry, died while keeping others safe. But God kept me from getting hurt too badly."

She sat quietly, thinking this over for a moment. "Okay. You can wead now."

I glanced at Mrs. Graves, who continued with her knitting. She didn't look up, but I could see her struggling with her tears. I cleared my throat again, and continued reading as Skin Horse explained to Rabbit what it meant to become real.

"'Real isn't how you are made,' said the Skin Horse. 'It's a thing that happens to you. When a child loves you for a long, long time, not just to play with, but REALLY loves you, then you become Real.'

'Does it hurt?' asked the Rabbit.

'Sometimes,' said the Skin Horse, for he was always truthful. 'When you are Real you don't mind being hurt.'

'Does it happen all at once, like being wound up,' he asked, 'or bit by bit?'

'It doesn't happen all at once,' said the Skin Horse. 'You become. It takes a long time. That's why it doesn't happen often to people who break easily, or have sharp edges, or who have to be carefully kept. Generally, by the time you are Real, most of your hair has been loved off, and your eyes drop out and you get loose in the joints and very shabby. But these things don't matter at all, because once you are Real, you can't be ugly, except to people who don't understand.'"

I kept on reading for a little while longer, until Hope's breathing deepened, and her eyes closed. Then I put the book down and gently lifted her into my arms. I stopped in front of Mrs. Graves on my way to the side door. "Thank you for helping me," I whispered.

She smiled up at me. "You're a good father, Matthew. You and Hope will get through this, and she'll be all right."

I prayed she was right. I took Hope across the dog run and into her bedroom. Then I laid her on the bed with Velveteen and Skin Horse, covering them up. She rolled onto her side and let out the deep sigh of peaceful sleep. As much as I ached for Ruby, I was grateful for the moments I'd just shared with Hope.

I knelt beside her bed, folding my hands together. "Lord, bless us with Your presence and mercy. Help me be the father You desire me to be. Comfort Ruby tonight. Give us all the peace of knowing You are in control, and that we can trust our lives in Your hands."

CHAPTER THIRTY

Ruby

September 25, 1945
Cullman County Jail, Alabama

I realized fairly quickly that my prison stay this time would be very different from my first time. Not only was I allowed visitors only on Tuesday and Sunday afternoons, but I was on a strict schedule of eating, restroom breaks, and one hour of exercise each day. When he was around, John Frost barely spoke to me, or even looked at me for that matter. Mostly, the other two deputies took care of everything.

There were three men locked up with me, and I did my best to keep to myself, but it was difficult to ignore them. Mr. Cain was charged with drunkenness and beating on his wife. Mr. Phillips had robbed some stores. Mr. Dodson had stolen cash from a family farm where he'd been working. I didn't speak much to any of them.

I was thankful that at the very least, I had a cell to myself at the end of the row. I spent nearly all my time reading Daddy's Bible and praying for Hope and Matthew. I counted down the hours until Tuesday afternoon, when I could see them again.

About two o'clock, John came into the cell area and walked to my door. Once again, he barely looked at me. "Ruby, I'm taking you over to the courthouse to meet with your lawyer and Mr. Norton to discuss your case. Just so we understand each other, you will be handcuffed the entire time. I expect you to comply with any order I give you. Understand?"

I stood from my cot, unsure if I should walk to the door or stay where I was. "John, I told you. I won't be any trouble. I'll do whatever you say."

"It's not you I have to worry about," he muttered, turning the key in the lock. He stepped into the cell and held out the handcuffs. "Come on over here and stick your hands out."

I did as he said, and he locked them on. The metal dug into my wrists, but I didn't say anything. Taking me by the elbow, John led me down the walkway and out into the main office. He released me long enough to stop at his desk and get some things out of a drawer, before gripping me by the elbow once again and leading me down the hallway behind the office. We passed several doors before exiting into the bright sunshine and hot air.

"John?" I said as we turned for the courthouse. "Why are you so tense around me?"

"Tense? I'm not tense. Just wary, maybe."

We walked up the four cement steps that led into the back of the courthouse, and John opened the door for me. We headed down one more hallway before stopping at one of the doors. Inside, Stanley Pierce and Matthew stood near the window. I didn't want to make John any more nervous than he was already, but as soon as I saw Matthew, my heart leapt. I stepped to the side as Matthew came to me and wrapped his arms around me. I slid my cuffed hands over his head and hugged him close.

"How is Hope? Is she all right?"

"She's just fine. She misses you and asks for you every day, but we're getting through it."

He released me, and I slipped my hands back over his head. I turned to John and held my hands out, expecting him to unlock the cuffs, but he shook his head. "You gotta wear those the entire time you're out of your cell. Already went over that."

"Is that really necessary?" Matthew asked, his voice tight with frustration.

John looked at Matthew like he was mad. "Look, I was nearly killed the first time she escaped. I'm not risking anything of the sort again."

"But we came back willingly," Matthew insisted.

John's expression hardened. "After nine years!"

"After being trapped in a war!"

"All right, fellas," Stanley said, stepping between them. "Let's take this down a notch. Matthew, stop talking. You might say something you shouldn't. John, thank you for bringing Ruby over for our meeting. I trust you'll be waiting outside the door, and I'll let you know when we're finished."

John stared at Matthew a moment longer before turning to go. When the door was closed behind him, Matthew let out a huff. "That's ridiculous, and he knows it."

"It's all right," I said. "He's just doing his job."

There was a knock at the door, and a tall, lean man in a dark suit stepped inside. He looked to be about fifty, with graying sideburns and serious frown lines. He stuck out a hand to Stanley, who shook it quickly.

"Mr. Pierce," he said. "How are you today?"

"Afternoon, Mr. Norton. I'm well." Stanley gestured to Matthew and me. "This is Matthew and Ruby Doyle."

Mr. Norton sized us up. "So, the prodigal couple returns."

I felt Matthew tense beside me, but before he could respond, Stanley spoke up. "Shall we get down to business? I'll need to meet with my clients when we're done, and time is short."

Mr. Norton set his briefcase on the table and took a seat. Matthew and I went around the table to sit beside Stanley. He had no briefcase, no notepad. Nothing. Had he even prepared for this meeting?

Mr. Norton pulled out a file and slipped on his glasses. "All right, I'll be as brief as I can be. Right up front, I want to say that I appreciate you've both come forward willingly, and that I have taken that into consideration in putting together an offer for a plea. However, do understand that what we are about to discuss is the only offer on the table. I'm not here to negotiate." The solicitor looked at me over the rim of his glasses, as if he wanted to make sure I was listening, before returning his gaze back to the papers in front of him. "Now, we'll start with Mr. Doyle. Due to what's come to light, there is enough evidence to charge you with conspiracy to aid and abet Mrs. Doyle's flight from justice, accessory after the fact, and making a false statement to police."

"What false statement?" I asked.

"The statement you signed giving your account of what happened during and after the escape. It is clear now that you knew she was alive and did not disclose that to the sheriff's department."

"I had no idea—"

"Matthew," Stanley interrupted. "Let me do the talking." He leaned onto his elbows and turned his attention to Mr. Norton. "Now, Ernest, you and I both know you'd be hard pressed to prove that Major Doyle knew Mrs. Doyle was alive at the time he signed that statement. The truth of the matter is, he had no idea. Besides that, everything you want to charge him with lies outside the statute of limitations."

"You would prefer I pursue the other charges, then?"

"I would prefer you stick to charges that reflect my clients' actual conduct and character. As for Major Doyle, he has broken no laws. He came upon a scene that appeared dangerous to the life of Mrs. Doyle. He drove her away from the scene with every intent of returning her to the custody of the Cullman County Sheriff's department. Are you telling me you want to go to trial and try to prove to twelve men that Major Doyle—a man who risked his own life to save the lives of countless others in the Philippines, a recipient of a Silver Star—you want to try to prove that you know his intent on that day? I think you would better serve the Cullman community by dropping these ridiculous charges for Major Doyle. Then we can have a real conversation about a plea deal for Mrs. Doyle."

Mr. Norton raised an eyebrow and looked between us before letting out a sigh. "He is still guilty of aiding and abetting her continued flight from justice. The very fact they are married and were together in the Philippines confirms that fact."

"All that is confirmed, Ernest, is that Major Doyle discovered that Mrs. Doyle was alive only after the war in the Philippines began. Yes, they were together, but it was while the entire group of islands was under siege. Could he really be expected to return her to custody at that time? How could he have even achieved that? Let's be reasonable. As soon as he returned home from the war and was released from the hospital, he and Mrs. Doyle made their way back here to bring this case to a resolution. Like I said: You would be better off dropping any charges against Major Doyle."

I could see that Mr. Norton was giving way, and I silently thanked the Lord for sending us Stanley. He might not have looked prepared, but he had Mr. Norton singing an entirely different tune than when he'd first come in.

"All right," Mr. Norton said. "I won't press charges against Major Doyle. However, I will not waver one bit on the charges against Mrs. Doyle."

"I wouldn't expect you to," Stanley said. "Now, let's hear what your idea of a plea deal is for her."

I could see that Mr. Norton was none too happy with the way things were going. His back stiffened as he turned his attention to me. Matthew's hand slid over to mine beneath the table.

"Mrs. Doyle, although your conviction from 1936 was vacated, the indictment for murder still stands. You will still be charged with murder if you wish to go to trial, which still carries the maximum penalty of life in prison or execution. You will also be charged with fleeing from justice, conspiracy to escape, escaping custody, and the attempted murder of two sheriff's officers. Do you understand the charges as I've read them to you?" He peered at me over his glasses again.

"Yes, sir."

"All right then, if you plead guilty to voluntary manslaughter and fleeing from justice, I'll drop the other charges. I'll recommend the maximum sentence of fifteen years in the state penitentiary."

"Fifteen years?" Matthew said. "That's crazy."

"I assure you, Mr. Doyle, that this sentence is fair considering the seriousness of the charges. I believe your wife was sentenced to the electric chair after her first trial. I would think that fifteen years would be a welcome change in the outcome."

I squeezed Matthew's hand, and he didn't say anything else. Mr. Norton gathered his papers and put them back into his satchel. Stanley pushed up from his chair and extended his hand over the table to Mr. Norton. "Thank you for your time today. We'll discuss the offer, and I'll contact you as soon as they've come to a decision."

Mr. Norton took Stanley's hand with a deep frown. "I look forward to hearing from you. Like I said, this is a very reasonable offer. I don't wish to be unjust. But there were serious illegal acts committed, and restitution must be made."

"I believe we're all in agreement on that. Good day, Mr. Norton."

"Good day, Mr. Pierce. Major. Mrs. Doyle."

After the door closed behind him, I turned to Matthew with the most determined expression I could muster. "All right. So, I think we should take the deal. What do you think?"

Matthew turned in his chair and took my hands in his. "I don't like it one bit. You shouldn't have to serve fifteen years for something you didn't even do. Ruby, you've already suffered so much. How much is it worth? Are you willing to miss Hope's entire childhood to continue down this path?"

I couldn't fathom going fifteen years without being a part of Hope's life. My stomach swam with nausea. But I'd started down this path to protect Samuel from what I knew would be an unjust system. And there was no reason to believe that system had changed for the better.

I turned my gaze to Stanley, who'd taken a seat at the table across from Matthew and me. "What do you think we should do?"

He folded his hands together and laid them on the table, looking at us thoughtfully for a while before he answered. "I read over the transcripts from your first trial. And I read all of Mr. Oliver's notes as well. There were definitely some irregularities in that first trial that I believe will work in our favor this time. The footprint evidence for one. It never should've been admitted, and I don't believe it would be this time around. Judge Thorpe would likely preside over your case, and he's a stickler for procedure. That would work in your favor. There was also a damaging testimony from a pastor that I believe we could make sure was omitted. But all in all, I can't guarantee anything. There is a chance you could end up convicted of murder again."

"Just ain't right," Matthew said, standing and pacing the room. Eventually he stopped and let out a deep sigh. "Ruby, maybe it's just time to tell the whole truth and let God take care of the rest. Isn't that what this whole journey has been about? Turning yourself in and walking in the truth?"

"Matthew, you know I can't."

Stanley looked from me to Matthew, and then back to me again. "What's the *whole* truth?"

I met Matthew's gaze and gave him a slight shake of my head. He went back to pacing, so I answered Stanley's question. "I can't say."

"Well, my instincts tell me that you should take the deal. It's not the best deal I've ever seen, and there might be some ways to get the sentence down, but there's no telling what kind of sentence you might get if you go to trial."

Matthew stopped and leaned back against the wall. He ran his hands through his hair and then threw them out to the side. "Well, I reckon we've done started down this path of surrendering. We need to see it through and trust God knows what He's doing."

With all the fear swirling around inside of me, it did my heart good to hear Matthew putting his faith in God again, even if it wasn't very enthusiastically. I just hoped our faith and our family could weather another storm.

***

We decided to pray and give it a few days before we made a final decision about the plea deal. Stanley stepped out of the room for a few minutes to give me a chance to say goodbye to Matthew, and we stood together near the door, his arms around my waist, mine still cuffed around his neck. He pressed his forehead to mine, and I closed my eyes.

"I don't know if I can walk through this fire, Ruby," he said. "I've been reading my Bible, and I've been praying just about all day, every day. But I just don't know."

"I'm scared too."

"Remember the day you were being transferred to Wetumpka? I came with Asa and your mother to see you, and Asa read the story of Peter stepping out of the boat and walking on the water toward Jesus."

"I remember."

"You tried to tell me that day to hold on to my faith. You were right, and I didn't understand what you were saying. But I read that story again, and I got it this time. I saw what you meant. Peter took his eyes off Jesus. He looked at the crashing waves and the storm raging around him. That was when he began to sink. I get that I'm supposed to keep my eyes on Jesus."

My chest warmed, and I couldn't help but smile. "It only took you nine years to finally get it. But that's better than a lot of folks, I suppose."

He lifted his head and managed a smile. "I'm pretty hard-headed, I reckon. You want to hear the verse I'm memorizing? It's what gets me through every day right now."

"I'd love to."

"It's Galations 2:20. 'I am crucified with Christ: nevertheless I live; yet not I, but Christ liveth in me: and the life which I now live in the flesh I live by the faith of the Son of God, who loved me, and gave himself for me.'"

I laid my head on his chest and soaked up every ounce of the joy God had given us for this moment. "I love that verse. I'll keep it in my heart every day too."

There was a knock on the door, signaling our time was up. Matthew leaned down and kissed me deeply. "I love you so much."

"I love you too." I slipped my arms over his head and walked over to the door.

Matthew opened it for me, and we stepped into the hallway. Stanley shook Matthew's hand. "I'll be in touch soon," Matthew said. Then he turned back to me. "And I'll see you Sunday afternoon. I'll bring Hope this time."

Once again, John took me by the elbow and led me out into the parking lot behind the courthouse. We made our way back to the jail, heading down the hallway that would come out behind his desk. But about halfway down the hallway, my stomach took a nosedive, and I nearly lost my balance.

"Ho—hold on," I said, reaching for the wall to keep from falling over.

"What's the matter?" John asked.

"I don't feel so well." I closed my eyes, nausea making the bile in my stomach rise. "I think I'm going to be sick."

"Come on. There's a restroom up ahead."

He supported me now as he led me the rest of the way down the hall. We came out into the foyer of the jail and crossed the room to another door. I was nearly doubled over at this point, and John threw the door open. I rushed inside, bending over the toilet and heaving into it.

To his credit, John stayed by my side, keeping my hair out of my face as I retched again. When it finally stopped, I stood and leaned back against the wall. John went out and came back with a glass of water. He looked at me like he wasn't sure what to do with me. Then he unlocked my cuffs.

"I reckon you ain't going anywhere at this point," he said.

I drank the water, trying to get the taste of vomit out of my mouth. "Thank you," I managed.

"Are you sick?" he asked then rolled his eyes. "I mean, I see that you're sick, but do you feel like you've got something contagious? Maybe it's just nerves."

I put my hand on my stomach and drank another gulp of water. "I don't know yet. I just feel a little dizzy. But my stomach feels better now."

"Why don't you go lay down on your cot, and I'll check on you in a bit. If you think you need a doctor, I'll call one in for ya."

He walked me back to my cell, and I laid down on the cot. A few minutes later, John brought me an extra blanket. "Thought you might get the chills or something."

"Thank you," I said.

He stood over me like he wanted to say something else. He glanced around the cell and grabbed a chair from the corner, pulling it over beside my cot. "Ruby, can I ask you something?"

I nodded.

"That day your uncle shot me. Did you know? I mean, did you know what they were gonna do?"

"No. I would never have agreed to something that was going to hurt anyone else. I'm so sorry, John. I really had no idea what they were doing."

He sat back in the chair, his expression softening. "I reckon...I reckon I always knew that."

He went quiet for a few minutes. I closed my eyes, the nausea slipping back into my stomach. He cleared his throat, so I opened my eyes and looked over at him. He was leaning forward on his elbows, but he kept his gaze on the floor.

"Ruby...I...I need to ask you something else. That day, after I was shot. You helped me, didn't you?"

"Well, I tried. I helped get you into the car. And I did my best to tend to you. Matthew showed up, and we both tried."

"I heard you," he said, raising his gaze to mine. "I was gone. I was out of it, but I had this sense that I wasn't in my body somehow. And then I heard you praying. You asked God to bless my spirit, to work a miracle in my body and soul. You asked Him to heal me."

All I could do was speak the truth. "Yes. I did."

"And He heard you. He healed me. Whatever you...can do. Whatever your gift is...it worked. Even the doctors couldn't explain it. Said I had all the signs of being shot, just none of the actual blood loss. They said I should have bled to death. Same for Sheriff Peterson. No one could explain it."

"God loves you, John. He knew you'd serve a greater purpose one day. Your work on earth wasn't finished yet."

He let out a long breath and rubbed his hand over his face. "I got a couple of kids, you know. Sharon, she was just a baby back then. My wife, Sue, she'd have had to raise her all alone. But you...you did something amazing."

"God did something miraculous. It wasn't me."

"You're forgetting something. I was there that night old Emmitt Hyde tried to kill himself. I knew it then. I knew you did something. You healed him too, didn't you?"

"God healed him. I just obeyed."

He looked at me as if he didn't know what to make of all this. My stomach churned again. "John, I may need a pail or something."

He jumped up and left the cell, not bothering to close the door. Soon he returned with a metal pail, placing it on the floor by my bed. "I better get a doctor in here."

"I don't think a doctor's going to help matters," I said. I closed my eyes again, doing the math in my head.

"Why? You know what you got?"

I finished counting and opened my eyes. "Yes, and it's not contagious. It's a baby."

John's eyebrows shot up. Slowly, he backed away from me and sat in the chair. "That's something new. I ain't never had a pregnant prisoner before."

"God's got an interesting sense of humor, doesn't He?"

"That's one way to look at things."

I rolled onto my back and stared at the ceiling. God's timing was always perfect; I knew that in my heart. But I had to wonder at this particular instance. Was it really His plan for me to have a baby in jail? Didn't I have enough on my plate?

***

I spent the next few days trying to convince myself that I wasn't really pregnant, that I just had a stomach virus. I couldn't remember a whole lot about my first pregnancy, especially the first few months when I'd been so focused on finding Matthew. I couldn't even remember if I'd been sick since I'd been recovering from malaria at the time.

But this pregnancy was doing its best to sear itself into my memory. I spent most of the days on my cot or kneeling over my pail. It was awful. I could barely stomach any of the food John brought me. He finally started bringing me just plain toast and water. The other men in the cellblock complained about the smell, but there wasn't anything that could be done about it. John even called in the doctor, who agreed that I was most likely pregnant and just had to get past this bit of morning sickness. I took issue with that description. It was all-day sickness.

On Sunday, I was determined to appear as healthy as possible for my family's sake. There was nothing that could be done for me at the moment anyway, so adding another worry to Matthew's burdens seemed needless. By midday, I'd gotten myself cleaned up and was sitting in the chair awaiting my visitors.

But to my surprise, it was James that walked in to see me. I jumped up from my chair and met him at the cell door. He looked so much older than I remembered him. Much more like I remembered Daddy looking. His leathery skin was deep brown from being in the sun, and his dark eyes held the same hardness they always had.

"James," I said, unable to hide my surprise. "What are you doing here?"

He stopped at the door, clearly uncomfortable. He held on to a newspaper and slapped it against his hand. "I reckon I needed to see for myself that you was alive. It's just...so crazy. I mean, you were dead. But now, here you are."

"I'm so glad you came. I've wanted to say so many things to you over the years. I'm so sorry. So sorry for everything."

He held up his hand to stop me. "Now, hold your horses. We can get to all that in a minute. I don't have a long time for visiting today. I just wanted to see you for myself. You don't have to go apologizing."

"Oh, but I do. I was such a terrible sister. I never realized how much you sacrificed for us, and I made it seem like I was ungrateful for all you did to take care of me when I was growing up. And then, I kept that awful secret from you. I'm so sorry, James. I really am."

His eyes widened, and he came closer to the bars. "*You're* sorry? Ruby, I'm the one that needs to apologize. I was too hard on you and Henry. I didn't have to be that way. I know that now."

"It's all right," I said. "We can start over."

"And then I never supported you during your trial. That was unforgivable."

"Nothing's unforgivable."

He shook his head, his eyes filling with sorrow. "When you don't apologize to the people you love before they're gone...that's unforgivable. I don't deserve forgiveness. Especially when I've been so stingy in offering it myself."

"It's not too late."

"It's too late for me to make things right with Henry. He *is*...I mean...he's not coming back, is he?"

I shook my head. "He died in the Philippines."

"Yeah, I read about that in the paper back when they presented Mother with his Silver Star. I guess I just hoped that since you weren't really dead, and Matthew wasn't really dead...maybe Henry wasn't either."

Mother. James had called her "Mother." Maybe there was still hope for that relationship. We stood in silence again, and I thought of how Henry had always brought out the laughter our family needed during hard times. "I sure do miss him," I said. "He would have me laughing all the way through this awful situation."

"He did manage to find fun in the most dire circumstances. I should've appreciated that more. You know, when I heard that he'd died, I realized that I had no more family left in the entire world. Both my parents, and then you, and then Henry. It was the loneliest I've ever been."

"Can I ask you something?"

He nodded.

"Why did you shut Mother and Asa out of your life if you were lonely?" I moved over to the cell door and got as close to him as I could. "I know she isn't the woman who gave birth to you, but she loves you just as much as if you were her own. Can't you forgive her and Daddy? They meant well. They just wanted you to be happy."

"Were we?" he asked. "Were we happy?"

"I thought so. Until Daddy died. And then it got harder. But we still had joy. You started your own family, and I saw you with Abner. You were a wonderful father. I'd bet you still are."

"I have a whole houseful of young'uns now. You should come see—" He stopped as realization hit him. "Ruby, what's going to happen to you now?"

"I'm not sure yet. Probably prison for a long time."

He held up the newspaper in his hand. "You know, you've caused quite a stir. The entire state's fired up about the mysterious Ruby Graves, escaped murderess, whose conviction was vacated. Everyone wants to know where you've been. Some papers are reporting sightings of you in various places. I think someone said they saw you in New York, another said you were in Texas. Apparently you've done a lot of traveling while you've been hiding from the police."

"Let me see that," I said. He passed the paper through the bars, and I opened it up. It was the *Birmingham News*, and the front-page headline read, "Fugitives From Justice Return to Face the Music." The subtitle continued, "Where Has Ruby Graves Been Since Being Convicted of Murder in 1936? Sources Say She's Been On the Move."

"Oh my goodness," I said. "They're just making up stories about me."

"Maybe you should set the record straight."

"I hate newspapers. They crucified me the first time I was on trial. There's no telling how far they'll go this time. Now the *Birmingham News* is writing about me? I hope no one shows up at the farm. Hope will be so confused and scared."

"Who's Hope?" he asked.

"My daughter."

His eyes widened, and he took a step back. "You have a daughter? Wow, I think we have some catching up to do."

"How long do you have? It could take a while."

Just then, John appeared and approached my cell. "Ruby, your family's here. I'm going to move you to a meeting room so you can visit." He stopped at the door and looked at James. "You're welcome to come along if you like."

"I don't think so," James said. He stepped back from the door. "I'm sorry, Ruby. We'll catch up another time. I just...can't yet."

"All right," I said as John entered my cell. "Take care of yourself."

"You do the same." James watched me a moment longer before heading back out the way he'd come. I watched him go, my heart both glad for his visit, but sad that he couldn't find peace with Mother and Asa.

I turned to John and stuck out my hands. He grinned and shook his head. "I reckon you can walk to the meeting room without being cuffed."

I tried to smile, but a bout of nausea sprung up on me. "Thank goodness. I hate those things." I swallowed, and the feeling passed. We headed out of the cell and down the walkway. "John, don't say anything to my family about me being pregnant. I'll tell them myself when I'm ready."

"Sure thing, but how are you going to explain throwing up every ten minutes?"

"I'll just have to make sure I don't do it while they're here."

He glanced at me with raised eyebrows. "I'll put a pail outside the room, just in case."

CHAPTER THIRTY-ONE

Matthew

September 30, 1945
Hanceville, Alabama

I was learning new lessons each day, some of them difficult to swallow, others coming naturally. Playing with Hope in the evenings was my salvation from missing Ruby. In many ways, it was like having Ruby there with me. But spending each night alone in the bed, thinking about her and missing her, wondering if we'd ever be together again, was a hard lesson in trusting God. It drove me to my knees night after night. But the real lesson I learned in those dark hours was that joy was possible in the midst of much heartache.

I stopped begging God to save Ruby from prison or the electric chair. Instead, my heart began to desire God's presence and comfort for all of us, regardless of our circumstances. And in the moments when I felt the most sorrow, when I'd think on Henry's death and all the anger and sin that had followed, or the uncertainty of our future, a gentle, quiet presence came along beside me. If I was caught up in my pain, I would miss it. But most nights, I felt the Lord beside me, and I continued to ask for His wisdom and guidance.

Just when I thought I was making progress in my effort to completely surrender to God's plans for our future, we made our family visit to Ruby on Sunday afternoon. It started with a tense moment, with James coming out from the cellblock as we waited to see Ruby. I think Mrs. Graves gasped the loudest, but we were all surprised. He didn't say anything, but he did give a polite nod to Mrs. Graves before he walked on by. It was all I could do to keep from going after him. But I forced myself to stay in my seat, and instead, I prayed God would work on James's heart.

Once we were settled in the conference room and Ruby came in, things took a turn for the better. Although she looked pale and tired, Ruby set a bright smile on her face and made us all feel at ease. Hope clung to her mother the entire time, telling one story after another. She even ratted me out for taking her down to see the hogs in the middle of the night. Hope scrunched up her shoulders and giggled, while Ruby pretended to be mad at me.

"Well, sounds like Daddy is taking great care of you, sweetie," Ruby said. "But he might be in trouble for late night parties with the pigs."

Everything was fine until it was time to go. Then I learned another lesson about joy in the midst of sorrow. Hope sobbed, and she begged Ruby to come home with us. I could see how much it hurt Ruby to tell her she couldn't come yet. Mrs. Graves couldn't watch. She buried her head in Asa's neck as I tried to coax Hope away from her mother.

"We'll come back and see Mommy again soon," I said. "I promise."

"But why?" Hope sobbed. "Why can't she come home wid us?"

"It's hard to explain, sweetie. Mommy has to stay here for now. But we'll pray every night that she can come home as soon as possible."

Hope had wrapped herself around Ruby's legs. I couldn't bear to pull her away, but I had to. Tears streamed down Ruby's cheeks, and Hope squirmed in my arms. "Momma, please come home wid us. You don't hafta stay here."

I held on to Hope as she stretched her arms toward Ruby. *Dear God, what are we doing to her? Will she ever recover from this? Please help me calm her.* I pressed my hand against Hope's back, turning her into my chest and holding her as close as I could. I shushed her and rocked her from side to side.

"It's going to be all right, little bunny. Mommy is fine. And we are all just fine too. We'll just go home and take care of the animals, and keep the house ready for when Mommy can come back. Remember how much fun we had yesterday? That hog tried to dig under the fence, but you told him a thing or two, and he straightened right up."

She stopped squirming and slid her arms around my neck. "He was being a bad pig."

"Yes, he was. But you told him what's what, didn't you?"

"Yes, sir."

"We better get back to the house and make sure he isn't causing trouble again."

"Yes, sir." Her voice, so quiet and sad, broke my heart. But at least she was calm. I mouthed, "I love you," to Ruby, not wanting to get Hope worked up again.

Ruby pressed her hands to her chest, her tears still flowing, and mouthed, "I love you too."

The ride home was tough. Hope sat in my lap, straddling me with her face pressed against my chest. She kept her arms around my neck, and she barely moved the entire ride. I rubbed her back and prayed over her, asking God for peace in her little soul.

By the time we got back to the farm, Hope was asleep, so I carried her into Asa and Mrs. Graves's bedroom, where she took her naps every day. I laid her on the bed, and stood in the doorway watching over her for a few minutes to make sure she was asleep. That was when it hit me.

My lesson for that day was to make every moment with the ones I loved count. And that it was time to make peace with my father.

***

Later that afternoon, I stood on the doorstep of my childhood home, poised to knock, yet unable to do so. Although so much of it looked the same—the huge magnolia trees to my right and left, the blooming white ginger lilies my mother had cared for so meticulously, and their fragrant smell on the breeze—so much had changed. I knew when I walked through those doors, Mother wouldn't be there to greet me, and I already felt the huge hole of her absence.

I raised and lowered my hand countless times. They had to know by now that I was back in town and that Ruby was alive. It was all over the papers. Would they be surprised to see me? What would I say?

Lord, there's still so much hurt and anger in my heart. I don't think I can forgive Father. I don't have the strength. Only You can forgive him. Somehow, You're going to have to give me the forgiveness I can't muster on my own. Help me to see Father the way You see him. Help me to remember all that I've been forgiven for. Be near to me, and calm my spirit.

I took a deep breath, and rang the bell. Within a few seconds, footsteps approached, and Ellis swung open the door. He looked exactly the same as I remembered him: dark as night, slim, silvery hair, and a warm smile he didn't often share with visitors at the door, but had always shared with me.

"Mr. Matthew," he exclaimed, his face lighting up. "We been hopin' you'd come by, and now here you are!"

I stretched my arms out and walked right into a hug, which seemed to take Ellis back for a moment. I reckoned white folks didn't go around hugging the help, but as soon as Ellis had smiled at me, I'd been overcome with my love for him.

I patted him on the back before releasing him. "Ellis, I can't tell you how good it is to see you. How's your family?"

"Oh, everyone's doing just fine. I got grandbabies all over the place. You should see 'em. Running this a'way and that a'way. Can't hardly keep up with 'em, but I sure do try." We beamed at each other for another moment before he came to himself and gave a little start. "What am I doing? I need to go tell Mrs. Mary and everyone that you're here. I'll be right back."

He took off toward the back of the house, leaving me standing in the foyer. I looked around at all the portraits on the walls, most of them meaning very little to me. But when I came to Mother's, my heart grew heavy. I had so much regret to face, so much to try to make right. Was it even possible anymore?

Before I could think on that too long, I heard Mary calling out to me, and the next second she was running across the foyer. She threw her arms around me, and I wrapped mine around her waist. "You're here!" she cried. "You're really here!"

"I'm really here," I said, swinging her around as I hugged her. I set her down and stepped back to look at her. "I'm sorry it took me so long."

She laughed through her tears and took me by the hand. "You have to come see everyone."

"Everyone?"

"Yes! The whole family's here. We get together every Sunday afternoon."

I froze, suddenly apprehensive about seeing the entire family all at once. "How many people are we talking here?"

"Oh, I don't know. Tom's family, Frank's, mine...all of us. Daddy insists everyone come for dinner on Sundays, and we've been doing it for a couple of years now. Of course, Andrew and I live here, so we're always around. Come on! Come see all your nieces and nephews!"

She tugged on my hand again just as two little girls in matching flowered dresses ran into the foyer, their blonde pigtails bouncing. The oldest carried a toddler in her arms, who was clearly weighing her down. She handed the toddler to Mary with a big huff. "Mother, are you coming? Grandpa is about to start the race."

She turned them around to face me, her free hand on the older girl's shoulder. "Girls, *this* is your Uncle Matthew." Their eyes widened. "This is Rebecca. She's six." She patted the younger one on the shoulder. "And this is Martha, who will be four very soon. They've been dying to meet you for months now."

I squatted in front of them, amazed at how much they looked like Mary. "I'm so glad to meet you," I said. "You're both just as beautiful as your mother."

They looked at each other and giggled. Hope would love her cousins. Maybe I should have brought her along, but I hadn't known what to expect.

Rebecca looked up at Mary. "Mother, can we go back to the race now?"

"Yes, go ahead. We'll be along in a few minutes."

The girls ran out of the foyer toward the backyard, and I stood up again. "And who is this young man?"

Mary bounced the little boy on her hip, grinning at me. "This is my son. His name's Matthew, but we all call him Mattie. Andrew hates that. Says it sounds like a girl's name. I reckon he'll grow out of it though."

I smiled at him, and he ducked his head into Mary's neck. "Matthew?"

"Yeah. We named him after this fella we used to know. He was a hero or something in the war."

I couldn't find words for the love and regret coursing through me. How had I been so blinded by anger that I couldn't see how much my little sister loved me?

"Mary, I'm so sorry about not coming home for so long. Especially for not writing you more often. I should have—"

"Hey, all's forgiven. You're here now. That's what matters."

I cleared my throat, trying to keep my emotions in check. "So, uh, what race are the girls talking about?"

"Oh, that. Father had Ellis build a little track around the property with a few simple obstacles. The kids all run around it whenever the weather permits. Father insists on starting the race and being at the finish line for each of his grandkids as they come across. It's really quite wonderful."

I had a hard time picturing Father that way, but maybe Mary was right. Maybe he had changed. I was about to agree to go with her to the backyard when I heard a moan from behind me. It was a deep, guttural sound, almost like a cry. I turned around to see Father in his wheelchair at the door that led back into the kitchen. Ellis stood behind him, his hands gripping the handlebars. He pushed Father into the foyer.

My throat ached at the sight of him. He looked worse than when I'd seen him in Houston, his mangled hands twisted. He coughed as Ellis pushed him forward. "Mr. Matthew," Ellis said. "Your father wants me to tell you how happy he is that you're here."

I walked over to Father, still unsure of how I felt about all this. But I was determined to try to make peace with everything that had stood between us. "Hello, Father. It's good to see you."

He hit his little chalkboard in his lap with the chalk in his hand. I couldn't make out the scratches. But Ellis could. "He says he's very happy. We're all very happy to have you here today."

Mary came up beside me, her hand resting on my back. "Come on outside and see your brothers and their families. Stay for a while. We'll catch up on everything."

I hated to disappoint her again, but I wasn't ready for a big family production. "I really can't stay," I said. "I'll come back soon, though. I want you to meet my daughter."

Mary's eyes shone with happiness, and she nearly jumped in the air. "I knew it! That little girl in the picture. She has your eyes. I knew she was your daughter! Oh, when can we meet her?"

"I don't know. There's a lot going on. I assume you've read the papers?"

Mary looked over at Father, her smile fading. "Yes, we've seen them. Is Ruby really...alive?"

"Yes. And she's facing some serious charges. We have a lot to deal with. But I promise, I'm not disappearing anymore. I'll come back when I can, and I'll bring Hope next time. I'm sure she'd love to meet her cousins." I met Father's gaze. "And her grandfather."

A tear fell from the corner of his eye. He scratched something on his board, and I glanced up at Ellis for a translation. Ellis looked confused. "Mrs. Mary?" he asked.

She stepped over and looked at the board. "He wants to ask Matthew some questions." She turned to me. "Do you have a few minutes?"

"Ah, just a few. Hope was napping when I left. She's been upset and missing her mother. I don't want to be gone too long."

"I understand," she said. "Come on. We'll have a seat in the parlor for a few minutes. I'll help Ellis, and we'll figure out what Father wants to say."

"Where's the other fella?" I asked as Ellis pushed Father into the parlor.

Mary took a seat on the sofa next to Father's chair. "Mr. Fisher has Sundays off. It's usually just family here, so we don't need his services then."

"I see. So what does he want to ask me?"

Mary and Ellis looked over Father's shoulder while he scribbled on the board. Mary interpreted. "How's Ruby?"

My gut twisted. "I'd rather not talk about Ruby, if that's all right."

"He wants you to know he's sorry."

"I know," I said. "I'm working on forgiving him. But that's gonna take some time."

Mary erased his board for him and he scribbled again. "Did you look over the papers he gave you?"

"Yes. I gave them to Ruby's lawyer." I met Father's gaze. "I'm not interested in the property or the money, but I am grateful for what you did to get Ruby's conviction vacated. She at least has a chance at a fair trial now."

He scribbled again. "He wants to know if there's anything he can do to help."

"No. We're trusting in the Lord this time. He's all we need."

"What about money for the lawyer?"

"I have enough for now. My life insurance is covering a good portion of it."

"What about a job? Do you need work?"

I pushed up from my chair and took a deep breath, walking a few steps to keep my frustration from mounting. "Look, we have everything we need right now. I appreciate the offer for help. But I don't want anything from you. Please respect that."

Father gazed up at me, unmoving for a few moments. Then he nodded slightly. I was hoping he was through, but he scribbled again. "How are you feeling?" Mary asked.

"I'm fine."

She shifted in her seat, looking as though she was treading carefully. "I think what he's asking about is your health. I told him about what happened when I visited, and how sick you were. He's been worried about you. He wants to know how your health is."

"Some things have been tough to deal with, but I'm getting better."

"That's good to know," she said.

"Well, I need to get going," I said, anxious to put an end to all the questions. This was about as far as I could go down the path to reconciliation for one day. "I'll come back and visit again soon."

I gave Father a polite nod as Mary stood. She came over and hugged me, speaking into my ear. "Thank you so much. This means the world to me."

"You're welcome. I'll see you soon. I promise."

I shook Ellis's hand and let myself out the front door. I jogged down the steps, finally feeling like I could breathe again. I hadn't realized how tight my nerves were the entire time I was in that house. I climbed into Asa's truck and sat quietly behind the wheel for a few minutes.

"Thank you, Lord," I said out loud. "I know it's not exactly complete forgiveness, but it's a start."

***

The next morning we got off to an early start around the farm. The country had finally returned to its regular time, turning the clocks back an hour from what had been called "War Time." I hadn't slept well in so long, it didn't make any difference to me. But Asa was pleased as Punch.

"Ain't gotta wait around for the cows to get up to start on the chores," he said as we walked out to the barn. "We can get to work at a decent hour of the morning now. Get most of these chores knocked out before breakfast."

Indeed, we did get them knocked out before breakfast, which was fine by me. I got to take Hope down to see her animals for a tad bit longer, and seeing her smile after all those tears the day before did my heart good. She gave a good scolding to the hog, who by all accounts had spent the night lying flat on his side. But Hope was convinced he'd been rooting under the fence again, so he got a good talking to over the matter.

After her rounds, I took Hope back up to the house to help Mrs. Graves with the chores while Asa and I went down to the workshop. Hope registered her usual complaints about doing the girls' jobs, and I gave them the attention they deserved.

Then I went down to the workshop and set to planning the addition the Kramers had hired me to build onto their house down the road a piece. I suspected they were more interested in catching any gossip floating around me than they were in my work, but it was money I needed, so I'd accepted the job.

Late in the morning, I heard a car coming down the driveway. I figured it was either nosy neighbors or nosy reporters. I had a good mind to ignore it, but I didn't want Asa or Mrs. Graves having to handle my problems, so I went out to greet the visitor. A smartly dressed man climbed out of the maroon Chevy convertible, and he looked around the farm like it was a marvel. I could tell by his snazzy clothes that he wasn't from around these parts. When he removed his sunglasses, I recognized him immediately.

"Mr. Freeman!" I said with surprise. "What in the blazes are you doing here?"

His easy smile spread across his face, and he stuck out his hand. "Man, oh man!" We shook hands with enthusiasm. "Am I glad to see you made it off Mindanao alive. I thought for sure the Japs had gotten you, but here you stand. You sure are a sensation across the state of Alabama right now."

"Don't tell me you came all the way down here chasing a story."

Mrs. Graves and Hope came out of the front door. "Hello there," she said. "Can we help you?"

"I certainly hope so," he said.

"Mrs. Graves," I said, stepping up to the front porch and picking up Hope. "This here's Mr. Homer Freeman. He writes for *Time* magazine."

"Mr. Freeman," she said, her voice tight. "We're not interested in giving any interviews."

"I completely understand," he said. "But if you'll allow me a few minutes of your time, I can explain how I know this fine young man and his wife."

"You know Ruby?" She glanced at me with a furrowed brow.

"Mr. Freeman was in the Philippines with us," I said. "He escaped on the same plane that Ruby did."

"Like I said, ma'am. I only want a few minutes of your time, and maybe just a few bites of whatever smells so good in there."

Mrs. Graves looked back and forth between us before tossing her hands up. "All right then. I reckon if Matthew trusts you, we can trust you. I'll just go get Asa and let him know dinner's ready soon."

I passed Hope over to her. "Go with Grandma, sweetie. And pick me out a nice juicy peach for my dessert."

"Yes, sir," Hope said, giving a suspicious glance to Mr. Freeman.

Once they were off the porch, I held the door open, and Mr. Freeman came inside. "Can I get you a glass of sweet tea?" I asked.

"That would be splendid," he said, taking a seat at the table. I poured us two glasses and joined him. He didn't waste any time getting down to business. "Matthew, I understand Ruby's in jail awaiting trial for murder. Again."

"Yes, sir."

"Oh, don't bother with the formalities for me. I'm just Homer. And I owe my life to you. I'm the one that should be saying 'Sir.'"

"All right, Homer. Yes. Ruby's in jail, and she's been charged with murder and fleeing from justice. So, I reckon you've already figured out that what Natalie said on Mindanao was true."

"I worked that out a long time ago. Before I ever said goodbye to Ruby in Australia. I also worked out that Ruby didn't kill anybody. So what gives?"

I took a gulp of my tea. "It's a long story."

"Those are my specialty," he said.

"I don't want our business splashed all over the pages of magazines and newspapers. No offense."

"None taken. I do hope you realize that your business is going to be splashed on those pages whether you like it or not. This story has legs. It's spreading fast. And what I can offer you is a chance to tell the real story. To control the narrative. I don't want you and Ruby getting painted as outlaws. I know the courage and integrity that's inside you. I saw it that day on Mindanao. I want to help."

"By doing what exactly? Writing a story about us?"

"Not just a story. A series of articles. I want to show the country why we fought so hard against the Nazis. Why it was necessary to blow the Japs to smithereens. Your story isn't just about you. It's about all of us who suffered over there. It's about our boys who died. It's about the ones coming home to a shattered existence. The world needs to know that it's possible to rise above it."

"I don't want to do anything that would hurt Ruby's case."

"I don't either. I don't intend to write one word that you and your lawyer think will hurt her. But at this point, I truly believe if you get the public on your side, it can only help."

I drank the rest of my tea, considering what he was offering. Despite my best intentions to trust God and surrender to His control over the situation, I was perplexed over just what that meant. Had God sent Homer here for this very reason? What if this was another bad decision like I'd made before with Ruby's uncles? What if I did something to hurt Ruby rather than help?

"I tell you what," I finally said. "I need to think about this and pray on it. I'll talk to our lawyer tomorrow. I'm going down to see Ruby. We have to decide if we're taking the plea deal the solicitor offered us."

"Would you mind if I tag along? Off the record, of course. I sure would like to see Ruby again."

"She'd probably like to see you too. I don't reckon it would hurt anything for you to come by. We're meeting at the jail at two o'clock tomorrow." I stood and shook his hand. "Off the record?"

He took my hand and smiled. "Until you say otherwise."

***

I prayed long into the night for God to tell me what to do. But as usual, God was not that direct with me. I'd become sure that whatever I did, surrendering to God's hand in my life had to be the guiding principle of my decisions. I still didn't have a full grasp of what that meant. Maybe I never would. But I was determined to figure it out the best I could with my limited wisdom and stubborn determination for control.

There was no small voice whispering in my thoughts this time, but there was a quiet peace in my spirit. Somehow, even though I couldn't make sense of it, I was certain that God's hand was in all of this, even in Homer's arrival. And I found peace in knowing that whatever happened, God was with us.

I slept fitfully, still struggling with dreams of gunfire, blood, and regret. When I awoke the next morning, the sheets were so wet with perspiration, I could've rung them out. I went out to the well and doused myself with cold, refreshing water, washing away the darkness still trying to steal my hope.

After the chores were finished for the morning, and Hope was once again under the patient care of Mrs. Graves, I borrowed Asa's truck to head into Cullman. I arrived at the courthouse earlier than my scheduled visit with Ruby and Stanley, and went into the section of the courthouse where the judges and lawyers had their offices. I took a moment to say a prayer before knocking on Mr. Norton's door.

Lord, even Jesus asked for a way out before he submitted to Your will, so I reckon it's all right to ask. I know that You are able to remove this cup from Ruby. If it's Your will, please let me drink from it instead. I trust that You are able to accomplish this Lord. But even if You don't, my hope lies in You.

I pushed the door open, greeting a young woman at a desk who seemed quite busy. She glanced up at me over the top of her typewriter. "Can I help you?"

"I was wondering if I could speak with Mr. Norton for just a moment. It won't take long."

She pressed her lips into a hard line and rolled her chair over to another section of her desk. She scanned a date book, shaking her head. "I don't think I can get you in until Friday."

"Is he here?"

She huffed and rolled back over to her typewriter. "Yes, but he's on an important phone call."

"I'll wait. Like I said, it'll just take a moment."

"He has an appointment following the phone call. It's best to schedule a time to meet with him rather than simply showing up here."

"I completely understand," I said. "And I won't do it again. But this is very important."

She eyed me another moment, then took the pen out from behind her ear. "And what's your name?"

"Matthew Doyle."

Her eyebrow twitched, but her demeanor didn't change. She jotted a note onto a small piece of paper and disappeared into the office bearing the name *Sol. Ernest Norton*. She returned a few seconds later. "I gave him the message that you wanted to see him. I can't guarantee he'll make time for you."

"Thank you," I said, taking a seat across from her. I rested my head in my hands, and went back to praying.

About twenty minutes later, Mr. Norton stepped out of his office. I stood and offered my hand, which he gave a brisk shake. "I understand you want to see me, Major Doyle?"

"Yes, sir," I said. "It should only take a few minutes."

"All right, then. Step inside my office."

I couldn't help but notice the cold, minimal feel to his surroundings. Only a few books lined the matching bookshelves behind his desk, and they were aligned perfectly with the edge of the shelf. Everything, including his diploma and a picture of his wife in her wedding gown, was set apart in exact proportions.

"Take a seat," he said, coming around his desk. "Have you and Mrs. Doyle come to a decision about your plea? I expected to hear from Mr. Pierce on the matter days ago."

"I apologize for making you wait. Ruby and I needed some time to consider everything and pray over our options. I know to everyone else around here we must seem like resurrected fugitives, but there's a deep need in Ruby's heart to do the right thing. She's...she's just the most caring person I've ever known." Mr. Norton didn't appear to be moved, so I cleared my throat and focused on why I was there. "Mr. Norton, I understand all the charges as you explained them last week. I was wondering if I might be able to convince you to make a few changes."

"I already negotiated as much as I'm going to. Take it or leave it. Up to you."

"And I understand that, but what I mean to say is that...well, if you can come up with a deal where I'm the one who goes to prison instead of Ruby, I'd sure be glad to take it."

He lifted an eyebrow and leaned back in his chair. "*You* would go to prison instead of Ruby?"

"Yes, sir. I'd plead guilty to whatever you feel is appropriate to charge me with."

"Why would you do such a thing, son?"

I didn't particularly care for being called son, but I brushed that aside. "We have a daughter who's about to turn three. She's one of the reasons Ruby didn't come turn herself in as soon as she escaped the Philippines."

"Did you say three?"

"Yes, sir."

He looked toward the ceiling as if he was counting to himself. "So your daughter was...well, Ruby was pregnant when she arrived in Australia?"

"Yes, sir." It occurred to me that I might be saying more than I should. But I was determined to convince him that it was I who should be in jail. "Hope—she's our daughter—she needs her mother. She misses her every day."

"Wouldn't she miss her father as well?"

"Yes, sir. Believe me, if I could make sure my daughter had both of us in her life, I'd do whatever I could to make that happen. But that just isn't the reality we're facing. I understand that. I just want to do what's best for my family."

"I see." He pressed his fingertips together and seemed to consider this. "You know, I made a few phone calls and got a copy of your records from the army. You were awarded a Silver Star."

"Yes, sir."

"You aided the escape of twenty people from the island of Mindanao, charging into a Japanese patrol so the plane could take off."

"Yes, sir."

"And you commanded a guerrilla unit in Luzon for over two years."

"Yes, sir. But I don't see what that has to do with Ruby's case."

He leaned forward and studied me. "I reckon I'm just trying to get a picture of the man I'm looking at. Seems you're a bona fide hero."

I met his gaze. "Sir, if you really knew everything, I mean...*everything*...you'd know who the real hero is. And it's Ruby."

His expression softened, and for a moment, he actually seemed sad. "Mr. Doyle, the way I see it, the law has to apply to everyone equally. There can be no exceptions. Justice must be blind, even to heroes."

His answer didn't surprise me. "So, that's it. The deal is the deal."

"The deal is the deal."

I stood and offered my hand again. "I thank you for your time, Mr. Norton."

He stood and shook it. "I thank you for your service and your sacrifice, Major Doyle."

CHAPTER THIRTY-TWO

Ruby

October 2, 1945
Cullman County Jail, Alabama

I was just getting my feet under me when John came to my cell on Tuesday afternoon. I'd spent most of the morning bent over my pail. John looked in on me with pity every time he came to check on me, and he'd ask if there was anything he could do. I imagine he felt downright helpless, but there wasn't anything that could cure my nausea, except maybe going home.

John unlocked my cell door and glanced over at the pail by my bed. "You feeling up to a visit today?"

"I reckon I have to today," I said, pushing myself up from my cot. "We're making a decision about whether or not to accept Mr. Norton's plea deal."

"Oh." He dropped his gaze to the floor. "I sure wish there was something I could do to help you, Ruby."

"You've done plenty. You didn't have to spend so much time with me. I'm sure you have plenty of work to keep you busy." I walked over and held my hands out.

He fastened the handcuffs on my wrists again. "Thank you for being a model prisoner. You've made my job easy."

He took me by the elbow and led me along our same path to the courthouse, but this time there was familiar comfort to his touch. Despite the handcuffs, we might've just been two friends taking a walk together.

"What happened to Sheriff Peterson?" I asked when we'd reached the hallway behind his desk.

"He retired once the department came under investigation. No charges were ever filed, and there was never any real evidence of corruption, but public opinion is a harsh judge sometimes."

"Yes, I remember."

He pushed the door open to the outside and gave me a thoughtful look. "I reckon you do." We headed across the parking lot. John didn't even have a hold of me anymore. "Anyways, after all that business with your escape and the papers outright declaring him guilty of corruption, he decided it was best to retire and move to Mississippi where the rest of his family lives."

We reached the back door of the courthouse, and he opened it for me. Before going through, I met John's gaze. "I really am sorry for all the trouble. At least, for my part in things. I should've just come back right away. I was just so scared for everyone."

"Ruby, I appreciate your apology. Really. But I do need to remind you that whatever you say to me isn't protected. I'm still the sheriff."

"I know. It's all right. My future's in God's hands now, and I don't want to worry about being careful of what I say anymore. I'm just ready to live in the truth, and the freedom that brings."

"I'm afraid freedom probably isn't what's in store for you."

I smiled at him, remembering one of my daddy's favorite verses from the Gospel of John. "'If the Son therefore shall make you free, ye shall be free indeed.' This world isn't my home. Maybe my physical body won't be free for a long time, but my soul is. And nothing can change that."

Together we walked into the courthouse and down the hallway to the conference room. We stopped at the door, and John took my hands. He unlocked the cuffs. "I reckon you don't need these in here."

I looked into his eyes and we both smiled. "Thank you."

He pushed open the door, and I practically ran straight to Matthew. He held me close for a long while. I closed my eyes and shut out the rest of the world, soaking up the warmth of his hands pressed to my back, and his chest against my cheek.

"Are you all right?" he asked.

"Better now," I said, refusing to let go just yet.

After a few more moments, I finally stepped back and released him. I turned to the table, expecting to see Stanley seated there, but someone else was with him. "Mr. Freeman?" I said in delight, walking over to him with my arms spread wide.

He stood and gave me a hug. "Ruby, it's so good to see you again. I hope you don't mind me crashing your meeting."

"Not at all. But what are you doing here?"

He gestured toward Matthew. "I saw the stories in the paper, and I had to track this fellow down and thank him for saving my life. I'd like to do what I can to help."

"I don't know what you can possibly do at this point."

"Ruby," Matthew said, coming up beside me. "Homer wants to write some articles about us, explain our story to the public."

"Do you mean...in *Time* magazine?"

"Yes," Matthew said.

Mr. Freeman gestured to a chair. "Why don't you have a seat, and I'll explain what we've been discussing."

I sat down and studied the three of them as Mr. Freeman explained what he wanted to do. He leaned forward onto the table, his enthusiasm for this idea apparent. Matthew, on the other hand, leaned back in his chair beside me without saying much at all. And as for Stanley, I couldn't read him one way or the other. He appeared just as casual and mildly interested as he always did.

"Let me make sure I understand," I said when he'd finished. "You want to write a series that tells everyone in the country just about every detail of my life? I can't say I'm comfortable with that, Mr. Freeman."

"Well, I'm not suggesting a telling of your whole life's story. But maybe just yours and Matthew's story. He's shared a little with me about how you two met when you were teenagers and how you cared for him when he was sick. And for the past month, the country has been reading about the horrors of how our boys were treated in the Pacific, with nearly every paper publishing General Wainwright's account of what happened on Bataan and Corregidor. Honestly, I think now is the time to tell the story of two people who came through that horror and found hope. The country would fall in love with you two."

I glanced at Matthew. "And you think this is a good idea?"

He shrugged. "Honestly, I don't know. I prayed and prayed over it, and all God has told me the past few weeks is the same thing over and over. Surrender. Just, surrender. I'm done with running. I'm done with trying to control the outcome of our lives. And Homer here just showed up of his own accord. I reckon God brought him here for a reason. And I figure I'll just keep on trusting that things will work out the way they should."

I turned to Stanley. "What do you think we should do?"

"It's tough to say. It depends on whether or not you're going to accept the plea deal from Mr. Norton. If you aren't, and we're going to trial, then some positive press is probably a good idea, but it should be limited in what it covers. If you're accepting the plea deal, then I don't see how a series of articles could affect that outcome. It's up to you, really. What do *you* want to do?"

I slid my hand over my stomach. I had no desire for another trial, with every situation and every word uttered being twisted to mean something it never did in the first place. I was tired. And I wanted to rest.

"Matthew," I said, turning to face him. "I think we should accept the plea deal. That way, we know what to expect. And we can ensure that I'll be out someday to be with you and Hope again."

He took my hands in his. "I don't know if I can raise her on my own."

"You won't be alone. Mother and Asa will be there. And most importantly, God will be with you the whole time. You *can* raise her. You're a wonderful father."

He kissed my hands and held them against his cheek. *Fifteen years*, I thought. *Fifteen years apart. And he'll have to raise two of our children, not just Hope.* I ached for God to take this burden from us, to finally give us a chance to be together. *Your will, Lord, not mine. Not mine.*

I turned my gaze back to Mr. Freeman. "You can write your story. But I don't want it to be about me. I want it to be about all the amazing people who have been a part of our journey so far. Promise me you'll tell their story. Henry's, Janine's, Dr. Grant's..." I looked into Matthew's eyes, grateful I had so many memories to take with me. "...and especially the men and women who fought so bravely in the Philippines. Tell their story. Not mine."

***

Stanley notified Mr. Norton of our decision, and Judge Thorpe set my sentencing for October 30. Four weeks. That was all I had left to see Matthew and Hope before I would be transferred to Wetumpka again. And then how often would I see them? A few times a year? What about this new baby? Would the state take the baby from me? Would he or she even know me at all?

Four weeks.

I spent the first week occupying my time by reading Daddy's Bible. I figured I would start at the beginning and read all the way through it as many times as I could. I would hide every word of it in my heart, so I could pray every word of it back to God.

The following Sunday, Matthew came to visit, and John let him sit with me inside my cell. I tried not to cry when he didn't bring Hope, but he said she wasn't feeling well. My maternal instincts kicked in, and I peppered him with questions.

"Does she have a fever?"

"Just a smidge. Nothing too bad." He swept my hair away from my face, talking to me as calmly as possible. I sensed my anxiety growing, and if I'd thought about it rationally, I'd have known I wasn't upset about Hope being sick. I was scared of what lay ahead.

"Is she eating? She needs to get plenty of fluids if she has a fever."

"She's eating a little. She ate some apple butter your mother made for her."

"Apple butter? That has so much sugar in it. And with Daddy's diabetes—"

"She ate some chicken noodle soup too."

"Well, that's better, I suppose. What about her energy? Is she lethargic? Has she said anything about her throat hurting? Have you felt her glands near her throat?"

"Ruby," he said quietly. "She's all right. She just needed some rest."

I fell against his chest, and he held me close as I cried. I couldn't stop for a solid ten minutes, and he eventually walked me over to my cot and sat down with me. "I just miss her so much," I said. "I miss her little face, and her questions, and her excited little bunny hop. I miss reading *The Velveteen Rabbit* with her, and tucking her in at night. I miss praying with her and brushing her hair." I let out a sob from the depths of my soul. "Matthew, it just hurts so much."

"I know, love. I know you're hurting. I'm so sorry. If I could bear this for you, I would."

"I don't know if *I* can bear it."

I cried a little longer before finally exhausting my tears. I was so weak, so easily discouraged. What little faith I had! I was certain I was such a disappointment to God. I steeled myself and pushed away from Matthew. I couldn't fall apart. I had to find strength in the Lord, and stop looking at my own circumstances. I walked over to the small table that held my toiletries, and blew my nose in a handkerchief.

"Are you all right?" Matthew asked.

I nodded as I turned around. But a sudden swell of nausea overtook me, and I had to fly across the cell to the pail in the corner. As I bent over it and vomited, I sensed Matthew behind me within a second.

"Ruby? Ruby, are you all right?"

I took a few breaths before the second wave hit me. He held on to me as I finished, calling for John to bring me some water. I straightened and wiped my mouth with the handkerchief I'd used earlier. My eyes watered.

John came to the door with a glass of water. "Here ya go. Let me know if she needs more, or if she wants some crackers or something."

"Has she been doing this for long?"

John glanced at me before putting his hands up in the air. "I'm just here to help if you need it. Ruby, let me know if you want those crackers."

"It's all right, John," I said. "Will you bring me a few? And I'm sure I'll need another glass of water."

"Sure thing." He headed out of the cellblock, leaving the door open.

Matthew came to me with concern all over his face. "Ruby, what's going on? Are you sick? Do you need a doctor?"

"No, I'm fine. I'm just…I'm pregnant."

It took a couple of seconds for him to register what I'd said. His mouth fell open, and he stammered. "Wh—what? Pregnant? Are you sure?"

I nodded. "Morning sickness. Sore breasts. I'm terribly emotional, in case you can't tell. All the signs are there. And I missed my time of the month."

"Pregnant? How does that even work with...well, with you being in here? Are you getting medical care?"

"Yes. There isn't much to be done for now, anyway. I'm sure there are doctors and nurses down at Wetumpka that can take care of me when I get there."

Realization hit him, and he started pacing. "Oh, Ruby. No. No! You can't be pregnant now. Surely God wouldn't be so cruel."

"It's going to be all right."

"All right? *All right?* Is this what happens when you *surrender* to God? Everything goes belly up? Are you really supposed to have a baby *in prison?*"

"Shh," I said, tears pricking my eyes again. "Matthew, please. This is hard enough as it is."

He came to me and pulled me close again. "I'm sorry. I know this is difficult for you. I just have no idea how to take this. I thought we were doing the right thing. I thought if we listened to His voice, if we trusted Him, God would make things right. But things just seem to be getting worse."

"We are doing the right thing. We just have to keep trusting Him. 'For now we see through a glass, darkly; but then face to face: now I know in part; but then shall I know even as also I am known.' We can't see the whole picture right now, and what we do see seems bleak. But we just have to keep our eyes on the Savior."

I could say the words easily enough. But like Matthew, I was struggling to write them on my heart and mind. I couldn't see anything promising in my future. Only years and years ahead, where now, I wouldn't know either of my children.

CHAPTER THIRTY-THREE

Matthew

October, 1945
Hanceville, Alabama

I did everything I could to hold myself together while I was with Ruby, because I knew that was what she needed from me. But my fragile grasp of the new truth in my life, that freedom and peace would only come when I surrendered control to God, was severely shaken. Ruby was pregnant. *Pregnant.* What was God thinking?

I returned to the Graves' farm and worked the next few days with doubt and fear clinging to me with every step I took. I spent as much time as possible with Hope, because like her name, she reminded me of what was possible. When I was with her, just like her little bunny, I felt like I was real.

On Tuesday, October 8, *Time* published the first of Homer Freeman's articles on us. He brought a copy out to me to look over, and I had to admit it was good. In it, he explained how he'd first met Ruby on Corregidor, and he described the care he'd witnessed from all the nurses trapped in those tunnels. He drew the reader in to Ruby's story in particular, this mysterious young woman who seemed to care so deeply for others, an accusation of murder and escape, and his search ever since to come to the truth about who Ruby Graves Doyle really was. Then he promised a series of three articles, detailing the heroes he'd come to know: a young couple named Matthew and Ruby Doyle. It was enough to pique the interest, without yet telling our actual story.

We stood in the dining room, with Homer beaming at me, waiting for my reaction. "It's great so far," I said, setting it down on the table.

"The best part is, the Associated Press is picking up the series of articles too. Ruby's story will go nationwide."

"I'm still not sold on all this," I said. "Neither of us wants all this attention."

"I understand, and I've promised to tell your story honestly. I won't write anything you don't want me to. But my editor loved my notes, and he thinks this story is going to catch fire quick."

I tried to share his enthusiasm, but I just couldn't find any. "Homer, Ruby's pregnant."

His smile faded, and sympathy replaced it. "Geez, Matthew. What rotten timing. Does that mean she'll have to have her baby in prison?"

"It looks that way. I don't know anything about taking care of a baby. Hope is challenge enough, but add a baby and I'll be lost."

He wagged his finger at me thoughtfully. "You know, that could actually help her. A judge might show leniency, knowing she's pregnant. A jury probably would too. Are you both determined to have her plead guilty?"

"At this point, yes. I'm not sure anything can change that."

We fell into an uncomfortable silence, so I stood and changed the subject. "Would you like some sweet tea?"

"I'd love some."

I went over to the refrigerator and pulled out a pitcher, but before I had finished pouring, I heard a car coming down the driveway. I brought Homer his glass and went to the front door. I prayed it wasn't reporters already, but I recognized Stanley's Chevy and relaxed. I excused myself and went out onto the front porch to greet my lawyer.

Stanley came up the steps, looking a bit unsure of himself for the first time since I'd met him. "You're not going to believe this," he said.

"If it's about the article, I've already seen it. Homer's inside and brought a copy over."

"That's right. The article came out the other day." Clearly that hadn't been what was on his mind. He glanced over his shoulder at his car. "Actually, what I was referring to was the visitor I received this morning in my office. He shared a little of his story with me, and he wants to talk to you."

"Stanley, I don't want to start entertaining folks just because of these articles coming out."

"This has nothing to do with Homer's stories. Matthew, I think we should hear him out. He says he can help clear Ruby's name."

I'd already finished most of my work for the day, and Hope was down for a nap. I supposed it wouldn't hurt to give the fella a few minutes of my time. "All right then," I said. "But let's not make it too long. Once Hope wakes up, he's got to go."

Stanley turned back to his car and waved the man to come forward. The passenger door opened, and a young colored man in army dress uniform climbed out. He straightened and tugged on his olive drab jacket, walking toward me with his gaze to the ground. My heart thundered. I knew who he was, even before he looked up at me, but when his eyes finally came up to rest on mine, I was certain.

"Samuel?" My voice didn't come out as much more than a whisper.

"Yes, sir. It's me. I came to talk to you, sir."

It took a few moments to find my words. "Of course. Uh, come on in here." I opened the door for them, and Stanley followed Samuel into the house. Samuel removed his cap, and I took a moment to really see him.

He wore the wings of an airman, and the breast of his jacket was covered in colorful bars. "You're a pilot?" I asked.

"Yes, sir. I trained down in Tuskegee with the 332nd."

"That's...that's the Purple Heart you got there. And..." I looked more closely. "And the Distinguished Flying Cross."

"Yes, sir."

Then I noticed the black bar with red, white, and blue stripes on the ends. "You were a prisoner of war?"

"Yes, sir. About a year ago, my plane caught fire, and I had to bale out over Yugoslavia. Nazis got me two days later, and I spent the rest of the war in a prison camp."

I stood there in shock, taking in the young man I'd known as a boy. I hadn't seen him since he was ten years old. Back then, he'd been afraid of his own shadow, jumpy and suspicious of me. Now, he stood tall and dignified, though he still held an air of suspicion about him.

"So, Mr. Pierce tells me you want to talk to me," I said. "You want to come sit at the table?"

"This won't take long, Major Doyle. It is Major, correct?"

"Yes, but I'm not in the army anymore. You can just call me Matthew."

I glanced at Stanley, who walked over and took a seat in the rocking chair near the fireplace. He didn't say anything, just seemed content to watch with a fascinated expression.

Samuel cleared his throat and fidgeted with his cap. "Maj—I mean, Matthew, I read about what's happened to Miss Ruby in the papers. How she's been alive all this time and came forward to turn herself in. I was recovering in the hospital when I saw an article about it in the local paper. I couldn't hardly believe it. Mama told me what happened after Ruby's trial back in '36, and I just felt awful about it. I never shoulda run off like I did. I was scared, and I just done what Miss Ruby told me to do. But it was wrong. I know that now."

"Samuel, are you saying you want to come forward and tell everyone the truth?"

"Yes, sir. It ain't right for Miss Ruby to be suffering when all she ever did was help me and Mama. She's about the best white lady I've ever known. Well, 'bout the best *person* I've ever known. I can't let her take my punishment. Not when I'm the one who killed Chester Calhoun."

**

I couldn't believe it. Was I dreaming? Had the key to Ruby's freedom just waltzed right in the front door? I paced the living room, my brain racing through the possibilities. If Samuel came forward and told the truth, Ruby could come home. We could be a family.

Across the room, Stanley sat on the edge of his seat. "Did I hear him right?" he asked. "Did he just say *he* was the one who killed Chester?"

I nodded.

"And you knew this already?"

I nodded again.

Now Stanley was up and pacing with me. "This could change things. I need to think this through. And I need to know what really happened."

Samuel stood behind the sofa watching us, still fidgeting with his cap.

"Samuel, come around here and have a seat," I said. "Tell Mr. Pierce what really happened that day. He's Ruby's lawyer. You can trust him."

He moved around the sofa and sat down. "Well, I was working in the fields that day when I saw Chester walking toward the barn. I was about to go in there and confront him on account of how he treated me when I was a young'un. But Miss Ruby, she saw me and told me to get on back home, that nothing but trouble would come from me confronting Chester. As I set out for home, Chester saw me and told me to get in the barn and move some feed sacks. While I was in there, he started going after me again."

"Wait a minute," Mr. Pierce interrupted. "How old were you then?"

"I was fifteen, sir."

"And what do you mean by he was *going after* you?"

"Chester used to beat me with the horse whips when Mama and I lived on Calhoun's land. Calhoun told her she could come along and pick enough food to feed the two of us after the day's work was done. I reckon Chester thought it would be a good time to harass us. So he did. He did awful things to both of us back then." Samuel dropped his gaze to the floor. "That's how Mama got pregnant. Chester...he did that." He cleared his throat and during the uncomfortable silence that followed, Stanley and I exchanged looks. "That was how I met Miss Ruby. She helped us when we had nothing. Mama was afraid to go up to the farm and get food for us. We were nearly starving. But Miss Ruby brought us food and hope. And she saved us when the tornado came through and nearly killed us." Samuel glanced up at me, his eyes softening. "Well, I reckon you and Miss Ruby both saved us that day."

"All I did was drive the car. The saving came from God and Ruby."

"Well, anyway, after that, Mama and Miss Ruby stayed good friends, and Miss Ruby always looked out for me. That day in the barn with Chester, he started talking at me again, trying to anger me. I was all right until he started talking about my mama, about the things he was going to do to her. I just lost it, and we started brawling. Chester was beating on me pretty good, and I would've taken my lickin', but Chester wasn't just trying to lick me. He was trying to kill me. Told me so. Only thing I could do was get my knife out and try to keep him from killing me.

"We wrestled around some more, and Ruby even jumped in there to try to help me. But he flung her off and said he was going to kill her next. He came at me again, and that time we fell into the hay bales. When I came up, Chester was stumbling around with the knife in his chest. Honestly, I don't even remember doing it. Just happened all of a sudden."

"Samuel," Stanley said. "Why didn't you tell the sheriff all this when it happened?"

"Ruby said there was no way I'd get a fair trial. That the white sheets would have me strung up before I could even tell my story. I was so scared. And so was she. She said she'd tell 'em it was her that got attacked, and she told me to run. So I did. Reckon I been running in some way or 'nother ever since."

The room was deathly quiet while we all processed Samuel's story. It pretty well matched what Ruby had told me. "What do you think?" I asked Stanley. "If Samuel comes forward, won't that exonerate Ruby?"

"That would be the best-case scenario, but I can't say it would be likely. I'm afraid all it's gonna do is implicate Samuel, not clear Ruby. Even if Mr. Norton believes him, and the jury believes him, Ruby can still be charged with accessory to murder. Honestly, since he's a Negro, he's more likely to get convicted of murder, thereby ensuring Ruby gets convicted of accessory to murder, if not worse. I'm afraid Samuel coming forward doesn't guarantee Ruby will be cleared."

That wasn't the answer I was looking for, and it apparently didn't suit Samuel either. "But Mr. Pierce," he said. "I was the one who killed Chester. Miss Ruby didn't do anything except try to help him. That's the God's honest truth."

"It won't matter what the truth is, son," Homer said from behind us.

Samuel jumped up and turned around, quick as a jackrabbit. "Who are you?" His alarmed eyes darted from Homer back to me. "What's he doing here?"

I stood and tried to calm Samuel. "This is Homer Freeman. He's trying to help Ruby too. We're all trying to help Ruby."

Homer stepped into the room and leaned on the back of the sofa. "Like I was saying. It won't matter what the truth is. All that'll matter is the story people believe. You can't prove what happened in that barn nine years ago, just like the solicitor can't prove it either. It'll be your story versus his story, and whoever is more believable will win. Simple as that. And not to put too fine a point on it, but you live in Alabama. No jury's going to believe you over a white man."

Just then, Mrs. Graves came inside with a basket of green beans from the garden. She froze just inside the door, looking around at all of us. Her gaze stopped on Samuel. "I don't believe we've met," she said.

"Mrs. Graves, this is Samuel," I said. "He uh, he knew Ruby a long time ago. He wants to help with her case."

She looked at Samuel again, and I could see understanding dawning in her eyes. "You're the boy...you're that woman's son."

Samuel seemed to grow more and more uncomfortable. He went back to fidgeting with his hat, and his shoulders slumped. "Yes, ma'am."

"But how can you help with her case?"

I jumped in. "He was the one who helped me find Ruby when she was attacked by Chester, remember? I would've never found her in time without his help that day."

Stanley stood and came around the sofa. "Wait a minute. You also saw her get attacked by Chester the first time?"

"Yes, sir. I did."

Stanley turned to me with wide eyes. "Matthew, why didn't he at least testify to that in Ruby's first trial?"

"Ruby wouldn't hear nothing of it. Said she didn't want him or his mother anywhere near the trial. She was adamant. And when Ruby makes up her mind about something, there's no changing it."

Both Samuel and Mrs. Graves nodded in agreement. Stanley tossed his hands up. "Well, I reckon we can't do anything to go back and fix that first trial anymore. Technically, it never happened anyway. I'll take Samuel on home and get back with you in a couple of days. You can let me know if this changes anything about your decision."

We all said goodbye and shook hands, while Mrs. Graves took her green beans to the table. I joined her, and she slid a bowl over in front of me. "Hold 'em like this and snap off the end. Then snap 'em a couple more times. Snapping beans is good work for thinking."

I took a few in my hands and followed her instructions. She was right, it was good for thinking. I considered my options, knowing full well what I really wanted to do was march Samuel down to the sheriff's office and turn him in myself. That young man had been the catalyst of every awful thing that had happened to Ruby. How was it that God saw fit to allow him to go on about his life like nothing had happened? Why was Ruby, and our whole family for that matter, having to pay for his mistakes?

I spent the rest of the evening barely registering what was going on around me. I went through the motions of caring for Hope, bathing her, dressing her, and reading to her. I tucked her into bed, and we prayed together, but I couldn't tell you what she'd said to me all evening. All I could think about was finding a way to get justice for Ruby.

I couldn't go to bed for a long while. I paced back and forth next to the bed, playing out scenarios in my mind. If Samuel confessed, they'd arrest him. Would they then turn around and free Ruby? What would Ruby say if Samuel sacrificed himself for her? She'd never allow it. Somehow, she'd find a way to take all the blame on herself again.

Imagining Ruby's stubborn determination to protect Samuel fueled my anger again. My heart sped up, and the dizziness I knew signaled the rise in my blood pressure sent me to a chair in the bedroom. I dropped my head between my knees, taking slow, deep breaths.

It seemed so close. Samuel was *right there*. The truth was standing right in front of everyone, and if they'd only see it, Ruby and I could have our family back. We could raise our children together. She could sleep next to me every night. It was so close!

I had to find a way to make it happen. I had to find a way to get justice. I had to make things right. I crawled into bed well into the early hours of the morning, and I fell into yet another fitful sleep, full of nightmares.

CHAPTER THIRTY-FOUR

Matthew

April, 1943
Luzon Province, Philippines

My entire arm was on fire. I could hardly move it. Both bullet wounds were infected and smelled like rotting flesh. And I didn't care. I trudged through the jungle, past palm tree after palm tree, an endless sea of bugs and foliage. I wanted to die. How could I ever go back and look Ruby in the eye? I'd been a sentimental idiot, and because of me, Henry was dead.

Henry is dead.

I had to say those words to myself to believe them. How had I let it happen? How could God have let it happen? What good was praying? What good was fighting to stay alive if it meant I'd have to tell Ruby that her brother was dead?

As I worked my way through the jungle, following behind Diego's skillful bolo, I did my best not to move my left arm. It hung limp by my side, throbbing with excruciating pain. But I took it, and I refused to complain. I deserved it.

We were only a couple of days out from reaching our camp near Floridablanca when Diego came to me one morning as I was packing up my bedroll. He studied me for a moment before reaching for the disgusting, worn blanket. "Let me help, Major," he said.

I tried to jerk the blanket away, but it felt like a knife jammed into my shoulder, and I nearly dropped to my knees. I couldn't hold on to the blanket, and Diego easily pulled it from my grasp. He rolled it up tightly and shoved it into my rucksack.

"Major," he said. "There is doctor near small barrio not far from Meycauayan. I am told he treats Americans. You must go see him about shoulder wound. You are infected."

If he only knew how true that was. My very soul was infected. "I'm not going to Meycauayan. We need to get back to camp."

My head swam, and the earth seemed to take a dip. Diego felt my cheek with the back of his hand. "You have fever. We go."

And that was that. Diego led the way toward Meycauayan, and the closer we got, the weaker I grew. By the time we reached the barrio where this doctor was supposed to be, I could no longer stand, and my men took turns carrying me on a makeshift litter.

As I lay on the ground, I looked up at Diego speaking with a small Filipino man, the image of them blurring. A woman came from behind them, and she kneeled down beside me. Her hands caressed my forehead, and she turned to speak Spanish to Diego. Something about "peligro." I knew that word. *Danger.*

There was more discussion around me in Spanish, and I was lifted into the air. I floated about for a bit before landing on a table in a hut. The Spanish all ran into a slur of sounds. A large, dark-skinned man leaned over me.

"No sobrevivirá," said the deep, gruff voice. "He no survive. Infección inside the blood."

The female voice was emphatic. "No, look at his skin. His lips are blue and he's breathing rapidly. He's just lost too much blood. Keep him warm, and I will get Dr. Bruno."

The voices trailed away, and darkness took over.

***

When I awoke again, my head was pounding. I groaned and looked to my left. The woman I'd seen before sat beside me, her arm resting on a small table between us. Red surgical tubing ran from her arm over to mine. That made no sense. I looked again, and I realized the tubing wasn't red. She was giving me her own blood.

"Where am I?" I asked.

She looked up from the notebook she was reading, and I could see she was very young. Maybe just barely twenty. "My father's barrio. I am Malaya Baon. You are Major Doyle, sí?"

"Yes. Are you giving me a blood transfusion?"

"Sí. Your blood was dangerously low."

"You speak English very well."

"I went to school in Manila until the Japanese came."

"Why are you giving me your blood? Don't you need it?"

She smiled and went back to reading her notebook. "I will not give you that much, Major. Just enough for you to live on."

"What if I don't want to live?"

Her smile faded, and she sat up in her seat. "What a silly thing to say. You are Major Doyle. You are the one keeping my people's hopes alive. You are the one who will find a way to chase Japan out of our homeland. You must live another day. And another. And another."

I glanced down at my bandaged arm, noticing my hand. My wedding ring was gone. Probably lost during the battle with the Japs. And like Henry, it was lost for good. My chest grew heavy, aching for Ruby and

Henry, for peace and home. But that wasn't possible anymore. Ruby would never look at me the same once she knew I'd lost Henry.

***

It took a few days for me to get back on my feet. By that time, Harris and his remaining men had already left for Manila with instructions to set up a network of operatives that would communicate with me through Dakila Baon, the chief of the barrio, and Malaya's father. They were to organize as many people as possible who were in positions to observe the Japanese—restaurant owners, grocers, dock workers, night club owners—anyone who could put eyes on Japanese movements.

Malaya continued to sit with me, giving me another transfusion on the second day of my recovery. We didn't speak again of my desire to die, and I did my best not to think of Henry. Instead, I listened to Malaya talk about the history of the Filipino people, especially her own ancestors. And I decided I couldn't think of home anymore. I couldn't think of Ruby. I had to put all of that out of my mind and think only of helping the Filipinos. Nothing else in the world could exist if I was going to keep from descending into despair.

On the fourth day, I was well enough to get up and walk around the barrio. Doctor Bruno Cabrera had treated me over those days, and thankfully he'd concocted a mixture of pills that took the edge off my nightmares and sleeplessness. It even seemed to dull the ache that Henry's death had left behind. I was determined to continue in my duties, focus on fighting the Japs, and deal with those emotions later. So I invited Bruno to join our ranks as a lieutenant. He promptly refused.

After another two days, I'd had enough treatment. I ordered Diego to pack us up. We would be returning to camp. I approached Bruno once more, inviting him to stay in our camp with us and treat the wounded and sick in the area surrounding us. This time, he considered the offer.

"I will not join guerrillas," he said. "But I will travel with you, Major. I must make sure you do not ruin all my hard work in getting you well." The drugs coursing through my veins agreed with him.

I said goodbye to Malaya, who promised to bring word from Harris as soon as it arrived. I was surprised by the small lift in my spirits that gave me and looked forward to seeing her again.

We set out for my headquarters—Diego, Bruno, and the five bodyguards who'd remained at the Baon barrio with us—trekking through the jungle at a faster pace than we had before. *I* was moving faster than before.

We reached camp in a day and a half, and I immediately called a meeting of my staff. Diego and Garzon came inside, and it took every ounce of my control to ignore the fact that Henry was no longer there. It was like a piece of my own body had been ripped off, and the physical pain of his absence was more than I could bear.

After getting a report on the status of the camp, I pulled Diego aside. "Can you get Bruno in here?"

"Sí, Major."

Something inside of me blew apart, and I snapped at Diego. "Do not ever say that to me again. Understand? I hate that! Just say 'Yes, sir,' or 'Yes, Major.'"

"Yes, Major," he said.

I couldn't look him in the eye, but I felt the tension between us nonetheless.

Five minutes later, Diego came in with Bruno, who was so large, he barely fit through the door to my hut. "Thank you, Diego," I said. "You can go now."

He gave me a strange look before ducking out. I realized it was the first time I had intentionally asked him to step away when I was speaking with someone. But this was a matter that I intended to share with no one. Not even Diego.

"I need something to help me take the edge off a little more. Nothing crazy. Just something to keep my strength up during the day."

"Major, you are already taking medicine to help you sleep. Now you need medicine to stay awake?"

"Something like that. Just until I get a handle on some things."

He let out a sigh and shrugged. "I have something that can help. I will have to send for some supplies soon, though."

"Sure, sure. Whatever you need. Can you just bring me that medicine as soon as you can?"

"Yes, Major."

***

Three weeks later, a young Filipino man stumbled upon one of our sentries. He was carrying a basket of food back to his family, but he'd somehow gotten lost. At least, that was his story. I wasn't buying it.

Diego ordered Garzon to guard the man in the supply hut while we discussed what to do. But I had no intention of discussing anything. Before Diego even uttered a word, I ended all discussion on the matter.

"Kill him," I said.

Diego's eyes widened. "Major, do you mean—"

"Was I unclear in any way, Diego? Was there something I said that you did not understand? What is it in Spanish? Muerte?" I stepped over to the door and looked him in the eye. "From now on, we kill any suspected spies or prisoners. We don't have the capacity to keep them, and we can't risk setting them free. Have Garzon print up an order to send out to the cadres across Luzon. This is the policy from now on."

"Yes, Major."

And that was how I, Matthew Doyle, was responsible for the murder of twelve Filipino citizens over the next two years.

CHAPTER THIRTY-FIVE

Matthew

October 1945
Hanceville, Alabama

When I awoke it was still dark. I was so hot, it felt like my skin was on fire. And I was soaked through with sweat. I ripped off my shirt and sat up on the edge of the bed, trying to slow my racing heart. I tried to take deep, slow breaths, but I couldn't.

I'd killed them. I'd been responsible, not only for Henry's death, but for at least twelve more Filipino men and women. Up to now, I'd just been trying to imitate what I saw in Ruby. I'd been trying to do all the things it looked like others did when they gave their life to God. But I had failed. I'd failed in the most unforgivable way possible. I was the one who aught to be facing prison. I was the murderer.

I'm a murderer.

I couldn't sit still, so I went out into the dog run. The cool October breeze shocked my bare skin, but it wasn't enough. My guilt and shame still clung to me. So I went around back to the well and drew up a bucket

411

of icy cold water from the depths. I dipped my hands into it and splashed the water over my head.

Wash me, Lord. Wash my sin and cleanse me. I've tried so hard to trust You, but all I have are filthy rags. I'm nothing.

I tried again to splash the water over my face, my hair, my neck and shoulders. Finally I turned the whole bucket over my head. I had to wash it all away. But I couldn't. Not with well water.

The back door opened, and Asa's boots walked toward me. I looked up, and saw his curious gaze on me. "Son, you all right?"

"No," I croaked. "I can't do this. I can't wash away what I've done. I can't go back and change it. I can't stop looking backward. All I want is to be made clean. But I'm so filthy, inside and out."

He took a towel that had been hanging on a nail near the door and walked down the steps to me. He handed me the towel and waited for me to dry myself off. "Come on inside and get dressed. We have work to do this morning. Best to get an early start."

Asa was a man of few words. At least that had been my experience with him as a teacher of shoeing horses and mules. He would teach me something by showing me how to do it, and then making me do the same thing while he stood behind or beside me in silence. He often let me do something completely wrong from start to finish, never saying anything until I discovered my mistake on my own. Then he'd simply say, "Get it right the next time."

It was frustrating at first, but I learned quickly, and I learned how to pay close attention to what he did, not what he said. He taught through action. And this morning was no different.

I was still distraught over my earlier realization, but Asa didn't say a word about it. After our regular chores were done and breakfast finished, we went straight to work in the barn. He lit the coal in the forge, stirring it around as the coal turned a flaming orange. I took a seat on my observation stool, where I usually watched and learned.

"I do most of my forging from October through February," he said. "Too hot the rest of the year to fool with it, except in emergencies." He walked over to one of his wooden bins and came back with a piece of steel about two feet long and an inch or so wide. He tossed it to me, and I caught it. "Bend it," he said.

"What?"

"Bend it. Make me a shoe for old Ike over there. He's gonna need some new shoes come winter."

I studied him to see if he was joking with me, but he looked as serious as could be. "You want me to bend this and make a shoe?"

"Yup. Get to it." He walked back over to the bin and grabbed another long piece of steel.

"You know I can't bend this."

He came back over to the forge. "Sure you can. Put your hands on the ends and push real hard. See what happens."

I did what he said, but with not much effort. I felt like a complete buffoon. "Asa, I can't bend it and you know it. What's going on here?"

He let out a sigh and grabbed some tongs hanging on the wall. He used them to grip his piece of steel. "Think I can bend this one?"

"Well, if you heat it up first."

He smiled and pointed to his temple. "Now you're thinking." He put the steel into the coal, burying it. He watched it for a moment. "Think I can bend it now?"

I shrugged. "You're the expert. Can you?"

Lifting the steel out of the coals with his tongs, Asa brought it over to the anvil. He took a hammer hanging on the wall nearby and hit near the end of it. The steel didn't budge. "Didn't work," he said. "You know why?"

I shook my head.

"Fire ain't hot enough. And I took it out too soon."

He went back to the forge and buried the steel beneath the coals again. This time he reached up and turned on a blower. As it blew air over the coals, white-hot fire blazed up around the steel. He kept it burning longer this time. Every minute or so, he'd take the tongs and shift the steel around a bit, looking at it. This time when he pulled it out and took it over to the anvil, the steel glowed orange.

Asa held it over a rounded tip on the anvil, almost like the end of a bullet protruding out. He struck the steel over and over, bending it over the anvil. Eventually, after several hard hits from the hammer, it bent into a rounded "V." Asa turned it this way and that, striking it from different angles. At last he held it up and examined it. "Looks about right." He set the shoe aside and tossed the tongs at my feet. "You ready to try yours?"

I couldn't find much enthusiasm, but I went through the same motions Asa had. I wasn't as skilled at using the hammer, so my steel shoe came out looking pretty crummy. But swinging that hammer cut loose some of my frustration. I was grateful for that.

We set the steel into a cooling tub, grabbed a couple of Cokes out of the refrigerator, and went out of the barn to cool off for a few minutes. I watched Hope trailing behind Mrs. Graves as she pulled the sweet corn off the stalks to fix for lunch.

"You know, you're like steel, Matthew," Asa said out of nowhere. "God puts you through fire so He can shape you into the man He intends you to be."

I didn't know what to say, so I took a long sip of my Coke. Asa kept on going, undeterred by my silence. "Some of us are steel, like me. Like you. We need the fire to get blazing hot, and we gotta stay in it for a long while before we're ready to be molded. Some people, like Ruby, why they're more like gold. It still needs fire to be pure and be molded, but that fire don't need to be quite as hot. You see what I'm saying?"

"I think so. You're saying that God's putting me through this fire so He can make me a better man."

"Yes. The problem is, you keep looking for ways to jump out. You're so focused on getting out of the fire, you miss the Savior standing next to you in the furnace."

"You sound just like Ruby."

He smiled. "Or maybe she sounds just like me."

I had to chuckle. "Maybe."

"You know, I went through some pretty tough times myself. I made some terrible choices when I was young. And I wasn't the only one who suffered the consequences. It could have wrecked my faith. Well, I reckon it did for a long time. But I figured out that I could either keep looking backward at my failures, or I could look at Jesus's victory.

"Now, I don't know all that's happened in the years since your healing, but I was there that night, and I felt the Lord bring His mighty blessing on you. He didn't save you from one fire just to lose you in another. He knows what's transpired in your life. He knows what you've done. He knows your pain and your sorrow. And He's been with you every step, even when you couldn't feel Him. You have to know you're forgiven and loved. And there ain't nothing in heaven, or earth, or in hell that can change that."

A wave of emotions swelled up inside me. I wanted to be loved, to be forgiven and accepted. I wanted to be that man God wanted me to be. I wanted to show His love to my children. I wanted to be the husband Ruby deserved. And it all had to flow from the same river of Life. I didn't have to try to be all those things. I just had to trust in the Lord.

Dropping to my knees, I bent over and let the dam inside me break. I felt Asa's hand on my back, his presence kneeling beside me. It wasn't so much that I needed to cry, but I needed to release all the shame and regret I'd been carrying around for so long.

"Lord," Asa said, "You are the God who takes us by the hand and leads us through the valley. You stand with us in the furnace of persecution. You bear our cross of condemnation. Your wounds heal our hearts, and Your love lifts us out of the stormy sea when we begin to

416 | JENNIFER H. WESTALL

sink. Be with Matthew and Ruby as they face this trial. Keep their eyes on You, and only You. Show Matthew Your mercy and Your grace. Amen."

I had no words for that moment, only groans from my spirit. And a still, quiet voice came on the wind.

Surrender.

So I did. I gave up my shame. I gave up my desire to save Ruby. I laid it all down. And like the night I was healed, I felt the same loving presence wash over me, filling me with peace. I didn't have to figure out anything. I didn't have to fight anymore. I just had to surrender.

And whatever circumstances came our way, I would lean on the Savior standing beside me in the furnace.

CHAPTER THIRTY-SIX

Matthew

October 30, 1945
Cullman Courthouse, Alabama

There would be no last minute salvation for Ruby; at least, not in the sense of her prison sentence. I accepted that with peace in my heart, knowing her true salvation was secure. I was even able to look Samuel in the eye and tell him Ruby would be proud of the man he'd become. I could also tell him that he shouldn't turn himself in. Stanley, Homer, and I had all come to the same conclusion. It would only hurt both Samuel and Ruby in the end. It had been hard for Samuel to accept, but he agreed to stay away from the whole affair if it meant Ruby came out better off.

So, on the morning of October 30, I rode with Asa into Cullman while Mrs. Graves kept Hope at the farm. Despite having laid down my fear and intense desire to save Ruby, my heart was heavy as we drove through town. I prayed God would comfort all of us with His presence throughout the day. The only positive aspect was that it would be a short process, unlike Ruby's first trial. She would enter the guilty plea, receive her sentence, and be done with it.

As we neared the courthouse, my stomach filled with dread. The sidewalk and courthouse steps were flooded with people. A few held up signs, but I was too far away to read them.

"Well, what do we have here?" Asa asked.

"Not another circus," I said. "We should never have agreed to Homer's articles."

There'd been two more published with one still to come after the sentencing, and true to Homer's word, the Associated Press had picked up the story. Our lives were being discussed over breakfast nationwide. No wonder there was a zoo outside the courthouse today.

Asa found a parking spot a block away, and we walked through the crowd with our heads down, hoping no one would recognize us. The foyer was crowded as well, with a group of reporters and cameras all in heated discussion. I caught a glimpse of Homer talking to several men gathered around him who were furiously taking notes.

Asa and I turned down the side hallway that led to the conference room where we were meeting Ruby and Stanley. John stood outside the door, and he opened it as we approached. "Morning, Mr. Graves, Matthew."

I came into the room and went over to Ruby, who was seated in a chair near one corner. She was pale, and she held her arms over her stomach. I knelt in front of her. "You all right? Can I get you something?"

She shook her head. "I have some water and crackers. I'll be fine."

I pushed her damp hair away from her forehead. "You don't look well, baby." I turned to Asa. "Can you see if someone can get her a damp rag?"

"Of course," he said. "I'll be right back."

When Asa was gone, Ruby met my gaze. "Did you see all those people?"

"Yeah. Walked right through 'em. Crazy, huh?"

"We should've never let Homer write those articles. This is only going to make Judge Thorpe think I'm after publicity. I hate this. I never wanted those stories to be about me."

"I reckon we can't go back and do that over. But Homer did a good job. He told the country about what the Japs did to us, and how hard you and all the nurses worked to save as many of our boys as you could. I thought it was a real nice job on his part."

Asa came over with a cool rag. "Thank you," I said, taking it and placing it on Ruby's forehead.

She closed her eyes. "I'm ready for this to all be over."

"There have been some...developments," Stanley said from behind me.

I stood and faced him. "What do you mean?"

"Well, normally at a sentencing, the judge will ask you to enter a plea, you'll say you're guilty and give an explanation of what you did. Then you can speak on your own behalf and ask the judge for leniency. The defense can call a witness or two to speak about your character. The solicitor will call up the victim or the victim's family and let them have a say. Then the judge might retire for a bit to decide on the sentence, or he might have already decided on a sentence based on the report we submitted to him last week. It's usually a quiet and standard procedure. But circumstances are unusual today, as you saw trying to get in here."

"Is this circus going to make things harder for Ruby?" I asked.

"It's hard to say. But the crowd isn't the only thing that's unusual. Numerous people who want to speak on Ruby's behalf have contacted me over the past day or two. Honestly, I'm hard-pressed to decide on who should speak. We're talking about folks from all over the country: a pilot from Houston who's a war hero, a couple of army nurses, a baseball coach from San Francisco, even a colonel."

"A colonel?" Asa said, looking over at Ruby in awe.

420 | JENNIFER H. WESTALL

Ruby looked pretty surprised as well. "All those people...want to speak for me?"

Stanley nodded. "They sure do. Some were quite emphatic about it. But Mr. Norton will have a couple of people speak as well. You should be prepared for that."

"Does the judge know she's pregnant?" I asked.

Asa's wide eyes darted from me back over to Ruby. "Honey, you're pregnant?"

She nodded, still pressing the damp rag to her head.

"I included that information in the report I sent him last week," Stanley answered. "So he knows. With all these solid character witnesses, I'm beginning to think we might be able to get the judge to reduce her sentence."

"What do you think he might reduce it to?" I asked.

"I think it's reasonable to hope for eight to nine years, with her serving about five of those. It's a long shot, but you never know— miracles do happen."

Stanley smiled over at Ruby, and she gave him a weary grin in return. My hope stirred inside me. Maybe Stanley was right. Maybe Judge Thorpe would take all these things into consideration and give Ruby a lighter sentence. But I'd stood in this place before. I'd believed in a judge being reasonable and fair. I'd hoped for God to save Ruby from injustice nine years ago. And nothing had turned out the way I'd thought it would.

Because I was so busy looking at the fire.

I took a deep breath and resolved not to get distracted. "Why don't we all say a prayer before we go in there," I suggested.

"That's a good idea," Asa said.

Ruby stood, and we all came together in a circle. "I'll start," I said. "Asa, will you finish up?" He nodded.

We all wrapped our arms around each other and bowed our heads.

"Lord, we come to you today with humble hearts seeking Your grace and mercy, but most of all we ask for Your presence and reassurance. We've done our best to trust in You and to follow Your guidance. We are trusting that Ruby is in Your hands, that our family is in Your hands, and that You have secured our future in eternity. Remind us throughout this process to keep our eyes on You in every circumstance. And no matter the outcome, we will praise You and glorify Your name."

Ruby

I listened to Matthew's prayer with a full heart. When he finished, I had to take a moment to choke back my tears before I could add my part. "Heavenly Father, I want to thank you for bringing us together in these quiet moments. Thank You for giving us Your peace. I pray You'll give everyone here today wisdom and courage. I pray we'll rest in Your hands. Lord, You know how weak I am, how easily my focus wanders from You. I pray for Your strength today and in the days to come."

Asa cleared his throat and began. "Almighty God, we come to You today to worship You in Spirit and in Truth. To sit at Your feet and witness Your hand of mercy, grace, and comfort. I pray for Your blessings on Matthew and Ruby, on Hope, and the baby we've yet to meet. Help us to remember that when we are weak, You are strong. In Jesus's name we pray. Amen."

We all lifted our heads, but held on to our hug for just a moment longer. It was such a sweet moment, I didn't want it to end just yet. It was the first time all day I didn't feel sick to my stomach. Even Stanley seemed to be enjoying our closeness. But the knock on the door signaled it was time for us to move into the courtroom, so we dropped our arms.

"Let's go," Stanley said. "I reckon we're as ready as we can be."

"Who are you gonna call to speak for Ruby?" Matthew asked.

Stanley picked up his briefcase from the floor. "I figured I'd start with one of the nurses. She seems like the most compelling, and from there

I'll just keep on calling folks until Judge Thorpe tells me to stop. If we're lucky, we'll get two or three in, maybe even four if he's in a good mood."

"I don't think this crowd would put any judge in a good mood," I said.

We filed out of the door, and John walked beside me, giving my elbow an encouraging squeeze. Matthew accompanied me on my other side, taking my hand. We walked in through a side door to the courtroom and made our way over to the defendant's table. I couldn't help but think of the last time I'd been seated at that table. So much had happened since then, and I'd grown so much. Yet still I struggled to keep my faith secure.

I walked over to the table as Matthew and Asa went around to the pew right behind me. Homer made his way through the crowd and slid in beside Matthew. "How are you holding up?" he asked.

"Just fine," I said. "I think you've drawn us quite a crowd."

"Looks that way. I tell you what, every person I talked to so far is here to support you. They all want to see Judge Thorpe show you leniency today. I didn't overhear one person say anything negative."

That was a small comfort. I remembered how awful it had been to feel the scorn of the entire community in my trial and I thanked God. I turned to speak to Matthew, but caught sight of Mr. Doyle in his wheelchair, being pushed around the pews on the outside. He'd obviously suffered a stroke at some point since I'd seen him last. I recognized the slack in the left side of his face and the way his right side seemed to be frozen in place. My heart sped up at the sight of him. What if he was going to try to influence the judge again?

I had to squash that fear. If I could stare down four Japanese soldiers invading my tent with the intent to rape me, I could stand toe to toe with Mr. Doyle and his hatred, if that was his intent.

Behind the man pushing Mr. Doyle, I saw Mary walking toward us as well. She smiled at me and waved like we were seeing each other at a social gathering. I gave her a timid wave back. Matthew turned to see whom I was waving at, and when he turned back to me, his cheeks were flushed.

"Um, I wasn't expecting them to come. I, uh, I've talked to Mary and Father. He won't be interfering with anything this time around. In fact, he seems to want to help. But I told him to stay out of it. We'll see if he does, I reckon."

Mary and a man I assumed was her husband slid into a pew a few rows back, and Mr. Doyle set his wheelchair next to them. I decided I couldn't worry over that right now. Besides, a few seconds later, I saw James making his way over to the pew behind Matthew.

"Ruby," he said, "I just want you to know that I support you. If I can help a'tall this time, I'm here for you."

"Thank you," I said, leaning over the railing with my arms spread wide. James leaned over the top of the pew, and we made our best attempt at a hug.

When we straightened, he stuck out his hand to Matthew. "I want to thank you for looking after Ruby all this time. I understand you were with Henry to the end. That means the world to me."

Matthew took his hand, but could barely meet his gaze. "I just wish I could've done more."

My gaze fell on another familiar face, one I couldn't place. I tapped Matthew's arm. "Who's that man in the back, over there on the other side? In the suit. Tall. Black hair. I know him from somewhere."

"I'm not sure. He does look familiar, but...wait." Matthew put a hand on Stanley's shoulder. "Do you know who that is?" He pointed out the same man I'd noticed.

"Uh, yeah. That's Jim Davis. He's one of the jurors that claimed Ruby's verdict was tampered with. Helped get it vacated."

The clerk called the court to order, so everyone hushed and stood up straight. I faced the front and watched Judge Thorpe emerge from the door beside the bench. He climbed up into his chair and regarded the overflowing courtroom with a grimace, before taking his seat and rapping his gavel.

I'd never seen Judge Thorpe before. He appeared to be around fifty or so, with graying hair and a few wrinkles framing his eyes. As he looked out at the sea of faces, he pressed his lips into a tight line. But when he spoke, his voice almost seemed gentle.

"Let me start by saying a few words to you folks in the gallery. I understand the interest in the case being presented. I can read magazines as well as the next fella. However, this courtroom will operate in an orderly fashion here today, following every procedure to the letter. If even one of you folks speaks out of turn, or causes a disruption, I will have every one of you removed."

There were a few murmurs from the courtroom, but many members of the assembled crowd nodded their assent.

Satisfied, Judge Thorpe looked down at the stack of papers in front of him and began. "This is the case of the State of Alabama versus Ruby Doyle, also known as Ruby Graves, also known as Grace Doyle, and also known as Grace Miller. Let the record reflect that representing the State of Alabama is Mr. Ernest Norton and representing Mrs. Doyle is Mr. Stanley Pierce. Are the parties ready to proceed?"

Matthew

Sitting through Mr. Norton's description of what happened back in 1936 was almost as difficult as it had been the first time I'd heard the prosecution's ridiculous theory. Thankfully, he had agreed to leave out the most damaging part of the original theory, which was the speculation that Ruby was romantically involved with a colored boy at the time, and Chester had discovered them together in the barn. Instead, Mr. Norton described the encounter as coming about because of Chester instigating a verbal altercation with her based on her continued friendship with Negroes, which escalated to a physical confrontation. It wasn't a whole lot better, but it was better.

Next he launched into a detailed account of the escape, describing how Ruby's uncles had ambushed the sheriff and Deputy Frost, shooting them in the process. My face grew hot as he described my involvement in driving away with Ruby from the scene. In the end, he declared it had been Ruby's responsibility to turn herself back into custody, if indeed she was truly unaware of the escape plan, but she had chosen instead to go on the run.

"Your Honor," Mr. Norton concluded. "With the evidence of the witnesses and the statements of the defendant herself, the State believes that if this case were to go to trial, it would prove beyond a reasonable doubt the guilt of Mrs. Doyle in the voluntary manslaughter of Chester Calhoun, as well as her guilt in fleeing justice."

Mr. Norton took his seat, and Judge Thorpe turned his attention to the defense table. "Mrs. Doyle, is Mr. Norton's description of the events accurate?"

"Yes, Your Honor." Ruby's voice sounded so small.

"And are you pleading guilty to the charges of voluntary manslaughter and fleeing justice because you are, in fact, guilty?"

There was a slight hesitation before she answered, "Yes, Your Honor."

"Is there anything you'd like to say at this time?"

Stanley stood and straightened his tie. "Your Honor, at this time, I'd like to ask the court to allow a few folks to speak on Mrs. Doyle's behalf. They'd like to testify to her character and her actions over the past several years."

Judge Thorpe removed his glasses and leaned back in his chair, studying Stanley with narrowed eyes. "Yes, I'm aware of all the folks requesting leniency for Mrs. Doyle. I've received numerous letters over the past week extolling her virtues. However, I would like to get out of here sometime today, Mr. Pierce. So I will allow these statements on the condition that they are kept brief and to the point."

"Yes, Your Honor." Stanley looked down at his notepad. "The first to speak will be Captain Laura Beckett, who served alongside Ruby on Bataan."

A uniformed nurse stepped through the gate and came in front of Judge Thorpe. I didn't remember her exactly, but her face seemed familiar. She stood tall and confident and addressed the judge with a commanding, but sincere voice. "Your Honor, I served as a nurse on Bataan with Mrs. Doyle during some of the worst days of my life. We were constantly bombarded by Japanese planes, and we were starving to death under the siege. I'm sure the conditions on Bataan are fairly well known, so I won't go into further detail. What I will say is that I observed Mrs. Doyle performing her duties, and I can say without a doubt that she was the most generous, kind, and selfless person there. She would work herself nearly to death to make sure each and every soldier in her care was treated and shown the dignity he deserved. In fact, when she contracted malaria herself, she continued working until she passed out. She was relentless, and she was full of mercy and kindness. I ask that she be treated with the same here today. Thank you, Your Honor."

Judge Thorpe gave her a tight nod. "Thank you, Captain Beckett, for your presence here today, as well as for your service to your country."

Captain Beckett returned to her seat, and Stanley stood again. "Your Honor, Lieutenant Natalie Williams would also like to make a statement."

My jaw almost hit the floor as Natalie walked down the aisle and through the gate. What was she doing here? The last I'd seen her, she was getting hauled away from the plane after trying to rat out Ruby. Had she fooled Stanley into thinking she would be supportive?

"Your Honor," she began, her voice trembling slightly. "I also served with Mrs. Doyle on Bataan, but my experience was quite different from Captain Beckett's."

I knew it. I dropped my head into my hand, grinding my teeth. I should've taken a look at the list of people Stanley intended to call. *Lord, please shut her mouth like you did the lions in the den with Daniel.*

"When I knew Gr—I mean, Ruby on Bataan," Natalie continued, "I was terrified of dying. All I could think about was how I was going to get out of there. I didn't always consider the soldiers or my fellow nurses, and for that I'm ashamed. After the siege began, I figured out who Ruby really was because my aunt ran the boarding house where she lived at the time of her arrest. I used that information to blackmail Ruby for food nearly every day. We were starving and I was desperate. I even made her give me her medicine. That was how come she caught malaria. I was awful to Ruby." Natalie paused and brought her hand to her mouth. "I even left her behind at the hospital when we evacuated. But after all the terrible things I said and did to Ruby, she treated me with kindness in return.

"You see, Your Honor, I was among the twenty-four nurses that escaped Corregidor just before it surrendered. I was in the group due to be left behind on Mindanao because our plane couldn't fly. Terrified beyond reason, I took off running down the dock, hoping I could catch the one usable plane. When I saw Ruby standing in the doorway, I thought she'd treat me the same way I'd treated her. She'd close that door and let that plane take off without me. But she didn't. She encouraged me to run harder. She grabbed me as I leapt onto the plane, nearly falling out herself. She risked her life to save me when I'd done nothing but cause her misery. Ruby embodies grace and mercy. And I ask you to show her that same mercy today. Thank you."

As Natalie turned to leave, my heart swelled and my eyes pricked. Ruby had never told me that story. She must have been devastated that I wasn't coming to the plane as I'd promised, yet still she'd found the strength to save Natalie. *Natalie!* I didn't think my love for Ruby could grow anymore, but somehow, it did.

Stanley continued to call people up front to speak for Ruby. Homer came forward and told of Ruby's kindness and bravery. Colonel Nathan Hanson, who'd been the last man I'd sent back to the plane as I fought off the Japanese, testified to our actions that day. Even Emmitt Hyde came forward and told about the night Ruby had kept him from killing himself. Gone was the desperate man I'd seen nine years ago. He stood before the judge in a clean suit, shaved, and with a quiet dignity.

"Your Honor," he said in his gruff voice. "My life was on the path to destruction when I was locked up next to Miss Ruby in 1936. I'd lost everything, and everyone that I'd ever cared about. All I wanted was to die. But Miss Ruby, she helped me find hope. She helped me see that I could still be the man God wanted me to be. And she saved my life, Your Honor. I don't know how she did it, despite being behind bars herself. But all the same, she saved me."

Even back then, I'd scolded Ruby for helping Mr. Hyde, concerned only of how it would make her look to others. But here he stood, a testimony to the love and courage that overflowed from her. She'd touched so many lives, and finally, *finally*, I could see how wrong I'd been to try to keep her gift only to myself.

With each speaker, I tried to read Judge Thorpe's reaction. I kept expecting him to tell Stanley that was enough. But he didn't. He leaned onto the bench and listened intently to each story. He even asked a few questions now and again to get a better idea of the circumstances.

When Mike came forward, I caught the warm smile he shared with Ruby as he walked through the gate and stood before the judge. It still pricked my jealousy; I couldn't help that. He'd been there for Ruby and Hope when I couldn't. My gratitude outweighed my envy, but I couldn't rid myself it entirely.

"Your Honor," Mike said, "I was the pilot of the plane that flew Mrs. Doyle and the others off Mindanao. I saw first-hand the courage and honor of both Major Doyle and his wife, Ruby. As you've already heard, the only reason we were able to take off at all was because of the sacrifice of Major Doyle and the others who helped fight off the Japanese patrol nearby. In the end, Major Doyle chose to continue fighting them off on his own, so that the rest of us could escape.

"I became friends with Ruby after we arrived in Australia, and together we did everything in our power to locate Major Doyle, who was reported killed in action. Afterward, she and her daughter Hope lived with my parents in Houston while we continued to try to find information on what had happened to Major Doyle.

"Your Honor, Ruby is...an amazing mother, a kind friend, and selfless to her core. She puts the needs of others ahead of her own, even if it's to her detriment. She loves fiercely, forgives completely, and treats everyone she meets with dignity and respect. I don't know exactly what happened in that barn nine years ago, but I have no doubt that Ruby was protecting herself. And I ask you to show her and her family mercy. Thank you."

As Mike took his seat a few rows behind us, all I could think about was what a wonderful testimony to Ruby's character this was. After pouring herself out time and time again for others, sometimes nearly to the point of death, she was finally on the receiving end of all the love and grace she reflected on a daily basis. The sentence was going to be what it was, and there was nothing I could do about it, but I thanked the Lord over and over for allowing Ruby to see that the love she'd sent out over the years hadn't been in vain.

When all was said and done, Stanley had called six people forward to speak on Ruby's behalf. And I believed in my heart that every one of them was sent by God that day to let us know that He heard our prayers, and that He was with us.

Ruby

I sat behind the defense table in humble gratitude as one person after another spoke so highly of me. It was especially sweet to see Natalie again and to know we had put all the ugliness of the past behind us. I thanked the Lord for such a wonderful reminder of His love and care for me.

But I knew the time for reality would come fast, and it certainly did. Judge Thorpe asked Mr. Norton if any victims of my crimes would like to make statements.

"Indeed, Your Honor, there are two victims who wish to be heard on this matter. The first is Sheriff John Frost, who was shot during the escape."

My eyes found John as he stood and came from across the courtroom. He didn't look over at me, so I braced myself for his testimony. I couldn't have any hard feelings toward him. He had a right to have his say. He faced Judge Thorpe and set his shoulders back.

"Your Honor, I was with Sheriff Peterson back in 1936 as we were transporting Mrs. Doyle to Wetumpka to await her sentence. We spotted a wrecked automobile on the side of the road just as we entered Blount County. We pulled over to offer assistance, but once we were in the midst of assessing the two men we believed to be injured, I noticed a third man had gotten into the sheriff's car and was speaking with Mrs. Doyle. I yelled at him to get out of the vehicle, and that was when I was shot from behind. Much of what happened next is still a blur. But there are a few things that are crystal clear.

"First of all, I remember Mrs. Doyle helping to get me to safety inside the vehicle. I passed out after that, but I remember bits and pieces as I came in and out of consciousness. What I remember for sure is that Mrs. Doyle was frantically trying to save me. If she was determined to escape, she didn't show it. She stayed with me, prayed over me, and I am convinced I would have died if she hadn't treated my wounds in the car.

"Now, I'm not standing before you to say that she bears no responsibility for her original conviction. However, I believe in my heart that she did not willfully participate in the ambush of Sheriff Peterson and myself. I ask that you please take that into consideration when handing down the sentence. Thank you, Your Honor."

The courtroom fell silent for what felt like a full minute as John made his way back to his seat. He never made eye contact with me, but I hoped he knew how much his testimony meant to me. My eyes ached from holding back my tears, but I was determined to hold out a little longer. I glanced over my shoulder at Matthew, and I could see he was having the same trouble.

"I love you," he mouthed to me. That nearly broke my willpower. I quickly mouthed the same back to him and turned my attention to Mr. Norton as he stood again.

"Your Honor, the last victim who would like to speak today is Mr. Percy Calhoun, father of the deceased, Chester Calhoun."

There was mumbling in the crowd behind me as Mr. Calhoun stood from the back of the courtroom and made his way forward. The years since I'd last seen him had not been kind. His frail shoulders slumped, and his ragged overalls hung loosely over his body. He shuffled to the front of the courtroom, looking like he'd rather be anywhere but here. When he spoke, his voice was gravelly, and at first I had trouble understanding him.

"Thank you, Your Honor, for 'llowing me to speak today."

"Mr. Calhoun," Judge Thorpe said. "I'm afraid you'll have to speak up just a bit."

He grunted and started again, this time a little louder. "Your Honor, thank you for 'llowing me to be heard in this matter. I know everyone here has spoken in support of Miss Graves...er...Mrs. Doyle. I don't know nothing 'bout what's happened in the years since Chester's death 'cept in my own family. I can say it has torn us apart. I've lost my son, my wife, my reputation in the community, and just about all my business. However, I don't fix the blame on Mrs. Doyle entirely.

"Your Honor, the truth of the matter is that...well...Chester was not an easy man to get along with. He was harsh with our sharecroppers, and even more so with the Negro workers. I admit, it's quite possible he attacked Mrs. Doyle first. However, there were circumstances surrounding his death that never added up, and I can't say Mrs. Doyle is completely innocent. I believe the charge of manslaughter is appropriate here.

"Now I ain't no judge, so I leave the matter for deciding her punishment up to you. I got no recommendation on that matter. But I will say that I am prepared to accept whatever you deem to be appropriate. Thank you for hearing my statement, Your Honor."

After Mr. Calhoun returned to his seat, Judge Thorpe addressed Stanley. "Mr. Pierce, is there anything else the defense wishes to add at this time?"

Stanley stood and took his notes with him. "Your Honor, we would simply like to remind the court of the mitigating circumstances involved here. First of all, Mrs. Doyle has never changed her story about what happened in the barn with Chester Calhoun. She has maintained from the beginning that she was responsible for his death. Secondly, as the court has heard here today, Mrs. Doyle neither conspired with her uncles nor condoned their actions in ambushing the Cullman County Sheriff's vehicle while transporting her. In fact, she actively tried to stop her uncles and did everything she could to treat both Sheriff Peterson and Deputy Frost. Lastly, she has accepted full responsibility for her actions after the ambush in fleeing the scene and not returning to custody immediately. Despite being in the first trimester of pregnancy, having a young daughter who needs her, and a family to care for, she has returned of her own volition to face the consequences of her actions."

Murmurs of shock and concern sounded across the courtroom as those present assimilated the surprise news of Ruby's pregnancy and its implications. Judge Thorpe tapped his gavel and gave them all a stern scowl, before Stanley continued.

"We understand that the State will be recommending a sentence of no more than fifteen years in the state penitentiary. However, we ask that the court take into account all the testimony heard here today, as well as the many letters received requesting leniency."

Stanley shuffled his notes back into order and took his seat beside me. We were almost finished. My stomach swam from nausea, but I did my best to control it. *Just a few more minutes, and this will all be over.*

Mr. Norton stood up next to make his case for my lengthy incarceration. He cleared his throat and straightened his suit. "Your Honor, the State would like to acknowledge the circumstances Mr. Pierce has pointed out to the court. Mrs. Doyle has exhibited a willingness to accept responsibility for her actions. That is why the State is recommending a reasonable term of imprisonment of no more than nine years for the charge of voluntary manslaughter and three years for the charge of escape. We believe this is a fair sentence that reflects the seriousness of the crimes committed by Mrs. Doyle."

Had I heard him right? I glanced again over my shoulder at Matthew. His palms were pressed together, and his head bent forward, like he was praying. The sentence was down to twelve years now. *Thank you, Lord.*

Mr. Norton took his seat, and Judge Thorpe leaned back in his chair again. He folded his hands together and studied me carefully. "Mrs. Doyle, although I did not have a specific sentence in mind coming into today's hearing, I did have a general idea of how I would rule. I've read over the court proceedings of your first trial, along with the reports associated with this hearing. I've read all the letters submitted by your friends and family, and I've considered the testimony of the victims. However, I find that I may need a little more time to make my decision. Therefore, the court will stand in recess for one hour, and I will make my sentencing when we return." He slammed the gavel down onto the bench and stood, before leaving through the door at the back of the courtroom.

I turned to Stanley as everyone in the courtroom began talking at once. "Is this a good sign?" I asked.

He shrugged. "I'm not sure. Without knowing how he intended to sentence you to begin with, I don't know if he's considering a longer term or a shorter one."

Matthew leaned over the rail separating us and took my hand. He pulled me toward him and wrapped his arms around me. "He asked for twelve years instead of fifteen. That's a good sign."

"I sure hope so."

"How are you holding up?"

"I'm all right. I could use some water."

"I'll get it," Asa said. He disappeared into the crowd.

"Did you hear all those people standing up for you?" Matthew asked. "And Natalie! You never told me what happened between you two."

"I guess I haven't thought about it in a long time. I can't believe she came here. All of them! Laura, Mike, and Mr. Hyde. God has truly blessed me today, no matter the outcome."

CHAPTER THIRTY-SEVEN

Matthew

October 30, 1945
Cullman Courthouse, Alabama

By the time the judge returned an hour later, my nerves were shot. We'd spent most of that time in the conference room letting Ruby get some much needed quiet and rest. She threw up once, but swore she was fine to finish the day. It killed me to see her like that, her face so pale, and her body so weak. This couldn't just be due to her pregnancy; it had to be the stress of the hearing as well. As much as I was dreading the separation we faced, I took comfort in that at least this part would soon be over, and we could begin the process of waiting for our family to be whole again.

I had to wonder how Ruby's pregnancy would play out. Would she have to deliver the baby in the prison hospital? Would they let me be there? Would I be able to take the baby home with me? How in the world could I possibly care for a newborn? My mind began to race, but I caught myself again taking my eyes off God's provision for my family. I

435

would just have to trust that He would guide us and protect us along the way.

Putting the future to the back of my mind, I focused squarely on the judge as he prepared to make his ruling. My knee bounced up and down as he told Ruby to stand. Stanley rose with her. I wished with all my heart I could stand in her place, or at least stand beside her.

Judge Thorpe reviewed the terms of the plea agreement, a seemingly endless statement of all the charges we'd been discussing for weeks now and the rights of the State to recommend the sentence, and the rights of Ruby to request leniency. Finally, he got to the meat of the matter.

"Because the plea in this case was not a binding agreement, sentencing is at the discretion of the court," he said. "With that end in mind, I have considered several issues, which I will now outline. Firstly, it is my understanding that the defense has neither requested a reduction in the charges, nor an alternate sentence in this matter. The only request has been for leniency at the discretion of the court.

"Secondly, I have taken into consideration the willingness of Mrs. Doyle to accept full responsibility for her actions over the past nine years, as well as her voluntary return to custody even though she is currently with child.

"Thirdly, this court would like to acknowledge the courageous conduct of Mrs. Doyle during the time she was trapped on Bataan along with our military. It is evident that she served others with a selfless heart and dedication to those who were suffering unimaginable pain. Nothing said here in this court today can take away from your sacrifice, Mrs. Doyle. For that, I thank you."

He paused and seemed to gather his thoughts for a moment. "Lastly, given the testimony of the two victims in this case, it is the conclusion of this court that Mrs. Doyle did not act with any malicious intent during the ambush of Sheriff Peterson and Deputy Frost. However, rather than return to custody, Mrs. Doyle fled the State to avoid her sentence for her previous conviction. Even though that conviction was later vacated, at the time, Mrs. Doyle was legally incarcerated, and the escape was unlawful.

"Therefore, it is the decision of this court, in the matter of the charges involving the escape, that Mrs. Doyle's guilty plea is accepted. This court sentences you to no more than eighteen months in the state penitentiary."

Eighteen months. That was manageable. We could handle eighteen months. My hope began to rise.

"Now," Judge Thorpe continued. "In regards to the charge of voluntary manslaughter, it is the belief of this court that, although manslaughter was committed, there were mitigating circumstances, including a possible pattern of violent behavior by the victim himself. Mrs. Doyle, you have remained consistent in your story, and I believe it is compelling. Therefore, in the charge of voluntary manslaughter, I am accepting your guilty plea and fixing the sentence at three years."

Mumblings erupted through the gallery, and I couldn't help a small feeling of victory. Altogether, that was four and a half years we would be apart, but it was so much better than what I had been expecting.

Judge Thorpe tapped his gavel. "Order, please." He waited for quiet again. "In considering the larger picture presented here today, and considering the time you sacrificed in service to your country in the Philippines, and the fact that I do not want to sentence a baby to being born in prison, the court is suspending Mrs. Doyle's sentence, contingent upon her adherence to all laws from this point forward."

My heart raced. Did he say the sentence was suspended? I racked my brain trying to remember what that meant for Ruby. Stanley turned to her with a wide smile, so it must have been good news. Both my knees were bouncing by now.

"In other words," Judge Thorpe said, "you will be free to go as long as you do not ever break any laws in the future. If you do, you will serve out the sentence as I described it."

438 | JENNIFER H. WESTALL

He kept talking, explaining something about paying fines, but all I heard was the word *free*. Ruby was free! I dropped my head into my hands, unable to control the sobs of relief that came out of me. Several hands clapped my back, but I couldn't even look up.

Please Lord, let this be real.

Judge Thorpe declared the case to be concluded and brought his gavel down for the final time. Cheers erupted in the courtroom, and I jumped over the rail, wrapping Ruby in my arms. She laughed as I swung her around. "Easy, soldier!" she said. "I'm a bit seasick."

"Can you believe this?" I said. "Ruby, you're free!"

She wiped at her own tears and raised up on her tiptoes to kiss me. "It is hard to believe, isn't it?" She hugged Asa as he came around the rail, followed by Homer. Then, as if a floodgate had opened, one person after another lined up to congratulate her.

I stepped back from the crowd to let her enjoy the moment, but I stayed close, not wanting to let her get far from me ever again. She beamed with joy, and my heart overflowed with love. I bowed my head and closed my eyes once more.

Lord of Heaven and Earth, You have blessed us beyond our expectations, and certainly beyond what we deserve. Thank you, thank you, for being with us today and for setting Ruby free. You are the God of the furnace, the valley, the pit of despair, and You are the God of Victory.

Ruby

I don't know how long I stood there accepting hugs and congratulations from folks, some of whom I didn't even know. I alternated between elation and exhaustion from moment to moment, but I didn't want to miss any of it. Asa shook hands with everyone who'd spoken for me, inviting them over for a celebratory dinner the next day.

Matthew wrapped me in his arms once more, kissing me on the forehead. "I know a little girl who wants to see her mommy pretty bad. You ready to go?"

"More than ready," I said. I turned to Stanley and thanked him once again for all his hard work.

"It was truly my pleasure," he said.

"You'll come to dinner tomorrow?"

"I wouldn't miss it."

Matthew stuck his hand out and gave Stanley's a firm shake. "I have to admit, I had my doubts. But however you managed it, you gave me back my family. I cannot thank you enough." Then Matthew pulled him into a hug, while Stanley laughed.

When they released each other, Stanley picked up his briefcase from the floor. I caught a glimpse of a small, dark figure in the back corner of the courtroom, watching me. His eyes shifted away as soon as he realized I'd seen him. Everything around me seemed to go silent for one instant, and the still, small voice called my name.

Ruby.

Then just as quickly, everything rushed back. "Is that Brother Cass?" I asked Asa.

He looked to the corner where I'd gestured. "Sure is. Wonder what he's doing here."

"Probably looking for a way to condemn Ruby," Matthew said. "Let's not let him ruin our day. Come on, let's go home."

We made our way down the aisle, Matthew leading the way. I noticed Brother Cass moving toward us, and my stomach tightened. It wasn't that I feared speaking with him so much as I feared how Matthew would react to him. I didn't want anything to spoil our happiness. But there was the matter of hearing God's voice again, the way I had so long ago.

Ruby.

Matthew must have noticed him too, because he tightened his grip on my hand and sped up toward the door. Brother Cass got to the door just before we did, and he lifted his gaze to meet mine. He raised his hand as if to ask us to stop, but Matthew plowed right past him, pulling me with him.

On the steps of the courthouse, we ran smack into a flock of reporters. Cameras popped and men called questions out to me from all directions. "Ruby, how do you feel? Ruby, what will you do now?"

"I just want to thank all the wonderful people who came out to support me today," I said. "I'm truly humbled by the testimony on my behalf. And I especially want to thank Judge Thorpe. He showed me great mercy, and I plan on living a life that's worthy of that mercy."

"Ruby?" another man called from my right. "What made you decide to come back and turn yourself in?"

"I just knew it was the right thing to do."

They shouted more questions, but Matthew put his hand in the air and announced we were heading home to spend time together as a family. Then he pushed through the crowd, with Asa and me following behind.

The fifteen-minute ride back to the farm was the most exquisite agony. I couldn't wait to see the look on Mother's face when I arrived, and I didn't think I'd let go of Hope for a full week. Mother must have seen the truck coming, because she was waiting out on the front porch as Asa drove up.

I didn't even wait for the truck to stop moving before I threw the door open, climbed over a laughing Matthew, and took off for the steps.

"Ruby!" Mother exclaimed as I ran to her. "Wh—what in the world?"

"Mother, the judge let me go free!"

We threw our arms around each other, and wept together for a few moments. Then the front door opened and Hope came outside. "Momma!"

I scooped her into my arms as Matthew and Asa came up the steps. "Oh, my sweet angel, I've missed you so much."

She squeezed my neck so hard it hurt, but I didn't care one little bit. I walked over to the rocking chair and sat down, sitting her in my lap. Keeping her arms around my neck, she pulled her face back so she could look at me.

"Are you home now, Momma?"

"Yes, ma'am. I'm home for good now."

"That's good, 'cause I don't wanna do the girl chores wid Gamma anymore. You can do dose. I wanna do outside chores like Daddy."

I laughed in spite of my tears. "All right, sweetie. You can do outside chores. You can follow whatever path God sets before you. And don't let anybody tell you otherwise."

She climbed out of my lap, but took my hand and pulled on it. "Come on, Momma! I hafta show you the baby chickens!"

I wiped away my tears and smiled at Matthew as I passed him. I grabbed his hand and pulled him with us. "Come on, Daddy. Let's go see the baby chickens."

We walked down to the barn with Hope between us, swinging from our hands every few steps. I couldn't stop my tears from flowing, and I couldn't stop laughing at myself either. Matthew kept looking at me like he didn't know what to do with me.

We rounded the barn and went over to the chicken coop, leaning on the fence around the chickens' yard. Matthew lifted Hope and set her on the middle rail so she could see over the top.

Hope pointed over the fence at a group of fluffy yellow chicks huddling near the far corner. "See Momma, dey stay over dere 'cause dey get scared."

"Why do you think they're scared?" I asked.

"'Cause, they tink someting bad is gonna get 'em. But I keep telling 'em dey are safe here. God has dis fence around 'em."

I looked over at Matthew and smiled. "Yes, He's had His fence around them all along, and they never even knew it."

He dropped his head and let out a low chuckle. "Silly chickens."

Hope turned around on the rail and climbed back into Matthew's arms. Then she reached one arm out to me. "Come here, Momma."

I came close, and she put her arm on my shoulders. "What is it, sweetie?"

"Look at Daddy," she said.

We both looked him over while Matthew lifted his brow. "What are we looking at?" I asked.

"See?" She pointed to lines that had formed around his eyes. "And look." Then she pushed her hand through the thinning hair at the crown of his head. "It worked."

"What worked?" Matthew asked.

My eyes were already flooding because I knew just what she meant. "Yes, my sweet girl," I said. "You're right. It did work."

Matthew smiled faintly at Hope. "What worked?"

She put her hands on his cheeks and lowered her voice. "Daddy, you're weal now."

***

The next day, the farm was overrun with family and friends that had come to celebrate with us. Mother bustled around, bringing food out for everyone, but the guests brought delicious dishes to share as well. It was almost like a funeral reception, except it was full of laughter and joy.

I stayed by Matthew's side most of the day. Seemed like we were in constant contact, my hand on his arm, his hand on my back, or just holding hands while we talked. I don't think either of us could bear to be apart from the other for more than a few seconds.

Likewise, Hope clung to me most of the morning. But once guests began to arrive, she flitted around the room talking to everyone about her animals. She even led a procession of curious children down to the barn for a tour.

The most wonderful part was that I got a chance to really thank the people who had spoken up for me in court and supported me. Homer arrived before everyone else, and we spent nearly half an hour reliving the hearing and its outcome. "I'd planned to write a final piece for *Time* about your sentence and what lay ahead for you all while you were in prison," he said. "I can't tell you how proud I am that the story has such a happy ending. For one thing, happy endings sell better." He winked, and we shared a laugh.

"I certainly prefer them," I said.

Homer took a plate with him of Mother's roasted ham, sweet potatoes, creamed corn, green beans, and corn bread. Said he had to get busy on writing that next story. We wished him well, and promised to stay in touch.

No sooner had Homer driven away than James and his family arrived. My heart soared when they came into the house, and I flew over to hug Emma Rae. She gasped in surprise before hugging me back. "Oh, you have to introduce me to all these beautiful babies!" I said.

She pushed the oldest forward, and I recognized little Abner right away. He was the spitting image of James when he was a boy. "I'm sure you don't remember me," I said, "but I sure do remember you. My, you've grown into such a handsome young man!"

Emma Rae introduced Percy, who gave a quick handshake before running outside after Abner. The twin girls, Ellen and Jennifer, flashed bright smiles. They resembled Emma Rae, with perfectly curled blonde ponytails. "It's nice to meet you both," I said. "This is your cousin, Hope." I pushed Hope in front of me.

She looked up at her cousins curiously, then turned her face up to mine. "Momma, how come there's two of that girl?"

444 | JENNIFER H. WESTALL

Emma Rae and I laughed. "They're twins," I said. "They were in their mommy's tummy together and came out into the world on the same day. That's how come they look alike."

She smiled cautiously at them. "Do you like chickens?"

One of them—I couldn't remember who was who yet—wrinkled her nose. "Ew. Chickens? They just cluck and run around like crazy."

"I know," Hope said through her giggle. "They make me laugh! Want to come see the babies?"

Both girls shrugged. "Sure," they said in unison. And they followed Hope out of the door.

"My goodness," I said. "I don't know how you keep up with four of them. Hope is plenty for me."

Emma Rae leaned onto the back of a chair at the table, letting out a small laugh. "You'll get used to it. I hear you have another one on the way. Come and sit a while and tell me what you've been up to the past few years. I heard you did a bit of traveling." She winked, and I couldn't help but smile. It hit me that I had a sister now. And as happy as that made me, it also made me ache for Janine.

I caught a glimpse of James standing in the living room beside the fireplace. He was studying the picture of Henry and his medal. Matthew was approaching him, his head bowed.

"I'll be back in a minute," I said to Emma Rae. "Why don't you help Mother get everything to the table?"

I joined Matthew just as James was asking if he was really there when it happened. "That article in *Time* said you and Henry were guerrillas together for a while. You said Henry saved your life. Is that right?"

Matthew took the photo of Henry from the mantel and stared down at his smiling face. "One night, we were staying in this tiny little hut, starving and getting eaten alive by mosquitos, wondering if Japs were gonna bust through the door at any minute and kill us. And Henry starts telling me these stories about you two. How he used to follow you around everywhere you went. That you two used to go out on double dates sometimes and pull tricks on the girls. He got me to laughing so hard, I was sure we were gonna be discovered."

James's mouth broke into a grin. "He was something else, that's for sure. We fought more than we should have, but we sure did laugh a lot too."

Matthew handed the picture to James. "That's how I want to remember him. Laughing, cutting up, making fun of me. Yes, he saved my life. But not just on the day he stood in my place and took the bullets meant for me. He saved my life every day by reminding me that I was alive, and that there was more to the world than just suffering and evil. He was more of a brother to me than my own brothers ever have been. And that's how I choose to remember him. And I feel certain that he would want you to remember him the same way."

James nodded as he swiped at the corner of his eye. "Thanks for doing everything you could to look after him." Then he glanced over at me. "And you, I knew you were always too big for your britches. Running all over the world, fighting off Japs, dodging bombs, and flying planes. You were dangerous enough just behind the wheel of a car."

I grinned and slipped my arm around his waist. "So does that mean you won't let me take you up in a plane?"

"Goodness, no!"

"Oh, so you *will* let me take you up?"

He rolled his eyes and chuckled. "I reckon some things never change."

***

A little while later, as the living room was filling up with familiar faces, Emmitt Hyde pushed his way through the crowd. I'd barely recognized him the day before when he'd spoken in court. He'd stood tall and proud in his suit, his face shaven, and his eyes full of life. Today, he approached me with his arm around a woman that seemed only a little older than myself. She smiled at me with warm, blue eyes as Emmitt introduced her.

"This here's my wife, Eleanor. We been married about five years now."

I took Eleanor's hand. "It's nice to meet you."

"It's so nice to finally meet you," she said. "I've been hearing about you for years. What you did for Emmitt that night in the jail really turned his life around. He speaks to troubled kids now, trying to get them to change their ways before it's too late."

I hugged Emmitt's neck, remembering the dark shadow that had hung over him when we'd first met. "You are a beautiful picture of God's faithfulness, Emmitt. Don't ever forget it was God who saved you that night. He just allowed me to be a witness."

"Yes, ma'am. I know that. I hope you know how much I prayed for you these past few weeks. It's good to see God bless people who bring His blessings to others."

***

I had to excuse myself a few times during the afternoon to catch a breather. I even had a bout with nausea around one, which I lost miserably. I determined it would be best to stick with light, bland foods the rest of the day.

When I came out of Mother's bedroom, I saw Brother Cass standing near the front door by himself. He held his hat in his hands, shuffling it as he scanned the room. I glanced through to the dining area at Matthew. He made eye contact with me and smiled.

"You all right?" he mouthed at me.

I nodded, and pointed toward the front door as I made my way in that direction. As I passed the dining room, I told him I was just going to get some fresh air.

"Want me to come along?" he said.

"No, I'll be back soon. I'll just check on Hope and the other kids."

I came over to Brother Cass, who still hadn't moved from the front door. "Can I help you?" I asked.

He studied me without speaking at first, looking up at me. He'd always been a bit shorter than me, but with the slump in his shoulders he seemed even smaller. He took a nervous glance around the room. "Can we speak outside, Mrs. Doyle?"

I wondered if he'd choked a bit when he said my name. After all, he'd put great effort into keeping me away from the Doyle family. I didn't particularly want to speak with him at all, but I figured it was best to step outside. Better to deal with him myself than have Matthew get riled up.

"Of course," I said. I followed him out onto the front porch, but I realized that we'd be in plain sight if Matthew came looking for me. "Why don't we take a short walk?"

We left the front porch and headed for the path that stretched into the woods. I waited for him to begin, but he didn't speak for a few minutes. Not until we were out of sight of the house.

"I followed your story," he finally said. "I read about your time in the Philippines."

"With all due respect, Brother Cass, I don't feel comfortable discussing that with you."

"Yes, I can understand that."

"Why don't you just tell me why you're here?"

"I have...I have a request."

I nearly laughed out loud. A *request*? Of all the nerve..."What kind of request?" I asked with as much patience as I could manage.

He stopped walking and wrung his hands. "Well, you see...it's Mrs. Cass. She's quite ill. She's been to see several doctors and none of them can seem to figure out what's ailing her exactly. She seems to be losing blood, but they can't determine how or where it's coming from."

"I see." My heart softened just a little. But only a little, and only for Mrs. Cass. The one time we'd spoken, she was awfully kind to me. And I'd never heard a bad word spoken about her in all my years. "And you're coming to me because...because you want something?"

"Yes." He sighed and brought his gaze up to mine. "I'm asking you to come see her. To pray over her and do...whatever it is you do."

"But I thought you believed I was evil, that the healing I witnessed was sorcery or witchcraft."

He walked away from me a few steps. When he spoke again, his voice cracked. "I...I'm not sure anymore. I'm not sure about a lot of things. I don't know where your...your *gift* comes from. But I know my wife is the most patient and loving woman I've ever known. I've made some mistakes in my time, and I've been difficult to live with. I've demanded holiness from others, but never from her. She just seemed to naturally possess this...light inside her."

He stopped again, looking off into the woods. "It's shaken everything I believed in to watch her suffer. I've believed in a God that's just, that punishes sin, even accepting my own punishment from Him. But she's done nothing that she should be suffering for. And I don't..." His voice cracked and trailed off. "I don't understand," he continued after a few moments. "Would God punish *her* for my sins? How is that just?" He shook his head. "No, I can't accept that. I've begged Him to help me understand, to show me her sin or mine so that I can make it right. I've prayed for her healing and sat by her bedside day after day. And there's been nothing for nearly a year. Not a word from God at all. Until you showed up again."

I waited in silence, knowing in my heart what was to come.

He walked back to me, his palms up as he implored me for my help. "Ruby, I don't care where your gift comes from. It can come from the devil himself, for all I care. If I serve a God who won't show me how to make this right, a God who will let my beautiful wife suffer...I can't accept that. I know I don't deserve an ounce of pity. Lord knows I never showed any toward you. But I'm asking anyway. Please. Come see her and pray over her. If nothing happens, then so be it. But I had to try. I had to ask."

I'd known from the moment I saw him in that courtroom, when God had spoken my name. I'd known He was calling me to help heal Brother Cass's wounds. And like he'd shown me in the moments of grace with Natalie, God showed me now that His love was not just meant for those who deserved it.

"Of course I'll come," I said.

***

"You're going *where?*" Matthew asked, his voice rising. He walked away from me, shaking his head. "No. No...just...no."

I stood on the front porch, waiting for him to pace this out and get to the same place I'd gotten to already. *Lord, open his heart and show him what You showed me.*

"Ruby, you cannot give that man one ounce of yourself, do you hear?"

Lord, give Matthew peace.

"I cannot believe you are even thinking of showing that man compassion after everything he's put you through. Everything he's put all of us through!" He continued pacing, shaking his head the whole time. He muttered to himself about craziness, about taking compassion too far. "No one can expect you to forgive that man."

"Have you forgiven your father?" I asked quietly.

He didn't stop pacing, but he did stop muttering. "I'm working on it."

"Do you think God can't forgive Brother Cass?"

"Of course He can! He can forgive anyone He chooses to. That doesn't mean you have to go and expose yourself to his hatred again. What if he's setting you up? What if he has some crazy scheme to get

450 | JENNIFER H. WESTALL

you to break the law and force you to have to serve out your prison term?"

"God told me to go," I said.

He threw up his arms and walked over to the side of the house, leaning against it and closing his eyes. His mouth moved, but I couldn't hear anything. I hoped he was praying. After a few moments, he opened his eyes and looked over at me.

"Will this ever get any easier?" he asked.

"Will what ever get easier?"

"Surrendering. I keep thinking I've finally done it. I've finally laid down everything I can before the cross. But then God digs out something else I'm still clinging to. And it's just as hard each and every time. Why is it so hard?"

I walked over to him and slipped my arms around his waist. "I don't know. Maybe because throwing off sin isn't so easy. Maybe because our natural selves resist God. But we have hope that in the end, we will stand before God as a completely new creature. And there will be no more suffering, no more need for surrendering, no more sin. Just love. Pure unfailing love for eternity."

He rolled his eyes, a grin easing over his lips. "You're doing it again." He leaned down and kissed me. "It's not fair being married to an angel, you know. I don't get to win any arguments."

"Well, maybe you should start arguing with yourself. You can definitely win those."

He chuckled and rested his forehead against mine. "All right, but I'm going with you."

"Did you hear God's voice telling you to go?"

"Not exactly."

"Then you weren't invited."

He kissed me gently. "Then I'll drive you and wait in the truck."

"I can drive myself."

He pulled me close, kissing me deeper this time, and sending my stomach into flips. "Please be careful. Don't trust Cass."

"I don't have to trust him. I trust God."

***

By the time I returned from Brother Cass's place, most of the visitors had left. I pulled the truck up beside the last remaining car and sat in the overflowing peace that still filled me. God had returned my gift, and I finally felt whole again. Not only that, but I'd made peace with Brother Cass, at least in my own heart. What peace there was between him and God, I would never know.

I bowed my head and thanked God for calling me to Mrs. Cass's side, for allowing me to be a part of the indescribable holiness of His presence. I thanked Him once again, as I knew I would every day, for the mercy I'd received. I laid my hand over my belly, and I prayed for the new life growing inside me, and that Matthew and I would have many years of joy ahead.

When I came inside the house, only one visitor remained. Hope jumped down from his lap and ran over to me. "Momma! Look! Uncle Mike is here!"

I picked her up, and we walked over to Mike as he stood from the rocking chair. His smile spread across his face, and he wrapped me into a hug. "It's about time you showed up at your own party," he said.

Matthew came over from near the fireplace and stood beside me. I sensed a possessiveness that, in a way, was reassuring. "How did everything go?" he asked.

"Very well," I said, putting Hope down. "Mrs. Cass is feeling much better." I turned to Mike. "How long can you stay?"

"I'm heading out in the morning."

"Did you fly here?"

"Yes, ma'am."

Mother came into the room just then. "Mike and Matthew, do y'all want any more food before I put the last of it away?"

"No, thank you," Mike said. "I'm stuffed."

"None for me, thanks," Matthew replied then turned back to Mike. "Did you say you flew here? All the way from San Francisco?"

"Well, I stopped in Houston to let my parents know what was going on. They're anxious to find out how all are doing. Especially Hope. Mother misses her terribly."

"Tell her we'll be out to visit as soon as we can. Maybe next summer?"

"That would be swell," Mike said.

Matthew slipped his arm around my shoulders. "Mike, there's no possible way to thank you and your parents enough for everything you've done for my family. You've made it possible for us to have a future together. You've been a true gentleman, and a hero."

Mike's eyes flitted quickly to Matthew's arm before he smiled. "All I've ever wanted for Grace...I mean, for Ruby, is her happiness. And I don't think I've ever seen her happier than she is now."

"Well," I said. "There is one more, small thing that could make me just a smidge happier."

"What is that?" Matthew asked, his eyebrows lifting.

Mike began to laugh, and Matthew looked from me to Mike, and back to me. "Ruby, what is he laughing about? What is the one small thing?"

"It's nothing!" I said, but I couldn't hide my wide smile.

Matthew pinched the bridge of his nose. "I'm going to hate this, aren't I?"

I reached up and kissed him on the jaw. "Most definitely."

"Ruby..." Matthew's voice rose just a bit. "Ruby, you're pregnant!"

I slipped out from under his arm and linked mine through Mike's. "Now, where is this plane of yours?"

Hope

June, 1964
Smith Lake, Alabama

M y entire childhood, Mother told me I was destined for something special, that God had given me a gift, and it was up to me to find out what it was and how to use it to glorify Him. But when your Mother is Ruby Doyle, there's a certain height to the unspoken expectations you grow up with, and for a long time, I just assumed my gift would be something spectacular.

As a young girl, I envisioned myself with super powers. Not like the ones my brothers read about in their comics. I didn't see myself as being able to fly or see through things. Those weren't *real* powers. No, my powers made a difference in real people's lives. I could love people long enough and with enough conviction to change them. I could see inside their hearts, see when they were happy or sad, anxious or at peace. I *knew* things about people, even when I couldn't explain them.

Somewhere along the way, that changed. I didn't exactly stop believing in miracles. I knew God worked miracles, but they became distant, cold things I could only read about in the Bible. And the things that were warm and close, the things that held weight and could be measured, became more real in my life. Especially once I left home for college.

Like my father, I had a sense of space and numbers. I loved building things, especially things that seemed to solve problems or make difficult jobs easier. If I had to help clear rocks out of an area of Uncle Asa's field, I'd rig up a train of wagons to pull them. Since I only had one wagon, I had to improvise. So I studied how the wagon was put together, and I built myself two more. The pride in Daddy's face when he saw those wagons was something that stuck with me the rest of my life. I was only six.

So when I followed in Daddy's footsteps to the University of Alabama to major in engineering, it wasn't much of a surprise to anybody. At least, not anybody in our family. The boys in my classes were pretty surprised though. In fact, there were so few women in any engineering field, I had to get special permission just to be admitted to the program. I fought hard to get there, and in the end, got my way.

So, I knew it was going to come as a huge shock when I told my parents I was going to change majors. Not only that, I knew when I told them what I wanted to change my major to, things were going to get very uncomfortable.

The whole family was spending the summer at our house on Smith Lake that Daddy had spent most of my life working on in some form or another. He built a successful construction company ten months out of the year, and spent the weekends of January and February adding on to the lake house. By 1964, it was large enough to sleep all seven of our family, plus Grandma Graves and Uncle Asa, and at least six or so more cousins from either Mother's side of the family or Daddy's, depending on who was visiting at the time. My summers were full of memories of swimming and fishing, roasting marshmallows, and playing games with my siblings and cousins long after the lightening bugs stopped flickering.

Since Smith Lake wasn't far from home, Daddy could still drive to work each morning and be back in time for supper each evening. Of course, it took Daddy longer than it should to make that drive each day. For some reason he never explained to any of us, he refused to drive on Highway 69 between Hanceville and Birmingham, which just happened to be the fastest way to get to the lake house. It didn't matter, though. For every single one of my twenty-one years, I never once saw him drive along that road. And if you asked him why, all you'd get is a shared glance between him and Mother, followed by, "Just a bad road. Better to avoid it."

By the first weekend of our stay, I'd already been through the imaginary conversation where I announced my big plans no less than fifteen hundred times. And I still hadn't come up with a good way to broach the topic. So my plan was to divide and conquer.

I approached Daddy first. He was throwing the football with Henry and Stephen as he monitored the smoker where his famous pork butt would reach perfection later in the day. Aunt Mary and Uncle Andrew were due to arrive about noon to spend the weekend with us, along with their sons Matt and Arthur. So if I wanted to talk to Daddy, I knew I had to do it before the chaos of a football game began.

I crossed the soft grass in my bare feet, wearing my bathing suit beneath my shorts and tank top. The sun was already blistering hot as I passed my sister Janine dutifully watching over our younger sister, Maggie, as she splashed in the water's edge. Janine was starting high school next year, which worried me a little. She was quiet, and a bit shy. Always observing situations rather than participating in them. I hoped she would come out of her shell over the next few years.

Maggie, who would turn eight in a few weeks, was the quintessential baby of the family. Both Mother and Daddy spoiled her rotten, and she never had to do any chores. But her joyful smile and bright eyes were quick to win you over if you doubted for a second she didn't deserve all the adoration she received.

I reached Daddy just as he threw a pass to Henry. They'd been arguing all week over his plans for the fall since he'd just graduated from high school, so they'd finally called a truce and come outside to burn off the steam. Though, as I got there, I heard Daddy telling Henry that there were so many avenues out there he could pursue and be good at. I figured the truce hadn't lasted long.

"Daddy, can I ask you about something?" I said, setting myself up just behind him and off to his right. Henry was known for his pranks and wouldn't hesitate to belt me with the ball if it tickled his fancy.

"Sure, sweetie," he said. "What's on your mind?"

"I need to talk to you and Mother about something, but I was hoping to get your thoughts on it before I talk to her."

"You mean, you were hoping to get me on your side first so I'll convince her to let you do whatever crazy scheme is in your head."

"No," I said. "I really want to know what you think about it."

"Like when you wanted Uncle Mike to teach you how to fly? Of course, that one backfired on you, didn't it?"

I had to laugh because it was true. "How was I supposed to know it was Mother who would be more accepting of that plan?"

"Hope!" Henry called. "Look out!"

I ducked instinctively, throwing my hands up to cover my head. I heard the smack of the football hitting Daddy's hands and Henry's cackling laughter. I groaned as I put my hands down. "Henry Doyle! Are you ever going to grow up?"

Daddy threw the ball to Stephen, who was at least making an attempt to hide his laughter. "Come on, Henry. Leave your sister alone."

"Hey, Dad," Stephen said, throwing the ball back. "You think Namath is the best quarterback Alabama's ever had?"

"It's possible. Coach Bryant says he is."

I sighed. Getting Daddy's attention away from football could prove difficult, even when it wasn't football season.

"Didn't you play with Coach Bryant when you were a freshman on the team?" Henry asked.

Daddy threw the ball back to Henry. "No, son. I only practiced with him. There's a big difference. I had to quit the team, remember?"

Henry caught the ball and shook his head. "Why did you quit the team? What a waste. You could've had a national championship that year."

"Because I knew where my priorities lay," Daddy said with a hint of emphasis to his voice. Henry sighed.

"Daddy?" I tried again. "I really do need to talk to you."

"All right," he said. "Y'all save my spot. I'll be back." He turned and put his arm over my shoulder. "I'm all yours, little bunny."

"Daddy, please don't call me that."

"I'm sorry. Old habits die hard." We started up the slope toward the house. "Listen, why don't we just go face this head on, and you can talk to me and your mother about this at the same time."

"I'd rather talk to you first."

"I'd rather your mother not think I've been conspiring with you again. Besides, you're well past twenty-one now, and you don't need mine or your mother's permission to do anything."

We walked up the steps of the huge wraparound porch that had been a surprise for Mother the summer I was thirteen. "I know I don't technically need your permission, but I would still appreciate your blessing."

He grinned and opened the sliding glass door. "Well, this must be something big if you're this nervous. What is it, anyway? You joining the space program or something? Gonna be an astronaut?"

"Worse."

We stepped into the kitchen where Mother was cooking all the side dishes that would be devoured in a few hours. The smell of apple pie hit me, and my mouth watered. Daddy walked over and took a deviled egg from the batch she was working on, and she slapped his hand as he reached for a second.

"Save some for dinner," she scolded.

Mother smiled at him in that secret way she had that told him she meant business, but also that she adored him. I'd only begun to notice their secret language in the past few years, looks that passed between them carrying entire conversations no one else heard. It intrigued me, especially in light of what I'd learned in the last couple of months of my studies at Alabama.

Daddy slipped his arms around Mother's waist and kissed the top of her forehead. "Your daughter wants to talk to us about joining the space program."

"What?" Mother's eyebrows arched, and she took a glance over at me to see if he was telling the truth. "You're just pulling my leg."

"No," he said. "She wants to be an astronaut. I blame Mike for this one. If he hadn't flown her down to Cape Canaveral, we wouldn't be having this conversation."

"Daddy!" He wasn't helping things one little bit, and he knew it. "I do not want to be an astronaut. Mother, don't listen to him."

She smiled and moved out of his arms to finish working on the eggs. "It's all right, sweetie. I'm used to your father's teasing by now."

Daddy went to the cabinet and pulled down two glasses. He filled them with ice and set them on the counter beside me. His eyes met mine, and he tipped his head toward Mother as if to say, "Go on and get it over with." Then he went to the refrigerator and pulled out the pitcher of lemonade. As he filled our glasses and refilled Mother's, I gathered my nerve.

"There is something I want to talk to the two of you about, though," I said. "I've been thinking of changing my major."

Daddy finished pouring the lemonade and took the pitcher back to the fridge. "Well, the field of engineering has been growing and changing over the past few years. You have a lot of options. What were you thinking about? Mechanical engineering? You always did have a talent for building gadgets."

"No," I said tentatively. "I...uh...I was thinking of leaving the engineering program for something different."

Mother's eyebrows shot up and she stopped working on the eggs. "After everything you went through to get admitted? Your father worked very hard to get you into that program."

"I know, and I'm extremely grateful." I looked over at Daddy, who leaned back against the fridge and crossed his arms over his chest. His lean muscles bulged beneath his shirt. He was still strong, still as athletic as I had imagined he was in his youth.

"You're quitting the engineering program, and it's your mother whose opinion you're scared of? Good heavens. What are you up to?"

"Daddy, I've loved being in the engineering program. I still enjoy it, but a few months ago I had an assignment in one of my other classes, and it's led me down a path that...well, it's changed everything for me."

Mother wiped her hands on her apron. "Hope, we can see this is difficult for you, but let's not draw it out. Tell us what's going on."

"Okay, here goes." My stomach knotted. "A couple of months ago, in my English Composition class, we had to write a research paper. The teacher gave us some topics to choose from, and I decided to research my family history. I knew Daddy was in World War II, but he never says anything about it." I glanced at him, afraid of the stony expression I'd find there. He shut down anytime any of us asked about his time in the war. "Anyway," I continued. "I went through the newspaper archives at the library on campus, and I found a bunch of articles from 1945 about the two of you. Then that led me to some articles in *Time*—"

"Hope," Daddy interrupted. "Let's get to the point, shall we?"

My stomach twisted again. They were both staring at me now. Daddy walked over and put his hands on Mother's shoulders, like he felt some need to protect her from me. "I...I read the articles. I went back and found old newspapers from 1936 too. I researched all of it. The first trial. The escape. Your time in the Philippines. I...I just wanted to know you, both of you. I had no idea you went through so much together."

"And how did your research paper turn out?" Mother asked.

"I got an A."

"Good for you," Mother said. I couldn't tell how she meant that. She'd gone completely rigid. I actually hadn't expected this to be the hard part of the conversation.

"Why didn't either of you ever tell me about all this?" I asked. "Mother...did you really...did you kill that man?"

Mother dropped her gaze to the floor, but didn't answer.

"It was a difficult time in our lives," Daddy said. "We moved on and made peace with it. There was no need to live in the past. Then. *Or now.*"

I felt like I was ten years old again, getting scolded for taking Mother's new washing machine apart to see how it worked. I wasn't meant to see the inside, only the finished product. I realized that by digging into their past, I was intruding on sacred ground.

"I'm sorry, I didn't mean to be disrespectful."

Mother raised her gaze back to mine. "You were going to tell us about changing your major."

"Yes," I said, clearing my throat. "I guess, in doing all the research I did, I figured out that I really enjoyed it. I didn't just research my own past, but I read about the war and everything it's led to. It explains so much about what's going on now between the U.S. and the Soviets, why the tension in Vietnam is so high, why the world's up in arms about hydrogen bombs and communism. So I've thought about it a lot, and I've prayed over the path for my future. And...I want to study journalism."

"Excuse me?" Mother's face went from pale to red within seconds. "You want to do what?"

Daddy released her shoulders, and she walked toward me like she might just get a switch and wear me out. "Journalism," I said, my voice growing smaller. "I want to—"

"What on earth would make you want to study that?" she demanded.

I looked to Daddy for help, but he almost looked amused. "Mother, I know you don't like reporters, but I wouldn't be like them."

"Like what? Dishonest? Writing lies and distortions just to grab headlines and get attention? Destroying the reputations of innocent people?"

"Not all journalists are like that," I said. "I want to write about real events. I want to explore all the changes going on in the world. We're living in a time in history like no other, and I want to be a part of it."

Mother threw her hands up and stormed out of the kitchen. I looked at Daddy, my eyes stinging for a second before I got them under control. He let out a deep sigh and rubbed the back of his neck, before following Mother into the living room.

I couldn't decide if I should give them a few minutes or go in there and reason with them. Daddy was right when he'd said I didn't need their permission, but it sure didn't feel that way. Maybe I didn't need their permission, but I still didn't want to disappoint them.

I closed my eyes and did what they'd both taught me to do in situations like this. I prayed.

Lord, please give me wisdom and courage to speak with them. I want to honor them, but I have to make my own path too. Even if they don't like it. Please help me talk to them. Help me to honor You and them on this new journey.

I walked into the living room and found Mother standing by the window looking out toward the water. Her arms were folded across her stomach, and her brow furrowed with worry. Daddy sat on the edge of his recliner, his elbows resting on his knees, his hands folded together. I hated making them upset. Maybe I should just forget the whole thing.

"I'm sorry," I said.

"You don't have anything to be sorry for," Mother said without turning around. "You did an assignment, and you followed where it led you. You never know why God leads you down certain paths. But I hope you've prayed over this new direction for your life."

"I have," I said.

Mother closed her eyes and shook her head slightly. Then she turned to Daddy. "All right, then. I think she should come with us next month."

Daddy looked up at her like she'd just grown another head. "Come with us? Why, I haven't even decided if *I'm* going yet."

"We should go. And we should take Hope and Henry with us."

"Go where?" I asked.

"The Philippines," Mother said, her voice low, almost respectful. "Your father and I have been invited to attend a ceremony by the Philippine government. He's being honored along with some others who served with him."

"I don't think I should go," Daddy said. "You know what will happen."

"It happens anyway, every year around the same time. The dreams will come anyway. We should go." Daddy shook his head, but Mother ignored it. "We'll call Homer. I'm sure he would love to come too, and he can talk to Hope about her new career choice."

"Homer?" I asked. "You don't mean...Homer Freeman. You know him?" Mother ignored me.

"Ruby," Daddy said quietly. "I can't."

She stepped over and knelt in front of him, taking his hands in hers. "Matthew, it's been nineteen years. It's time to bring him home."

***

July 5, 1964
Nichols Field, Manila, Philippines

For four days in July of 1964, I watched my parents in awe, as if I'd never truly known them before now. The ceremony at Nichols Field near

Manila on July 5 was only the beginning of the drawing back of a curtain I'd never known was present in my own life. Before it began, Daddy shook one hand after another, slapped countless backs, and received so much adoration I couldn't help but be proud to stand near him.

He introduced me to a short, dark-skinned man named Raul Diego, who Daddy said kept him alive at least three hundred separate times. He laughed when he said it, but there was also something about the way he looked at Diego that told me it might not have been much of an exaggeration.

There was a big parade, and the Philippine Secretary of Defense personally pinned eight different medals on Daddy that day. I stood beside Mother and Henry as they called out the medals one by one—the Distinguished Conduct Star, the Distinguished Service Star, the Gold Cross, the Wounded Personnel Medal, the Philippine Legion of Honor, the Sagisag Ng Kagitingan, the Philippine Defense Medal, and the Philippine Liberation Medal with Bronze Service Star.

Mother shone with adoration for Daddy, standing tall with an occasional tear on her cheek. Henry, for once in his life, treated the whole thing with reverence and awe. He asked Daddy to explain almost everything, from the meaning of his medals to the rank structure of the guerrillas he'd commanded. I hadn't realized until recently how much the military interested Henry, or how much concern that seemed to cause Daddy. He colored every explanation with warnings about the true nature of war, about the horrors of what happens to a man who has to kill someone. But this didn't seem to deter Henry one little bit.

I could relate to how Henry felt. Mother insisted that I speak with Mr. Freeman about his experiences, and I could tell by his response that she'd prepared him for the conversation. He did his duty, sharing stories of bombs exploding, people dying, and the terror of being shot at. But when Mother wasn't around, I pressed him for the truth.

"Hope, I care deeply for your parents," he said when we were back at the hotel in Manila. I'd asked him to meet me in the restaurant while

Mother and Daddy rested from the day's activities. "I don't wish to undermine them in any way."

"I'm not asking you to undermine them," I said. "I just want to know what you really thought of being a war journalist. I mean, you were there, right in the middle of everything. If you had it to do all over again, would you change anything?"

He took a sip of his whiskey and pressed his glasses up the bridge of his nose. "All right then. Honestly...no. I wouldn't change anything. For me, traveling to all the places I've been, writing about the human experience in different places and different times, has made me the man I am today. In knowing the people around the world better, I've known myself better. And I've helped others to see outside their own little bubbles, to see parts of the world they would otherwise never know about. I love doing it. I can't imagine doing anything else." He paused and took another drink. "But if you tell your mother I said any of that, I will deny it until the day I die."

***

The next couple of days of our visit were difficult on so many levels, both physically and emotionally. Along with Diego and Mr. Freeman, we were accompanied by officials from the Department of Defense and a team of scouts to travel northwest in search of my uncle Henry's grave site. We first took a small private plane to Tarlac City, and from there loaded onto trucks to drive northwest for hours into the mountains. I tried to keep a basic understanding of where we were according to the map Mr. Freeman shared with me, but it was useless. All I knew was we were slogging through jungle.

When the trucks finally came to a stop, I thought we'd reached our destination. But we were only bedding down for the night in a tiny village Daddy called a barrio. We were tucked into various huts with total strangers, sleeping on cots with legs inside of tin cans filled with water. Mother said this would keep the ants from crawling on me while I slept.

"Is this what it was like when you were here before?" I asked her as we sat on our cots facing each other.

She pulled her long brown hair around her shoulder and began braiding it for the night. "No, dear. It was much worse than this. We were starving. Bombs were going off every day all around us. We were surrounded by sick and injured men. We were sick ourselves most of the time." She looked around the hut. "This would've been heaven on earth to us at the time."

After she made sure I was fairly comfortable, she stole out of the hut where we were to sleep. I figured she went looking for Daddy. My curiosity got the better of me, so I peeked out to try and find them. When I didn't see her anywhere, I debated on whether I should just return to my cot or look around for a few minutes. The screeches and chirps of the jungle around me convinced me not to go far. I stepped out of the hut and walked along a path that I knew led to the center of the barrio.

Off to one side, I saw them sitting together by a fire. Nothing extraordinary was going on. They just sat next to each other on a large log, Mother's head tilted over onto Daddy's shoulder. She ran her hand over his back, stroking up and down. I felt like I was trespassing, so I went back to my cot.

The next morning we hiked further into the jungle. Daddy and Diego led the way, pointing and conversing in Spanish and English. Henry stayed by my side, helping me climb over rocks and push through heavy palm leaves. At one point he leaned over and said quietly, "Did you know Dad could speak Spanish?"

"No," I said. "But I'm realizing there are a lot of things about Daddy and Mother I didn't know."

"Me too," he said. "Did you see the way he moves through the jungle? Like a cat or something. Did you know about all this already?"

466 | JENNIFER H. WESTALL

"About what?"

"This. His time fighting as a guerrilla with Uncle Henry. He never told me a single thing about it."

"No, he never told me," I said, glad I was able to answer honestly without explaining everything I did know.

After several hours of toil through the jungle, our procession stopped. Daddy and Diego walked in a small circle, pointing at trees and muttering to each other. I came up beside Mother and took her hand.

"You doing okay?" I asked.

She squeezed my hand and nodded her head.

"You think Daddy is okay?"

"He's as well as he can be. This will be a difficult day for him. He loved your Uncle Henry like a brother. They were very close. Losing him was one of the toughest things your father ever faced."

"What was Uncle Henry like?" I asked, noticing my brother had come up on the other side of Mother.

She slipped her arm around his back and laid her head on his shoulder. "Much like your brother, actually. He was fun-loving, a great athlete, loved to play pranks, and he kept me laughing through some very difficult days. I've missed him every day of my life since we were separated."

After some bustle near one of the thickest palm trees, Daddy stepped out from the group and looked over at Mother. "Ruby, you want to come over here?"

She let go of us and walked over to Daddy. Henry and I trailed behind, not wanting to intrude. The group of men stepped back from the tree, where they'd worked to clear some of the overgrowth. A long mound of rocks lay beside the tree with a makeshift cross at the head. Vines had overgrown the cross, and it was nearly tilted over.

Mother let out a deep sigh and held a handkerchief to her nose. Daddy wrapped an arm around her, his own face showing signs of struggle to hide his emotions. Then Mother knelt beside the grave, her hand resting on top of the rocks.

"I know this wasn't your final destination, and that you aren't even here anymore. I just want you to know that we still think of you every day, and that you were loved beyond measure." She stood and took Daddy's hand as he came alongside her. "So when this corruptible shall have put on incorruption, and this mortal shall have put on immortality, then shall be brought to pass the saying that is written, Death is swallowed up in victory. O death, where is thy sting? O grave, where is thy victory?"

Daddy cleared his throat, and when he spoke, his voice strained with emotion. "Lord, we come here today to honor our fallen brother, Lieutenant Henry Graves. He was brave and true to the end. He made us laugh, and he gave us strength. Thank you for allowing us to find him and bring his earthly remains back home with us. We know this earth is not really our home, and that Henry is rejoicing along with the saints of old. We thank you for preserving us, and we wait with hope for the day we can all be together in Your kingdom. Amen."

Mother and Daddy turned away as several men stepped in to begin the excavation. Daddy reached out for Henry, and Mother put her arm around me. We held onto each other in that sacred place, together and whole. Daddy finally released just a fraction of his sorrow with a short sob. He pulled Henry even closer. "Do you understand how much I love you, son?"

Henry nodded his head. "I do, Dad."

"I only want you to live a life that honors God and the gifts He's given you. If that means serving your country like I did, like your Uncle Henry did, then so be it. I'll make peace with that somehow. Just...please, pray over it. Be as sure as you can be. And serve God with your whole heart. Surrender to Him completely. It's the only way to truly find peace."

"I will, Dad."

Daddy looked over at me, his eyes damp. "That goes for you too, little bunny."

I managed a small smile, and squeezed in tighter with Mother. I even put my arm around Henry to complete our circle.

"Listen, both of you," Mother said. "Remember the things your father and I have taught you. Fear and doubt and loneliness...they'll all come at some point. But remember the verses we've taught you. Remember the lessons you've learned at church, from your teachers, from us, about who God is, and who you are as His child. He says in Isaiah 41, 'For I the Lord thy God will hold thy right hand, saying unto thee, Fear not; I will help thee.' Remember that always. Your salvation is secure. Nothing on heaven or earth can separate you from your heavenly Father's love. Nor ours."

***

On our last day in the Philippines, the four of us went out on our own with Diego. We left Manila carrying two shovels and a short curved sword Diego called a bolo, and took a boat across the bay toward the Bataan peninsula. Mother told us all about her trip across the bay just after Christmas in 1941. Our boat landed only a kilometer west of where that boat had been when Japanese planes bore down on them. Mother had dove to safety, leaving her suitcase exposed on the beach.

"When I finally recovered it," she said as the wind whipped strands of hair across her face, "there was a bullet hole in the corner, and the gun your father had given me was destroyed. But your grandfather's Bible was untouched."

Henry shook his head in amazement. "Why have I never heard these stories?"

"They may seem like amazing experiences now," Daddy said, "but they were terrifying at the time. We don't remember them as adventures, son. We remember our friends who died. We remember how hungry and exhausted we were, and how close we came to death. We don't relive those days willingly."

We climbed out of the boat and caught a ride on a truck that was heading west. Daddy and Diego sat in the front, telling the driver what to look for. Mother sat in the back with Henry and me.

"Where are we going?" I asked for the tenth time that day.

"Probably nowhere," Mother said.

I couldn't understand why she and Daddy wouldn't just tell us, but I decided to stop asking. After only a few kilometers, the truck slowed down. I saw Daddy pointing at a marker on the side of the road. We drove past it a little ways, and then the truck turned off into a dense section of jungle.

"Mother," I said, with a bit of alarm. "This isn't a road!"

"I know," she said. "Hold on to something. It could get bumpy."

We bounced along in the truck a while longer, finally coming to a stop in what looked like the middle of nowhere. There was no town, no barrio, no road. Just palm trees, and dense vegetation.

Daddy got out of the truck and helped Mother climb out of the back. I hopped over the tailgate after Henry, and we both looked around, bewildered.

"You think this is it?" Mother asked.

"As best I can tell," Daddy said. "It doesn't exactly look the same."

Daddy thanked the driver and got the shovels out of the back of the truck. He handed one to Diego and they began walking further into the jungle with Diego leading the charge with his slashing bolo.

I threw my hands up and followed. "Mother, what is going on?" I asked again.

She sighed and continued picking her way through the leaves and vines. "We're trying to find the site of the hospital where I was a nurse."

"Why?"

She shrugged. "We figured we'd take a chance that it was still here."

I couldn't understand why it was so important, or why we were bringing shovels. But I decided it could be interesting, and if I was going to be a journalist, I needed to follow challenging roads to find worthwhile stories.

After turning around a couple of times, arguing over the location of the dental clinic—"Ruby, I helped build it, I think I know where it is!"—and uncovering a few rusted pieces of shrapnel, Daddy and Mother finally agreed that they had found it.

"Found what?" I asked. "I don't see anything but jungle."

Diego kept on slashing away at vines. "Here you are," he said.

I walked over to the area he'd just cleared. There were bamboo bed frames completely overgrown with vines. Mother walked around the area in a circle. "It's just so overgrown," she said. "I don't think I can work out where it would be."

Daddy walked several yards away from her. "I think this would have been the front of the ward. Henry and I came up from that direction...maybe." He pointed behind him. "I think your tent was about over...there." He walked another several yards away.

"This is silly," Mother said. "We're never going to find it."

"Can't hurt to try," Daddy said, thrusting a shovel into the ground.

Diego took his bolo and started cutting away at the growth near Daddy. He called Henry over and handed him the other shovel. So Henry and Daddy dug several holes in an area about ten feet by ten feet.

"We're never going to find it," Mother said. "I'd rather go find the river if it's all the same to you."

Daddy looked at his wristwatch. "Let's give this another hour. Then we'll go find the river. We'll need it by then." He smiled over at her, his face red and covered in sweat.

After they'd pretty well covered the area with holes, Daddy sped away and walked around it again. "You know, we might not even be at the correct ward."

"That's what I've been saying," Mother said, her tone increasingly exasperated.

Daddy held up his hand. "Hey, have a little faith, all right? Have I ever let you down?"

"Do you want me to start a list?"

He grimaced. "As long as it starts after 1945 it should be pretty short."

He studied the area again, walking about thirty yards away from us. He walked in another circle, uncovering more debris, and waved Diego over to swing his bolo again. Then they marked off another area, and Daddy and Henry went back to digging.

Just when I thought Mother was going to order them to stop, Daddy called her over. "I think I found something. Come look at this."

Mother walked over and looked into the hole Daddy had been digging. She gasped and covered her mouth. "It can't be."

Daddy bent down and lifted a filthy rectangular shape out of the ground. He dropped it and hit it several times, knocking the dirt off. Then he stood and gestured toward it. "Go ahead, Ruby. Look it over and see if it's yours."

She knelt down and looked over what appeared to be a very old suitcase. She stood it up and knocked some more dirt off. I could just make out a hole in the top corner. She laid it flat again and juggled the latch several times before it finally popped open. I watched as my mother sat back on her heels and wept.

"What is it?" I asked as I came closer.

Mother reached inside and lifted out what was probably once a white dress, but it had yellowed somewhat. It was covered in tiny red roses. She held it up and showed it to Daddy, who smiled from ear to ear.

"I told you we'd find it," he said.

Mother brought the dress to her chest, still crying. "Thank you," she said. She leaned over the suitcase again, moving items around and laughed as she pulled out the mangled gun. "I guess this isn't any use to anyone."

Daddy chuckled with her. "Why did you even keep it?"

She shrugged. "Because it was from you."

She dug around another few seconds before her eyes flooded with tears again. "Oh, Matthew. Look."

She held up a small square in her shaking hand. Daddy reached for it, and I came to look around his shoulder. It was an old picture, nearly faded. Four people stood together smiling, and I recognized Mother and Daddy. It took me a moment, but I also recognized Uncle Henry.

"Who's that other girl?" Henry asked. He'd come up on the other side of Daddy.

"That's your Aunt Janine," Mother said. "Henry married her the same day your father and I married."

I looked more closely at the photo. They were all gaunt, with their cheeks sunken and their bones protruding. Mother had on the very dress she'd just held up, along with huge army boots on her feet. They were a mess. All four of them. And they radiated happiness.

Mother stood and came over to us. Daddy handed the picture back to her. "All right," he said with a gentle smile. "You happy, Mrs. Doyle? Can we go home now?"

Mother nodded and came into his embrace. "We can go home now."

"Good," he said. "I've always hated the jungle." He released Mother and picked up her suitcase. "Diego, my friend. Thank you so much for once again helping me to find my way. Now, can you please help me find the fastest way out of here?"

Diego threw his head back and laughed. "Sí, Major!"

The End

AUTHOR'S NOTE

Writing the Healing Ruby series has taken me on a journey I would never have expected. In the kitchen of my Aunt Sharon's house in April of 2011, where I first heard stories of my grandmother Ruby's mysterious gift, the idea that first hatched in my mind was born out of my reluctance to accept something so preposterous.

Like Ruby Graves, my grandmother grew up during the Depression. She lost her father to diabetes, and soon thereafter, the family lost everything they had. Just like many American families during these years, they struggled to survive while building deep connections with their family and neighbors.

Since publishing the first book in the series, I've had the privilege of hearing even more stories of my grandmother's childhood, of how her two older brothers, George and Percy, teased her to no end; of her devotion to my grandfather, Homer, and her six children; and her independent spirit that has passed through several generations of Hays women. We've laughed at her exasperation every time Homer would call her his "little girl" just to rile her. We've argued over who was her favorite grandchild (just for the record, writing a series of books based on her as the main character has put me *way* ahead of the rest of you). We've remembered so many of the little things that made her special to each one of us.

But the "gift" has always been something that's difficult for me to accept. I'm a believer, and I accept Jesus as my Savior based on faith. And I believe God heals. But I still look for logical patterns, evidence that rings true, and above all else, *truth*. Ruby's experience of the supernatural bothered me, even as I wrote about it. Even though I knew my dad and my aunts wouldn't lie to me about my grandmother, so she must have had this gift. Their testimony rang true, but it still unsettled me.

Early on, I knew that Matthew was the character I related to the most: his doubt and fear, and in this last book, his reluctance to accept his security as a child of the one true God. I've often asked myself why it's so easy to believe the lie that I'm not loved, that God doesn't see or hear me when my world shatters. Why do I feel alone when I cry out to Him?

No one speaks agony of the soul like David, and Psalm 42 is the cry of my heart in those most lonely moments:

> [1] As the deer pants for streams of water,
>   so my soul pants for you, my God.
> [2] My soul thirsts for God, for the living God.
>   When can I go and meet with God?
>   [3] My tears have been my food
>   day and night,
>   while people say to me all day long,
>   "Where is your God?"
>   [4] These things I remember
>   as I pour out my soul:
>   how I used to go to the house of God
>   under the protection of the Mighty One[d]
>   with shouts of joy and praise
>   among the festive throng.
>   [5] Why, my soul, are you downcast?
>   Why so disturbed within me?
>   Put your hope in God,
>   for I will yet praise him,
>   my Savior and my God.
>   [6] My soul is downcast within me;
>   therefore I will remember you
>   from the land of the Jordan,
>   the heights of Hermon—from Mount Mizar.
>   [7] Deep calls to deep

> *in the roar of your waterfalls;*
> *all your waves and breakers*
> *have swept over me.*
> [8] *By day the Lord directs his love,*
> *at night his song is with me—*
> *a prayer to the God of my life.*
> [9] *I say to God my Rock,*
> *"Why have you forgotten me?*
> *Why must I go about mourning,*
> *oppressed by the enemy?"*
> [10] *My bones suffer mortal agony*
> *as my foes taunt me,*
> *saying to me all day long,*
> *"Where is your God?"*
> [11] *Why, my soul, are you downcast?*
> *Why so disturbed within me?*
> *Put your hope in God,*
> *for I will yet praise him,*
> *my Savior and my God.*

In the end, writing these stories has brought me along in my own walk with the Lord. I can't understand why He has allowed the pain I've experienced, but I know it has nothing to do with His love for me. Like David above, I can only conclude that no matter my circumstances, no matter the fire that surrounds me, I put my hope in God, and I will forever praise Him.

So I came to the place where I can accept that my grandmother had a gift I don't understand. It only makes me love her more, and it makes me praise God even more. I don't have to understand it. How God works through each person is unique. It's what makes Him infinitely "other" than us, and at the same time, infinitely able to understand us.

I say all this to hopefully encourage you. When you are in that darkest of places, when you cry out from a depth inside your soul known only to you and God, He sees you. He hears you. He feels your pain. He

478 | JENNIFER H. WESTALL

has suffered with you, but more importantly, He has suffered *for* you. He will not lose you in the fire. Take your eyes off the flames, and put them on the Savior standing beside you.

Yes, our Savior died a horrible, gruesome death for us. But that wasn't the end of the story. Jesus lives. And we serve a Savior who is still standing beside us, still speaking truth to our spirit, if we will only listen and believe.

RECOMMENDED READING

The titles below were invaluable during my research into the guerrilla warfare that took place in the Philippines after the U.S. surrendered, along with the effects of the war on soldiers once they returned home. There are many more books available that I simply do not have the space to list. But if you're interested in reading more on these topics, this is a great beginning.

Lieutenant Ramsey's War by Edwin Price Ramsey and Stephen J. Rivele

Agent High Pockets: A Woman's Fight Against the Japanese in the Philippines by Claire Phillips

Soldier from the War Returning by Thomas Childers

The Hidden Legacy of World War II: A Daughter's Journey of Discovery by Carol Schultz Vento

Behind Japanese Lines: An American Guerrilla in the Philippines by Ray C. Hunt and Bernard Norling

Once a Warrior—Always a Warrior: Navigating the Transition From Combat To Home Including Combat Stress, PTSD, and mTBI by Charles W. Hoge

MORE FROM JENNIFER H. WESTALL

Historical Fiction:

Healing Ruby, Volume One of the *Healing Ruby* series

Breaking Matthew, Volume Two of the *Healing Ruby* series

Saving Grace, Volume Three of the *Healing Ruby* series

Abiding Hope, Volume Four of the *Healing Ruby* series

Contemporary Christian Romance:

Love's Providence

ACKNOWLEDGEMENTS

This book has been a journey into my own soul from start to finish, and I have to thank God first and foremost for bringing this story to the page. I have a thorough process of outlining an entire book before ever writing a scene, and a thorough process of planning and outlining a scene before I write it. Every time I sat down to type out a scene I had meticulously planned, something took over my fingers and a scene I did not recognize would appear. I fought this for a while, getting frustrated that I kept having to erase my plan and rewrite it, but much like Matthew, I finally surrendered to it and stopped planning everything my own way. What happened inside my own heart was beautiful and something I'll never forget. I know that my words aren't perfect, and to say that God wrote this story might be a bit dramatic, but in my heart, I know where the words came from, and it wasn't from me.

I must also thank my beautiful family, David, Brody, and Fox. You guys make life so much fun, and you make the best distractions any writer could hope for. My parents have continued to be a huge encouragement, always listening when I need to talk out my what-if questions. There's nothing like a family behind you to give you wings to chase your dreams.

I also have to thank my editor, Bryony Sutherland. I always hesitate to expound on her enormous contribution to my career, because with each successive book she is harder and harder to schedule. I'm afraid if word gets out how amazing she is, I will have to plan books for years in advance. And Bryony knows how that whole planning thing goes for me. She is wise, patient, steady in the face of my whirlwind writing schedule, and she always has a word of encouragement when I need it the most. I can say without a doubt that this series would have never been possible without her. Thank you, Bryony. I cannot say it enough.

Lastly, I want to thank all the readers who have emailed me or commented on my Facebook page their enjoyment of the series. You've all been patient as I slowly delivered one installment at a time, encouraging me, and sending so many prayers up when I needed them. I've prayed for many of you as well. You're all a tremendous blessing, and I love the community of believers we've built. I hope we keep adding to our numbers! Thank you to all of you who have so enthusiastically shared these books with family, friends, neighbors, and fellow church-goers. Your excitement has been so encouraging. And I love you all so much!

ABOUT THE AUTHOR

Jennifer Westall is the author of the beloved *Healing Ruby* series, an enduring love story spanning the Great Depression and World War II. She's also the author of *Love's Providence* (2012), a contemporary Christian romance novel that navigates the minefield of dating and temptation. Over her short publishing career, she has moved quite a bit, and looks forward to one day settling down with her husband and two boys. She homeschools by day and writes by night, thus explaining those pesky bags under her eyes. Readers can connect with her at jenniferhwestall.com or find her on Facebook and Twitter.